I0608584

The Nyctalope
vs. Titania

IN THE SAME SERIES

Jean de La Hire. *Enter the Nyctalope*
Jean de La Hire. *The Nyctalope on Mars*
Jean de La Hire. *The Nyctalope vs. Lucifer*
Jean de La Hire. *The Nyctalope vs. The Antichrist*
Jean de La Hire. *The Nyctalope vs. The Master of Life*
Jean de La Hire & Others. *The Nyctalope Steps In*
Jean de La Hire & Others. *Night of the Nyctalope*
Jean de La Hire / Emmanuel Gorlier. *The Nyctalope and The Tower of Babel / The Cross of Blood*
Jean de La Hire / J.-M. & Randy Lofficier. *Return of the Nyctalope / The King of the Night*

Jean de LA HIRE

The Nyctalope
vs Titania

translated by
Michael Shreve

BLACK COAT PRESS

Introduction Copyright © 2025 by Jean-Marc & Randy Lofficier.
Titania translation Copyright © 2025 by Michael Shreve.

Cover illustration Copyright © 2025 by J.O. Ladrónn.

Visit our website at www.blackcoatpress.com

ISBN 978-1-64932-395-8. First printing: June 2025. Published by Black Coat Press, an imprint of Hollywood Comics.com, LLC, P.O. Box 17270, Encino, CA 91416.
All rights reserved. Except for review purposes, no part of this book may be reproduced or transmitted in any form or by any means, electronic or mechanical, including photocopying, recording or by any information storage and retrieval system, without permission in writing from the publisher. The stories and characters depicted in this anthology are entirely fictional. Printed in the United States of America.

TABLE OF CONTENTS

Jean de La Hire

Introduction

The Nyctalope vs. Titania was first serialized in France under the eponymous title *Titania* in the newspaper *Le Matin* from 20 April to 23 July 1928. It was then reprinted as two slim volumes respectively entitled *Titania* and *Écrase la Vipère!* [Crush the Viper!] by publisher Jules Tallandier in 1929 in its imprint « *Le Livre national* » Nos. 677 et 678.

This made little sense from an editorial standpoint, since *Titania* was a direct sequel to *The Antichrist*, serialized in *Le Matin* in 1927, but not collected in book form until 1932 by publisher Arthème Fayard.

An updated bibliography of all the Nyctalope novels and related books was included in a previous volume in this series, *The Nyctalope and The Master of Life*.

Jean de La Hire, the creator of the Nyctalope, was born in Banyuls on January 28, 1878, into a relatively obscure, aristocratic family which had long been impoverished by various social upheavals. His birth name was Adolphe-Ferdinand Célestin d'Espie de La Hire. His family claimed descent from one of the knights who fought with Jeanne d'Arc, although its most famous member was the mathematician and astronomer Philippe de La Hire (1640-1718), who has a theorem and a lunar mountain named after him.

La Hire began his literary career with high ambitions, selling his early work to Fernand Xau, the editor of *Le Journal*, and to the humorous periodical, *Gil Blas*. He worked for a while as secretary to Colette's husband, "Willy," and wrote a brief memoir of that time.

La Hire's first successful serial was *La Roue Fulgurante* [*The Fiery Wheel*] (1907)[1], the extravagant account of an alien abduction by a spacecraft which appears to anticipate the now common notion of "flying saucers."

His most enduring creation, the Nyctalope, was one of the first modern superheroes—a crime-fighter who can see in the dark and, as it was later revealed, also sports an artificial heart and is seemingly gifted with an unusual vitality and longevity. To modern readers, the Nyctalope is bound to seem rather feeble next to the likes of Superman and Spider-Man, but he compares well to Doc Savage or The Shadow. His powers are ultimately less important than his symbolic status as a paragon of moral and scientific enlightenment.

After World War II, La Hire was arrested in May 1945 for having collaborated with the Vichy régime and was tried in December; the judgment confirmed his permanent exclusion from the world of French publishing. He escaped from

---

[1] Available in a Black Coat Press edition, ISBN 978-1-61227-217-7.

custody in February 1946 while being transferred to a hospital, but was condemned *in absentia* in 1948 to ten years' imprisonment and the loss of his citizenship rights. He never returned to serve his sentence, and was still in disgrace when he died on September 6, 1956.

Then, the Nyctalope and its creator fell into literary oblivion, until, after an absence of fifty years, the character returned in our anthology series *Tales of the Shadowmen*, where he proved to be immediately popular. Thanks to the indefatigable Brian Stableford, ably succeeded by Michael Shreve, several translations of the original works have since followed, and today, the Nyctalope has reclaimed his title as one of the pioneers of superhero fiction.

New readers may be surprised by some *Harlequin*-like aspects of the story. One should remember that, in the United States and England, pulp magazines were bought mostly by men. However, in France, a daily newspaper like *Le Matin* had a sizeable female readership, often comprised of secretaries, salesgirls, etc. Therefore, it was important for any author of *feuilleton* fiction to incorporate both adventure and romance in their serialized novels.

Maur Korridès, who plays a major role in this novel, is a mad scientist who first appeared in La Hire's *Le Trésor dans l'Abîme* [The Treasure in the Abyss] (1907). He is believed to have died at the end of that novel and is only mentioned occasionally in *Le Corsaire Sous-Marin* [The Underwater Corsair] (1912-13), in which the Nyctalope has a cameo.

In reality Korridès, as we find out later, traveled to Mars with his second wife, Marguerite. We are never told what happened on Mars, but when he returns in 1917, he is alone, bitter and vengeful, and soon agrees to work for the Bolsheviks. Eventually, Korridès married Titania in 1926, just prior to the beginning of this novel. They have a son, Hugues, who will later fight the Nyctalope under the nom-de-guerre of "Belzébuth" in the eponymous 1930 novel.

Maur Korridès has a brother, Prosper, who is a kind and benevolent scientist, and the hero of La Hire's *Les Grandes Aventures d'un Boy Scout* [A Boy Scout's Great Adventures] (1926).

Pierre is the son of Leo Saint-Clair and Sylvie Mac Dhul, his third wife; he was born after *The Antichist*. He appears in this novel and *Belzébuth*. There, he should be one year-old, but La Hire incorrectly states he is eleven. He returns in *Gorillard* (1931) and *Les Mystères de Lyon* [The Mysteries of Lyon] (1933) where he is portrayed as a young man in his twenties, which is impossible to reconcile with his mother's age.

In the series of short stories featuring the Nyctalope initially published in *Tales of the Shadowmen* and collected in *The Nyctalope Steps In* and *Night of the Nyctalope*, We have postulated the existence of two Pierres: one born on Mars in 1912 from Xavière de Ciserat (in *The Nyctalope on Mars*), and another, "Pierrot", born in early 1927 from Sylvie Mac Dhul—the one featured in this book.

8

This Pierrot probably died in 1928 in heretofore unrevealed circumstances, and the Pierre featured in *Gorillard* and *Les Mystères de Lyon* is the other, elder Pierre.

Sylvie presumably passed away in 1931, also in unrevealed circumstances. Emmanuel Gorlier revealed in his story *"The Lesson of Captain Danrit"* (in *The Nyctalope Steps In*) that the older Pierre eventually joined De Gaulle's Resistance, while his father, as we know, collaborated with the Vichy régime.

Now, read on!

Jean-Marc Lofficier

2 fr.

Jean de LA HIRE

TITANIA

Collections hebdomadaires du
LIVRE NATIONAL
ÉDITIONS JULES TALLANDIER
75, Rue Dareau, PARIS (XIVᵉ)

THE NYCTALOPE vs. TITANIA

PART ONE: TITANIA

CHAPTER I
A Pile of Ashes and a Wooden Pedestal

"Don't you think we can walk a little, Leo?"

Saint-Clair chuckled and raised his wife's bare hand to his lips to give it a kiss.

"After a year of marriage, Sylvie, we love each other like the first day because we feel and think the same thing, in the same way. I was just about to say the exact same thing to you."

"Darling," she sighed.

He spoke into the ear trumpet, "Vitto, stop!"

Ten yards on the coupe pulled over to the curb. The driver jumped out, opened the door and the couple got out of the car.

"Go on ahead of us," Saint-Clair told him. "We're going back on foot."

The driver got back in the car and took off right away.

On this calm, quiet, splendidly moonlit night in May the deserted avenue was perfect for a stroll, especially after a long night at the Opera.

Wrapped in her coat, Sylvie took her husband's arm, squeezed it affectionately and they walked together in that light, smooth, steady pace of fit and healthy people.

In this sparsely populated neighborhood of Satory, southwest of Versailles, there were very few cars at one in the morning. But there was silence, such total silence that the two pedestrians did not even hear the muffled sounds of their slow footsteps.

All of a sudden a loud noise broke the silence. The loud noise of a human voice, a long, harrowing, terrifying cry that faded into a groan and was cut short by a shriek...

"Oh!" Saint-Clair said.

He had stopped with Sylvie beside him, whom he held with a protective arm. They were frozen in astonishment. But suddenly in a silence more profound and sinister, it seemed, in the clear night, a call for help rang out very nearby.

"Help! Help!" And with deep despair, "My God, it's over! Oh, oh, help!"

"A woman," Sylvie whispered.

"There, behind the trees." A moment of hesitation and then: "Let's go see."

"Yes, let's go," Sylvie agreed bravely.

The "trees" were a garden surrounded by a low wall topped with an iron grill lined with metal in the inside. More than once, passing by here in their car, Saint-Clair and his wife had remarked about this property so well tucked away from all eyes and whose entrance must be through a forest path since the protected wall revealed no opening all along the avenue.

"Have to go around to find the entrance, it could be far," Saint-Clair said. "Let's climb. It looks like there are lots of trees so we won't be seen."

For Leo Saint-Clair, a.k.a. the Nyctalope, there might be obstacles difficult to get through but never impossible. And if one knew even a little of the athletic prowess of Sylvie Mac Duhl, one could guess that with the help, if needed, from the man who had been her husband for a year now, she would never stay behind when he was on the move.

Under the light fur, her shoulders were covered with a silk scarf. She took it off and twisted it longways to make a strong cord that she tied around her waist, cinching the coat that protected her shoulders, arms and thighs but left her limbs free to move nimbly.

"Do you have a weapon?" she asked.

"No, but it doesn't matter."

Sylvie, no less than Leo, could not resist the call to adventure, danger and mystery. Plus, it was a woman who had called for help.

Sixty seconds after the woeful, desperate call that had followed the heartrending shriek, Leo and Sylvie were climbing the wall, which was easy. The grill was ten feet tall. But its bars were huge. Leo climbed, one hand grabbing the horizontal bar that connected the perpendicular ones. Once on top he leaned over and held his hand out for Sylvie. She grabbed his wrist…

"Get a good grip on the crossbar. Perfect. Pull up. Watch out for the spikes, they're sharp. Got it? Good…" Words barely whispered, advising, accompanying and admiring the action.

An agile leap together and the bold couple was on the ground, the moist ground of a garden crowded with tall trees, a lot of pine trees. The spring foliage of the others was full enough not to block the pale light of the stars.

Leo and Sylvie took three steps to get away from the wall and were in darkness.

"Your hand, Sylvie."

Because he was the Nyctalope, for whom there was no night, for whom there was no blindness, whose eyes always saw. And he feared nothing because twenty years of adventures and war had taught him to have no fear, even primal fear, that his will knew how to control and conquer. As for Sylvie, she was the Nyctalope's wife and loved him.

Thus, then, without weapons and in the night, they walked through the private park towards a house whose windows were probably open and from where the awful shriek and urgent call for help most likely came. Unless it was from outside, in a clearing or an arbor, on a path, in a courtyard? No new clues. The call for help did not repeat.

"Watch out," Saint-Clair whispered. "A pavilion, a villa…"

But he did not stop.

A moment later Sylvie whispered, "I see… look, on the ground floor, an open window."

They were on the edge of an open lawn bordered by a narrow path of white gravel. Beyond the lawn, directly across from them, the path opened up into a little esplanade in front of a two-story villa. In the left-hand corner an overhanging turret. Then, from left to right, six windows upstairs, four on the ground floor with a front door. All the wooden shutters were closed, as well as the door. But on the right, downstairs, the last window was open, its shutters against the wall, panes invisible, meaning it was wide open.

The moon fully lit up the mysterious facade where the open window bore a black hole, tempting, menacing, sinister.

"We have to go through the window," Sylvie said softly.

"Yes," Saint-Clair agreed.

"But if there's someone armed in the room, they have every right to shoot us, being on private property…"

"My lord."

"I'm afraid for you, Leo."

"Me too, Sylvie, I'm afraid for you. We are indeed unarmed. What if you were to wait here, behind a tree? I could go around the lawn…"

"No, no, I'm following you. I'll go around with you."

"You're right. Come on."

It was crazy! Everything pointed to a tragedy happening in this mysterious house. But Saint-Clair could not resist the temptation of some madness. Besides, there might be someone he could save in this house. How could be step back now?

"Come on, Sylvie."

As light-footed as Mohicans on the hunt, the couple resumed their walk. Still under cover of the trees, in the dark, they got to the right corner of the house.

"Can you see into the darkness of the room?" Sylvie whispered in her husband's ear.

"Yes, I see," he answered. "Nothing strange. Looks like a reading room. Shelves of books cover the walls, a table, two armchairs. The window sill is too high from here for me to see if the floor is parquet or carpeted. The table's empty, polished wood. There's only one thing on it. What in the world is that? Weird! A kind of block that doesn't look like anything I've seen... A block or a stand, a little pedestal... all alone on the corner of the table. What's it doing there?"

"And nobody?"

"No, nobody I can see."

"Let's go, Leo. We can stay on the cobblestones around the courtyard, then along the wall there's cement strip. We won't make any noise and we'll stay out of the line of sight of anyone who might be hiding in the room."

"Right, let's go."

When, with their throats a little dry and their hands tingling, they were both against the moonlit wall next to the open window whose shudder they could touch, they stood there puzzled for a moment. A very brief moment. Because almost right away Saint-Clair leaned over to his wife and whispered:

"I'm going to jump in. If there's someone in there, they don't know that I'm out here. I'll take them by surprise. You, wait here until I call for you. It has to be like this, got it?"

"Yes, I'll wait.

He kissed her lightly on the corner of her mouth and slipped away, his back to the wall.

At the window he swung around, grabbed the sill, lifted himself up and jumped in.

He did not have to go far into the room to see that there was no one inside. The furniture was arranged so that no human being could have been hiding there. In the back of the room, two doors, one on the right of the wall, the other on the left, both closed. Locked? Quietly, deftly, Saint-Clair went to check. No, just closed. But both doors had locks. Saint-Clair pushed them open one by one.

He went back to the window and leaned out a little to call out softly, "Sylvie!"

She held up her arms and he helped her climb into the room.

"Well?"

"Nobody. Two doors back there. You can see a little, I think. Look at the thing on the table. What do you think it's for?"

She was leaning over the pedestal-shaped wooden block when a moan echoed through the house, grew louder, rose like through a musical scale and then suddenly broke into sobbing. Moaning and sobbing so sorrowful, so horribly heartrending that Leo and Sylvie both stiffened up, grabbed each other and stood there staring at the back wall.

Silence, laden with dark menace. Sylvie and Leo feared and desired, at the same time, to hear again the desperate, dolorous moan. But the silence loomed. Loomed so heavily that Saint-Clair felt an unbearable dread.

All of a sudden he scolded himself for doing nothing while in this very house the same voice had earlier called out for help. Someone was in trouble and they could still be saved. He shook his wife out of their embrace.

"Sylvie," he said, "I have to know."

"I'm not leaving you."

"Well then, let's go together."

They walked. They believed that they remembered the moan coming from the middle of the house. So, it was the left door they had to take. Saint-Clair turned the doorknob and pushed gently. The darkness of a hallway, but he could see. With his left hand he took Sylvie's right hand and they stepped into the gloom.

They moved forward and soon had the impression that the tragic mystery was moving away from them at every step. Unimpeded, without difficulty, without the slightest incident, they opened doors, stepped in and inspected the rooms. In a few minutes they had seen the whole ground floor of the mysterious house. Nothing out of the ordinary and not a living soul. Comfortably furnished in good taste. Everywhere showed clear signs that the house was inhabited. But nothing gave the slightest clue for the noise, the calls for help, the moaning and sobbing.

There was a small door under the stairs that led to the basement.

"We'll go down later if we don't find anything upstairs," Saint-Clair said. "Let's go and don't worry about me, I'm armed."

"How's that?" Sylvie asked.

"I found a loaded gun in a drawer."

She was reassured as they started climbing the stairs.

They had realized downstairs that the strange house had no electric lights. Therefore, they did not have to worry about a light suddenly turning on unless it was a lamp whose flame was quickly lit. But the Nyctalope would see the adversary before he could do anything, if, that is, the upstairs was not deserted like the ground floor.

But it was deserted, completely.

Four bedrooms lined the hallway that, like below, ran from one end of the house to the other. They were furnished, beds made—they had all been slept in. On the night stands were candles more or less burned down. On some tables were kerosene lamps ready for use.

In short, an inhabited house but with no inhabitants.

And that was all. No stairs, no ladder, no trapdoor to an attic. There must have been one up there but it was closed off and unused.

"Well now", Saint-Clair said aloud when their visit was over, "this makes no sense at all. I'm going to light a candle so you can see what I've seen, Sylvie."

From a pocket of his tuxedo jacket he pulled out a gold box full of matches. He struck one and lit a candle on the night stand. He kept the revolver in his right hand, took the candlestick in his left and very calmly, despite his gnawing anxiety, said softly:

"Sylvie, let's go back through everywhere. Stay on my left."

The young lady was quivering with curiosity. In the candlelight she eagerly devoured everything that her husband had seen with his Nyctalope eyes. They went from bedroom to bedroom. The idea flashed in them of a secret door, a hidden room. But reason prevailed.

He phrased it like this: "The house is a long, narrow rectangle flanked by a tower. The windows in the hallway look out on the paved courtyard. The bedroom windows face the lawn. The corner tower has got a staircase. We've seen the inside downstairs and up here, wall to wall. There's nothing else."

"There's the basement," Sylvie said.

"Yes, let's go there now. But the moaning and sobbing didn't come from a basement."

In the basement were three big cellars. One was empty of everything but dust; the second had some unused furniture and empty crates; the third was the proper cellar: rows of bottles, two casks, three demijohns.

"I wasn't expecting anything down here," Saint-Clair remarked. "Let's go back up. I noticed in the vestibule there was a door that must lead to the courtyard."

The key was in the door.

Saint-Clair blew out the candle, put the candlestick on a sideboard and pulled the door open.

Together the two explorers went out. Lit by the moonlight the paved courtyard was a big square between the mysterious house and an old, one-story building. Leo and Sylvie walked quickly to the door. A big, old prison lock bolted it closed. Saint-Clair slid the bolt and the heavy door creaked on its hinges.

"Yes, a big garage. And a beautiful car, I say!"

"Oh, Leo," Sylvie said, "the radiator's hot."

"Huh?"

He touched it. The radiator was indeed hot. Saint-Clair put his hand on one of the front tires.

"The tire's warm."

He tried the others and all were still warm from a speedy drive.

Sylvie added, "Plus, it smells like a car that's just been driven."

"My word, there's no doubt about it. This car was on the road less than thirty minutes ago. It got back here right before we heard the call for help. Whoever was driving and the woman who cried out and the person moaning and sobbing when we were in the reading room… where are they? By God, I intend to find out. Let's go, Sylvie."

"Let's go."

Saint-Clair, revolver in hand, led the way. Sylvie followed him with the candle lit again as they revisited the house. But nothing unusual or suspicious. Nobody.

Leo and Sylvie went out into the garden on the opposite side that ran parallel to the street. It was separated by a very high wall without a grill from the forest road beyond which the Satory woods stretched silent and deserted. To the right and left, far from the mysterious house, the walls abutted the property of a summer home that Saint-Clair remembered having seen closed up and therefore uninhabited since he had moved here a month ago with Sylvie, their child and their domestic help into the Bligny chateau, which is at the west end of Avenue Bois-Robert.

"I'm totally stumped about this night," he grumbled after half an hour of investigation with Sylvie found them once again in front of the window of the reading room.

But then he thought of the block of wood, the pedestal.

"Let's go back in, Sylvie."

The moon had dipped in the sky so that its light, still bright on this clear May night, shined directly on the bare table whose polished wood glistened. On the corner of this table the wooden block was still there.

Leo and Sylvie examined it.

It was pedestal made of ebony wood, round, in the shape of an upside-down Doric capital whose largest diameter measured barely eight inches. So, a small pedestal and nothing more...

One detail, however: its entablature was pierced by four screw holes equidistant apart.

"And that's it," Saint-Clair said. "This pedestal must have held a vase, a cup or maybe a statuette that was screwed in here." And he swore angrily. Then he growled, "Leaving here without knowing anything about this woman who screamed, cried out for help, moaned and sobbed... from this crazy house... that car... Oh, what's going on here?"

Head down, grumbling under his breath he had walked into the middle of the room. And he suddenly stopped in front of something new. Sylvie jumped to his side. Her eyes followed his hand, still holding the gun, and bewildered she saw...

She saw a pile of ashes. It was on the carpet in the middle of a somewhat light-colored rosette, making a gray spot with irregular black streaks. A perfect cone but a little truncated, maybe ten to twelve inches in diameter at the base and half that in height. Right around it the carpet was heavily singed, proof that the object was burned there and the ashes had not been brought from somewhere else.

Saint-Clair rushed over to the fireplace and lifted the mantel. Inside was clean except for a little soot that had fallen from the flue.

"These ashes didn't come from the fireplace," he said, "because they haven't had a fire in here for a long time. Odd."

He went back, squatted down and with his left hand took two handfuls of the inexplicable ashes, which he dropped into his coat pocket.

"Why that?" Sylvie asked.

"To get it analyzed."

"And the pedestal?"

"I'm taking it too."

On saying this he grabbed the ebony block.

"We're leaving, Sylvie, but let's go out the back that leads to the forest road. I noticed the key is in the lock."

Therefore, bringing with them the ashes, the pedestal and the revolver Leo and Sylvie crossed the garden using the only usable path between the wild, dense trees, a path that led to the paved courtyard, a very winding path whose every turn was a blind corner.

Once through the small door in the back wall they were on a narrow forest road.

"This road," the Nyctalope said, "should connect up to the avenue by some alleyway."

"Surely," Sylvie agreed.

They walked quickly without talking. The tension from the dramatic mystery was gripping them physically and tyrannizing their minds. They were thinking of the outrageous situation they had stumbled into on this astounding adventure. But while Saint-Clair was becoming more and more determined to know and understand everything, Sylvie was starting to get more and more worried, feeling deep down an awful foreboding of a disaster that she and the love of her life might fall victim to.

Back at Bligny everything was normal. Leo and Sylvie went up to their bedroom and got into their pajamas and sending their domestics straight to bed. After taking a loving look at the crib where their son, Pierre, an adorable three-month old baby, was sleeping and seeing that the nanny was next to him, sleeping with one eye open, they went back to their room, smoked, talked and did not go to sleep until dawn.

But Saint-Clair was up the next day, Wednesday, May 25, at 9 a.m. An hour later he was in Paris, in the laboratory of his old friend, the renowned chemist Charles Noissan, to whom he handed a box right away and said:

"My friend, here are some ashes. I'd like to know what was burned to make them. It's serious and urgent."

"Have you got some shopping to do until noon, my dear Nyctalope?" the scientist asked with his usual good humor.

"No."

"Then sit down and you can have breakfast with me."

"If you'd like."

"Of course. I'll do the analysis and then after washing my hands we can eat. How's that sound?"

"Sounds good."

"Very well."

An hour and a half later, having just finished the analysis, but also having heard the whole story of the Nyctalope's nocturnal adventure, Charles Noissan, as conclusive as he was confident, gave it to him straight:

"My friend, the pile of ashes from the mysterious house is the residue produced by the combustion, strangely but without a doubt instantaneous, on the carpet, of a human body, *standing up!*"

CHAPTER II
The strange meeting

In the tiny dining room separated from the laboratory by a reading room, Noissan and Saint-Clair ate breakfast together, served but the chemist's old cook who was deaf as a post. They went over and commented on all the incomprehensible data of the tragic problem with many unknowns. Conclusion:

"Inform the police?" the Nyctalope said. "No, at least not yet. I'll act alone but with Vitto and Socca at my side."

"Your guard dogs?"

"If you'd like."

"Don't forget that I'm entirely at your disposal, Leo."

"Thanks. I'll use you plenty."

"I'm counting on it. But be careful, my friend, the mystery man who found a way to instantly reduce to ashes a man standing on his own two feet is no ordinary citizen. Of course, you're not ordinary either, but still, watch out!"

"Dear me."

And Saint-Clair went to the garage where Vitto his mechanic was waiting for him with the coupe. Socca had stayed in Versailles to take care of a little investigation.

"Let's go home, Vitto."

At Bligny the Nyctalope found Sylvie anxious: she was worried about their son Pierre's health since diphtheria had been running rampant in Versailles over the past week.

"Is Pierrot okay?" he asked straight off.

"Just fine," his wife replied. "The nanny's walking him in the garden. But read this."

They were in the sitting room of their private quarters upstairs on the second floor. In plain, almost men's pajamas Sylvie stood before her husband who had left his hat in the vestibule and was slowly taking off his gloves. Without touching the paper he read the typed lines that his wife was holding in front of him:

Monsieur Leo Saint-Clair, famously known as the Nyctalope, is kindly requested to send back or bring back to the Sycamores the small ebony pedestal and the loaded revolver that he unduly appropriated on Wednesday, May 25 at 1:30 am.

Respectfully yours,

Dr. Maur Korridès

"Good God, where did this come from?"

"Socca brought it in with the envelope opened. Should I call him."

"Yes, yes."

She pressed a button. After a short wait, during which they sat side by side on the divan and reread Dr. Maur Korridès' demand, basically justified but so surprising, two short knocks on the door got Saint-Clair to announce, "Come in" and Socca appeared.

"Explain this!" the Nyctalope demanded instantly.

The man was just a butler before his employer but a loyal ally before his boss. In a rather military stance, looking straight ahead, simply and quickly the 30-year old Corsican, short, wiry and dark, rattled off:

"I made the summary investigation. The house called *The Sycamores* is occupied by Dr. Maur Korridès. He doesn't exercise. He is married. His wife, who lives with him in *The Sycamores*, is very beautiful. They often go away for a long time, always by car. They are believed to be very rich. Everything is paid in cash. No known relatives. Never any visitors. Domestics: a black chauffeur and a mulatto maid who does everything, not married. As far as information, that's it. As for the letter Madame is holding in her hand, do I need to say?"

"Yes, Socca," Sylvie said softly. "I didn't tell him the little story you told me."

"Well, here goes" the Corsican livened up a little. "When I'd got all the information, I came back for breakfast. Then I thought that while waiting for you to come back it might be a good idea to take a little look-see at *The Sycamores*. I got to the door in the wall on the forest road and walked around smoking my pipe like on a casual stroll. I was in the area around five minutes when it opened and a tall negro walked up to me—the chauffeur I figured. He wore no hat. He smiled at me and said, 'G'day, f'end. You ah Socca, de butlah of massah Saint-Clai?' I hesitated to respond but he kept smiling and went on, 'Oh, dun say no. We know. Take dis. From my massah to yohs. G'day.' He handed me a rolled-up piece of paper, turned around and hurried off. The door closed behind him. I unrolled the paper. An unsealed envelope. I took out the letter and read it in case immediate action was necessary. But I saw the only possible action was to give it to Madame since you, Monsieur, were still in Paris when I got back. And that's it."

"Very good, Socca," Saint-Clair showed no emotions. "Go arm yourself and tell Vitto to do the same. Wait for me in the vestibule."

The Corsican bowed to Sylvie, saluted the Nyctalope with his right hand to his forehead, turned around and left.

Saint-Clair and Sylvie stood up.

"Are you going to *The Sycamores*?" she asked, worry showing in her beautiful blue eyes.

"Yes and with my two guard dogs. But come on, dear... you're so brave, so strong!"

She was moved, took his hands, hugged him and almost moaned, "Yes, Leo, yes, I know. Alone or together, we've both faced so many other dangers and have always come out on top. But this time, really, I'm scared... I'm scared and I don't know why. If it weren't for little Pierrot, I'd come with you. But my place is with him... and I'm scared for you. I don't... Listen, Leo, couldn't you just send back the pedestal and revolver with Socca or Vitto or both of them and not go yourself?"

"Oh, Sylvie, can it be? I still hear the scream, the call for help, the desperate sobs. I can see that house that's lived in but was deserted. And the ashes, do you know what they were?"

"What?"

With a shudder Saint-Clair repeated exactly what the great chemist said, "The residue produced by the combustion, strangely but without a doubt instantaneous, on the carpet, of a human body, *standing up!*"

"What are you saying? What a nightmare! Can it be?" Sylvie was shocked. "No, no, you won't go. Or I'll take Pierre in my arms and go with you."

Leo Saint-Clair had never seen his wife—the brave and sportive Sylvie Mac Duhl—in such a state of frightened alarm. It touched him but not enough to weaken his resolve. He hugged her, caressed her back, spoke to her and managed to calm her down and even convince her. Together they went into the garden to kiss little Pierre who was playing in the sun on a blanket with some tiny balls that his nanny was rolling around him.

Walking back to join Vitto and Socca in the vestibule Saint-Clair repeated, "I'll have two bodyguards, armed, vigilant, ready to kill—because I'll give them strict orders. I don't know where or what I'm walking into, but rest assure, dear, I'll kill before I'll get a scratch. I have to know and right away. I have to, especially since this letter adds bluster to the mystery. With such a puzzle before me I couldn't live with myself if I didn't do everything possible to solve it. Sylvie, in two hours or so I promise I'll be back. Yes, in two hours I'll stop whatever I'm doing and come back here. I want to. I'm sure I'll be able to."

"To God's ear, Leo! But in such a situation who can be sure of what will happen in two hours? Still, I understand you. Without Pierre I'd be with you. Go, Leo, go on then! But be careful!"

Five minutes later, flanked by the two Corsicans, Leo Saint-Clair was striding down the avenue towards the alleyway leading to the forest road by the Sycamores. He was wearing a soft hat, a three-piece suit and tanned gloves. In their city clothes (cap with leather visor, double-breasted jacket with silver buttons, "aviator" boots) one of the Corsicans was carrying a long, flat package (the revolver) and the other a short round one (the ebony pedestal). In the outside right pocket of the jackets they had seven-round Brownings. The boss, as usual, was without any weapon except for his intense eyes, his quick reflexes, his agile body, strong muscles and expertise in boxing and jiu-jitsu.

The three men were quickly at *The Sycamores*, the house of the horrible and hopeless scream, of the pile of human ashes and of the disquieting Dr. Maur Korridès.

Neither doorbell nor ringer of any kind. With his fist Vitto, who was small, thin and dark like Socca, knocked twice on the metal gate. A short wait and the little door on the right opened slowly. Taller than the height of the opening a ne-gro in a striped coat bent down, stepped through, stood back up, smiled, bowed three times and spoke subserviently.

"Massah Saint-Clai', I believe. Please entah... and also his men. Massah Mau Ko'idès is honahed to expect you..."

Thus, eating all his Rs and lisping a little, the black servant led in the Nyc-talope and his two "guard dogs".

Never among the countless twists and turns in his adventurous life had Saint-Clair ever burned with as much curiosity as at this moment. Everything in this affair was so completely unexpected and so clearly bizarre with a tragic un-derbelly! A hundred questions came to his rational but currently troubled mind. He had rejected all hypotheses as they formed since the unsettling moment that he had left the mysterious house the night before. And after the wild discovery of Noissan about the ashes, Saint-Clair had forced himself not to ponder the matter.

"Think only about the facts, the bare facts!" he told himself.

But go and try to shackle your thoughts!

The Nyctalope had a real sigh of relief when he, followed by Socca and Vitto, finally entered the unforgettable reading room. Yes, Saint-Clair was re-lieved because in the room was a man, a living human being whom they could fight, from the perspective of bare facts.

"Dr. Maur Korridès?" the Nyctalope stopped three feet inside the room and took off his hat.

"Yes, monsieur. And you are Leo Saint-Clair. Very well!"

A brief silence. In two mutual blinks of an eye the two adversaries assessed each other. And they judged each other worthy.

And yet, just from the physical aspect, the Nyctalope was obviously supe-rior. He was tall, slender and strong, built like an athlete, lithe and limber, solid muscles and nerves, an intelligent and energetic face with eyes... eyes whose gaze was irresistibly seductive or hypnotizing and full of domineering power.

On the other hand, Korridès looked like the typical puny, pathetic profes-sor, poorly built, poorly dressed, scrawny and weak. But his face was impres-sive. Not Mephistophelian but Plutonian. He united the dark spirit of the under-world with the rough majesty of the Olympus of the heroic age. A face wide, long, sharply chiseled. His big, dark eyes, deep-set under a brow that looked huge with his natural proportions, were the "equal", but somehow *on a different moral plane*, to the Nyctalope's. Close-cropped, barely graying hair, clean-shaven with no wrinkles, the mysterious man could have been forty or fifty years-old.

Korridès started in right away. He had a low, deep voice with a vague hint of sarcasm.

"I didn't think, monsieur, that you'd be accompanied by two bodyguards... I'm alone."

Saint-Clair shot back, without fearing to sound too wary since he was only being wise, "I hate carrying packages."

The response was sharp, "And yet last night..."

Saint-Clair made it plain, "Last night I didn't have them with me."

Then an immediate follow-up, "And I didn't know then what the pile of ashes was."

Casually, he continued, "Coming here, monsieur, to your house that all my senses feel disturbingly suspicious about, I'd be a fool to think of showing off my bravery. The bravery of the Nyctalope is never in question. Therefore, accept as fair and square or better with good cheer the presence of these two men. They'll only be leaving when I do."

Blunt and hard he added, "And I won't be leaving until I'm satisfied."

He made a discreet sign with his left hand. Vitto and Socca knew the order. They followed it. One of them put on the table (still bare) the revolver, lightened earlier of its bullets; the other set down the ebony pedestal in the shape of an upside-down Doric column. Once done, they stepped away and went to lean against the walls on opposite sides of the room near the two doors that Saint-Clair had noted were opened from the inside. Each of them put their hand in the coat pocket and stood completely still, calm, vigilant.

Standing behind the table, between it and the window whose paned glass was closed, Dr. Korridès had shown no sign of emotion. It was as if he had not heard Saint-Clair's comments and as if the attitude of the "bodyguards" meant nothing to him. But when the Nyctalope automatically glanced down at the place where the ashes had been, Korridès spoke very simply and emphasized his final words:

"The ashes you're looking for have been swept up, just like yours will be some day."

"What?" Saint-Clair reared up.

Korridès smiled, continued to speak simply, "But of course, monsieur. See, as strong as you may be, I believe that I am stronger than you. I think rightly, no, that you're not going to have me killed, not now or later, by your nice servants. You're a fighter, not a killer. Therefore, our battle, I imagine, will be a fair fight. But a fight to the death... I warn you... Monsieur Saint-Clair, by entering this house last night and going down into the basement, by taking some ashes and having them analyzed by the famous chemist Charles Noissan, your friend, by not forgetting that you heard a scream, a cry for help, groaning and sobbing in this house, you have tacitly but categorically declared war on me. I accept. I

would have gone to your home to formally accept if you hadn't come here...
But every declaration can be retracted. You're giving me back the revolver and
the pedestal, that's good. Forget about the scream, the call for help, the sobbing
and the ashes and it will be even better. Also forget about *The Sycamores* and
about Dr. Korridès and it will be perfect. Meaning, retract your declaration of
war and I, too, will take back the discourteous remark about sweeping up your
own ashes."

He stopped talking.

During this strange, nuanced speech, Saint-Clair was impassive. He waited
a few seconds and then he too spoke very simply.

"Monsieur Korridès, have you nothing else to say to me?"

"No, Monsieur Saint-Clair."

"And before confirming or retracting my so-called declaration of war, let
me ask you a few questions?"

"Maybe I'll answer, monsieur, but in that case, won't you have a seat and
allow me to do the same."

With a poise and precision of movements that was unexpected from his
physical appearance, the extraordinary doctor grabbed a stool, slid it next to the
table, sat down and leaned his elbows on the table. Saint-Clair sat in a leather
armchair four feet in front of Korridès. At the back of the room, against the two
doors, Vitto and Socca watched, listened, waited, all their senses on alert, their
right hands still holding the Brownings in their pockets.

Saint-Clair had decided not to beat around the bush. Right away he took
the offensive and attacked head on. Glaring across from him, he snapped out:

"Was the same person who was screaming last night in this house also the
one who groaned in despair and sobbed in sorrow?"

"Yes, monsieur, yes!" Korridès answered immediately.

"A woman?"

"Yes."

"You tortured her?"

"No."

"So, what did you do to her?"

"I killed her husband."

The Nyctalope was prepared for any eventuality, but he had not imagined
that his questions, indiscreet to say the least and with no legal necessity to back
them up, would get such precise and terrible answers. When he heard "I killed
her husband" he stiffened up and thought for a second that this Korridès was
crazy. But this thought really did not last for more than a second.

The troubling individual, always calm, with such expressive eyes, had a
look that could not have hidden any hint of madness. The doctor's face forced
Saint-Clair to regain his composure.

"You killed?" he asked, leaning a little forward and staring hard into the
big, serene, black eyes of his incredible adversary. "In self-defense?"

"No," is all Korridès said.

"Why then?"

"Vengeance?"

The Nyctalope lowered his voice to keep his emotional reactions under control. "The pile of ashes?"

"Yes," Korridès said, "it was that man."

Saint-Clair straitened up again and a brief shudder ran down his spine. He murmured, "And his wife witnessed this... scientific murder?"

"Yes. His wife saw the preparations and the execution. That's why she cried out. A little later, when we were taking her away, she groaned and sobbed... You were in this room then, Monsieur Saint-Clair, with your wife."

"But where were you?"

The dreadful Dr. Korridès had a pale smile and responded with an apologetic wave of his hand, "Allow me not to answer that particular question. To keep you from asking any futile questions, let me tell you that I won't satisfy your curiosity about the fate of the dead man's wife, my servants, my wife or myself since you and your wife already paid a visit to... I'd rather say made a search of this house."

The tone of the unimaginable doctor was slightly sarcastic. Saint-Clair was having a hard time controlling his anger. He stood up, took two steps forward, put his right hand on the table, then leaned forward and loomed over the doctor who did not take his eyes off him, just raised his head a little.

"Monsieur," Saint-Clair spoke in a low voice, "you must be very sure of yourself, very proud of your power to dare to tell me such things in such a tone of voice and all this after threatening me, which I will never forget. Reduce me to ashes like you did to a man last night! And if I strangle you right here and now? You're not scared, you told me, of Saint-Clair becoming a murderer. But if I killed you, it wouldn't be murder, it'd be an act of justice and protection!"

"As you want, monsieur," Korridès replied calmly. "But I warn you first that your attempt to strangle me will fail, even if you've got strength and numbers on your side. And I warn you further that in the improbable case you succeeded, a great and tragic sorrow will be waiting for you at home. Yes, at your Bligny chateau."

Saint-Clair rocked back on his feet and growled, "What are you saying?"

Still in the same calm voice the doctor said, "Do I really need to explain? No, monsieur. Keep that calm you had in much more tragic circumstances in your life. Did I call you here last night? Are my affairs any business of yours? Because a woman screamed and cried out for help, does that give anybody the right to break into a private house? If you thought there was a crime being committed here, you just had to inform the police. I'll tell you right now that they would have seen nothing, understood nothing and their questions would not have been answered with the candidness with which I honor you. Anyway, perhaps you haven't finished questioning me. I'm waiting, listening and ready to answer again, but this time within the framework of a certain order that I have clearly drawn in my mind."

The Nyctalope felt a little flustered. His adversary had the upper hand. But this prompted him get hold of himself. He went back to the armchair and sat down. He thought for a moment before speaking sharply but calmly.

"Monsieur, the ebony pedestal I took, not to study and analyze like the ashes but simply to have something physical to remind me that I wasn't dreaming. So, this pedestal, what's its purpose?"

In a friendly voice, like someone volunteering information, Korridès replied, "The pedestal is what I screw a little machine onto. A machine of my own invention. Two flashes dart out, three seconds apart, and that's all it takes for a man to be reduced to a pile of ashes."

"What for? Why such an eccentric murder? And why this vengeance, as you yourself called it?"

"That, monsieur, is my secret."

"I'll figure it out," the Nyctalope grumbled.

Korridès shook his head and spoke very solemnly, "I sincerely hope you do not because when you know, even though it is only part of my cardinal secret, you will have signed your death warrant, so to speak. Oh, not a quick death unless I'm forced to kill you in self-defense. No, you, the Nyctalope, will feel my power in a different way. I will say no more."

Korridès stood up. He walked over to Saint-Clair and touched his arm, then continued:

"I've decided not to answer any more of your questions. I want to get back to the main idea that started our conversation. Yes or no, do you acknowledge the declaration of war that you made upon me today?"

Slowly, Saint-Clair stood up and looking directly into the eyes of his incomprehensible enemy he answered with admirable serenity, "Yes, I acknowledge the declaration of war. Your means sound formidable to me and you believe they're invincible. I don't know your goals any more than I do the causes that are making you do this, but so be it, you should know that I will find out and I will defeat you!"

While talking the Nyctalope pointed his left index finger at Korridès' forehead and with his right hand gestured to the ebony pedestal on the table. A moment of silence followed before he resumed.

"You alluded vaguely to a second threat. Do you have the courage to specify it?"

Without hesitating one second Korridès answered with startling intimacy, "Nyctalope, there are three chinks in your armor: your son, your wife and your hubris, your excessive pride, which quite rightly has given you so much success in all aspects of your life. Before killing you and before telling you why, I will strike at these three chinks! If you had tried to strangle me just now, a great and tragic sorrow, I said, would be waiting for you at home. I wasn't exaggerating, I assure you. I never exaggerate.

"You recognize that my means are formidable and you think I believe them to be invincible. I do more than believe, *I know they are*. And in so much so that I can terrorize you, the Nyctalope, whom nothing has ever terrorized. Yes, my means will terrorize you when you find out what they are.

"Believe me, Saint-Clair, if you want to save your child, your wife and your pride from annihilation, renounce this war you feel you have to wage against me to find out my reasons, goals and means.

"This time I've said all I'm going to say. It is, I think, almost 4 p.m. At 8 p.m. if you haven't sent me a paper with the word '*Peace*' written on it and your signature, I will consider the war between us commenced.

"Oh, I won't attack you right away. I will act when I feel like it. At first I'll just defend myself. But watch out because sometimes to keep up a good and effective defense, one has to unexpectedly go on the offense."

When he had finished talking Korridès took a few steps back, which put him against a bookshelf. He leaned casually on it. And immediately a section of the bookshelf opened up like a door and out stepped the tall, black servant.

"Hamed," the doctor said, "show these messieurs out."

With a quick and agile movement he himself slipped into the hidden passage and disappeared into the dark. After this, just as quickly, the bookshelf slid back into place.

For a moment Saint-Clair was deeply tempted to chop the negro under his left breast and go search the house with Vitto and Socca, Brownings out in the open. But as brave as he was, he was still affected by the unnerving cynicism and the obvious power of the diabolical Korridès... He thought of Pierre and Sylvie.

He shouted inside his head, "No, no! Don't do anything crazy! First take care of them!"

He turned around and ordered, "Vitto, Socca, let's get out of here."

CHAPTER III
What the Nyctalope did

When he was back on the forest road Leo Saint-Clair felt like had just woken up from a horrible nightmare. The kind of feeling that gives you goose-bumps, a chill, a shiver down your spine and almost at the same time a kind of relief making you sigh, "Ah, it was just a dream".

However, since this was no dream but very real, the feeling of relief did not ensue. Nevertheless, the Nyctalope's mind was even more acute in a certain sense.

"Vitto, Socca," he said, "hurry up, by God, get a move on!"

He did not run, as impatient as he was. He forced himself to walk fast, but still just walking and not sprinting. He figured that if Korridès was watching him at the moment, the enigmatic but highly intelligent doctor would know why Saint-Clair was hurrying.

At either side of their boss, Vitto and Socca were marching at the same, steady pace. They were both pale, half crazed with anger. Only their deep-rooted habit of strict discipline kept them from lunging together at Korridès in the reading room and completing the strangulation that had flitted through the Nyctalope's mind.

Yes, discipline alone held them back. But to themselves they had promised to sacrifice everything they had in the world, even their own lives, to bring down, at the first opportunity, the horrible man whom their common sense considered demented, all the more dangerous since his madness looked like brilliant scientific acumen.

See, Vitto and Socca were educated and intelligent.

Although they worked for Saint-Clair the Nyctalope as chauffeur/mechanic and butler, these roles were, in fact, only secondary. In reality, they were very often the Nyctalope's collaborators like adjutants are collaborators of a general or better yet like two exceptional police inspectors, in certain serious cases, are direct collaborators of the police chief.

They understood not only every chilling word Korriès said but also the meaning behind them.

Back in Bligny Sylvie was waiting impatiently. She let out a cry of joy when, from the window of her small sitting room, she saw her husband and his two partners crossing the courtyard. She knew that he would come straight to her, therefore she did not move.

In the vestibule, at the foot of the stairs, Saint-Clair told the two Corsicans, "Vitto, get the town car. Socca you get the roadster. Be ready to leave in an hour or so. No bags for you, we'll be coming back. If it takes too long, you can buy what you need on the road."

29

Then he went upstairs.

As soon as he saw his wife, he smiled and spoke calmly, "Dear, it's going to get tough. I'll explain, but first we have to act. You and Pierrot have to leave with Adele. I'll come with you. Clothes and necessities for a month-long holiday. But only the strict necessities since you can buy whatever else you need. In an hour we have to be on the road. Tell Brigitte that you're visiting a sick friend in the countryside. She'll be staying here. And hurry. I've got some orders to give."

He hugged her tenderly and went back downstairs to his study. He called for Briard, the head servant, and Lucas, the footman, and told them, "I'm leaving on a trip with Madame, the child and the nanny. I'll be back in a few days. Let no one in the house, Briard, and let Dubosc know. Any letter delivered by post or by hand is to be kept under lock and key. If they ask for information, just say that Madame is with a sick friend who called for her urgently. I, of course, went with her.

"Until I get back, take turns, you two and Dubosc, to keep watch day and night. If anyone tries to sneak in or break in, use guns on sight without warning. Run straight to the police after the incident. Needless to say, don't leave except for the cook to do the shopping. Keep an especially close eye on any delivery-men coming here. In short, a state of siege! Got it?"

"Got it, monsieur, yes," they said together.

"You have enough money for a couple of days, Briard?"

"Oh, yes, monsieur, and more than you think. I received the rents from Normandy today."

"Good. Spend it as usual. Now go and be careful."

He went back upstairs. In the bedroom, at the head of the bed a big chest was hidden behind a tapestry and a door opened by a secret mechanism. Saint-Clair opened the chest and took out a wad of big bills and from a drawer he removed a flat holster, a little like a Browning but smaller and squatter. He dropped it into the outside right pocket of his jacket. Then he went into the bathroom and washed away the rush of blood to his head with a wool glove heavily soaked in ether, rubbing his face and neck. In the adjoining dressing room he put on a waterproof traveling coat. And he was ready.

In the garage, which was one of the old outbuildings of the chateau, he joined Vitto and Socca. The town car, a comfortable family car, was ready, luggage rack and straps prepared for the bags that Briard and Lucas were bringing down for Sylvie. The roadster, a tight-fitting four-seater, was also ready—the vehicle that the Nyctalope used for fast drives and quick trips.

He said, "Vitto, you'll drive the town car. You have to be in Orléans for the Southern Express night train. We'll always be somewhere behind you. Keep an eye on your mirrors to see if anyone's following you. If so, it'll mean a fight. Shoot out their tires. From Etampes to Orléans the road's smooth as silk, so don't miss. If no one's following, all the better, keep the gun in the holster."

He checked the two cars: gas, water, oil, electrical, all set. He already knew it. But he had accustomed his staff not to forget that the "eye of the boss" never closed.

A ring sounded.

"The bags," Socca said.

He dashed off. A double door opened onto the small service steps. Socca helped Briard and the footman. Saint-Clair watched them load. Five minutes later Sylvie and the nanny Adele, who was carrying the sleeping baby, climbed into the town car at the back of the main courtyard.

Forty-five minutes after getting back to Bligny from the visit to *The Sycamores*, the Nyctalope shot his roadster onto the road to Orléans, two hundred yards behind the town car. He had still not given any explanation to Sylvie who knew neither the why nor the where of their hasty departure.

All the way to Etampes the distance between the two cars did not change more than ten yards, but once this city had been passed Saint-Clair told Socca, "I'll slow down a lot at the first turn. Watch behind us. I'll keep an eye on the rear-view mirror. If a car shows up that's not an old clunker, I'll let it pass. Then we'll follow it. If it doesn't try to pass the town car, which I ordered to slow down when another car came up, then it means we're being followed. We'll catch up to the suspicious car and when I pull up beside it, if I say 'Fire!', shoot out the tires. Got it?"

"Yes, boss."

"Good."

It was just like out of the movies, all action. Was it going to end in tragedy?

The shrewd Nyctalope had guessed correctly.

Two minutes after he had slowed down in the turn a car appeared, barreling down the road. It sped past the roadster. It was a single chassis with a long hood, two bucket seats and three spare tires behind them, with a huge gas tank in the back.

"Damn," Saint-Clair muttered, "it's ready for a race. It left Versailles a good fifteen minutes after us, I'm sure. Korridès' troops do a good job. Someone tailed us from Bligny and when we took the road out of Orléans, the doctor was informed and off goes the sports car."

But the sports car was seen again two miles on and quickly caught up to first because the Nyctalope's roadster could outrun the best car on the road and then because Vitto had orders to maintain a maximum speed of 50 mph. So, since the sports car was not passing the town car, which would have been easy, it meant that Korridès had sent it to "tail" the Saint-Clair family on their trip.

"Here we go!" the Nyctalope said to Socca. "Get ready! Take out your gun!"

An instant later they were behind the sports car and signaling it let them pass. For a full minute they kept in line. Saint-Clair saw the two people in the bucket seats but he could not identify them. In any case, it was not Korridès or his black servant.

"Weird," the Nyctalope mumbled to himself. "The one at the wheel looks to me like a woman. The chin, the lips, the nose... Too bad the cap is pulled down and with glasses hiding their eyes... But really, I'll bet it's a woman. The gal drives well. I'll double my bet that the car belongs to Korridès. If I'm wrong, oh well. But it's better to apologize later and maybe pay a fine than to let Korridès know where my wife and son are going."

He turned slightly to Socca and said, "Three spare tires! If you shoot out the front two, they'll only have ten minutes of work and they'll catch up with us. Then it'll start all over again and maybe worse than now. We have to take a chance and hit them hard! Get ready, Socca! Now, take the gun and threaten the driver. Yes, right now..."

Getting on his knees on the seat Socca brought the rifle up to his shoulder as his boss had ordered.

Saint-Clair looked over at the sports car and shouted, sharp and clear, "Hey! Pull over. Stop the car! And hands where I can see them! Or else we'll shoot! Pull over! Hands up!"

He himself slowed down.

On his right the brakes screeched. The car rolled for another twenty yards before stopping. The passenger had already raised his arms, hands open. When they were completely stopped the driver did the same. Saint-Clair parked his roadster in front of the other car and jumped out onto the road.

"Lord," he grumbled, "I sure hope no car passes us and tries to help the people it looks like I'm attacking."

He was instantly beside the sports car's left door. He was holding a big Browning, which he pointed inside the car.

Calm but brusque he said, "You belong to Korridès. I don't like being followed. I have nine bullets to use, seven for your tires and two for you if you make a move. And the rifle over there is aimed right at you." He shouted, "Keep them in your sights!"

He walked around the sports car. Quickly and accurately he put a bullet into the two left tires, the three spares and then the two on the right.

Tranquil and haughty, he said, "Madame, since I'm sure now that you are a woman and a very good driver to boot... Go back to Etampes very slowly, rolling on the rims. Back there you can repair or replace your tires. And at Versailles tell Dr. Korridès that I will carry on with this war until either victory or death. When I find out what I don't know now, it'll be a success to add to the final victory. I'm used to not getting flustered any more than Oedipus before the Sphinx, even it it happens to be a She-Sphinx, madame... Now, watch it, keep your hands up! Or I swear on the life of my son I'll kill you both!"

He backed up to his roadster and got inside.

"Keep an eye on them, Socca. If they lower their hands, don't shoot, duck."

He himself bent forward so that the back of the seat was protecting him and he started the engine. The roadster pulled away.

The "lady" in the sports car had guts. She was the first to drop her arms.

Socca shouted to his boss, "Watch out!" and he ducked down.

A shot rang out, then another. But the roadster was already speeding down the road. Four more shots were fired. Three of them hit.

"It's just the body," Socca said.

"We're clear now," Saint-Clair breathed.

They were out of range and behind them Korridès' sports car was out of the race.

In three minutes the roadster caught up to the town car. Saint-Clair put a whistle in his mouth and blew a shrill call. The town car slowed down, pulled over and stopped.

"Socca, get behind the wheel. Go ahead of us to the station in Orléans. Get a compartment with three berths for Hendaye on the Southern Express that leaves around 10 p.m. I'll follow in the town car."

Saint-Clair got out, walked around the car and saw that two bullets had hit dead spots in the back of the car.

"Go on, everything's fine," he called out.

He went to the town car and climbed in across from his wife after giving orders to Vitto.

Sylvie was visibly struggling to stay calm. She was horribly worried and totally ignorant of the reason for and the destination of this hasty trip. She had not heard the gunshots but when her husband's car disappeared from view for a few minutes she waffled painfully between giving the order to stop or doing her duty, which was to let Vitto follow his orders.

She did not ask questions.

After smiling at Little Pierre, who was sleeping on his nanny's breast, settling into the left corner of the car with some soft cushions, Saint-Clair looked at Sylvie.

"Now you'll understand. First, I'll sum up my talk with Dr. Korridès."

He told her briefly but without leaving out any essential details.

Then he continued, "My first duty was to get you to safety, you, Pierrot and Adele without a second to lose. It was a possibility, now it's a certainty. As I guessed I was being spied on. We were followed but I stopped the car sent by Korridès this time.

"At Orléans you'll get on the Southern Express. Vitto's going to park the town car at Marçon's where it'll be safely hidden. Like that your trail will be cold for any subsequent search. We'll deal with it later, as soon as you've arrived in Spain. After changing trains at the border, if you don't see me, go to

Saint Sebastian where you'll wait for me where we usually stay. I'll be coming in the roadster with Vitto and Socca. Can you guess where we're going?"

"Yes," she said, very calm now, "to the Duke of Arandar."

"Exactly."

She laughed lightly and a little nervously. "In fact, I think that as a secret hideout, inaccessible and well defended, the castle of San Lorenzo can't be beat. And the duke will be delighted because besides Gnô Mitang there's not a man in the world who loves and admires you more than he."

"I think so too," Saint-Clair agreed.

"Very well," Sylvie went on, "and what are you going to do? I can guess that too... You want to uncover the mystery of the Sycamores and defeat Korridès."

"Yes."

Taking her hands in his, in a voice that was emotional but forceful, he said:

"Sylvie, I'm absolutely certain that it wasn't yesterday that got us involved in the unfathomable existence of this Dr. Korridès. It's possible that last night's adventure was pure chance. All we had to do was not get out of the car and we never would've heard the scream that lured us into the Sycamores. But I believe it was only an excuse for Korridès to cross swords with me.

"When I was with the man I had the distinct and deep impression, unarguable and ineradicable, that I had been an enemy for a long time in some tragic game of this man. What past is he hiding? Who was the victim whose ashes I picked up? What's at the bottom of this abominable mystery that I'm sure is criminal behind all the darkness obscuring it? I want to know. I have to know. I feel I must. Otherwise it would mean little Pierre, you and I becoming victims of Korridès like sheep for a butcher. He'll lead them to the slaughterhouse without them suspecting a thing. He'll kill them without them expecting it. Well, you understand that it's impossible to live with this in your head and this threat constantly looming.

"Therefore, Sylvie, appreciate your role, which is huge—keep our son safe! Me, by more or less roundabout ways, I will fight our enemy! This fight would be impossible and I would surely lose if I didn't know you were safe, at least as far as human intelligence can know such things, in the castle of San Lorenzo with the Duke of Arandar."

Sylvie's face expressed such calm determination that Leo did not need a response to know that she understood, approved and would not try to appeal to his love for her and his great affection for his son to turn him away from the urgent and fierce battle against the mysterious Korridès.

They squeezed each other's hands in a passionate union of their vital forces and said nothing else.

At the Orléans station they were met by Socca who had the necessary tickets in his hand.

"That's great!" Saint-Clair said. "Come with us. Don't leave us. I'm going to check in the luggage, then all of us will wait for the train together. My order: watch everything around us and keep an eye on any suspicious individual. Of course, I don't think Korridès is trailing us now. He couldn't have predicted the stop at Orléans or the Southern Express. I stopped his stalkers and no one could've beat us here. But still, in such a short time this man has already shown me such prowess that we have to always be on guard, especially for the unexpected.

"You, Vitto, when the bags have been unloaded, go park the town car at Marçon's. He knows you. Just tell him that I'd like him to hide it, all right? Hide the car in the abandoned stable at the back of his garage. You park it there yourself and then get back here."

"Okay, boss," Vitto said.

A little later the Nyctalope kissed his wife and son in the three-berth compartment on the Southern Express train. Afterwards, he and Socca waited on the platform until the train had departed.

During the whole time they were in the station they had seen no suspicious coming or going around their small group first in the waiting room, then around the luggage and finally on the platform.

"I feel better," Saint-Clair said. "Now it's up to us to drive fast enough so that my wife doesn't wait too long in Irun on the border."

Across from the station Saint-Clair and Socca filled up the gas tank, added some oil, checked that the radiator was full, that certain bolts were tight, then bought some sandwiches and chocolate as well as bottles of mineral water. That was all the provisions they took to go from Orléans to Irun.

"Do you have enough tobacco?" Saint-Clair asked.

"Yes," Socca answered.

"Good."

See, when they took long road trips the three men liked to smoke their pipes.

Right after they had bought everything Vitto showed up.

"Boss, Marçon says hello and he's sorry he can't see you and not to worry about the car being spotted by anyone. I thought it best to tell him to take detailed notes on anybody he or his help caught snooping around his house or yard."

"Very good, very good," Saint-Clair was satisfied. "Get in and let's hit the road."

The Nyctalope got behind the wheel with Vitto on his left. Socca sat behind them with the tobacco, pipes and food. They each buckled on their hats, adjusted their glasses, knotted their scarves and buttoned up their leather jackets. As the clock in the roadster showed 11 p.m., they left Orléans on the road to Blois.

Blois, Tours, Poiteirs, Angoulême, Bordeaux—the long route, straight to the junction of Dax and Bayonne—then right away to Bayonne-Hendaye. And Irun!

The 450 miles of this trip were driven by the Nyctalope (with the advantage of being able to drive in the middle of the night without the need for headlights and only needing to squint his eyes not to be blinded by the oncoming cars) in 8 hours and 27 minutes.

When Bordeaux was behind them he said, "If nothing breaks down, it's not my wife who will be waiting for me but me waiting for her and my son."

Nothing broke down. Saint-Clair arrived in Irun three hours ahead of the Southern Express. He would not, therefore, have to cross the border in the car and drive all the way to San Sebastian. He went straight to the train station and got three passes for Burgos and told Vitto and Socca:

"I'll meet my wife on the train. She won't get off before we head to Burgos. You, listen up, take the car to Rue de la Reine Christine, which is over to the left at the end of the avenue. Number 10 is a little café-restaurant. Have a quiet breakfast. If you don't see me again before 10:15 at the latest, it's because all's well and I'm on the train on the way to Burgos.

"Then you get back on the road. By Saint-Jean-de-Luz, Saint-Pée, Espelette, go to Saint-Jean-Pied-de-Port. On the way, being sure to take all the usual precautions, put on the spare license plate. At Saint-Jean find a cozy hotel, park the car at the back of a garage or a shed, anywhere it won't be seen, and act like Italian tourists. As usual, you have all the necessary papers for it."

"Yes, boss," Vitto and Socca chimed in together.

"Walk around, go see Roland's Breach in Roncevaux, hang out, but not too much, with the locals. Let your beards grow, one pointed and the other cut straight, but full, up to the ears. It'll make you look different than in Versailles. One day, even if you can park the car without being seen, go and paint it flat gunmetal gray. Since it's a glossy yellow, it'll change it. Then go to Bayonne and put the car in a big garage that you'll rent for three months in advance. Lock it up good and say you're going to Italy on urgent business and you'll be taking a plane, the Bayonne-Toulouse-Nice-Gênes flight. In the Bayonne train station buy two first-class tickets for Bordeaux, but get off at Morcenx where you'll get tickets for Tarbes. From there, on a local train in third class, head to Lourdes. Be simple, very ordinary pilgrims. You'll wait for me at Lourdes unless I get there before you. But you'll be staying a month at Saint-Jean-Pied-de-Port. Got all that?"

"Yes, boss."

"Here's 20,000 francs. Oh, find some time to go target shooting, just to stay sharp, with both the rifle and the Brownings. Some out of the way place in the mountains shouldn't be too hard to find. Also practice your knife-throwing. We have to be ready for and capable of anything. Got it?"

"Yes, boss."

While talking he had taken out of his pocket a wad of bills. He gave ten to Vitto and ten to Socca. To wrap up, he clarified:

"At Lourdes, everyday without exception, at 10 a.m. and 4 p.m., park for fifteen minutes in front of the grotto next to the parapet. That, I hope, is where we'll meet. That's it. Do you have anything to say?"

Clearly affected the two men looked at each other.

Vitto responded, "No, boss, nothing to say. It's all plain as day. Everything will be carried as you ordered, like always. But..."

He hesitated, his brown skin turning red.

"Well?" Saint-Clair said.

"Boss, we'd like to shake your hand..."

"Good Lord, do you really think I'd leave you in a situation like this without shaking hands?"

He held out both hands and clasped the iron grips of his faithful friends—and after an affectionate but authoritative gaze that pierced them to the depths of their soul, he said:

"Vitto, Socca, my friends, goodbye. At Lourdes in five or six weeks, I hope. Unless I come see you before 10:15 this morning, which means everything's gone haywire. Go on, goodbye!"

He turned around and went back to the station carrying the light suitcase he had got from Socca at the last minute. He went to eat because he was starving.

Because he had nothing else to do but wait for the Southern Express, he wanted to ponder the "mystery of *The Sycamores*" but he could not, as he had so far, suppress the worry he had felt since he had arrived so early in Irun. Immediately this worry formed in his mind very precise words, a tyrannical repetition:

"Was I wrong to leave Sylvie and Pierre? Should I have stayed with them on the train in Orléans and let Vitto and Socca take the car? This Korridès is undeniably strong, especially against me since I don't know all the aspects, the means, the instruments of his hidden power. Wouldn't he use my separation from Sylvie and Pierre to attack them?"

But at the same time, logical thinking argued:

"Come on! As strong as he is, Korridès couldn't have foreseen such a swift departure. I stopped his trackers and threw him off the trail. It's not humanly possible to predict everything about the Southern Express at Orléans and me driving without my family to Irun. In the train, in their locked compartment, Sylvie and Pierre and the nanny are out of reach. Plus, Sylvie is on guard. She has her Browning. She's brave. She knows how to stay level-headed. She has our love, our son and our happiness to defend. They can't catch her by surprise. They'll never surprise her. So, in 45 minutes now I'll give her and Pierre a big hug..."

"Sure," worry said, "but this Korridès..."

And the same counter-arguments arose, relentlessly.

A little hidden in a dark corner of the café, smoking a lidded pipe, which Vitto had filled up and slipped into the pocket of his leather jacket, before replacing his driver's cap with a Basque beret from the suitcase, and the driving gloves with simple traveling gloves, the Nyctalope was chomping at the bit like this, constantly glancing at the clock over the long counter, watching the tortuously slow march of time.

But the slowness of time was only relative. In reality, the expected hour always arrives, inevitably. And Saint-Clair, in the end, jumped on the steps of the same railroad car of the Southern Express on which he had put his family in Orléans. He could not help laughing, loudly and ecstatically, when he saw his wife and son and the nanny in the corridor followed by a strapping gal, the sleeping car's attendant in charge of the luggage...

An hour later the Spanish train left for Burgos, Avila, Madrid. In a compartment with bunks that changed into padded benches and comfortable seats, Adele was breastfeeding Pierre and the Nyctalope was whispering to Sylvie about the arrangements he had already made and those he would be making soon to carry on this fight against Korridès, a fight that very likely would coincide with the investigations into the mystery of *The Sycamores*.

CHAPTER IV
How Korridès reacted

"Rosario has Madame returned?"

"Yes, Monsieur, just now."

"Is she alone?"

"Yes, Monsieur."

"Go and ask if she can see me right away."

"Very well, Monsieur."

Rosario, the mulatto, leaving the doctor to take off his hat and coat in the vestibule, sprang up the steps of the grand marble staircase with a magnificent wrought iron railing.

Dr. and Madame Maur Korridès had lived in Versailles for a year. They leased an old house on Rue des Bourdonnais that had had its interior renovated years before into modern style and comfort by the previous tenant. They said or were said to be English. The fact is that the Korridès were often invited to receptions at the British Embassy in Paris and sometimes gave a big welcome to English visitors, obviously genuine and from high society, to tell by the looks of them. But in Versailles they socialized with none of the locals. They had, however, an excellent reputation in the neighborhood because they led an affluent but austere life, they paid cash and their butler, a Hindu, only haggled over bills so as not to look stupid or stingy. People knew they had a garage with living quarters near Buc that had a direct telephone line to the house on Rue de Bourdonnais. Their mechanic, also a Hindu, lived there with a junior butler who sometimes served as footman. They had two cars: a very comfortable sedan for the drives in Paris and casual outings; and a sports car for the long trips that Jane Korridès like to take, being a very sportive woman. Hadn't they seen her picture in a big illustrated newspaper as one of a very few European female aviators at an international banquet? And didn't they know that she had twice won automobile races in speed and distance, open races in which the daring woman driver and mechanic had beaten many a male "ace" driver?

"That Englishwoman, she's one-of-a-kind!" they said in certain salons in Versailles when talking about Madame Jane Korridès without knowing anything more about her.

And no incriminating fingers could be pointed at her lifestyle. It was the general rule to hold her, along with her husband, in the highest esteem—concession made, no doubt, by the Versailles "society" to the *Entente Cordiale*, that cordial agreement that was "so necessary to peace in Europe".

The only subject they allowed themselves to speak freely about was the work of Dr. Korridès. This "doctor" was particularly a chemist and physicist. He had a reputation of specializing in "explosives". They were therefore afraid that thanks to this English experimenter the district of the diocese would some day blow up like a powder keg.

That was all the public opinion had to say about the Korridès.

So, this evening the doctor sent the mulatto Rosario, the chambermaid, to ask if her mistress would see him. While waiting for an answer, with, hands behind his back and brow furrowed, he paced up and down the large vestibule at the foot of the grand staircase. The answer from Madame Korridès took only as long as it took the maid to climb the stairs and come back down.

"Madame is waiting for you, Monsieur."

"Good."

These little ceremonies in their relations in the presence of third parties came to an abrupt end as soon as the doctor closed and locked the padded door, also furnished with a thick, heavy curtain, of the vast room that was all in one a bedroom, smoking room and study.

"Hey," Korridès snapped, "Back already? You know that..."

"I know," the woman cut him off coldly, "love, marriage and fatherhood haven't weakened the Nyctalope one bit and it's going to be hard for us to succeed."

"He caught you by surprise?" the doctor hissed, pale and narrowing his eyes into a sharp and bitter glare.

"He stopped me on the road and made it impossible for me to follow him."

"Tell me."

"Well..."

Madame Korridès told how after Etampes Saint-Clair's roadster and the Browning took out the hot rod, its tires and the spares.

She was still wearing the brown suit and aviator boots that she usually wore when driving. The gauntlets, leather cap with a chin strap and the goggles had been tossed onto the couch next to a big leather armchair in which she lounged, legs crossed, while speaking.

A very beautiful woman, tall, svelte, graceful and strong, with sensual lips, magnificent black eyes, dark-skinned with a hint of saffron, Jane Korridès looked like she was probably a little over thirty, fifteen or twenty years younger than her husband who, being scrawny and quite ugly, made a surprising contrast to her. Her hair was cut short, like an athlete; her hands were long and nervous; her figure sleek and lively; her perfectly proportioned limbs were exquisite archetypes of the modern woman in whom Venus, Diana and Minerva are commingled. She spoke with a warm, controlled voice. She told of her defeat calmly.

She wrapped up, "The Nyctalope won. I concede. But I'll have my revenge. In the meantime, be on your guard, Maur. The war is on. So far we've only seen outlying skirmishes, most of them unknown to the enemy. But the enemy is only him, Saint-Clair, the Nyctalope. And he is alerted now. Without a doubt he wants to know and understand. With his wife and son hidden away he will come back against us. For him we are the sphinx of the mystery... So, watch out!"

Korridès was sitting on the couch across from Jane. He just shrugged and grinned.

"Bah! Our intelligence services are too well organized and too bloodthirsty for a woman, child and nanny, with or without the Nyctalope, to escape their eyes of Argus and their ears of a Sioux. The best plan, I believe, is to immediately give the order called for by the situation."

"Immediately!" she agreed without hesitating. "Against only the Nyctalope we'll just barely be able to defend ourselves. But against Saint-Clair, the husband and father, we can attack. Let's attack. If we don't strike first and deal a crushing blow, we'll be done for. And you know, Maur, what the consequences of defeat will be."

"I know," the man grumbled, "and I know even better what the price of victory will be. Let's go!"

She gave the man a smile and a look that got his blood boiling. He jumped up and leaned over, grabbing her by the shoulders with his tense, trembling hands, and in a raspy voice, through clenched teeth, bared like an enraged, hungry wolf, he said:

"Ah, Jane, I'll kill you. Yes, I'll kill you if the day comes when your presence, your smile and your looks, by the will of fate, are nothing but false promises... I will kill you..."

Staring icily into the man's gray eyes, she replied, "You've already told me, Maur. You've told me many times. And me, I'll answer once and for all— Watch out! If your love gets so easily exasperated, while waiting, and just turns into a lethal threat of hate, I'll make the first move. Before you kill me, I will kill you, Maur."

With these chilling words she reached out her arms, pushed away her husband, gently but forcefully, stood up, gathered her gloves, cap and goggles, turned around and marched off. Then she pushed aside a curtain and disappeared.

The doctor shuddered, frozen there for a few minutes, staring at the curtain. Was he hoping that his wife would come back? Everything about the man, admirable and unnerving in his face, pitiful in his body, exuded passion—a passion both frenzied and stubborn, capable of endless patience and rabid violence. He waited. And he became calm again... and thoughtful. All of a sudden he lowered his head, wrung his hands and muttered:

"Yes, I love her, would do anything for her, would put up with anything from her, up to a point..."

He paused, turned to the only window in the room and shook his fists.

"Saint-Clair! Saint-Clair! If I have to kill your wife and son with my own hands and then torture you until her hatred be gratified, until your death finally satisfy her, I will do it... But afterward, that she be my slave, or else..."

He paused again, swore like a sailor, stomped across the room and slammed the door behind him. He went to the ground floor, down a wide hallway and at the end of it entered a big room that had been converted into a chemistry lab. He did not stop. He opened an iron door, went through, closed it and stood inside a study/work room whose four walls were invisible behind shelves stuffed with books. As furniture, four stools, a rolling ladder and a table cluttered with files, papers, ink and pens. An electric globe in the ceiling automatically turned on.

Korridès stood before a shelf like all the others. He took out three bound volumes that he kept in his left hand and stuck his right hand into the rectangular cavity. A faint click was heard. Quickly the doctor replaced the three volumes and took three steps back.

With a suddenness and violence that, if he had not stepped back he would have been hit hard enough to floor a bull, the entire bookshelf swung open a quarter circle. A tapestry was plastered to the wall. A tapestry of Cordoba leather with relief drawings. Korridès stepped forward. With his thumb, index and ring finger he pressed three points in an equilateral triangle and a door opened in front of him. He went through. The bookshelf closed behind him and the door as well while the globe turned off.

But in front of the doctor, below him, six electric lights turned on one by one. They revealed a stairway.

The doctor went down thirty steps, crossed a small rotunda, put his left foot on a certain flagstone, his right foot on another one a little behind it and pushed down hard one after the other. He was in front of a low door recessed in a squat archway. It opened without a sound. It was very thick and made of two steel panels with insulation stuffed between them. There, too, Korridès hurried in and the door closed while the lights in the stairway turned off. A vast ceiling light turned on in the cellar he had just entered.

This cellar looked like a wireless radio booth on board a dreadnought battleship. A specialist technician would have admired the high quality of the recognizable equipment and been passionately interested in the unknown devices found there.

Korridès had long ago mastered the experimental system whose improvements and novelties, both secret, were his own invention. He had designed, made and installed everything. He sat at one of the three tables. For a good half hour he worked at the device.

Then he went back the way he had come and on the ground floor entered the dining room where he told Jane, who was reading a newspaper while waiting for him, "Shall we eat?"

"At once."

Her foot pressed an electric button on the carpet under the table and the butler appeared right away.

That same night, in the main towns of all the departments in France, in the capitals and main towns of the provinces, counties or cantons of all the countries in Europe, in Egypt, in Tunisia, in Algeria and Morocco, and finally in the biggest cities on every big island in the Mediterranean and East Atlantic—a man, woken up by special alarm, heard a musical phrase over the radio, repeated five times. Using a special, secret, decryption key each of these men rushed to translate clearly—and in French—the musical phrase that was immediately written on staves by a small device attached to the radio.

CHAPTER V
The invisible threat

In Spain there is no region wilder, rougher and less inhabited than the mountain range called the Sierra de la Demanda. It stands to the east-south-east of Burgos in Old Castile spreading over 125 miles long and 60 miles wide. Its highest peaks rise up less than 8,000 feet, but they are surrounded by the most horrific chasms. Jumbles of gigantic rocks and impenetrable forests cling to the mountainsides and crowd the steep, winding valleys where rushing rivers roar.

In this irregular trapezoid of 12,000 square miles there are barely a dozen communities that could to be called villages. There are just as many little settlements with land for grazing or logging, which make up the properties of four hidalgos, three of whom live in Madrid and have a house in Burgos. Only one of these landowners—the first or the fourth, as you want—decided to live as a country gentleman like in days of yore. He lived in the mountains all year long.

This was Duke Pedro d'Arandar y Salas, a Spanish grandee, an inveterate hunter and a skilled lumberjack. With expertise he handled the extra-light modern rifle that looked like a plaything and the medieval axe, which is a giant's weapon. At fifty, he was still as strong and agile as a thirty year-old. Although rough in appearance he was a charming man, able to strip off the Castilian arrogance when called for and endowed with a purity of soul and a naivety that anywhere else but the wild estate of San Lorenzo de la Demanda would make him prey to the worst of criminals.

A widower without children, Don Pedro d'Arandar lived in his castle with a maid servant who, through respect, admiration and natural fear, held her role as head servant. A dozen female servants under her and as many men, some married, some not, made up the household staff of the castle. There was a whole brood of kids and babies but they never left the property and the Duke completely ignored them. On the land were two gardeners and six shepherds with their families whose total number was unknown to Don Pedro. Only one man knew the state of the house and property: the steward, priest and chaplain of San Lorenzo, Padre Felipe, a Franciscan monk, specially assigned to this kind of extremely rural parish thanks to the castle's chapel.

As for the Castle itself—on the southern slope of Mount San Lorenzo, twelve miles by shortcuts from the nearest village, named Salas—it was a medieval Castilian fortress in all its magnificent, rugged and terrible splendor. Built with big, square blocks of hard rock, cemented with lime mortar and sand and joined with iron spikes, the walls had remained perfectly intact since the days of El Cid who was born in Burgos in 1026.

The whole line of Arandars had never touched the exterior architecture. Therefore, (we can see in our 20th century just as it was in the 10th) the castle of

San Lorenzo kept, without any decay, its crenelated outer wall with its gate-house and barbican, its fortified ramps on every level, its central building with corner towers, round towers, peaked towers, watchtowers, its stately dwelling and its chapel, its main courtyard, its roof garden, its outbuildings, its stables, its cellars and cisterns, everything surrounded not by a moat with still water but a veritable torrent that roared down from a deep gorge in the mountain, split upstream from the castle, poured its howling waters around the castle and rejoined its two branches farther downstream. Thus, San Lorenzo was an island fortress.

There was only one way to enter or leave the castle. From one end to the other of this route there were: the crenelated ramp on each of its eight levels with a barbican and gatehouse with three doors, the portico of two towers with a gate, its portcullis and drawbridge and its single-arched bridge across the river.

However, the interior of the castle, without losing anything of its general structure, had benefited little over the course of the centuries from the mellow-ing of human customs or at least from the appearance of mellowing that material progress created among men in civilized nations. The furniture had changed gradually and stopped (for good it seemed) in the Philippe IV style, which corresponds to our Louis XIII style. But the current Duke Pedro d'Arandar himself did not want electricity even though perfect waterfalls surrounded the castle, nor central heating even though furnaces could have been fed to capacity with dry wood starting on the first evening of autumn all the way through to the first morning of spring without the forests losing a bit of their incalculable wealth. In the San Lorenzo castle, even last year, they used candles in candlesticks or can-delabra or chandeliers and they heated with logs burning freely on andirons in huge fireplaces with large mantels. True, the chandeliers were from old Venice, the candelabra and candlesticks were of sculpted silver, splendid porcelain and precious wrought iron. True too, the andirons and firedogs paired in the various firebacks were pure masterpieces of Spanish metalwork from the time of Charles V...

And that was the place, truly fantastic in our age, even in Spain, even in Old Castilo—where Leo Saint-Clair the Nyctalope wanted to shelter his beloved wife and son.

Now, on Wednesday May 25, around 5 p.m., Don Pedro d'Arandar was getting back to his castle after a whole day spent surveying, with one of his game wardens, the paths of different herds of boars for which he was planning a big hunt. He had just come onto the hard, mountainous, rutted path that ran from the castle to the distant village of Salas. With the rifle slung over his shoulder and the warden behind him, the Duke had the springy, quick, steady gait of a mountaineer. Dressed in dark velvet, he wore an old, red, felt hat and tall, un-lined boots that were very supple. Except for the extremely modern rifle he was pretty much the picture of a hidalgo from the times of Charles V, with his short, gray, square-cut beard, his stern look and his hair cropped close.

Since the road, from a hillside left barren by a recent fire, widened into an big empty space before descending into the lowlands, the Duke stopped short and turned around.

"Ho, Antonio," he said, "did I hear the bells of mules?"

"Yes, sir," the game warden replied, a short, thin man, dark-skinned with the head of Don Quixote.

"Is it in front of us?"

"I think so."

"The coalmen are still a ways off from this area. Who could be going to the castle?"

Very intrigued because he had no friends coming before the hunting season and also a little worried for his solitude, which he loved, Don Pedro started off again, a little faster, hoping to catch up to the mules before they reached the castle. They could only be going to San Lorenzo since this path led nowhere else. They were not far ahead because the bells sounded very clear and could not be going very fast because the path was very bumpy and in bad shape from the hard rains of the last storm.

After barely fifteen minutes after his attention, curiosity and worry were almost simultaneously aroused, Don Pedro stepped around a huge mossy boulder and saw the animals a hundred feet in front of him. There were four of them. Two were carrying trunks and suitcases. The other two had women on them. Two women, one of whom was hugging something that looked like a swaddled child. Behind the mules were two men with sticks in hand. One was a peasant, a native mule driver. The other...

"Good God," the Duke swore as his face brightened.

He tossed his rifle back to the game warden with a "Ho!" as a warning and ran like a young man feeling strong, nimble and terribly excited.

But they heard him first. The two men turned around and stopped. There was a brief exchange of words. One went to stand in front of the mules. The other walked, hurriedly, to meet the hunter.

"Saint-Clair!"

"Don Pedro!"

Hands met, squeezed, and released. Then arms opened for a hug.

"Saint-Clair, you're here? And the ladies?"

"My wife and son and the nanny."

"What a surprise! But I didn't get a letter or telegram..."

"I didn't send one. The situation is very grave." Saint-Clair hesitated.

The Duke encouraged, "You can talk. My game warden doesn't know French... No, wait, don't talk. My surprise, my joy has made me rude. We'll talk later. After such a trip... Madame must be tired. And the child... Good Lord, I've lost all my manners!"

He walked quickly, but with dignity, hat in hand, up to Sylvie Saint-Clair, bowed deeply, kissed her gloved hand and in a voice turned hoarse with emotion said:

"Madame, my beautiful and charming friend, excuse my thoughtlessness. I'm holding up your arrival at my home, delaying dinner, I'm a lout. Your son! The angel. I'll play grandfather to him. Let's go! Mule driver, onward! And step on it!"

Sylvie smiled. Her husband walked behind the Duke, still holding his hat in his hand, next to the mule carrying the young lady. In front was the mule driver holding the bridle of the animal on which Adele was clearly fighting off sleep. In the rear followed Antonio the game warden, bare-headed, two rifles slung over his right shoulder.

Not a word was spoken all the way to the castle. After they passed the drawbridge Sylvie and Adele got on the ground. The Duke ordered the driver and his mules to spend the night in San Lorenzo and not go back to Salas until tomorrow. Then came the somewhat formal introduction of the unexpected guest to the guest rooms, which were always kept ready. After a meal of soup, eggs, fresh cheese, fruits and jams, Sylvie and her son, along with Adele, went to get some much needed rest. Thus, the Duke d'Arandar would finally satisfy his burning and anxious curiosity, which he had had the strength, out of Castilian courtesy, to keep absolutely silent.

In the smoking room next to his bedroom, doors closed, curtains lowered, a box of cigars opened, he pushed a big armchair over to Saint-Clair, sat down in another, and sounding a little shy, said:

"My friend, now that the basic, important obligations of hospitality are pretty much taken care of, try to stave off your own fatigue and please give me some explanation that my affection for you..."

"Don Pedro," Saint-Clair cut him off with a smile, "you haven't changed. I admire you, respect you and adore you. I don't know that if I were in your place I'd have had so much patience. It was a little bit wicked of me to accept all your strict laws of hospitality."

"You're welcome, my friend," the Duke was both content and confused.

"Anyway, you will wait no longer for the explanation I owe you. It's a crazy story. Here goes."

And the Nyctalope told the Duke everything that had happened since the tragic and mysterious evening of May 21.

He concluded, "I want to know who this Dr. Maur Korridès is, what he does and what he wants. There's a war going on that won't end except in the total defeat—or death—of one of us. My love for my wife and son make me too vulnerable. I'm asking you to take them under your protection, keep them here in your castle, defend them against any possible attack, in short save them. Nowhere else in the world can Sylvie and Pierre be safe except here in San Lorenzo. None of my friends have the respect, trust and affection that I have for you, Don Pedro. If you would accept…"

"If I'd accept!?" the Duke shouted, stood up and placed his two hands on the shoulders of his friend. "But am I not the godfather of Pedrito? And besides, didn't I tell you one day, that day in Saint Sebastian when you saved my honor that was so horribly compromised by that woman and my folly… Didn't I tell you that my goods, my respect, my strength, my life belong to you? Since then I've seen you five or six times, only for short visits, relaxing breaks that you honored me with… I don't know your wife except through the photograph you sent me of your wedding. And your son, I only know about him from the last letter you sent when he was already three months old. But you three are a holy trinity for me. I'm all yours. Don't ask anything, just give orders!"

Saint-Clair hid his gratitude behind a friendly smile. He stood up.

"God forbid I order anything," he said. "Don Pedro, I'm leaving tomorrow. While I'm gone, please watch over my wife and son as if they were your own. And consider that an awful danger is looming over them. I'm going to fight an incomprehensible enemy, incomprehensibly powerful, whom I imagine is ruthless, and my wife and son are the only chinks in my armor."

The Duke stepped back, turned toward a crucifix hanging on the wall over an old prie-dieu and with his right hand raised he solemnly pronounced, "I swear!"

The next morning, with the mule driver who had brought him to San Lorenzo, Leo Saint-Clair went back to Salas. But instead of returning to Burgos, he went over the mountain to the station of Arandar de Ducro on the Valladolid-Saragossa line, and got back to France through Lerida, Barcelona and Portbou.

From that day on, the lives of Sylvie, Pierre and Adele were structured. The Duke offered them a program that he thought best for the situation and the people involved.

"Madame Sylvie, the meals will be served in your rooms along with your child and nurse or sometimes with me in the dining room at the times I take it upon myself to set it… The music room is all yours. My blessed mother had a piano that I've kept and that someone from Burgos comes to tune when necessary because I love to play and I can also hold my own on the violin and cello. Music and hunting are my sins… My library is full of French and English authors because I speak both languages almost as well as I do Castilian… My stable can provide you with good mountain horses since I know you're a skilled and intrepid rider. But please don't go out unless I escort you. And my game wardens will discreetly keep an eye on us… Freedom, madame, total freedom, but under my constant protection. And my entire house is at your service, from my steward and chaplain, Padre Felipe, whom I will introduce you to later, to the lowliest of my kitchen maids, the gruffest of my farm boys. As for me, I am yours to command, the humblest of your servants…"

"Monsieur," Sylvie responded, still pale and teary-eyed from the separation, "all that is very nice and I'm deeply touched. But be like my father, please. I'll have my meals with you and at your regular times. When I need some exercise I'll go out with you. For Pierrot and Adele, a little stroll every day on the sunny ramparts of the castle or in the roof garden and in the shaded cloister of the chapel will be enough fresh air. Our rooms are big and opened at noon so my son won't feel too imprisoned, as it were. We'll play music, I'll read, embroider... and we'll talk, especially when we get news from my husband. I'm not worried about feeling bored because I know very well that with you as company and as caretaker it would be impossible, even if my personality were prone to, which it's not. I think, therefore, that..."

But next to her on the couch transformed into a little bed, Pierret cried out. For a moment his eyes opened and his pink hands started shaking at the ends of his pudgy white arms. He cried, he howled. Sylvie turned and leaned over him with a big smile, but the nanny was already running in from the next room and with her Toulouse accent (since she came from a village in the Haute Garonne) she said:

"Oh, the little one wants his milk."

He was swept up, cradled in the hefty arms and almost right away his two hands gripped the swollen breast. The Duke d'Arandar was enthralled, Sylvie was smiling and they did not talk or move, just watched the baby son of the Nyctalope until he was full and back to sleep.

On this first day, during which they did not leave the castle, Sylvie met the chaplain, Padre Felipe, tall, fat, colorful, glib and suave, more like a Norman monk than a Spanish Franciscan. By chance she met the brown-haired, pretty, quiet but alert Blanca, the maid servant to whom Leo had given some indispensable information and Blanca knew what to say to give Sylvie confidence in her utmost dedication. First of all, Sylvie had let her know, by example, about her limited but adequate knowledge of the Castilian language; Blanca could therefore talk and be sure to be understood. Then two servants, specially assigned, were introduced by Blanca: two young and strong girls from Aragon in white camisoles and short red skirts, legs and feet bare, as spry as squirrels, clean as a whistle and whose names were Rita and Sabel.

The next day, May 27, in the afternoon, Sylvie took a two-hour walk in the forest accompanied by Don Pedro. Fifty or a hundred feet ahead, to the side and behind four game wardens armed with loaded rifles surrounded them while trying to remain unseen.

May 28 it rained all day long. Music, reading, conversations, long meals, cigarettes...

May 29 was a Sunday: mass at eleven in the chapel...

And it was at the end of this mass that Sylvie had the uneasy feeling that this castle of San Lorenzo, isolated in the middle of the wild and deserted sierra, might not be the safe haven that the Nyctalope believed it was. Where did this feeling come from?

The eyes, the weird eyes of a man and the words, even weirder, of a child.

For the Sunday services and feast days, the chapel of San Lorenzo was open to all.

"It's a tradition that dates back to the very day of the consecration of the *capilla* in 1213 on August 10, the feast day of Saint Laurent," the Duke told Sylvie. "The tradition has never been neglected except for one time in July in 1320 when the castle was surrounded and besieged by a big group of Aragonese in a fight with the d'Arandar of the time. Now, we're neither surrounded nor besieged, but it's still important that the tradition be broken if it threatens your safety. There are two ways: the simplest and surest is that you don't go to mass."

"And the other?" Sylvie pressed him since she did not want to miss the quaint pleasure of the anachronistic and curious spectacle that she expected from this ceremony and its participants.

"I told Padre Felipe and Blanca, to whom I only gave half of your name, that you were one of two relatives I have in France and that no one here has ever seen you. You're Señorita Via, my niece. Furthermore, no one has heard the name of your husband or your real name. So, there's no way to identify Sylvie Saint-Clair, wife of the Nyctalope, with my niece Via, come here with her husband, her son Pedrito, my godson, and their nanny, the nurse... Are you following me?"

"Very well," Sylvie smiled.

"Therefore, you can go to mass with your head, shoulders and chest wrapped in a big shawl. And if you bury your face in the prayer book, it'll be easy to hide it from the faithful, not only because you'll be sitting at the lord's pew to the left of the altar in a dark little side alcove, but also when we come in last and leave first, as is fitting, we'll be passing by everyone kneeling down... Still, the safest would be for you not to attend the mass."

"I see!" the young lady did not want to deny herself the pleasure. "But the absence of your niece, surely very devout, will surprise the chaplain and all your servants and the faithful as well, who know nothing of your relative's visit to San Lorenzo. But they've seen me here. They gave me chocolate in the morning and sang to make Pierrot laugh. It wouldn't work to pretend I'm sick, especially since I wouldn't like to pretend to be sick... I'd have to be sick for the rest of my stay..."

"That's true, you're right, *caramba*!" the Duke grumbled quietly. "Unexplained or badly explained, your absence would start people talking more than your presence. And it would go all the way to Salas, all the way to Burgos. If you don't go to mass, they'll gossip all day long. If you go, they'll only say that Señorita Via, one of the Duke's nieces, is at San Lorenzo... and that's all."

"So I'm going?"

"Yes. But still, hide your face, which doesn't look a bit Spanish, I assure you. Use the shawl and the prayer book."

"Don't worry. But don't forget that the mule driver from Salas, his wife and their child saw my face. And the padre, Blanca, the game wardens and servants have all seen me too and will keep seeing me."

"That's true. *Sacramento*! Well, I don't..."

"Come on, Don Pedro, you can't accomplish the impossible regarding my safety seeing that I couldn't be invisible when I entered Spain. Between recklessness and discretion, there's a middle ground. Let's find it, as wisely and cautiously as possible. Leo, despite his justifiable fears, didn't intend to lock up his wife and son in a prison. So, I'll go to mass and I won't hide my face except as is normal for Christian modesty."

There was some irony in the thoughts, words and tone of the young lady. Before marrying the Nyctalope she had faced much more terrible dangers, at least closer and more concrete than this abstract and distant threat. This, along with her natural courage, drove her to be bold in spirit and not faint of heart. Besides, as inflexible and authoritative as he was with others, Don Pedro d'Arandar could be nothing but gentle, accommodating and supportive with Sylvie Saint-Clair.

He did not catch the irony. He did see the truth in her reasoning and he concluded, "Bast! You're right! In any case, there's no great risk when you're inside the castle walls. Outside, my men and I will always be watching over you. So, go to mass. But what about Pedrito? And the nanny?"

"Oh," Sylvie chuckled, "I imagine the little cherub, as you say, will excuse his nanny from Sunday services."

The Duke laughed too. His religion, like most great lords in Spain who are not Carlists, was very lenient about rituals. Here he caught the innocent sarcasm of the young lady and he figured that everything had worked out for the best.

Therefore, on Sunday, instead of being alone walking solemnly from one end of the chapel to the other right before the *Introit* and sitting stiffly under the heraldic canopy, Duke Pedro d'Arandar led his niece, his gloved left hand holding her bare hand, and took his place at the lord's pew after she had knelt down.

As expected, as soon as she could, discreetly, positioned herself so that she could see everything and everyone in the chapel.

Usually, the Sunday mass attracted not only the staff, interior and exterior, of the castle, but also many men, women and children who lived on the domain. Only in the winter, because of the snow, fog and floods, were there few people in the nave. But on this beautiful Sunday in spring, people came from as far as four miles away.

Moreover, something that happened often enough so that no one was surprised, on May 29 in the chapel of San Lorenzo, devotedly awaiting the mass was a whole tribe of gypsies. These "Bohemians" of Spain spoke not only their own mysterious idiom but also Castilian, Majorcan, Catalan, Languedoc and even Basque because they spent their lives wandering between Albaicín in Grenada, the crypt of Saintes-Maries-de-la-Mer and the church of Cangas in the bay of Vigo.

Now, the gypsies were naively brash, which sometimes bordered on rudeness. Furthermore, they loved a spectacle. The spectacle of a mass, as sacred as it was, was something they soaked up in every detail, these swarthy men and children, long-haired and scruffy, these women in scarfs, dressed in six colorful skirts and lighter blouses, all very clean, as it happened.

The whole tribe, numbering around fifty people, were gathered as near as possible to the tall grill that separated the dark, bare nave from the bright, golden altar. Behind these occasional intruders were the Spaniards from the region, normal worshipers, kneeling here and there in families or alone. The castle servants had their place, by tradition, along the small columns of the side chapels on the right side of the nave almost directly facing the lord's pew.

Blanca, prudently modest, was among them and Sylvie had trouble spotting her. But she was more interested in the gypsies and could not help glancing at them, even staring at times…

She did not notice right away the eyes of a man who was staring back at her. No individual among the Bohemians really caught her attention until the reading of the gospel, but then, very suddenly, she felt a kind of magnetic vertigo in her nerves by the insistent glare charged with mysterious electricity produced by a powerful mind.

Involuntarily, she turned her head and was right away seized by the bright flash in the man's eyes. He was a gypsy with a white beard, kneeling down in the front row. He looked like a stern, disgruntled patriarch. His dark eyes shot sharp daggers straight at the young lady. What this look meant Sylvie did not bother to ask herself at first. He was inflicting an almost painful discomfort on her, so troubling that she wanted to turn away and escape the despotic, potent, eerie gaze. But a force, stronger than her will, kept Sylvie from making the slightest movement. She remained dominated, virtually enthralled.

Nevertheless, her mind was free. She thought. She finally told herself, "It's me and me alone whom this man is watching. What does he want from me?"

So, what did this Bohemian's stare mean? Rational but troubled, Sylvie perceived both an examination and a threat, both insolence and defiance. At the same time, she noticed that the features of the man's face grew tense, hardened in the oval between his beard and white hair. And this face suddenly expressed bitter hatred…

It was then that the bells announced the Raising of the Host. The people on their knees lowered their heads. Eyes closed, faces buried. Freed, Sylvie leaned over the front of her pew. When she looked up and glanced over at the old Bohemian, she saw him praying, eyes lowered, looking calm.

She made a gut decision.

"Don Pedro," she whispered to her side.

"What is it?"

"Do you see that old gypsy, third from the left in the front row?"

"Yes, I see him. What of it?"

"Please watch him on the sly for the rest of the mass because he worries me. I'll tell you why later."

"*Bueno.*"

But the "*Ite, missa est*" was recited without the suspicious gypsy raising his head again. Once the final prayers were said and Padre Felipe had gone back to the sacristy with his two attendants, the Duke and his "niece" had to get up from the pew and leave the chapel ceremoniously by crossing, as was the custom, from one end to the other. When they passed by, the old man did not look up.

When Don Pedro and Sylvie arrived at the holy water font at the right of the main door, the Duke dipped two fingers in order to pass on a drop to the young lady for the last sign of the cross. But a little girl, a young gypsy, jumped out of the shadows, plunged her whole hand into the basin and held it up to the Duke. While Don Pedro was crossing himself, having turned to the altar according to the rite, on the forehead, chest, shoulders and lips, the quintuple sign of the cross, the little girl stood up in her bare tiptoes, grabbed Sylvie's neck and made her bend over. To the astonished woman the little gypsy spoke excitedly but very clearly:

"*Aplasta le vibora... Matala!*"

And in a flash, she ran away.

Remaining composed, Sylvie had the presence of mind to "sign" herself according to the Spanish custom at the very moment when the Duke turned back around. And together they left. They only had to cross the courtyard to reach the lord's dwelling. Curious to know the reason for Sylvie's concern about the old Bohemian, the Duke hurried his step. And the young lady, even more disturbed after the incident at the font, walked faster.

Spurred by her motherly instincts she said, "Let's first go see Pierrot."

"As you wish."

When Sylvie saw her son playing in the sun with a ribbon with the colors of Spain, which Adele was fluttering in front of him, she let out such an intense sigh of relief that the Duke got scared.

"*Qué suspiro!*" he said. "Were you worried about him?"

"What, no, I don't know," Sylvie answered with a shaky voice. "But listen."

And right away her beautiful face and big, blue eyes regained the calm energy that was the true essence of her character, without losing any of her feminine charm. Sylvie rattled off not only the eerie episode of the insistent, menacing, hateful glare of the old gypsy, but also the even weirder incident with the little gypsy girl.

She concluded, "Why tell me that, quickly, secretly, as if she was afraid of getting caught talking to me—Crush the viper... kill it!"

The Duke stood up straight and exclaimed, "So, she said '*Aplasta la vibora, Matala*'?"

"Exactly."

"*Desacrado!* Please, stay in this room. Wait for me." And he ran out.

The Duke d'Arandar was a man of fast thinking and prompt action. Maybe he sometimes did not think long enough, which could lead him to inappropriate actions, even though with the best intentions. But in this situation, the solemn and lofty opinion he had of his responsibility to the Nyctalope kept him from following through on the impulse that pushed him down the stairs and into the main courtyard where he saw all the faithful walking leisurely out of the chapel. The sight of his servants, the game wardens, the farmers and their families, behind whom would probably come the gypsies, this same sight made him foresee the turbulent and long-term consequences of what he had come to do.

Halfway across he stopped.

"No," he said, "not like this. I'm about to do something stupidly impetuous. Let's be smart about it."

Smiling but sternly he shouted, "Antonio!"

Hat in hand his chief game warden came over alone while the small crowd stopped in front of the chapel doorway.

"Did you see a family of gypsies at the mass?"

"Yes, of course."

"*Bueno!* The *señorita* knows neither their dances nor their songs. I want her to enjoy hearing and seeing them. Tell the head of the family that they will eat here. Bring them to the common room... My servants and my mountain workers are also invited. No one will leave until after the entertainment. It's a big party at San Lorenzo today."

While speaking the Duke stepped closer to his game warden. When they were face-to-face, he whispered quickly:

"I'm ordering all the exterior doors of the castle be closed. They will be reopened only on my orders. If anyone tries to leave, they must be stopped, but amiably, saying that I want everyone who was at the mass to eat, drink and be merry at my expense. Understood?"

"Understood, my lord."

"*Bueno!*"

With a gesture both noble and condescending the Duke greeted the small crowd that was surprised and delighted, then he went back into the castle.

In the bedroom doorway he waved over Sylvie. She put Pierrot in the arms of Adele and in the adjoining room learned what Don Pedro had just done.

"Devil take me," he wrapped up, "if I don't find the little gypsy girl so you can question her... and get a look at those old gypsy's eyes."

"Great," Sylvie approved.

But just then she remembered the Duke's tone of voice when he exclaimed, "So, she said '*Aplasta la vibora, Matala*'?" It was the tone of someone hearing words that bore a known tragedy. Without pause she added, "Tell me Don Pedro what the gypsy girl meant by those weird words: 'Crush the viper. Kill it!' And what's her relation to this present situation, if there is a relation?"

The Duke slowly wiped his worried forehead. He did not sit down. He did not think of asking the young lady to sit down. Standing before her, who was medium height and a head shorter than him, he took her hand and looked at her with tender concern.

He answered very gravely, "You're asking me too much, Sylvie. If I could answer your questions, everything about the two incidents in the chapel would be clear. But you're right—before hearing you say those words, I knew them. A fateful decree. Listen, I'll tell you everything I know about it. You'll think it's trivial. But maybe we'll find out more before sounding the alarm. When a gypsy fortune teller reads your palm, if she sees a very serious danger coming directly or indirectly from a woman, she pronounces a phrase, both a warning and an incantation, both advice and command: 'Crush the viper. Kill it!' If the danger is coming from a man, animal or a natural phenomenon, the soothsayer says nothing else about it. She'll just say, for example, 'Beware a blond man' or 'Watch out for horses' or 'Don't travel by sea'. But I repeat, if the danger seen in the lines of the hand is the work of a woman, the gypsy will always whisper in the ear of the person at risk, '*Aplasta la vibora. Matala!*' That's all I know."

"Well now," Sylvie said, "that makes things even more mysterious. The little gypsy girl hadn't read my palm. Therefore, if we take this seriously—and everything is serious in my present situation—we're right to suspect that Dr. Korridès has accomplices in Spain and these accomplices are already informed about me and on the attack. They can identify me without ever having seen me, like that old gypsy who's obviously one of them or sent by them, and finally that the gypsy girl is on my side or with people on my side who are trying to warn me... a warning that also tells me that it's a woman I should watch out for... Could it be that woman who was driving the sports car stopped by my husband on the highway from Etampes to Orléans? What do you think, Don Pedro?"

"My God," the Duke tugged nervously at his beard, "I think your reasoning is logical. And I hope that this afternoon we'll learn something by watching the old gypsy and questioning the little girl."

But a great and very troubling disappointment darkened the shadows that Syvlie and Don Pedro were starting to be surrounded by. An hour later, when they were sitting in two armchairs placed at the top of the front steps outside the castle and when they scrutinized the Bohemians gathered to the right, while the Spanish formed a big half-circle to the left, the two of them did not see the old man or the little girl among the gypsies.

"Antonio!" the Duke called out.

The game warden ran over.

"Not all the gypsies are here. I believe I saw at the mass an old, bearded man with long, white hair and a little girl around twelve or thirteen years-old... I don't see them here. Did anyone leave the castle?"

"No, my lord. No door or portcullis has been opened or lifted since the start of the mass. Nobody left."

"Well, where are the old man and the girl? Go find out."

Sylvie and Don Pedro kept a close eye on the game warden. They saw him stop in front of the Bohemians, go from one to another asking questions. The gypsies, stood up, gestured, laughed, surrounded the warden, all of them speaking at the same time, very loudly but so confusedly that twenty feet away not a word could be understood.

The game warden extricated himself and came back while the gypsies went back to sitting on the ground, as calm as could be.

Antonio stood on the next to last step and said, "My lord, the old man is dead drunk. As for the girl, she's got a strange illness: she falls asleep all the time, anywhere, and sometimes goes two or three days before she opens her eyes again. This sleep hit her only fifteen minutes ago. She and the old man are lying on straw mattresses in the mule drivers' courtyard.

CHAPTER VI
The musical phrase

Now, on the night of May 22, while the Nyctalope and Vitto and Socca were coming from Orléans, remember they drove at top speed to San Sebastian, the capital of Gipuzkoa province, where a man was suddenly woken up by a sharp, fast clicking.

This man reached out, pressed a button on a wooden bulb hanging off the night table and the bedroom lit up. The clicks were coming from a table between two windows on which sat a very new, very advanced radio-phonograph.

The man did not balk for a moment. He threw off the sheets and blanket and barefoot in pajamas he ran to sit at the table, flipped some switches, turned some knobs and waited, frowning, his whole, young, thin face showing utmost attention.

There were three silvery tones, spaced apart, then the radio-phonograph emitted a musical phrase of around thirty notes. Ten seconds of silence and the phrase was repeated exactly the same. Again the silence and again the repetition, then another, and a final one... The musical phrase was broadcast five times in all.

"Very good," the man muttered. "No possible mistake. It's the boss. Let's see what he wants."

In front of the radio-phonograph on the table and connected to it by electrical wires was a mahogany box in the shape of a portable typewriter case. The man opened the front side of this box, grabbed a metal tab inside, pulled and brought out a piece of paper that he unhooked from two studs holding it on the sides. Letting the tab spring back into the box, he looked at the paper. It was lined like sheet music and on it was printed the phrase from phonograph as if played by a violin.

"That's an easy one," the man mumbled. "Bet I don't even need the code key."

With his eyes glued to the paper he strained his memory, grunted, and then read out loud:

"Watch the possible passage of four one. Follow them everywhere and report to me every day."

Standing up, waving the paper over his head, the man danced a little jig, laughed and spoke out in a normal voice:

"Darlecq my friend, you've hit the jackpot this time if luck has it that the four one crosses the border into my sector! For prey like this the bonus is three million francs. I can't miss it. Put on my rags and double time! As long as my pals aren't on a bender like when that Pole and his wife went back to France through Irun and I missed it and the guy in Bordeaux spotted him..."

His pajamas flew across the room. In five minutes Darlecq was fully dressed. He slipped a Browning into his right inside pocket (specially made bigger than normal) buttoned up his coat, slapped on his fedora, left the room, the apartment house and walked quickly (without running) down the port road (Calle Puerto), then down a side street that led to the convent of Saint Theresa and he vanished under the archway of an old house.

At that very moment, two o'clock chimed from the church of Santa Maria.

The same clock sounded the quarter hour when Darlecq reappeared in the light of a streetlamp not far from the archway. Five men showed up with him and the group followed behind him to the intersection at the Plaza de la Constitución. There, without a sign or a word, they split up.

Paul Darlecq was an ex-sergeant of the colonial infantry who, at forty, turned bad. "Fell into the civilian", as he called it with a kind of cynical nuance of regret, he became a traveling salesman. Simply put, he was on the payroll of a secret society that hired him for jobs in which his unquestionable qualities of intelligence, determination and courage, his good health, his quick and calm reactions were indispensable elements, not to mention his lack of scruples, his rejection of the law and his contempt for human life. Paul Darlecq had a deep and fierce passion: he needed money and lots of it for his woman—the object of his passion—to remain faithful, really, truly faithful. Paul Darlecq would have killed someone every day to maintain this fidelity!

But this man had not yet killed anyone. He had done worse. He was ready to do more. And ultimately, if the woman he loved cheated on him or "dropped" him, he was prepared to kill her or himself. But as long as she stayed loving and faithful and therefore as long as they were together and continued to live in their present happiness, Darlecq saw the most criminal actions as trifles, jokes or simple distractions if they earned him more money than a man like him could earn from honest work.

Such was this dangerous man, as young and strong at forty-three years-old as he was at thirty who was launched into the field in San Sebastian at 1:30 a.m. by the musical phrase sent from Versailles on the night of May 22 by Dr. Maur Korridès.

Paul Darlecq was a born officer of the first rank. His superiors were never able to notice him in the regiment. Perhaps that was why he turned bad. Since he had turned "civil" the man happened to fall "under the thumb" of a boss who recognized and knew how to use him.

On this morning of May 23 at 8 a.m., while his underlings were posted in various parts of the city and on the roads across the Pyrenees in the San Sebstian area, Paul Darlecq himself "spotted" Saint-Clair the Nyctalope at the station in Irun and soon after saw him with Sylvie, Pierrot and the nanny transfer from the French train to the Spanish train bound for Madrid—because the rails did not have the same width, the trains had to stop at the border and the passengers in all classes had to transfer. Thus, Darlecq went on the road.

In Burgos he had time to buy a cloak after getting hold of a saddled mule. Alone, sometimes at a gallop, sometimes at a trot, sometimes merely walking, he followed the path of the harnessed team of mules that transported the Saint-Clair family and the nanny (the four one) from Burgos to Salas.

On arriving in Salas he had what could rightly be called "devilish luck". While Saint-Clair was leaving for the castle of San Lorenzo, Darlecq ran into some Bohemians on the outskirts of the city. He recognized the chief right away—a wiry but strong, white-haired, old man looking either venerable or sinister whom he had once been ordered to use for a child's kidnapping in Bayonne.

A sign from one to the other, a quasi-masonic sign, and contact was made.

Twenty minutes later Paul Darlecq abandoned the idea of going all the way to San Lorenzo. The band of gypsies went instead. He waited, hiding in the Bohemian camp and the next day saw the Nyctalope coming back from the castle.

The trip journey went on: Arandar de Duero, Saragossa, Lerida, Barceloa, Portbou...

In Barcelona Darlecq sent to Korridès a telegram written in a secret code. At Portbou he received the reply. It decoded as: "Watch the mother and child and pick up my orders every two days in Burgos."

Satisfied, since he knew the main prey he was hunting here was not the Nyctalope but his wife and son, Darlecq had no doubt that at the end of this adventure he would get at least two-thirds of the bounty, meaning two million francs. He got ready to take the train back the way he had come.

He had not left the station because the telegram from the boss was waiting for him in the cafe. Not another thought for Saint-Clair who stayed in the train since the transfer would be made in Cerbère on the French side of the border, while he checked the timetable for the Spanish trains.

"Well, I have two hours to wait. I'll get some lunch, not at the cafe but in the city. Easier to kill time that way."

But on the narrow, very steep street that goes into the small border town of Portbou, as the shady, dangerous man turned a corner he stopped short and could not hold back an "Ah!" uttered both in surprise and out of fear. Leo Saint-Clair the Nyctalope was standing in front of him.

In Portbou, in the month of May, around noon, the sky was clear and it was hot, so the sun-drenched streets were deserted. Saint-Clair and Darlecq were alone.

In a low voice, his face showing no emotion and his eyes cold, the Nyctalope said, "You, monsieur, I've seen too much since Saragossa. You're not Spanish. In Barcelona you sent a telegram to No. 10, Box 25, Central Post Office in Versailles. In Portbou here you got one in return, no doubt an answer to yours. It's all very suspicious to me. In this town I can get you arrested and sent to Girona, capital of the province. Like that I'll stop you shadowing me. It'll take eight days to realize the mistake that I'll just have to apologize for. Then you'll be free. But I'll find you and it'll be worse for you since I'll have got your papers and everything in your pockets sent to me beforehand. Get it?"

"So," Darlecq put on a brave front.

"Understand as well that I can save you from all this trouble and forget all about you if you tell me for whom and why you've been following me since Saragossa."

"I understand but I'm not buying it."

Saint-Clair narrowed his eyes and growled, "Watch out! I will have you arrested, imprisoned and sent to the State prison in Girona. In half an hour I'll be examining everything in your pockets. I'll know what you want to hide from me."

Darlecq was pale but held his own, "I dare you!"

"When you get out of prison, better watch your step."

"I'm not afraid of you."

"That's your final word?"

"Yes."

"Too bad for you!"

Before Darlecq could raise his fists or step back or duck or lunge to the side, he was punched on the chin, which made him stagger. A second punch, lighter but better placed, knocked him unconscious before he even hit the ground.

When he came to he was sitting in a chair in a squad room. His hands were cuffed behind his back. To the left stood two officers; to the right a table on which he recognized his Browning, his open wallet, keys and papers scattered. Behind the table sat a guy with a square, black beard who spoke to him in French but with a Barcelona accent.

"You're not the Spanish Sanchez Darro on the papers I found in your wallet, although they're perfectly legal. You're the French anarchist Robert Duvalle, sentenced in absentia to ten years of hard labor by the court in Grenoble and whose arrest warrant demands extradition because the French authorities have known for a long time that you're here in Spain. I'm transferring you to Girona where you'll be locked up until we can send you back to the French police. What do you have to say?"

Paul Darlecq shrugged his shoulders and said, "Nothing."

He knew that protests and denials were utterly useless. A man like Saint-Clair the Nyctalope does not do things like this without being absolutely certain that they cannot be fouled up by anyone or anything. He was smart enough to think that after knocking him out in the deserted street, Saint-Clair had searched him thoroughly, leaving only the gun, keys, money and false identity papers on his body. Regarding the telegram from the station, no need to ask for it from the police chief—Saint-Clair had stolen it.

"Check and mate!" Darlecq thought to himself. "Let's hope they don't keep me too long in the Girona 'carcel' and that the Nyctalope won't be waiting for me when I get out. I'm so stupid for thinking it was so easy in Irun when I got lucky to run into my prey at the start of the hunt. Didn't I know the reputation of Number One? The boss warned me in case the day should come… Idiot! Moron! But it doesn't matter, I held my own against the enemy. My courage, at least, didn't fail me. Better to be caught than to cave in. It's not all lost. For the moment, let's toe the line so they don't go too hard on me…"

Less than an hour later the fake Sanchez Darro, the real Darlecq, whom the Spanish police believed to be the anarchist convict Robert Duvalle, left Portbou on a local train. He was between two guards armed with their ever-present rifles and he had long chains running from his hands to the guards. Moreover, the second-class compartment—no aisle—where the trio embarked was not a "private". Four other passengers, two of whom were women, also got on at Portbou. After a few naturally curious glances the passengers paid no more attention to the prisoner and his escort. The two women, facing each other in a corner started gabbing. A man had fallen asleep in another corner, across from one of the guards. And next to the sleeper the fourth passenger had taken out of his pocket a pencil and paper.

The latter was a very young man, could not have been more than twenty-five years-old. He was decently dressed, not without a touch of elegance. He was clean-shaven, his fedora hat firmly stuck on the back of his head and baring his forehead, his soft collar with a simple tie made him look fashionable. He was writing, but in a weird way. First he drew some parallel horizontal lines and then with a stiff, quick movement he spun his pencil to make dots that on different lines.

Darlecq, who had nothing else to do but look around him, at first watched the young man abstractedly, then more deliberately and finally with rapt attention. From time to time the young man raised his head and looked sharply straight ahead. The guards were nodding off, eyes open but blank. They were Castilians. Darlecq knew it because he had heard them talking at the police station. And he also knew that they did not understand French.

He was thinking: "This young man is writing music. He doesn't have lined paper. If he's a real composer, he'd have music paper in his pocket to note down his musical ideas and not this wrinkled stationery that's probably been in his pocket for days. And that look he keeps giving me. I'm going to wink the next time…"

At that moment the other stopped writing, raised his head and stared straight into the prisoner's eyes.

Darlecq did not even think. His right eye winked three times and watched the face across from him. Immediately a smile, barely noticeable, for a fraction of a second, crossed the young man's lips as he discreetly eyed the two guards. He turned the paper on which he had been scratching for fifteen minutes so that the prisoner could see what was written on it.

The hunch Darlecq had had electrified him as he read the musical phrase on the paper.

And his mind was made up right away. He had to talk with this young man who was a "comrade" and who knew him, Darlecq, as a "comrade" as well. But, for starters, he had to make the guards believe the conversation was only about music and, secondly, anything important had to be said in French so that the guards would not understand.

Darlecq had come up with a good plan but he told himself, "As long as the two women and the sleeper don't know French. No matter, we'll see."

In Castilian, in a normal voice, with the obvious intention of being heard and understood by the two guards, he said, "Caballero, I see you're writing music. Might you be a composer?"

"*Si, señor*," the young man answered with a smile.

"Me too," Darlecq went on, still in Spanish. "I'm a composer, too. You might recognize my name. I'm French, Léonce Nittol."

The young man raised his hands and, in French this time, exclaimed, "But me too, I'm French. How is it that you, Léonce Nittol, ended up handcuffed here between these two policemen?"

Darlecq, in turn, spoke in French. Worried about being understood by the two women or the sleeper, even though he really seemed to be sleeping, he talked about hating the police. But after a minute of empty babble he and his new accomplice could see that the women were paying no attention to them and the sleeper was not pretending. The two guards, though they were both holding one of the prisoner's chains, showed complete incomprehension and indifference to the conversation between their captive and the passenger. So now the two conspirators had no need to put on an act.

"I'm Julien Peul," the young man said, "agent of the Ko in Cerbère and Portbou of the 4th I.C.[2], like you're… where?"

"Irun and San Sebastian," Darlecq replied.

"I thought you were in Saragossa. Doesn't matter. On the night of May 22 I got a musical message about the four one. Since then my men and I have been on the lookout in our sector. I spotted the big One this morning coming off the train from Barcelona. I followed him. I saw him attack you on the corner of the deserted street in Portbou. After knocking you out he went through your pockets, wallet and papers. Then he picked you up and took you to the nearest police station. I waffled between you and him because he sped off in a motorboat— he's got rich and powerful friends in Portbou—heading to France before I knew what was happening. So, I settled for you. They're taking you to the Girona prison and I know about the trumped up charges. You've got at least two or three weeks… I thought, because you were tailing the One like he'd said, since Saragossa, that you, too, might have received the musical message. It was easy

---

[2] *Internationale Communiste.*

to prove. Write the musical phrase sent by Ko and show it to you. If it made you flinch, I figured, you're a comrade. That's it. What do you think? Can I take your place? The One is lost for the time being but there's his wife, son and the nanny. They're as important as he is."

"More so!" Darlecq almost shouted. "I was following the four One since Irun. I saw the family being sent to safety and I kept on the tail of the big One. In Barcelona I sent a telegram to Ko about what I knew and what I did. But in Portbou Ko's answer ordered me to keep an eye on the mother and son and get further orders every two days in Burgos."

"From Matello, the head of the sector?"

"Naturally."

"Good. So, I'm not sorry for losing the One since Ko's orders were basically to stop following him. Will you let me take over for you?"

"Got no choice," Darlecq grumbled, shrugging his shoulders.

"Even if you're out of commission and I succeed, we'll share the reward."

"I'm counting on it, comrade."

"It's only fair. So, tell me, where are the woman and child?"

Before answering Darlecq looked at the two women, the sleeper and gave a sidelong glance to the two guards. Although reassured, he still took the precaution of leaning over and putting his finger on the homemade sheet music as if he was talking about specific notes.

He whispered, "San Lorenzo castle, Duke d'Arandar, Sierra de la Demanda, east of Burgos."

"Great! Understood and noted."

"And in the nearest town, Salas, there's a tribe of gypsies whose patriarch is with us."

"His name?"

"Escarpaz."

"Very well. Live in peace in Girona, comrade. I'll do the work for both of us. When the French police inspector sent to Girona sees that you're not the anarchist Duvalle, you'll be set free. Afterwards, go to Cerbère, to the cabaret *Le Phare*. Say I sent you and give them this code: '3+3=7'. They'll put you up, feed you, give you news from me and you can wait for me or go back to Irun, your choice. Is that all right?"

"All right."

With that Paul Darlecq broke out laughing. The young traveler laughed even harder, tearing to pieces his sheet music and throwing it away. In fact, the "musical phrase" was no longer of any use. It had done its job.

And the two comrades went on talking but intermittently, sometimes in Spanish, sometimes in French, about unimportant things. When the train stopped in the Girona station the so-called composer shook the hand of the so-called Leonce Nittol, falsely accused of being the anarchist Duvalle and on whom someone had bizarrely planted (or so he claimed) the papers of one Sanchez Darro, a name he was hearing for the first time.

In short, Paul Darlecq and Julien Peul parted on very good terms. The former stepped onto the platform with his two armed guards; the latter headed back to Barcelona. When the conductor showed up Julien Peul gave him his ticket, which was good only to Girona, and was given another in exchange, good to Burgos. Henceforth in good standing, he sat in the corner seat left empty by one of the guards, closed his eyes and imitated the passenger across from him, who was still sleeping, not even woken up by the noisy stop in Girona.

CHAPTER VII
The rays of light

The powerful speedboat covered the two hundred nautical miles in ten hours, from the cove in Portbou to the harbor in Villefranche (Maritime Alps). The boat was barely docked in the small, calm, sleepy port under the stars of this serene spring night when Saint-Clair the Nyctalope crossed the short walkway, waved one last goodbye at someone staying on board, and buttoned up his hooded raincoat because the air was cool from the sea and the still snowy Alps. He walked quickly across the steep town to reach the road that led to the peninsula of Saint-Jean-Cap-Ferrat. He did not stop on the peninsula until he got to the entrance gate of a property known in the area as the Nopals Castle. At this gate he rang the bell.

It was 2 a.m. Nevertheless, the Nyctalope waited less time than he thought he would. Thirty seconds after the bell rang a light step crunched softly on the graveled path in the garden whose massively thick trees and exotic plants hid the habitation. A short man appeared carrying a round and red paper lantern.

"Hello Sou!" Saint-Clair said. "Why are you awake so late, prowling around the trees?"

"Oh, monsieur. And why have you, if I may ask, come here in the middle of the night?"

"Am I not the Nyctalope?" Saint-Clair smiled back.

"Indeed, monsieur. Excuse me. The day is your kingdom but the night is your empire."

With a tiny key chosen on a keyring he had taken out of one of his pockets, Sou opened the gate. Saint-Clair stepped through.

"Is my friend Gnô doing well?" he asked.

"Very well, monsieur. The journey was rough and he was a little tired. But now his health is perfect. His Excellency is going to be very glad to see you. I'll tell him you're here as soon as he wakes up?"

"Thank you, Sou. Does Lord Mitang still wake up at 6 a.m.?"

"Yes, monsieur. And if you'd like to get some sleep, you'll have a full three hours to do so. Your room is always ready, of course."

"Thanks, I think I will get a little shut-eye."

"Would you like to eat or drink anything before?"

"No, but will you tell me, Sou, what you were doing out here when I rang?"

"Gladly, monsieur. It rained around midnight. I'm fond of snails. The downpour brings them out. So you see, since I don't sleep much and only very lightly, the sound of the rain woke me up and I came out to go snail hunting. I found many."

"Where are they?"

"In a special box, monsieur, which I left at the foot of a tree when I heard the bell. What a surprise! At two in the morning a visit is rather extraordinary but it's unwise for a man like me to be surprised when I know that the Nyctalope is the friend of my master and that his room is mandated to be always ready to receive him at any hour of the day or night."

"Very well, Sou. You can leave me. Are you going back to hunting?"

"If you don't mind, yes, monsieur."

"I don't mind and I hope you get heaps of escargots."

"One hundred will do. I am moderate in my passions. Have a good rest, monsieur."

"Thanks, Sou."

Saint-Clair went alone to his room where he got undressed, quickly cleaned himself up, put on some pajamas he found in the wardrobe, turned off the lights and lay down on the bed. He was asleep almost immediately.

At 5:30 a.m., he woke up and jumped out of bed.

At 6:30 a.m., shaved and fully dressed, he followed Sou who had come to announce that "His Excellence" was waiting for him.

The Japanese Gnô Mitang, the secret advisor to the imperial government, was bound by solid friendship to Saint-Clair the Nyctalope eighteen months before during a great, secret adventure that resulted in the destruction of an international terrorist plot against freedom, prosperity and the peace of civilized nations. The architect of the plot, Leonid Zattan, vanquished by the Nyctalope and his friends, had been rendered harmless; his accomplices had been killed, dispersed or arrested; his organization completely annihilated.[3] At any rate, Saint-Clair and his friends and the governments involved in the momentous secret believed in its destruction. They knew, however, that every revolutionary organization could, like the Phoenix of old, be reborn from its ashes. But they also thought that because of the truly complete destruction and disarmament of Leonid Zattan, this rebirth, if it ever became possible, would take at least ten or twelve years with a new generation of spirited and rebellious minds.

After the victory, Leo Saint-Clair had married Sylvie MacDuhl, the subject of prophecy of Nostradamus, the fateful virgin rescued from the claws of Leonid Zattan. Gnô Mitang had been raised to a secret, prominent position in Japan. The other friends of Saint-Clair and Gnô were living peacefully in their various professions.

Gnô Mitang was a short man, but well-built, muscular, and cold, around 40 years old, stone-faced, but with the polite look of a modern Japanese. Dressed in a light, white linen "suit" for the house, Gnô welcomed Saint-Clair with two open arms and a glowing face in the small salon of his personal rooms, which he occupied in Nopals (owned by Sylvie Saint-Clair, née MacDuhl) during his se-

---

[3] See *The Nyctalope vs The Antichrist*.

cret sojourns and no less secret conferences of official and unofficial ambassadors who were delegated by their governments to meet and talk there about international affairs of State, far from reporters and spies.

Looking as humble as could be, with a dozen tried and true servants under his command, old Sou was a top-rate caretaker at Nopals.

"My dear Leo," Gnô said, "what a pleasure to see you here so soon. When I telegraphed you from Port Said, I figured I wouldn't see you until next week and at your house in Versailles. How are your wife and son?"

"Thank you, Gnô, they're doing well. At least, I think so."

"Only think so? And why say that in such a tone of voice? What's happened?"

"It's to tell you," Saint-Clair replied, "and to talk about it that I took a speedboat yesterday in Portbou and came here to Nopals this morning. But I'm hungry. Let's eat."

"Yes, lunch first, we can talk afterwards. I know you and made provisions for your morning appetite. There are eggs, ham, a bottle of Madeira, coffee and the little crispy bread you like. Me, as usual, I'm having just lemon tea and buttered toast."

Two valets—two Annamites (Vietnamese)—came in, one holding the door open, then bringing in a small table and two chairs, the other carrying a huge platter.

The lunch was quickly consumed in silence. With one ring of a bell the two valets reappeared and the table, chairs and platter disappeared along with them.

"Well, Leo, I'm all ears," the Japanese said.

"Here goes."

Simply but precisely, without omitting any important detail, without adding one pointless word, the Nyctalope told what had happened from the moment he and Sylvie, on the night of May 21 in Versailles, had hopped over the wall of the Sycamores up to when he dropped off the so-called Sanchez Darro at the police station in Portbou. He wrapped up:

"Among the papers I found in this guy's pockets there was only one that might have any bearing on this matter."

He handed Gnô the telegram that "Darro" had received in the cafe.

The Japanese read aloud, "First the two and three One and every other dial, consult Campéador."

Gnô thought for a minute and then, "You've studied this, of course?"

"For ten hours during the trip here."

"And it doesn't mean anything to you?"

"Nothing."

"Gee."

He raised his head, looked at his friend and said softly:

"My dear Leo, what I'm about to tell you is going to upset you much less if you keep in mind how much I adore your wife, admire you and feel a tender affection for your son whom I haven't met yet. Well, turned husband and father, the Nyctalope has lost much of his intrinsic power. Before, you were the only one involved and the only danger you feared was for yourself, so it was nothing. Now you fear for your wife and son. Despite your strength of character, your intelligence and the passionate devotion that their safety, inevitably, forces you to act in their defense, you are less strong because you feel fear for them.

"In this affair, I only know what you just told me. I haven't been able, like you, to observe this Korridès. I'm missing all kinds of information to ponder, to judge, which you can do. Therefore, I'm less qualified than you to decode the telegram. And yet, I'm going to decode it with almost absolute certainty of being correct."

Saint-Clair responded very gravely, "What you just told me is what I told myself in Portbou when I saw the message for the first time. That's why I came directly here to see you, Gnô. In some circumstances I'd be stronger and quicker than you. In others, I know, precisely for the reasons you just gave, it's you who are more lucid than I. Decode it, I'm listening."

And so, in the clear, monotone voice of a didactic professor lecturing for the umpteenth time before a new generation of students, Gnô Mitang spoke.

"Let's examine why this Korridès, whose name I'm hearing for the first time, is your enemy, Leo. According to what you told me he said, he considers you his main adversary. But he includes your wife, son and even your nanny whose milk is keeping your son alive and healthy. It is, therefore, normal that in the coded language we have you, the mother, the child and the nanny are on top of Korridès' list of enemies. Why wouldn't he call you the 'four One'? Well, the expression 'the two and three One' means your wife and son.

"If we examine the circumstances of your adventure and if we remember Korridès' threat, the expression 'First' means that the man trailing you, not since Saragossa, as you believe, but in my opinion since the western border of Spain, meaning Irun-San Sebastian, the word 'First' means the guy is supposed to deal with the mother and child and leave you alone."

Gnô stopped talking. Saint-Clair did not say a word. After a full minute of meditative silence, the Japanese continued:

"The phrase 'every other dial' means every other day. That's obvious. And 'consult' needs no explanation. As for Campéador, well, I just need to know that you got off the train in Burgos and the Duke's castle is in that province. Remember that Burgos is the homeland of El Cid, nicknamed Campéador. So, 'consult Campéador' means do as I told you in Burgos, which proves, by the way, that your Korridès has a decent sized organization in Burgos, big enough for his agents to get all their orders."

"Clearly," Saint-Clair said, "your translation is right, my friend, and in hindsight it seems childishly easy. The sender could be none other than Korridès and this man, contacting one of his agents ordered to follow me, didn't have to make the message hard to decode. It just needed to get by the telegraph operators without being understood. It's astonishing that I, even though I'm directly involved in all this, spent ten hours wracking my brain in vain.

"You see, Gnô, you were right just now, identifying my weakness in this case. Can you believe that I haven't realized it since the start of this affair, meaning since my meeting with the mysterious Korridès?

"Not too long ago, in the adventures against Lucifer and Zattan, even in the most trying times and when it looked like all was lost for me, I never doubted my strength or my luck, never doubted by comeback and ultimate victory. Today, if I look closely, it's not doubt I see in myself but fear, a special fear, precise, pinpointed, that my ultimate victory will be won at a heavy price and maybe, God forgive me, by the death of my wife or my son or both! And this, unquestionably, is hampering my thoughts, my decisions, my strength. What can I do? Should I give up the fight? No, not at all. Besides, my enemy or enemies wouldn't let me. And that's the crux of the matter I'm asking you about, Gnô.

"What does Korridès want and why attack me? The hatred he's showing towards me is beyond reason, even considering the minor episode of my intervention in the mystery of *The Sycamores* that night. I don't understand.

"Since our victory over Leonid Zattan, all the reports I've gotten from various police around the world have convinced me that his international terrorist organization is destroyed, completely wiped out and even the actions of the 3rd International have nothing to do with this, I repeat, defunct organization.

"Korridès, therefore, is a totally new problem in my life. Why? What's his goal and what am I getting in the way of? The conversation I had with him gave me no clue about this or anything else. So, you now you know, Gnô, as much as I do about what's happening and what I think of it. And what do you think?"

The Japanese had listened to the Nyctalope with rapt attention. At every conclusion he nodded approvingly. But he hesitated a little before answering.

"Well, before expressing my opinion about everything, allow me to ask you one particular question that might be a little touchy... This telegram, you know now, is a direct threat against your wife and son. Is there nothing you can do immediately to repel the danger?"

"Immediately, no. The recipient of the telegram is in prison in Girona for at least two weeks. All evidence points to him being alone on my trail. I called the chief of police in Girona to keep the guy out of sight. So, we shouldn't have to worry about Korridès finding out. It'll take a few days, surely, for him to suspect that his man has been exposed and taken out of the picture, at least for the time being. That's why I have time to talk with you and reflect. When we've shed as much light as possible on the different facets of the problem, I'll make a decision. If we figure it's best, I'll go back to the castle. Until then, I truly believe that Sylvie and Pierrot are safe."

"Good," Gnô said. "Well then, here's the thought that came to me as you were speaking. I'm not as sure as you are about the extinction of the terrorist fires that Leonid Zattan lit. There were a lot of beds of coal. The complete files of Zattan told us about them and I'm not saying that there are beds of coal we don't know about, just that some of them might have, under the ashes, mind you, a few embers still burning."

He paused, lowered his head and stayed a good five minutes thinking quietly. Then he looked up and his lively black eyes stared into Saint-Clair's calm, waiting gaze.

"In Japan, when alone, I thought a lot about our grand adventure. Now, of the many people who stand out to a greater or lesser extent as protagonists in the affair, there are three whom I, personally, did not know. Of these three, I believe you knew only one. This one I'll name right off: Ignace Kiewicz."

"Of course I remember," Saint-Clair said. "He jumped in at the last minute, became my partner in the final struggle against the terrorists who'd been thrown into turmoil by the defeat, capture and incarceration of Zattan. But didn't he retire with his brother and some woman on whom they had taken out their vengeance?"

"Yes," Gnô said. "And they are my three people. This woman you mentioned is Diana Ivanovna Krosnovief, the Red Princess. She dreamed of marrying Zattan, of sharing his conquest and being, in a way, the empress of the world. All her hopes were crushed. All her ambitions were drowned in blood. She herself, as you said, disappeared with the Kiewicz brothers who had carried out some kind of family vendetta against her.

"That's it, right? All the copies of the police reports you regularly sent to me dealt with other Zattan collaborators and we know how they all died or retired or even reinstated themselves in everyday society around the world. But the only people, I repeat the only ones, who were not mentioned in the police reports were Ignace and Stanislas Kiewicz, former lieutenants of Leonid Zattan who later rallied to our cause but were always suspicious, and this Diana Ivanovna Krosnovief who, basically, was our main enemy even though, thanks to extenuating circumstances, you and I never saw her.

"Well then, in this new affair in which Korridès suddenly pops up against you, isn't there the Red Princess? Isn't it this woman who is out to satisfy a hatred that her wronged love and her failed ambition have stored up in her heart and mind?

"Mind you, Leo, this is only a hypothesis but really, if you take it seriously, it explains a lot of what you've been mixed up in over the past few days. No, no, don't say anything yet. Let me think and take this theory to its logical conclusion…"

Once again Gnô lowered his head and got lost in silent thought for a few minutes. Then in a cautious voice, as if the idea was coming to him little by little as he was talking, he said to himself:

"Consider this, my friend, the guy who was turned into a pile of gray ashes in *The Sycamores*, could he have been Ignace Kiewicz, made a victim of the woman he was getting revenge on? The poor woman whose screams and sobs you heard, the poor woman whom Korridès' cynical confession admitted was at the transformation of the guy into lifeless ashes, couldn't she be Nadine, the beloved slave and devoted lover of the Ignace Kiewicz?"

Many times during the fight against Leonid Zattan the Nyctalope had valued the powers of reasoning, logic and intuition, even divination, that Gnô Mitang's sharp mind possessed. As the Japanese was speaking, prudently but precisely, it seemed to the Nyctalope that a dark veil covering his eyes was parting, ripping open in places and through these gashes he could see faces, scenes, like in a film, real and vibrant in a bright light.

"That's it," Gnô said.

His sinking back into the armchair, his two hands dropping and the expression on his face signified that he was done voicing his thoughts.

With the calm but powerful suppleness that his changed attitude adopted, the feline agility of a lion and the fearful might of a tiger, Saint-Clair the Nyctalope stood up. He put his fists on his hips, stared straight into his friend's eyes and after a short laugh, declared:

"Gnô, you'll never know how good you are for me. Really, you've brought me back to myself. Since May 22, the day of my meeting with Korridès, I've felt my personality dissolving into something dark and dank, unspeakable and incomprehensible. You've pulled me out of this murky morass. Now I'm back on solid ground in the full light of day. Thank you, Gnô. Your hypothesis might be absolutely correct or only partly correct or perhaps wrong in every way. Do you admit that?"

"Of course," Gnô's face brightened with amused satisfaction.

"Well, whatever the future might hold, I will accept your hypothesis as the god-given truth. It fits the situation and the people involved so perfectly! It is, I repeat, on this solid ground that I can move forward. You talked about the weakening of my fundamental qualities. Well, my dear friend, you won't be mentioning that again, thanks to you. From this moment on, I can tell you without pride but with certainty that Saint-Clair the Nyctalope will be the man you've always known."

"And whom," Gnô added, "I've always loved. The Japanese, you know, may be impassive to most people but to their friends there is nobody warmer. Now come and hug me, which you didn't do when you came in because you were too tormented. But now you feel better and I'm glad to see my old Saint-Clair back!"

It was a warm hug of true brotherhood in which these two men expressed their even greater mutual respect and friendship. When they were done, they sat down.

The past was now clarified, at least by the hypothesis that was logical enough and preferable to nothing, to the unknown, to darkness. So, the two men felt the urgent need to consider the future.

"Let's see," Gnô began, "when you decided in Portbou to come straight here to see me, you made a detour from your original route. Where were you going? What were your plans?"

"Short-term plans," the Nyctalope answered. "I didn't know anything, couldn't come up with anything. But I wanted to know. My immediate goal, therefore, was to go to Paris alone and in disguise, as I often did in the past, observe the comings and goings of Korridès. I figured on spending two, three, four weeks at it as long as Sylvie and Pierrot were safe with the Duke and while my two faithful allies, Vitto and Socca, would let their beards grow, change their appearance as much as possible and wait for me first at Saint-Jean-Pied-de-Port, then in Lourdes. Then, depending on what I'd find out, with my unrecognizable partners, I'd launch the attack on Korridès and, by all possible means, fight to the death or the imprisonment of this enemy. But now it's another story;"

"What do you mean?" Gnô was all ears.

"Well, my friend, the first fact that despite all my precautions I was trailed from Irun or Saint Sebastian, at least from Burgos, by a guy on Korridès' payroll; the second fact revealed by the telegram that Korridès has a permanent contact in Burgos, which means an organization that must be pretty big; and lastly the fact that someone connected to Korridès knows where my wife and son are hiding… When we get right down to it, it doesn't matter if this guy doesn't do anything for two or three weeks. So, all these facts are telling me to forget about Korridès for the moment and go back to San Lorenzo to organize new and better, stricter safety measures so that Sylvie and Pierrot really have nothing to fear and I can deal with Korridès without worrying about my family. What do you think?"

"I think you're absolutely right. The earlier you get back to San Lorenzo, the better it will be. Believe me, Leo, the Spanish police can do their best to keep secret the guy you turned over to them, but I'm not at all sure that this guy won't find a way to contact the organization in Burgos and therefore Korridès himself about where you left Sylvie and your son. I like having you around and I'd be really happy to have you stay here for a few days, but I have to sacrifice my selfishness—the consequences could be very serious. Do you want my advice?"

"You don't have to say anything," Saint-Clair stood up, "I can guess. Leave here at once, get back in my speedboat and head for Barcelona, then to Burgos on a fast train."

"Exactly." And the Japanese stood up in turn and put his hand on his friend's shoulder. "One more thing. At what address is your wife supposed to be sending you news?"

"A bank in Paris to a good, honest young man who works there and whose connection to me is unknown to anyone. I alerted him in person before leaving Paris and I'm certain I wasn't seen or heard by anyone else."

"Good," Gnô said. "Here's a pen and paper. Write a note to the kid telling him to give me whatever messages he's got or will get. I have to go to Paris by plane. I'll be there tonight. If I find a letter from Sylvie, I'll read it… if that's all right with you?"

"Naturally. Please do."

"And I'll send it on by radio to Barcelona in the French consulate in the name of the consul without mentioning your name. The consul won't understand until you talk to him. So, go see him. You never know. It might be helpful to get some news before you go to San Lorenzo."

"Let's hope not," Saint-Clair furrowed his brow. "It would mean bad news."

"Yes, but better to be warned. From what you've told me and looking closely at the facts, this Korridès is powerful. I think he might be more powerful and more dangerous than Leonid Zattan. Before we were dealing with a warrior, a gang leader who fought out in the open through fiendish plots. Here, on the other hand, we're dealing with the head of a secret organization who is more formidable for being camouflaged as a man of wealth, living the life of luxury in Versailles.

"I have the feeling that this case, which started off so strangely and kind of petty and insignificant, is hiding something very dire for us. Be careful, Leo. Although you're back to your old self, don't abuse the power, intelligence and self-confidence of the Nyctalope. Anyway, enough talking, are you going?"

"I'm off," Saint-Clair said.

While listening to his friend, the Nyctalope had written the note to the bank clerk. In one corner of the paper he put the name and address of the bank and the name and personal address of the employee. At the bottom of the letter he signed it but with a small cabalistic sigil to authenticate the signature. He grabbed both of Gnô's hands and after a long, hard, deep look to communicate their feelings, they separated without another word.

Fifteen minutes later Saint-Clair was climbing back into the speedboat that was waiting for him at the dock in Villefranche and immediately hit the open water, not returning to Portbou but heading straight for Barcelona.

It was Sunday, May 29.

It was this Sunday, in the castle in San Lorenzo, that the strange episode with the Bohemians took place when Sylvie heard the mysterious phrase of the gypsy girl, so ominous and menacing: "*Aplasta la vibora. Matala!*" (Crush the viper. Kill it!)

73

CHAPTER VIII
The sect of the Hashshashins

Especially in times troubled by a great war, by the birth of a new religion or by natural disasters, Humanity, in its turmoil, produces sects, each composed of a greater or lesser number of people who, in their fanaticism, place themselves outside the common law, religiously, politically or socially. These people, in fact, are heretics.

Their close bond forms a sect that almost always pushes the outcomes of their beliefs or their original theories to the extreme. All religions, all great political or social movements had, have and will have their heretics who persist in their dissidence, exacerbate it, and very quickly become fanatical sectarians and often dangerous because they do not recoil from individual or collective acts of criminality.

Russian Soviet communism might be considered one of these secretions. Its so-called universal organization bears the name the Third International. It claims, in fact, to have a dogma and it works to impose it by breaking down all the nations of the world. Now, although all the schemes of the Third International are known, what we know less about it are its heresies since even the Soviet dogma has its heretics. At first on the fringe, then completely outside the Third International and soon against it, several heretical sects have been formed. Only three or four leaders of the Third International know about these and they keep quiet. The rest of the world is ignorant and the present story is the first public revelation ever made of them, or at least of one of them.

On Sunday, Saint-Clair the Nyctalope left Gnô Mitang after having the conversation that shed some light on the dark, dramatic mystery; the same Sunday when in San Lorenzo, in the mountains east of Burgos, Sylvie started to fear for herself and her son; and on this same Sunday, May 29, a kind of council of some of the Third International heretics was meeting in Versailles, in the same villa of the Sycamores that been the starting point of this strange and perilous adventure, a maelstrom from an unknown abyss into which Saint-Clair and his family and friends had been dragged.

If, out of idleness or curiosity, a forest ranger, for example, happened to be watching at 8 am the little path that ran parallel to the grand avenue along the dark garden of the Sycamores, he would have observed, no doubt with a great deal of surprise, that every fifteen minutes or so, coming from both directions, men stopped in front of the entrance grill. After a cautious glance around, each visitor made a gesture, every one the same: the right hand placed on the left shoulder with the forearm crossing the chest. Right way a small door next to the grill opened, the man entered, disappeared behind the canvas covering the grill and the door closed.

But there was no forest ranger. On Sunday morning the path was usually deserted and the five individuals who, between 8:00 and 9:15 a.m. made the gesture and entered the property were seen by nobody. Either they were familiar with the grounds or they had been well informed because without a guide the five men walked in the same way without hesitation. They followed the winding path that led to the villa, went around it to the right, fiddled with the latch of a service door and went in. In the narrow vestibule inside the door, a tall, strong mulatto woman was waiting for them and questioned:

"Hasan-ibn?"

Each man answered, "Sabbah!"

Then she led the visitor down the stairs into the cellars. When they passed the first cellar, the woman put a whistle to her mouth and gave three short, screeching blows. Immediately, a pile of dusty barrels and old crates slid all together from right to left, suggesting (rightly) that the messy mass of objects was on a movable platform. Thus was revealed a wall that itself slid from left to right uncovering an opening the size of a normal door, a rectangle that was completely invisible before. Once the man passed through, everything closed up again and the mulatto went back upstairs to wait in the vestibule for the next visitor.

The basement, where the five men met together at 9:15 a.m., formed a huge room, very comfortably furnished as a bedroom with two beds and flanked by a curtained alcove turned into a tiny bathroom. In the middle of the room sat a big, round table with seven desk blotters and inkwells. Between the two beds facing each other a wall disappeared behind long, overlapping shelves of books. A thick, wall-to-wall carpet covered the wood or tiled floor. What could be seen of the wall between the furniture and a few impressionist paintings was covered in dark red. No windows. The ventilation was supplied by two electric fans and probably a system of ducts to purge the bad air and let in the fresh because the atmosphere in the basement was absolutely normal. Electric radiators sat in the four corners looking like tiny, elegant fireplaces and providing a constant temperature. In short, everything in this peculiar room was designed to give the utmost comfort.

Given the arrangement of the basement and the way it was hidden on the edge of the cellars of the house, it could have been used as an inviolable refuge.

The five men there knew one another, seeing that each newcomer was welcomed by his predecessor with friendly smiles and amiably open hands.

After the usual small talk, each man sat in a chair before one of the blotters. When all five were present, there remained two empty chairs next to each other. But the absence did not last long since one or two minutes after the fifth man came in, the door slid open again and a man walked through, followed by a woman who wore a black cloth mask over her face from the top of her forehead to the middle of her neck and from ear to ear.

Tall, slender and supple, hair cut short, hands long and nervous but sleek and strong, shapely and perfectly proportioned, the woman must have had a very pretty face, judging by the sparkling splendor of her magnificent dark eyes that gazed out calm, domineering and mysterious at the same time through the eye-holes of the black mask. She was wearing one of those light, very modern dress-es that left her legs and part of her shoulders and arms bare and that hugged her body at every movement.

She made a strange contrast to the man in front of her. Almost deformed, puny, with an almost monstrous head that was too big for his body, he was dressed severely, romantically in a black frock coat belted at the waist and with long coattails.

At the sight of the weird couple, the five men stood up, bowed deeply, straightened up together and in one voice pronounced the Arabic greeting:

"Salam!"

The couple responded, "Salam."

They went and sat in the two empty chairs and the five men did the same.

Right away the woman spoke. "According to the rites of the Fidawis Hashshashin, name yourselves."

The man to her left, who had arrived at the Sycamores at precisely 8 a.m., said, "Number seven, Sams."

Then one after another:

"Number six, Freitag."

"Number five, Donners."

"Number four, Mittwoch."

"Number three, Diens."

"Number two, Montag," the woman's companion said.

And the woman herself, "Number one, Miss Sunday."

After a brief silence her beautifully resonant voice added:

"Behold the holy surah of the Fidawis Hashshashin. In the beginning Ha-san Ibn Sabbah, to satisfy Justice and Vengeance, founded a corps of assassins whom he called Fidawis, meaning the devoted.

"These men were ready to assassinate everyone whom their master told them to. In exchange, for his own life, which he sacrificed up front, the Fidawi was promised paradise. After putting him to sleep under the effects of hashish, Hasan ibn Sabbah transported the assassin to the garden of delights where he could enjoy all the pleasures of the Muslim paradise. He lived for a few hours in this garden of delights and then was put to sleep again to bring him out of the mysterious place. Henceforth he was ready to do anything to get back to this Eden for eternity since he had barely glimpsed it.

"We don't believe in the Muslim paradise or any other paradise after death. We believe that Man has only one conscious life and if he wants to know happi-ness, he has to create his own paradise here on earth.

"For us, the Fidawis of a new Hasan ibn Sabbah, happiness is, in both dream and reality, the unbridled satisfaction of our individual passions and our collective ambitions. For dreams we still have hashish. For reality, we have the physical actions determined by our will, carried out by our cunning and by our strength.

"We are above the laws instituted by men bound by societies or submitted to governments. We want to tear down these laws, destroy these societies and wipe out these governments. That is why we are the seven Fidawis of a new Hasan ibn Sabbah and why we have a myriad of comrades under our command who want to destroy everything like us but who are not so enlightened.

"And afterwards, if anarchy and death reign on earth, it doesn't matter to the Fidawis Hashshashin! Amen!"

"Amen," number two, Montag, repeated.

And the five others intoned, "Amen."

What monstrous fanaticism, what diabolical deformity of the meaning of the human character was revealed in this abominable gospel! No words in any language could truly describe it.

Nevertheless, as the words came forth out of the woman's red lips, lips that were fully visible through the slit in the mask, the faces of the six men exhibited a kind of ecstasy, more and more extreme... The "Amen" came out as a gasp from them, a voluptuous moan more than an actual word.

Obviously, the six Fidawis were regular consumers of hashish and it only took the musical influence of the deep, passionately toned voice of beautiful Miss Sunday reminding them of the fundamental principles of the sect for them to be, imagined or not, under the influence of the "divine drug".

But this abrupt, ecstatic trance was cut short after the brief silence of Miss Sunday when she opened her desk blotter and in the sharp, clear voice of the president of an administration meeting declared:

"Here's the report of the month's work. It's a summary of all your reports along with the actions taken by me and Montag."

She held out a piece of paper in front of her and read aloud:

"On May 15, the 64 centers of anarchist Hashshashins were finally established. Consequently, there is not a single nation of earth in which our council, devised by us here, doesn't have a militant organization ready to work for the fulfillment of our plans.

"From now on, each of us and our 64 comrades who make up the college of 71 Fidawis can, within the scope of our general action, pursue his or her own individual passions: hatred and the joy of revenge, love and the delight of possession, the acquisition of wealth, the thrill of power, etc.

"Already, certain actions, the easiest because they're carried out in a limited context, are starting to see the light of day: Paraguay has been in the grips of a bloody revolution for eight days; the Dominican Republic is split into four factions fighting one another with pillaging, fires, rape and murder; in Ethiopia our chief Fidawi has aroused a new pretender to the imperial throne, a whole province is already in flames; in Bulgaria the anarchists have made a secret pact with the communists of the Third International. That's it for general actions. It's only a start. But it's enough since the 64 centers were only set up definitively a few days ago.

"As for individual actions, there are many but there's only one that deserves our attention."

Miss Sunday dropped the piece of paper, clasped her hands together on the blotter and with a smile that bared her white teeth, after a brighter sparkle in her black diamond eyes she said:

"The hunt for the Nyctalope has begun. He tried to hide away his wife and child. We know where they are. Our comrades in Northern Spain—the 25th center—are informed. Week by week, day by day, if necessary hour by hour, we'll be kept up-to-date on the progress of the hunt. In any case, I've given orders that Sylvie Saint-Clair and her son be kidnapped and taken to one of our hideouts. The order should arrive in Burgos this morning, so it'll be carried out soon. I hope that before the end of the week we'll be able to make Leo Saint-Clair do whatever we want."

Number four, Mittwoch, raised his hand.

"Speak," Miss Sunday said.

Mittwoch's eyes, face and build were typically Russian, more specifically Muscovite. However, he spoke impeccable French without an accent, which he was very proud of, like any cultured Slav in these times of the Soviets just like in the times of the Tsars.

"My dear friend," he began, "I don't approve of you already attacking the Nyctalope. Of course I know the secret history of our time and I'm aware that the goal of the Hashshashins is not the same as that of Leonid Zattan and his cronies. They wanted to rule the civilized world; we want to destroy it. They called themselves communists but were really just autocrats working to conquer; we are proponents of anarchy, of total anarchy in which nothing will remain that might oppose the hotbed of human passions. Yes! And we're not offering our enemies the same vulnerability, the same chances of victory as Zattan did to his enemies led by Saint-Clair. That's obvious! But I still don't think it's prudent or clever, when we're chasing hares and deer, to wake up the sleeping lion. See, at the start, when our centers are able to go into action only in small countries like Paraguay, Ethiopia and a few others, we're chasing hares and deer. To attack the Nyctalope, to stir him up against us, it might be better to wait until we're stronger, until a good quarter of the earth is thrown into anarchic disorder. Saint-Clair is a force to be reckoned with. I'd rather reckon with him later."

Since the woman made a gesture and was about to speak, Mittwoch jumped back in:

"Yes, yes, I know, you have your revenge to satisfy. But revenge, as they say, is a dish best served cold. You haven't let the dish cool down enough, Miss Sunday."

"Have you finished?" she sounded annoyed.

"Yes, but I know my comrades. We're seven Fidawis here, counting you. I'll bet five agree with me because Montag will undoubtedly side with you."

"No," the companion of Miss Sunday said. "I took up the fight against the Nyctalope in spite of myself. Although she brags that our superiority over the enemy is clear..."

"This superiority won't last long," Number seven, Sams, cut in sarcastically.

"Let me finish," Montag replied calmly. "Miss Sunday would, in fact, prefer to wait for us to be stronger, Mittwoch. But our hand was forced."

"What?" With the same surprise, in French or English, Diens, Mittwoch, Donners, Freitag and Sams all exclaimed together.

Miss Sunday had calmed down when she said, "Here's what happened."

And she told, quickly but thoroughly, what had happened at *The Sycamores* on the night of May 21 and on the afternoon of May 22, that is to say the Nyctalope and his wife climbing into the garden, their inspection of the villa and the meeting with Dr. Korridès.

"Bloody hell!" shouted Freitag (an English sailor, no doubt), "goddamn! You should've killed him when you had him!"

Miss Sunday broke out laughing while Montag, on the contrary, feverishly nodded his head.

She stopped laughing. "Kill the Nyctalope! What are you thinking, Freitag? Is that a vengeance worthy of me? A victory worthy of us all? Kill the Nyctalope without making him suffer, without him seeing who's reveling in his suffering, without him knowing why he's dying? Come now! The Nyctalope must die only after the torments of a painful, hideous, diabolical agony! You five and you, too, Montag, you six, then, do you know nothing about what I have suffered? My revenge began precisely on the night of May 21. Since then, it has continued every day, for a few minutes every day, because I already have one piece of the puzzle and I will make his suffering last for a long time. This, of course, is just a little taste to whet my appetite."

Gently, Montag put his hand on Miss Sunday's bare arm and said, "My dear, you're getting worked up for nothing. It's the Nyctalope, let me finish."

Turning to the five Fidawis, he went on:

"My dear friends, the Nyctalope has been alerted by an unfortunate, unexpected accident, but unavoidable now. Circumstances conspired against us to be able to grab Saint-Clair and his wife during their nighttime search of the villa. I would've had a hard time killing him during the meeting, even if I wanted to because he was on his guard and accompanied by two men whom we'll call his 'lambs' or his 'dogs'. You see, in all this there was the hand of fate. Saint-Clair is now alerted against us, so we'll have to fight under the threat of being caught, exposed, defeated and annihilated by him. Therefore, let's not argue about what Miss Sunday has done but let's work so that the consequences of it will bring us victory."

"So be it!" Mittwoch declared. "But the deed is very serious. I fear the Nyctalope surrounded by a half dozen of his friends who will soon be at his side. I fear him, even alone, more than all the police in the world put together. I propose, therefore, that this council, the seven of the central committee of Fadawis Hashshashin, make once and for all only one decision."

"What's that?" Miss Sunday asked.

"Let me put it this way: Letting for the moment the 64 centers deal with the anarchist actions following the plan unanimously adopted by the general council of the Hashshashins, the central committee of the Fidawis will have no other objective but the capture of Saint-Clair the Nyctalope, which will be carried out in such a way that it will amount to the death and annihilation of the captive. In accordance with the statutes, I ask that this decision be put to a vote."

"Mittwoch," Miss Sunday smiled and held out her open hand across the table, "thank you. What you ask is what I was going to propose. I vote 'Yes'."

"Yes," Montag said.

Yes, yes, yes, all around the table. Seven hands were raised.

"Adopted!" Miss Sunday cried out triumphantly.

She stood up and with an odd sweetness to her voice said, "I'm going to send in the divine jam. See you tonight, my friends."

"Til tonight!" they all replied.

She backed up. Without turning around she touched the lower part of a three-pronged sconce with her left hand. The door slid open behind her. She backed out through the opening, her big eyes casting a fiery gaze upon the six men, then she disappeared into the cellar darkness while the door slowly closed.

A few minutes later the negro Hamed and the mulatto woman Rosario entered the underground chamber. The six Fidawis had already completely changed. The bare table had shrunk bizarrely and was now barely twenty inches tall. The chairs had been pushed back and lined up by twos or threes along the wall between the beds and bookshelf. The chandelier and electric wall lights had been turned off. The only light was very dim and cast a pale blue glow over the room. It came from the tiny bathroom that was shaded by layers of muslin. On the carpet all shapes and sizes of soft cushions were scattered around in a harmonious jumble. There were some on the beds, too, which had been transformed into huge divans.

As for the six men, they had taken off their clothes and were wearing only pajamas with baggie pants and billowing shirts. They were sitting Turkish style or lounging like Romans on the cushions around the table. Their faces bespoke a serene gravity, like philosophers listening to the words of a master.

But there were no Socratic thinkers here, only fanatics of the most divine (or the most satanic) artificial paradise—hashish eaters!

The servants put two platters on the table. One held six small crystal bowls containing a green paste, which filled the room with the unmistakable scent of hashish. On the other were six cups and a white porcelain coffee pot along with six spoons with thin heads and long necks.

The platters were emptied quickly, spoons, cups and bowls placed directly on the table in front of each of the six hashshashins. Hamed poured the coffee while Rosario mixed a spoonful of the green paste in each cup. The six men drank slowly. A second time the cups were filled and six spoonfuls of green paste mixed in.

The two servants left, taking the platters with them. With childish laughter, which soon faded away to be replaced by more profound and more intense experiences, the Hashshashins entered paradise in the center of which, beyond the limits of time and space, they would soon find the kind of indescribable bliss of a multitude of colors, tastes, scents, sounds and sensations, of a multitude of divine thoughts that the Orientals named with an untranslatable word: the Kief.

CHAPTER IX
The man from Burgos

Sunday, May 29, was truly a wealth of simultaneous events that foreshadowed grave developments like certain clouds forming at particular points on the horizon announce a coming storm.

In fact, on this Sunday, Sylvie Saint-Clair had heard the fateful phrase in the San Lorenzo castle. In the Nopals castle in Saint-Jean-Cap-Ferret, Gnô Mitang and the Nyctalope were shedding some light on the dark mysteries. In Versailles the disturbing council of the Hashshashins was being held. And finally, the comrade Julian Peul, who had bid farewell to Paul Darlecq in Girona, was arriving in Burgos a little before noon.

The affiliate of the Hashshashins for Cerbère and Portbou was not personally acquainted with his comrade Juan Matello, head of the Burgos region or province. But by rule he knew his address. He had to go to Calle San Francisco where Matello lived at the end of the street.

The young man followed the streets bordering the left bank of the Rio Arlanzon that ran through Burgos. At the San Pablo bridge he checked again with a police officer and from there he went straight into the old city.

At the very north of Burgos Calle San Francisco starts from San Gil Square and heads out into the countryside, lined on the right by buildings and gardens of the monastery of Trinidad and San Francisco, and on the left dotted with dispersed little houses, half-bourgeois, half-rural, backed against the hill that overlooked the forts and fortifications of Castillo.

Don Juan Matello was well known in Burgos as a fanatic of bull-fighting. He was one of the most renowned aficionados of the province. He said (and they believed him) that he was a gentleman of leisure from Madrid, settled for two years in Burgos after a bullfight he just happened to be there to attend. It had captivated him so much, all the public reactions to the various events of the corrida had seemed to him so insightfully passionate that he had told someone sitting next to him in the stands:

"Now this is a place where they understand even better than in Seville the traditional art of bull-fighting."

The next day he rented a kind of villa on Calle San Francisco across from the monastery of Trinidad. He bought furniture, hired a servant who was half-blind, nearly deaf and three-quarters mute but a wonderful cook. Since then, he had not left Burgos except for touristic outings, quite frequently, in the countryside (or so they thought) and to go two or three times a year to the grand corrida in Seville and Madrid.

Don Juan Matello, therefore, had earned the general respect of people in the city of El Cid and nobody suspected that he might have other occupations besides reading newspapers and bull-fighting magazines, talking endlessly about past, present and future bullfights, visiting farms in the area and never missing a bullfight, no matter how small, in the Plaza de Toros. Moreover, he was very pious and became fast friends with the monks in the monastery.

The house stood almost on the corner of Calle San Francisco and San Gil Square. It was set off from the street, surrounded by a garden and backed against a steep hill covered with thick trees. From the street one could clearly see the front of the two-story house with a roof-top terrace. Besides the big front gate set in a low wall on the street, there was a smaller door leading to the back and located in the corner furthest away from San Gil.

Naturally, Julien Peul went to the front gate. He pulled the rusty iron cord of the doorbell, which brought running a tall virago with a right eye whitened by leukoma and a left eye that never stopped blinking, a mustache on her upper lip and a generally off-putting air emanating from her thin, bony face wrapped in a black scarf knotted under her chin.

"I would like to see Señor Don Juan Matello," the visitor said very formally.

She did not answer but she opened the gate. Julien Peul followed her across the front yard and was led into a dark, rococo salon whose walls were decorated with old engravings of religious piety and bull-fighting. He waited two or three minutes. Entering through a different door than he came in he saw a man whose first impression on him was of intellectual refinement and physical power united in one person.

"I am Juan Matello. To whom do I have the honor of speaking?" The master of the house used the most polite forms of Castilian formality.

Julien Peul answered in kind, "The honor is all mine. I come on behalf of Ko. I hope you will favor me with a warm welcome because we have serious matters to discuss."

Juan Matello spread his arms to indicate the whole room, including himself, and said, "At your disposal."

Then Julien Peul put his right forearm across his chest, his hand resting on his left shoulder and bowed slightly while pronouncing, "Hasan ibn?"

"Sabbah!" Matello bowed in return.

The two men shook hands and the man from Burgos said to the man from Cerbère-Portbou:

"Let's go to my bedroom, please. I trust my servant, who is almost deaf and mute anyway, but my house is open to visitors and I have a lot of friends in Burgos. Here we might be caught in the middle of a conversation. In my bedroom, on the other hand, we'll be overlooking the garden and the side entrance and we won't be interrupted."

"As you think best."

Julien Peul was very familiar with the Iberian peninsula, having traveled there, as well as Portugal and other parts of Spain, as a student. He noticed that the Castilian used so comfortably and formally by Matello had a faint but un-mistakable accent from Lisbon. Moreover, the shape of his face and the solid bulk of his body made the young Frenchman think that his host was not Spanish but Portuguese.

He thought to himself, "It doesn't matter." But he thought of it again when they entered the bedroom.

It was a huge room that must have taken up two-thirds of the upper floor and was bright as the downstairs salon was dark. Here were no pictures of bulls or saints but in beautiful frames there were thirty or more photographs of the countryside and cities of Portugal. Peul's sharp eyes noticed right away that the sheer curtains that fell from the ceiling around the bed were made of silk in the colors of the Portuguese flag.

In the bright sunlight pouring in through the two big windows he could al-so see much better than downstairs the clean-shaven face of Matello, the sharp lines and prominent cheekbones, a generally domineering expression.

He thought, "For a fact, the comrade from Burgos is no ordinary man. I'm glad to know him and would be very surprised if his only game is with the Hashshashins."

Matello closed the door and locked it. A big curtain, wider than the door it-self, covered the wooden rectangle.

"The whole floor is mine," the man from Burgos said. "Two-thirds of it are taken up by this bedroom, the other third by the bathroom and stairs. The walls are thick and only the garden is next door. Nobody's on the rooftop terrace. My servant Chimena is the only one downstairs. If anybody comes here, we'll hear the bell and can see the visitor before he even enters the house. So, Señor Peul, you can speak freely. No need to whisper. In here, the walls do not have ears. But first, please sit down."

Matello's big, dark eyes and grim expression were concentrated on the small, brown eyes, observant and sparkling with intelligence, of Julien Peul, who met the imperious gaze of his host. But he felt at ease when he spoke, using Castilian, which he was fluent in.

"On the night of May 22 I was woken up by Ko's call and I heard the mu-sical phrase relating to the four One."

"Me too," Matello said.

"Investigation and surveillance all over my sector. Nothing until May 28. On that Saturday I saw the One at the train station in Portbou. He was walking, I followed. I quickly realized he was following another man whom he accosted at a corner of the streets, which were deserted in the hot sun, and after a brief, heated exchange, he knocked the guy out with two punches. Then Saint-Clair searched the guy, pocketed some papers and carried him to the nearest police station.

"An hour later, on the train from Portbou to Barcelona, I talked to the guy. He was a comrade, Paul Darlecq, from Irun and San Sebastian. He'd been trailing Saint-Clair from Irun. At Portbou he'd got a telegram from Ko ordering him to deal with the Nyctalope's wife and son and get further orders from you every other day.

"Darlecq was taken to Girona by two guards to be incarcerated because the Nyctalope had turned him in as someone named Duvalle, a French anarchist sentenced in absentia and thus deserving extradition. Saint-Clair himself took off to who knows where in a speedboat and I, replacing Darlecq and off the board for the moment, have come to tell you, the sector chief of Burgos, that the wife and son of the Nyctalope are in the Duke d'Arandar's castle of San Lorenzo in the Sierra de la Demanda."

"I know," Matello nodded his head.

This "I know" flustered Julien Peul a little, but he let nothing show and sounded delighted when he said, "Good, I'll take my orders."

In a simple but forceful voice, Matello declared, "Go back to Cerbère. I'll take Darlecq's place for you. I'll deal with the three One who are in the region where I am in charge of the Fidawis Hashshashin."

Julian Peul was not expecting this, which made it none of his business. By replacing Darlecq, rather cleverly, he had hoped, and rightfully so, to get half the reward promised to whomever of the Fidawis or even the simple comrades would capture in whole of in part the four One. Peul went even further. He was hoping that such a capture would go smoothly, without a hitch, without a fight, and he figured on standing out in the affair so that of all the men of the secret brotherhood, ready to do anything for Korridès, he would be the one elevated into the council of Fidawis, the true leaders and main benefactors of the international anarchist movement that was already proving its extreme violence and its fervent tenacity in a few small countries, sure signs of total success.

Now, with Matello wielding his authority as sector chief and maybe a member of the council, if he alone took control of the Nyctalope affair, Paul Darlecq and Julien Peul, being officially dismissed, had no hope of seeing any profit, glory or advancement from their work.

Imagine, therefore, how bitter was the young man's disappointment. This time he showed it: his face turned pale, rigid, his hands gripped the arms of the chair and he let out an uncontrollable moan.

At the same time, he felt himself being scrutinized by his superior. He was aware that his huge disappointment was apparent and he felt bad that he did not yet have enough self-control to hide his thoughts and feelings. This all made him look as young as actually was.

Juan Matello stood up and started laughing.

Julien Peul had not yet been degraded, like a Paul Darlecq for example, by the harsh discipline of the Hashshashins. He did not have the fearful fetishism that makes the hierarchy of Fidawis so powerful.

(See, it's a recognized fact, without exception, that members of secret societies most devoted to fomenting unruliness, disorder and anarchy are subject, in their own lives, to a very strict and severe authority, order and discipline.)

Julien Peul was outraged by the mocking laugh after being summarily dismissed by the higher authority of Juan Matello. He puffed himself up like an angry rooster and flushed with fury as he spoke out in French:

"Monsieur, you have the right to give orders and I have the duty to obey. But you mock me—that's going too far! One day you might be my direct boss, unless I become yours, but I will never be your friend!"

There was silence.

Motionless, standing firm on his two spread legs, his head slightly bowed with a piercing gaze, the man from Burgos observed the youth from Cerbère-Portbou who was having a hard time calming down after his vicious outburst. All of a sudden Matello, in a slow, calm, authoritative voice, spoke in French, rendering his Portuguese accent more audible than in Spanish.

"Peul, my boy, congratulations. This is the first time since I've been a Fidawi that I've seen a comrade react like that after being whipped. I have more than one file on you, so I know you're intelligent, brave and ambitious. I didn't know you were capable of personal dignity and outrage. Now, in my view, without that you're not a man, you're just a tool, a piece of equipment...

"Right! Sit down, please. Our relationship is only just beginning. Come on, sit and do me the pleasure of answering frankly the questions I'm going to ask. I believe your entire future lies in your answers."

Surprised, disturbed and proud all at the same time, Julien Peul sat back down in the armchair he had just jumped out of.

Juan Matello remained standing, his back against the corner of a window, his hands behind his back and his head lowered before looking up at the young man.

He said, "If you weren't on the payroll of Korridès, what would you be doing?"

Peul responded without the slightest hesitation, "Militant writer and soldier... a warrior of the new age, a modern mercenary!"

Matello raised his eyebrows, so Peul explained:

"I was too young to fight in the Great War. I wept tears of rage. Not that I was a patriot! Oh, no... War for war's sake! In my opinion, war is the height of adventure. The clash of so many nations impassioned me. But it was nothing new. At eight years old I was reading about wars—Turenne, Frederic II, Napoleon. At twelve I knew by heart the Commentaries of Caesar. So, you can understand why I tell you that the military service I did in France deeply disappointed me. I didn't know then that the barracks, for almost everyone, were the necessary entryway to battle. When I got out, I ate up my 40,000-franc inheritance running around Spain and Portugal as a field study of the conquest and eviction of the Moors, the crossing of Hannibal, the invasion of the Roman legions, the little wars of unification and then Napoleon's fight against the Spanish and English. That's why I know the peninsula very well and also why I'm convinced that you're originally from Portugal.

"Penniless, I thought about joining the foreign legion in order to learn at first hand what the life of a soldier was like, in spite of the peaceful times, and to get some practical experience at it, which the barracks only gave a boring glimpse of. Then I devoted myself, to a certain extent, through books and in my imagination, to reliving the great wars in which I kind of childishly regretted not being a commander of armies and I wanted to write books on war. At the time, I would've volunteered as an officer to the irregular troops spawned once in a while by revolutions in various parts of the world. But luck would have it that I met Korridès and I was seduced by some of his views, which you can easily imagine after what I've just told you. There you have it!"

"Very good," Matello said. "So, you're free to devote yourself entirely to the whatever you want to do, whether or not it conforms to your status as a Hashshashin comrade."

"Yes," Julien Peul smiled. "But you know as well as I do that if my actions transgress the oath I took as a comrade, I'll find myself laid out flat on the ground, dead, with a knife in my heart or a bullet in my neck."

"Yes," Matello said, "I know that... But it won't happen if I cover for you. Besides, for this great adventure, you won't have to worry about knives or bullets if I'm taking the same risks as you."

"Yes, that's true," Peul sounded excited. He jumped up again, carried away by an irresistible impulse that was born not only out of his own fervent feelings but also out of the potent fascination that the eyes and words of Matello exercised over him.

"Well then," the man from Burgos said, "You'll stay here. I'll get a replacement for you in Cerbère and Portbou. I'll assign you to myself as a comrade lieutenant. After a few days, maybe a few weeks of observation, either I'll initiate you into my secret or I'll turn you back over to the central committee."

Julien Peul felt both seduced and submissive, but he had regained his self-composure.

"So be it! I accept. I won't know until later whether I should thank you. But that's the future. The present is Saint-Clair the Nyctalope. What are we going to do about him?"

"No," Matello said. "The present is two-fold—it's about Sylvie and Pierre Saint-Clair."

"That's right, sorry. All the more reason, what are we going to do?"

"Well," the Portuguese answered snidely, "we're going to obey the orders of Ko... of Korridès... of the central committee of Fidawis... or rather the sovereign will of Titania."

"Eh?" Peul was stupefied. "Titania? Who's that?"

"Aha, my young friend, you still have a lot to learn, even about the sect of Hashshashins to whom you, like me, have sold yourself 'body and soul', according to the cynical expression of the oath. I'll tell you someday about Titania. For now, all you need to know is that her will is behind the orders expressed in the telegram Darlecq got in Portbou commanding him to come here. The order told him to get hold of Sylvie and Pierre Saint-Clair and put them in a safe and secure place. Easier said than done. It doesn't matter, we'll obey it and do our best to succeed."

"Good," Peul was satisfied. "And the three million franc bonus?"

"Phooey," Matello snorted, shrugging his shoulders. "Are you so grubby? Be patient and I think this whole thing will bring in a lot more than three million francs for you. For what I plan to tell you, it'll be more like ten, twenty, thirty million and more. I just hope the Nyctalope and the Hashshashins together can get it for me. But enough talk, it's past noon. Let's have lunch. One more thing, however."

He put his hands on Peul's shoulders, who was confused but subdued, and in a severe, serious voice said:

"Answer frankly like I asked you to a little while ago. Are you all in?"

"Yes." The young man was now decided.

Matello saw his mind was made up and was content. "Great. Deep down, you don't really care about universal anarchy, do you?"

"That's true."

"Your affiliation with the Hashshashins is just a matter of luck, circumstances, a reckless adventure, right?"

"Exactly."

"So, your soul is free and your body can be liberated. Well, I'm offering you, with or without or against the Hashshashins, it depends on unforeseen events, I'm offering you a rationally thought-out adventure that will bring you wealth, glory, power and honor."

"Oh ho! Why offer all this to me, Julien Peul, whom you've never even seen before?"

"Because I need a few strong young men like you. I've already got three who are working and waiting. You'll be the fourth, no different than the others in your duties and rights. I want six. We'll search for and find two more. Do you accept to be one of mine, more sincerely and more wholly than you were for the Hashshashin?"

"Well, sure, yes, I accept."

"For better or worse, for life or death?"

"Yes. *Per fas et nefas, per vitam et usque ad mortem!*" Julien Peul pronounced with his eyes ablaze.

"Bravo! Let's have lunch. There's a bullfight this afternoon that looks good. We'll go because I'm a fanatical aficionado. Tomorrow morning we'll leave for the Sierra de la Demanda where I'm expected."

"By whom?"

"By a man who should be seeing today, if all goes well, Sylvie Saint-Clair and her son Pierre. He's the patriarch of a Bohemian tribe. He's called Escarpaz. We're going to make use of him. Unfortunately for him, after he's played his part, we'll have to kill him."

"Eh?" Peul flinched.

"Ah, my friend, if this is going to be your first stabbing, tell yourself that on the path you've chosen, with the Hashshashins or with me, it won't be the last. If you have some sentimental respect for human life or fear of the law that wants to protect this life, kill yourself right now because the 'comrade' you are will soon be on the receiving end of the stabbing that he refused to give.

"But enough talk. I'm starved. Let's eat!"

CHAPTER X
Matello at work

The next day, Monday May 30, Leo Saint-Clair, coming from Barcelona on the fastest, most direct trains, arrived in Burgos in the middle of the afternoon. He went straight to a house in the Artillery district where he knew a chief mule-driver. He rented two mules and a driver and left immediately for San Lorenzo. He did not take the relatively good road but made a long detour that went by the village of Salas, then directly onto mountain paths that, despite their meandering zigzags, ended up cutting the journey in half. (From Burgos to San Lorenzo is 25 miles as the crow flies. It turns into at least 35 miles on the back of a mule). And the two mules were good. The driver knew the mountain and the distance was covered in nine hours, including the thirty minutes for a bite to eat at nightfall.

By chance, this May night in the mountain region of Burgos was splendid. The air was so pure that all the stars in the sky were visible. Even the paths most deeply cut into the rock got enough light to be able to walk at night. And it was fortunate because neither the mule-driver nor the two mules had night-vision like the Nyctalope.

Finally, around midnight, Saint-Clair stopped his animal at the bank of the raging river that encircled the castle. He took out the whistle that the Duke d'Arandar had wisely given him and blew a series of shrill warbles.

It was, in fact, the only sound that could be heard over the deep rumble of the river. The man on watch heard it. A light turned on in the narrow window of the watchtower over the drawbridge. The window was open and a man's head appeared in the light. Then the head and the light disappeared. One minute later the drawbridge slowly lowered and its iron-tipped edge dropped into the stone casing it was fit for.

"Anda," the driver grunted. The two mules stepped onto the mobile bridge.

Fifteen minutes later the mules were in the stable, the driver sitting in the kitchen before a plate of ham, bread and wine, and Leo Saint-Clair was entering his wife's room, having been left at the doorway by the Duke after Sylvie had been woken up by a bell and opened the door.

It had taken only a few minutes for Saint-Clair to inform the Duke of the events that had forced him to come back so unexpectedly. But it took a lot longer to tell the same thing to his wife because with Sylvie he omitted no details and reported his conversation with Gnô Mitang word for word.

Of course, before saying anything Saint-Clair and Sylvie went arm in arm to check on Pierre sleeping in his crib near the bed where Adele the nanny was also asleep.

The the couple went back to their adjoining bedroom. When the thick curtain was carefully put back over the connecting door without a sound, they talked. After telling her all about his own adventures and the conversation with Gnô, he wrapped up:

"I came back to warn you and the Duke. Your refuge here is known to the enemy, but we know that now and that's enough to prevent Korridès and his accomplices from doing anything to hurt you and Pierrot. Be even more cautious. The Duke will be on constant alert. This castle is an impregnable fortress built by man and nature. You and Pierre just can't go out so that, even if you're surrounded by enemies, which is physically impossible, you won't be in any danger."

"Yes," Sylvie shuddered. "What about you?"

"Me? I'm onto them. I'm absolutely certain that my arrival in Barcelona in the speedboat wasn't seen by anyone. Even if the guy I had arrested in Portbou managed to communicate with Korridès or another accomplice, he would've have said I was going back to France through Portbou or Cerbère. In fact, I'll be going back through Irun and Hendaye.

"At first I wasn't sure which strategy to take. I wondered whether it might not be better to stay in San Lorenzo with you. This idea, you can imagine, Sylvie, was very tempting. But by doing that I'd be leaving the field open to the enemy and I would learn nothing about what I want and need to know. And since we can't stay here forever, since sooner or later we'll have to leave, then we'll end of running into an enemy that's even stronger because I did nothing.

"Gnô's hypotheses are only hypotheses. But the light they shed on the obscurity of this mysterious adventure they make sense, on the grand scale and in a few specifics I want to investigate. But should I even investigate? In short, the sooner I can expose, fight and defeat Korridès, the sooner we'll can live in peace.

"That's why, Sylvie, my dear, my love, I'm going back tomorrow, not to Burgos where Korridès has eyes watching for me, but through the mountain to Miranda de Ebro, which has a train station on the line from Madrid to Irun.

"Of course, I could've written to you to set up a safe and secure mode of communication, but I needed to see you, to see little Pierre, to reassure myself that San Lorenzo is well protected and make sure that the Duke can guarantee all the new means of defense."

"You did well to come," Sylvie smiled with a cheerful glint in her eye. "I was going to write to you because I, too, have news to tell you."

As her brow darkened and her expression suddenly turned serious, Saint-Clair got worried.

He asked, "Bad news?"

"You'll be the judge of that."

The young lady recounted one by one all the incidents of the day before: the mass in the castle chapel, the Bohemians present there, the fateful phrase pronounced by the gypsy girl, and then she added:

"Sunday evening all the gypsies left, taking with them their dead-drunk patriarch and young Huronilla in a deep, almost cataleptic sleep. That night was very quiet, just like the day before. One of the Duke's game wardens who had secretly followed the Bohemians saw them go back to their camp next to Salas. I'd gone to bed and was sleeping calmly when the bell woke me up."

"Well," Saint-Clair said, "it all seems to fit the typical weirdness of the gypsies who wander around the world with a hoard of legends, superstitions and mysterious mutterings. It's not so surprising that the gypsy girl gave you a warning against a menacing danger from a woman. Gnô based all his hypotheses on the hatred of a woman toward all the people who defeated Leonid Zattan, therefore against you and me. If it's only a coincidence, it's still food for thought.

"It's too bad the Bohemians left the castle. Still, finding them now to question the girl and the old man wouldn't be wise since under these circumstances, no Bohemian on his guard would utter a word. Here we could've separated the girl from the old man and the old man from the rest of the tribe..."

Sylvie broke in, "Yes, the Duke and I thought about that. He Duke even planned, at one moment, to stop the Bohemians from leaving, but on second thought we figured that there was no justifiable reason for keeping them here. The old man's drunkenness and the girl's sleep were just meaningless events that they're used to. All things considered we'd have to have forced them to stay here. If there were only a handful of them the Duke wouldn't have hesitated, but it was the whole tribe except for three or four old women who stayed back in the camp to guard it."

"You were right," Saint-Clair said. "In any case, with these gypsies and the weird words of the young girl, now that we're warned about the enemy we have no choice but to consider San Lorenzo as a fortress closed to all strangers. You and Pierrot should be safe from danger inside this fortress."

"I think so too," Sylvie agreed as calmly as could be.

The conservation between the couple ended here.

In the morning, after a few hours rest, Saint-Clair and Sylvie joined the Duke in the dining room for breakfast. At the table they discussed only trivial matters, but then the three of them retired to the smoking room next to the Duke's bedroom and once again the whole situation was thoroughly examined. The conclusion was the same as what Leo and Sylvie had decided in their private conversation.

"You can leave with a serene heart," the Duke said. "For one, Sylvie and Pierre won't leave the castle where there's plenty of space, fresh air and all the comforts necessary for their health. Plus, no human being will cross the drawbridge without being seen and then interrogated and then accompanied until they're allowed to."

Saint-Clair asked for a knapsack filled with the necessary provisions for two meals for two men hiking in the mountains. They added a small wineskin and some oats for the mules. At 11 a..m Saint-Clair walked out of San Lorenzo, once again leaving what he held dearest in life to the care of the Duke d'Arandar.

After he had gone, the Duke had a long talk with Padre Felipe, then all the castle inhabitants (without the exception of a single person) were assembled in the chapel. In the name of the Duke the chaplain gave a speech explaining that a kind of grave danger might come from outside to threaten Sylvie and little Pierre, whose identity was revealed to everyone in San Lorenzo. On the Gospel held by both the Duke and the chaplain, men and women alike swore to keep vigil and, if called for, fight to the death in defending against any and all perils. In effect, since the enemy knew about the refuge, the once carefully guarded secret had become pointless.

Now, on that same day, Tuesday May 31, early in the morning on the mountain about half a mile north of Salas, Juan Matello and Julien Peul met the old patriarch of the Bohemian tribe. A pre-arranged meeting seeing that the first words out of the Portuguese's mouth were:

"Escarpaz, you're here. Good. Time is precious. Losing even one minute can result in irreparable losses."

The meeting place was in the woods at the top of a bare, rocky ridge. The summit of this ridge was jagged with rocky spurs jutting up on either side. Sitting attentively in the middle of the natural chaos the men could talk without fear of being heard or caught off guard. In fact, the ridge overlooked the edge of the woods where two or three paths converged in a kind of uneven clearing that was too far for their conversation, even if they shouted, to be heard by anyone hiding in the surrounding trees. And if anyone came and tried to climb up to the ridge, the hidden conspirators could easily escape down the opposite side.

The man who had chosen this place knew the mountain very well.

Without bothering to introduce his companion, Matello said, "We came from Burgos on mules. The animals are hidden over there, muzzled and tied up. If all goes as planned, Escarpaz, I'll show you where and you can get some men from your tribe to pick them up. I imagine you're farther than a mule's ride from here…"

Escarpaz laughed.

Up close, the Bohemian seemed a lot younger than he had looked at the castle of San Lorenzo. His white hair and beard had not changed but the expression on his face and the way he held himself were completely different! He was no longer an old man, bent double, hands trembling, bowlegged, bleary-eyed with a wrinkled brow and drooping lip, but here was a sturdy man, alert, with sharp, stern, even cruel eyes. All his movements, his whole attitude betrayed a strong, supple, perfectly fit body whose only marks of age were the white hair and beard. Patriarch? Perhaps, but chief, a rough and ready chief, for sure!

Sitting a little apart from the two men, Julien Peul contemplated the gypsy whom he knew had been sentenced to death. For, the Portuguese had informed the young Frenchman of his immediate plans: First, use Escarpaz and his tribe to kidnap Sylvie Saint-Clair and her son, then stab Escarpaz so that it will look like his brother gypsies killed him. If the kidnapping plot and the diabolical murder planned down to the last detail is accomplished, the result will be three-fold: Matello and Peul will have the hostages, Escarpaz, who already knows too much and will know even more after the kidnapping, will be killed and finally the whole tribe will be trapped by the police and Spanish justice system who will be searching among the gypsies for the murderers of the "patriarch".

Julien Peul had accepted this catalog of crimes and sworn to see it through to the end. Perverted by his inclination (surely atavistic) to worship fanatically "war for war's sake", ambitious for wealth and the freedom and power that he believed wealth gave to those who possessed it, lacking all moral compass, all patriotism and therefore all scruples, proud of being above the law, this veritable anarchist willfully started on the path of crime, which his joining the sect of Hashshashins had already opened but he had not yet bloodied his shoes.

With this cynicism, this will for wickedness, which perverted souls revel in when they think they have been matured by life whereas they have only been spoiled, Julien Peul contemplated the gypsy and snickered to himself:

"Stupid old man who thinks he's sly and strong and who's racing headlong into a death trap."

Headlong? Um... More experienced than his new student and partner, Juan Matello was not so sure that the dreadful web was being woven so smoothly, without knots and tears. He would be on guard. The game they were starting was rife with countless possibilities. He would do anything to win. If he did lose, basta! He would not even consider this possibility.

The Portuguese and the gypsy talked for a long time, attentively observed by Julien Peul who knew better than to butt into a discussion in which he had nothing useful to contribute. Escarpaz first told them everything he knew about the castle. Matello laid out his plan, changing a few details to fit the information he had just received. Then the two men went through the possibility of this and the difficulty of that, the chance of this or that happening.

When the conversation started to heat up Matello said, "Hold on, Escarpaz! You'll see!"

He unbuttoned his bulky hunting jacket and from an inside pocket he pulled out a big oilcloth envelope. He opened it, took out a piece of paper and unfolded it. It was a blueprint of the castle of San Lorenzo. He spread it on a flat rock and pointed with his index finger.

"Look! Here's the laundry room whose basement window is big enough for Huronilla to get into the castle. And here's where they slaughter the animals and she can open this little door that leads to the river. Follow my finger. Can't we get all the way to this storeroom for wood next to the kitchen without being seen? The night watchmen, no matter how many there are, will be in the towers... one, two, three... where they can see the whole line of ramparts and the courtyards... We won't go into the courtyards, unless there's a fire."

"*E verdad! Verdad!*" Escarpaz remarked with a short burst of laughter.

After this the two men talked without any more arguing. With the map spread out before them, they agreed on the every last detail. When it was done, when the blueprint was back in its waterproof envelope and safe inside Matello's buttoned-up jacket, Escarpaz just said:

"Señor, I have done a good job for you, which you paid for in advance, isn't that right?"

"That's right," Matello's voice was full of friendly, condescending recognition.

"Bueno! So, let's talk about the conditions of this new work. It'll be hard and dangerous. Lives will be at risk. If it turns bad, the police will get involved and my whole tribe will rot in prison. If even one of my children dies in chains... There's a price to pay!"

"I agree," Matello nodded solemnly.

"A high price!"

"Could be. Name your price, Escarpaz."

The Bohemian's gray eyes sparkled as he grunted, "*Veinte mil duros!*"

"Oh ho, 100,000 pesetas... You're ravenous, hombre."

Escarpaz did not reply but his eyes narrowed, then closed while his jaw clenched and his beard jutted forward. This obviously meant that the patriarch was not going to haggle. Nevertheless, Matello ruthlessly or at least very firmly did haggle.

Quite amused by the scene, Julien Peul thought, "Very smart, boss. The old man might as well ask for a million douros and get them... promised! What difference does the amount make to Matello since he won't be giving him a sou? But he's haggling. He's a smart one."

The bargaining did not last long. The Portuguese argued for barely thirty seconds when the gypsy stood up, slapped on his greasy hat and turned his back on them.

"*Adios, hombres!*"

He walked away. He was really walking away!

Matello stopped him with one word: "Deal!"

But he was wise enough to unleash a string of the crudest curses one could utter in Castilian slang and he stood up to shake the old man's hand. He added gruffly:

"You know I don't walk around with 20,000 ecus in my pocket. On my word, I swear, you'll be paid in Burgos, in the first *capilla* to the left in the cathedral, the *capilla* dedicated to Santa Tecla, next Sunday at 10 in the morning..."

"Bueno!" Escarpaz agreed calmly. "But you do have a pen, señor, to write with and I can read. Write for me that Don Juan Matello owes 20,000 douros to the tribe of Zapatan gypsies represented by Escarpaz or in the case of his death by his successor to the patriarch."

"Touché!" thought Peul.

But Juan Matello must have planned for this, too. However compromising, dangerous and costly this paper might prove to be for him in the future, he did not hesitate to fulfill Escarpaz's wary demand. But he took the opportunity to pose a question that had not yet been discussed.

Taking a pen and wallet out of his pocket he said, "Agreed. But if the plan doesn't work?"

Here Escarpaz let out a light but cocky laugh, "It'll work, señor. And I'll give you immediate proof, after which all talk will be meaningless. But your companion is young and there are secrets that are better kept for seasoned brains. Lean forward."

Peul was greatly disappointed and started to hate the old man with a passion at this point as Escarpaz whispered quietly and quickly into Matello's ear. The Portuguese's face lit up, truly, nothing fake about it. The "proof" must have been conclusive, convincing and complete because Matello shouted out, sincerely and triumphantly:

"That's it! That's it! Success is guaranteed! Bravo, Escarpaz!"

On a small white sheet of paper torn out of a notebook he wrote a few lines, a date and signed it.

"*Bueno. Muchas gracias, señor.*"

The mutually criminal pact was made: Juan Matello had the guarantee that in three or four days Sylvie and Pierre Saint-Clair would be in his hands and the gypsy Escarpaz was carrying a paper that was (unsuspected by him, of course) an irrevocable death warrant!

Matello and Peul remained silent until the Bohemian disappeared down one of the paths that led into the woods.

Peul spoke first, "What do we do now?"

"We're going to hole up and hide, my boy. Nobody must see us except for Escarpaz who knows where we'll be within the hour. Get the mules and let's get going."

"What did the old man whisper to you?"

It just came out, impulsively, without thinking. Peul was so brimming with curiosity that the question just spilled out. But he saw right away how foolish it was. Matello's face turned hard and haughty and scornful like the mask of some old Roman emperor. This face had beauty but a terrible beauty that mortified Peul when he heard the deep, menacing voice pronounce slowly:

"Are you crazy, young man? You have a lot to learn. I'll teach you if things don't get busy. Now the matter is closed. Follow me."

Angry at himself because he knew this scolding was justified, Peul followed his master, who was indeed his master from now on seeing that, instead of getting upset at the rude remarks, Peul thanked him as if he had done him a great favor.

The two men had left their mules half a mile from the rocky butte in a ravine whose bottom, watered by a little stream, was hidden by a leafy arch that the spring had already made thick enough for men, animals and bulky objects underneath it to be unseen by anybody who happened to be passing by on either side of the top of the ravine. No path led down to the bottom, but if you knew the mountainous terrain and had mules used to such land, you could go and down the steep sides that looked, at first sight, impossible to negotiate.

Matello and Peul dragged their animals out of the ravine, mounted them and trotted down a rather wide, cleared path that led them away from San Lorenzo towards Burgos. It only lasted fifteen minutes.

At a crossroads in the middle of the woods Matello angled his mule to the left and took a much narrower and uneven path, often blocked by bushes and low branches. It was hard going for Peul because he had neither the experience nor the ingenuity of his boss and in the end was guided more by his mule than by his own initiative.

Here again they traveled for fifteen minutes until they reached a bowl-like clearing on the slope of which was the wide opening of a cave.

"Here," Matello said, "no one will find us. I know the mountain of San Lorenzo backward and forward. This area we're in is completely void of game. Moreover, it's off the paths leading from the castle to the various farms and few villages in the region. I've never known why there's no game here, neither bird nor beast. The fact is it's a desert. But it doesn't matter why, we'll make good use of it. We have enough provisions for at least 24 hours. If we have to wait longer, Escarpaz will bring supplies.

"Dismount, my boy! Try to set up at the back of the cave as comfortably as possible. There's no water, it's as dry as a bedroom at noon. We won't get arthritis. But we we'll have no water to drink since we won't be leaving here except to go straight to San Lorenzo. Luckily our skins are full of wine that's light enough to quench our thirst and not worsen it."

The gestures, the glances and the voice of the Portuguese was full of kindness. Julien Peul was glad for this. He was afraid that the earlier scolding would continue or get worse.

So, he responded cheerfully, "Boss, seems like everything's going to plan. I hope you don't find me too green as a 'camper', as they say in England and even in France."

"The problem," Matello said, "is that the mules will get thirsty. I didn't want to ask the patriarch to bring a supply of water since he'll already be burdened with fifty pounds and as strong as he is, he could get careless in such rough terrain. So, when he comes to either stock us up or to take us away, he mustn't be seen by any game wardens or coal-men from the Duke d'Arandar. With a supply of water he couldn't go just anywhere or hide quickly. There are no roses without thorns—in fact we should be happy that the thorns are so often accompanied by roses."

The cave was spacious and, indeed, very dry. It must have been used more than once as a hideaway for long or short periods of time because the whole back of it was covered in a thick layer of dry leaves carefully stripped of twigs and needles. It made a huge, soft, safe and sound bed where a dozen men could sleep side by side.

The mules were tied in a corner of the cave. The two men, with their coats and supplies, sat at a rough stone table around which were chunks of rock arranged orderly enough to serve as seats. And so, sometimes silent, sometimes talking without really needing to, Matello and Peul waited for the night.

After using their provisions for a quick, light meal, they wrapped up in their capes, stretched out in the middle of the bed of leaves and were soon fast asleep.

Nothing disturbed their sleep. The next morning, June 1, the sky was cloudy and it rained with intermittent downpours, from 11 a.m. to 4 p.m. Then gusts of wind cleared the air. The sky was blue, the forest sunny. But all this lasted only until sundown, precisely, when the wind died down, mists rose from the ground, clouds gathered again and the cold, dark twilight heralded a night of bad weather, therefore a starless night.

During the whole day the two men did not leave the cave where they passed the time sleeping, dreaming and talking. They took the risk of smoking a few cigarettes, cautiously so that the smoke could not be seen outside. As little frequented as the place was, an unexpected patrol by some game warden was still to be feared.

In their occasional conversations Matello and Peul went over and over the plan of action that had been adopted with Escarpaz and they agreed that it had all the chances of success, even disregarding the important secret the gypsy patriarch had whispered to the Portuguese, a secret that proved, at least according to Escarpaz and believed by Matello, the favorable outcome of the plan. Asking again about this secret had naturally been avoided by Julien Peul.

The night was falling on the woods when a darker shadow suddenly appeared in the cave's entrance.

"Escarpaz!" Matello breathe a sigh of relief.

It was indeed the Bohemian.

"Hello," he said. "Here's some bread, goat meat and water. Eat and drink. You still have half an hour, then we go to San Lorenzo. It'll happen tonight."

"*Demonios!*" Matello exclaimed, "I knew it. It'll be cloudy and no stars. The night will be dark. All bodes well for us."

"Yes," Escarpaz said. "I'd decided to wait for three full days. On the third night we'd act, even if the moon and stars were out, which, of course, would make it harder and more dangerous for us. In the darkness of this cloudy night, it'll be more challenging but safer."

"Where are Huronilla and your people?"

"On their way to the castle. We'll meet up with them before getting to work. They have the rope and cork boards. Don't worry."

Matello laughed, "Oh, I'm not worried. You know, Escarpaz, my fortune hangs on the outcome of this plan as much as yours does. And I'm determined to risk my life if necessary. This kid here, whom you can call Juanito, is as committed as I am. So..."

"That's what needed," Escarpaz cut in, nodding his head.

And that was the end of the conversation.

The mules would have to stay in the cave where their masters would come get them soon if the plan worked. Otherwise, the poor animals would die there, tied up, of hunger and thirst unless they went into a frenzy, which seemed inevitable, and broke free to escape into the forest where their instinct would lead them to the sea or to a river. Anyway, Matello had bought them recently and was not attached to them, so he did not really care. Of course, Julien Peul cared even less than his master. Therefore, the conspirators left the cave without a glimpse of pity and followed Escarpaz.

They walked quickly and quietly through the forest. It took them 45 minutes to reach the castle of San Lorenzo. Relative to the river they were upstream on a rocky peak that overlooked the whole slope of the mountain. They sat and waited. The night was dark. However, a few clouds on the southern horizon had a kind of glare that emanated not a glow, let alone a light, but a kind of dusky halo. This halo moved slowly with the clouds, nudged by the light wind, silhouetting the castle, the medieval mass of San Lorenzo, as a darker shadow against the night.

It might have been around 10 p.m. when they heard an owl hooting, ten times in the same place, very clearly over a monotone rumbling of the river and rustling of the leaves.

"That's my people," Escarpaz whispered.

He responded right away with a single hoot. The sound of the nocturnal bird was so perfectly imitated that if Matello and Peul did not know better they would have believed owls were nearby and not the men and girl they were waiting for.

The gypsies showed up soon, black shadows moving across the peak of gray rock. There were eight men and a girl, Huronilla, maybe thirteen years old (already a woman as was always the case with Spanish gypsies), the same mysterious creature who had pronounced the fateful phrase in Sylvie's ear: "*Asplata la vibora, matala!*"

Matello and Peul, their eyes now accustomed to the dark, saw that the gypsy girl was not carrying anything, but the men were lugging coils of rope, thin but strong, and curved boards of cork, still keeping the shape of the tree trunk they had been torn off of.

"The night will be chilly and the water ice-cold," Escaprpaz said. "Luckily my boys can move fast and anyway the heat from the fire will dry them off. And you will see, señor Juan, that the 100,000 pesetas I demanded is money well spent."

"I don't doubt it," Matello replied. "Do we start right away?"

"No, it's too early. Usually everyone in San Lorenzo goes to bed at this time except for three guards in the watchtower, but it's better to wait an hour more so we'll be sure to surprise them in their sleep. Anyway, it won't be wasted time. We're well placed here to see all of San Lorenzo. Let's keep an eye on the side we'll have to approach. My young men and the girl know what they have to do. The longer they have to observe where they're going to attack, the better prepared they'll be. And you, señor Juan, get a good look because you're going into the castle with us."

"What we need," Matello said, "is for the wind to break up those clouds a little so we'll have light now and again. Sure, really faint but at least the glow from a star, briefly, for a minute, hidden again by the clouds... it would make our task a lot easier."

"Yes," Escarpaz said, "but better to have this darkness than a night lit up by the stars and by the bright dust of the Milky Way. But as you said, it'd be nice to have a little light now and again. Hold on! The wind is picking up, I think, from the east. The clouds look a little scattered now... You're a lucky man, caballero. Even nature seems to want to answer your prayers."

It was true. Barely fifteen minutes passed and in the southeast the mass of clouds broke apart, revealing a rift of twinkling stars. The whole landscape was transformed.

Standing to the north and above the castle, the adventurers, whom we can, in these circumstances, call bandits, saw all of San Lorenzo lit by the stars, in detailed silhouette against the completely black background of the mountains framing the horizon to the south. The tear in the mists widened, the stars multiplied, the castle made brighter, especially in comparison with the darkness cast by the architectural mass in the northwest.

"Caramba!" Escarpaz said. "All the demons in hell are on your side, señor Juan. Now we can see very well and if we keep to the shadows of the castle we can act without being seen."

Julien Peul shivered and straightened up. For the first time he dared to butt in between Matello and Escarpaz. Still intoxicated by what lie in store, he said, "Wait a minute longer. It's tempting fate!"

"Right you are, my boy!" Matello agreed. He turned to the patriarch and ordered, "Let's go!"

"Let's go," Escarpaz said in return.

The terrible trio left the peak where they had waited and watched and headed downhill toward the castle.

The high crenelated wall, the barbican, the fortified ramps, the central body with its corner towers, its round towers, its peaked and hooded towers, the lord's quarters and the chapel, the communal buildings, the stables and storerooms, in short the whole, huge castle of San Lorenzo built like an amphitheater on the steep flank of the mountain was surrounded not by a moat with a level surface of water like castle's in the plains but by a circular torrent that roared out of a deep cleft in the mountain, split upstream from the castle, circled it and rejoined downstream, thus making the castle an island fortress where there was apparently only one means of access—the drawbridge.

Since the day Leo Saint-Clair had entrusted his wife and son to the noble Duke, this drawbridge was always raised and it lowered only to let in the game wardens, coal suppliers and servants who were known and recognized but still checked on entry by the guards. Meaning the castle of San Lorenzo looked impregnable. In fact, it was. It was for everyone except for people like Juan Matello on the one hand and Escarpaz the gypsy on the other who had decided to bet their lives on a criminal undertaking whose first move was to sneak into the castle.

The river ran fast and furious. The natural canal split into two branches where the water rushed around the castle was around thirty feet deep on average and 40-50 feet wide in its twists and turns. Except for the place where the river was straddled by the drawbridge, which was narrower. But this place was the most guarded with sentinels on watch day and night to man the bridge, the gate and the huge double-doors of the entrance.

It was on the right flank, on the northwest side, and just a few feet above the split in the river that Escarpaz and Matello had decided to get into the castle. On this side were some communal buildings, mainly the laundry and after two thick walls separated by a small courtyard was the butcher-house.

See, in San Lorenzo everything was organized so that the lords and their servants could satisfy all their needs. For example, the meat was provided by the cattle, goats and sheep on the domain, which were brought to the castle alive and slaughtered and treated like in any butcher shop in the city or town.

Now, in the laundry there was a basement airvent to drain the water on the slightly slanted floor and it emptied directly into the river, barely a foot and a half over the current. In case of a flood the vent was blocked off by a hermetically sealed valve coated with a custom-made layer of oakum and cork. It was the same for all the numerous openings around the castle that could be flooded during the heavy rains in October. But in normal weather this vent and the other small openings remained clear for air circulation.

The gypsies' path led them into a wide cone of shadow cast by the castle. Escarpaz, Matello and Peul were in front. They stopped right across from the tower in the northwest corner, upstream from the part of the wall behind which stood the laundry building. Matello knew the castle blueprints by heart. Escarpaz had visited the grounds last Sunday. Therefore, they were sure there was no mistake, although in the darkness of night on this side, they could not see the air vent that was their first goal according to the plan of attack.

At their feet the right branch of the river flowed by, glistening upstream but invisible in front of them since the water reflected none of the stars shining in the southeast. Here the current made no sound but the rumbling of the waterfall downstream from the drawbridge at the juncture of the two branches was so loud that they could talk in a normal voice without fear of being heard by the sentinels probably on guard in the watchtowers, but there was always the chance that some insomniac might be wandering around on the ramparts.

"Señor, this is it," Escarpaz said. "Should we go?"

"Yes," Matello shot back.

"Anda! Huronilla!"

The gypsy girl was in the back of the group. She stepped forward, felt rather than seen by Escarpaz, Matello and Peul. The patriarch grabbed her, took off her clothes and rolled up her clothes, which he tied to her head.

He said, "Like this your rags will be kept drier than if you wore them. They'll warm you up when you put them back on in the laundry. I won't repeat what you have to do. Do you remember everything?"

"*Si, padre.*"

"*Bueno.*"

With a long, wide, very strong, colorful belt that the Spanish called "fafa", Escarpaz girdled the girl's waist. One of the gypsies gave her a rope and a cork board, tied fast to the end of the rope. The cork was put on the ground and Huronilla laid down flat on top of it, her hands stretched out clutching the front and her legs straddling the sides.

"*Vamos!*" Escarpaz barked. "Be careful, Huronilla, the clippers are folded into the fafa on your belly." And he repeated, "*Vamos!*"

Using the rope, the makeshift raft was lowered into the water and immediately swept up by the current. Escarpaz and two gypsies behind him slowly, carefully let out the rope. They could not see Huronilla, but they were sure she was going where she needed to go.

The trick had been devised, studied, calculated and prepared in advance. In this spot, the water rushed around a bend and ricocheted off the banks like a billiard ball, then rushed straight down to the ramparts. Therefore, any floating object dropped into the river here was bound to be thrown against the opposite wall.

She gave the rope slack very slowly so that she would reach the wall without getting hurt and after rearing up on the raft the girl could feel around for the rim of the air vent.

The air vent, a Roman vaulted arch, measured around three feet high and two feet wide at its base. It was fitted with two crossed bars behind which was an iron grill. To work loose or saw through the bars was long, hard work and that was why they used Huronilla who was thin, supple and strong enough to slip through one of the four open segments. Cutting the grill, on the other hand, was quick and easy, especially with the cutters she had in her belt.

"Be careful! Be careful!" Escarpaz called down.

The rope was slack and the current was no longer tugging at it. Therefore, the goal was reached. They waited, not without anxiety.

Suddenly, the rope went taut again and was given three tugs, which were felt by the men holding it. It was the signal that the girl was on the edge of the air vent and the cork raft was about to be abandoned to the current.

"Hey, my boys, heave it up!" the patriarch ordered.

The two gypsies holding the rope obeyed and soon they were back in possession of the rope and the cork board.

"*Muy bien*," Matello remarked contentedly. Then, loud enough for everyone to hear, "According to our plan, Escarpaz, I should go third, so only after you. But I'm the boss. I want and need to set an example. So, I'll go first. Juliano will follow me. Then the six chosen men and finally you, Escarpaz. That's it! I'll carry the girl's raft that will be needed for the return."

"As you wish," Escarpaz said.

Two gypsies were to stay on the bank: the two who had held and heaved in the rope. They had been chosen for their strength, their composure and their swimming skill. In case one of their brothers were in danger of drowning, they could jump in the river and save them either in the branch here or downstream where the two rivers met in the deep, funnel-shaped basin where the current was obstructed by an iron barrage equipped with a wooden flood gate that was not lowered in the summer when drought could sometimes make the river so low that it barely reached halfway up the banks.

For the second dip in the water (meant for the men) they went a little farther downstream. The goal was no longer the air vent of the laundry but the low door of the butcher-house, a door that Huronilla was supposed to open from the inside.

In fact, a blockhouse had been renovated into a slaughterhouse of cattle, sheep, pigs and goats to feed the many people living in San Lorenzo. This slaughterhouse was lit by two high windows over the river, meant only for ventilation and by a low door built at the same level of the air vent in the laundry and used to throw out the blood and unusable waste from the animals into the river. They also poured out the scalding water from the skinned pigs and the water used to clean the butchery as it was filthy with all kinds of waste. The river carried it all away. A very useful door, therefore! But it had been built only at the end of the Carlist Wars. It must have been awful for the inhabitants of San Lorenzo.

Awful, yes, like it was about to be on this night of June 1.

"*Anda!* Lower me down!" Matello shouted.

He was undressed and had his clothes tied to his head. He gripped and straddled the raft he lay on face down. The rope spun out, then slackened, left hanging for two minutes and finally was yanked three times. This meant that Matello had succeeded, that the door was open and the raft was safe and sound inside the butcher-house. See, to leave the castle they were counting on using the same system of rafts and ropes.

"Good," Peul said, "the boss got in. Now it's my turn."

The young anarchist wanted to show courage, endurance, skill and strength—all qualities he knew he would need to be initiated into the Secret by Juan Matello, an initiation that would make him, Julien Peul, a partner of Juan Matello…

What he feared the most was the icy contact with the invisible, rushing water and the mundane worry of catching bronchitis or pneumonia. But this fear of his was eased by the thought of getting quickly dressed again inside the butcher-house in clothes that would not be soaked during the operation because he would keep them held high and then he would be back on the move to recover any lost heat.

They prepared him, lowered him and he disappeared. He reached his goal without a problem as the rope loosened, tightened and was pulled three times.

Then very quickly, since the gypsies were ready, Escarpaz and his young men made the strange crossing. The last two to leave used a double board of cork because Matello was hoping they would need two extra rafts for the return.

Between the low door and the riverbank where the two big gypsies stayed behind, the dozen ropes were attached on one end to a big ring of the fattest rope, itself looped around a rocky spire, and on the other end were tied to the door with a simple knot made by Escarpaz himself using a small pocket flashlight given to him by Matello.

The dozen cork boards were lined up inside the butcher-house so that the ropes would not get tangled up.

Tonight, Sylvie went to bed right after Adele had put little Pierre to sleep. She was tired out as much from the emotion of having seen her husband so unexpectedly as from the fact that she had been woken up in the middle of last night and could not get back to sleep.

Tired as well, the Duke d'Arandar had gone to his room right after dinner. Of course, Blanca, the head maid, and the servant girls, Padre Felipe and the male servants all did likewise because the life of the master determined the life of all the regular residents of San Lorenzo.

Consequently, by the time the curfew was sounded by one of the guards, the lights in the castle were already off in all the rooms.

Antonio, the game warden, was on duty tonight as a kind of sergeant of the watchmen. Not counting Antonio there were six of them: two in the castle, two in the barbican and two in the watchtower. Out of these six three would sleep until midnight and be woken up by their partners who would take their place on the cots.

Antonio had to make a patrol every two hours, going from the castle through all the courtyards and up to the top of the watchtower, then back again.

Thanks to these precautions the Duke was truly peaceful because his mind found it impossible to imagine the castle could be invaded in the middle of the night by a group of men. Like him, all the residents were convinced it was impregnable once the drawbridge was raised, the portcullis lowered and the solid gate was closed.

This conviction was so firm that the Nyctalope and Sylvie were bound to share it. That was why nobody had the will, wiles or determination (like Escarpaz) to search for the chink in the armor of San Lorenzo—it holds true that at the start of a battle the attacker will prove more resourceful than the attacked. And always in life the offense will have an advantage over the defense.

With the watchmen posted at three points where they could see all of San Lorenzo, with the sergeant's patrol every two hours, checking the castle grounds and all the doors, the Duke d'Arandar figured he had made any attack impossible by men who might have been able to slip in during the day, which seemed sufficient to guarantee security at night. As for an attack in broad daylight, it was really unthinkable because Sylvie was so alert and the Duke was constantly checking on her and Pierre and sending others out to check the grounds.

Certainly, the incident with the Bohemian girl uttering that eerie, menacing phrase was not forgotten. But it was feeling more and more like just another oddity from a crazy gypsy because since Sunday nothing had happened that might lead them to believe there was any real meaning to it.

The fact that the phrase, as the Duke explained it, was pronounced by gypsy fortune tellers to people threatened by a danger coming from a woman, and side by side with this the fact that according to Gnô Mitang's theory a woman was the shadowy criminal inspiration behind Korridès—these two facts must have been a mere coincidence like observant people see all the time in their everyday lives. All this explained why, on the night of June 1, Sylvie Saint-Clair was sleeping as peacefully as her son Pierre and why the Duke d'Arandar was dead to the world in his deep slumber, a legacy of his youth.

As for Blanca, the sweet maid, and Padre Felipe, they of course had complete confidence in the Duke concerning the impregnability of the castle. Besides, they did not know that the gypsy girl had whispered to Sylvie, "*Asplata la vibora, matala!*". And that was a pity because especially in the superstitious mind of Blanca and the servant girls such a phrase would have loomed like a constant, terrible threat and unbeknownst to the master they would have taken precautions that feminine ingenuity might have made more effective than the quasi-militant measures of the Duke.

In fact, his precautions did not prevent Huronilla from entering the laundry, getting dressed, slipping into the butcher-house and opening the small door leading to the river. Juan Matello climbed in, did what he had to do with the cork-board and rope and was putting on his clothes when Peul arrived with chattering teeth. Matello turned on a flashlight, which he wisely covered with his hand to narrow the beam. He helped the young man get dressed in a hurry, then the band of gypsies piled into the butcher-house.

The nine men and the girl knew exactly what they had to do. Everyone had their roles. Now pride as much as self-interest would add cleverness and strength to their willpower. Each man was armed with a long, Catalan switchblade, stronger and deadlier than a common knife, but only to be used as a last resort to defend themselves against certain death.

Matello scanned their faces with the flashlight.

"*Bueno*, we're all here. Anything to say, Escarpaz?"

"Nothing. Let's go."

The high, wide door of the butcher-house, mounted on wheels, faced east. It was therefore in the full starlight that was faint by getting brighter as the clouds dispersed. The gypsy girl had only cracked open this door a few inches, just enough for her slender form to slip through. Matello carefully rolled the heavy, iron-rimmed door a little more. He was the first who was supposed to duck into the courtyard but he suddenly saw a man carrying a four-sided lantern standing in the archway of the castle keep whose gigantic base sat at the far end of the long courtyard.

"Hey, Escarpaz," Matello whispered.

But the old Bohemian had seen him too. He grabbed the iron handle of the door and closed it almost completely, leaving a crack just big enough to peek through. He watched the man as he marched past the communal buildings.

So quietly that Matello was the only one to hear, he said, "It's Antonio, the game warden. He's making his rounds."

Here the Portuguese proved he was the head of the expedition and for the first time earned the wholehearted admiration of Julien Peul.

"Watch out, boys!" he said quietly but loud enough for all the men behind him to hear, knowing that the constant rumbling of the river would drown his voice, especially at the distance where the guard was at the moment. "Watch out, I'm changing part of the plan. Juliano and I will be leaving the castle on horseback and not on the river. Now get ready to back me up. I'm going to capture this guy... Here we go... On your toes everyone! Back up, line up behind me to the left, back there... You, too, Escarpaz! And you, Juliano! Quickly... Good, now quiet! When you see me jump out, you jump out... and grab hold of the guy!"

What he said was understood and obeyed.

He himself stepped aside, not much, just a few feet, and he plastered himself to the back of the door. Then covering and uncovering his light he flashed a dozen brief rays at the thin opening. What Matello was counting on happened: the light beams were seen by Antonio. The game warden was surprised by them and by the fact that the butcher-house was open. He must have figured that a servant was trying to sneak out some extra meat because he came over directly, without taking any precautions. He pushed open the door, stepped in, raised his lantern to get a better look inside and…

But he was hit hard on the back and buckled under the weight of a body whose arms wrapped around him. He wanted to cry out but his mouth was blocked, his lips, chin and nose being crushed by a cloth rag while a scarf was being tied over his eyes. The lantern dropped out of his hand but was caught in mid-air. In no time he found himself lying on the tile floor, bound and gagged. Nevertheless, he did not lose his head.

He thought, "They've come to get señorita Sylvie and señorito Pedro. Shame on me for getting caught! If these wretches let me live, I'll never be able to look señor the Duke in the eye again!"

"Hey, Antonio," Matello spoke quietly, "I need the keys that you certainly have on you. I'll also need your cap and coat and pants and shoes. I'll give you mine, which won't give me away because I've removed any evidence of who made them or wore them. They're good quality, custom-made, almost new. You're getting a good deal."

While speaking like this in a mocking, condescending voice, Matello undressed his victim. He was ably helped by the gypsies, one of whom kept checking that the blindfold and gag were not disturbed by all the agitation.

"Fine!" Matello said when he was done. "Tie him back up and put him in the pig scalder. I'll toss him my clothes. He can wait there comfortably until someone finds him. Make sure the gag is tight enough that he can't rub it against something to loosen it."

Escarpaz had been alert enough to close the door. He looked like he was supervising the scene. He smiled to himself and mumbled, "Better off throwing him in the river. Later he'll have time to think about revenge. One of us will suffer the consequences if there's the slightest clue to who we are."

"No!" Matello snapped. "I forbid you to kill anyone here unless your life depends on it. Later on, do as you please. You swore you wouldn't kill, Escarpaz, and your men swore too."

"Maybe we were wrong, caballero," the patriarch muttered, shrugging his shoulders.

The Portuguese did not deign to respond. Having taken off his own clothes he hurried to put on the game warden's. But he had to keep his shoes because Antonio's were too big and would keep him from walking normally, which was indispensable. In the outside left pocket of the livery jacket he had found a ring with five small, modern keys made for safety locks. And in the right pocket a regulation Browning for Spanish officers. Since his flash of inspiration to change the plan Matello had been counting on these two finds. So, he was very satisfied.

"*Anda!*" he said. "Antonio in the scalder!"

The game warden was laid out in the long, wide recipient that looked like a kneading machine where they dumped the pigs in boiling water to make it easier to scrape off the bristles and hair off their skin. They tossed in Matello's clothes after he had taken everything out of the pockets and the band of gypsies gathered around their chief. Huronilla was holding the lantern. Matello took it and said:

"You all follow me a few feet behind, keeping to the shadows even when I sometimes step into the light. First we'll take the part of the castle that controls the portcullis and drawbridge. Only after that will we go back to the original plan with a few important changes in the details. Escarpaz and the rest of you, do you understand?"

"*Si, si!*" they barked with a kind of cocky savagery.

"Great. Let's go! Julien, my friend, stay with Escarpaz."

"Very well."

To get to the main courtyard of the castle they had to pass by the barbican, which is a kind of small fort between the castle itself and the overhang of the ramparts. On top of this structure a guard was pacing back and forth. Matello could see him through the gaps in the crenellation, a shadow puppet against the starry sky.

"Better and better," he thought to himself contentedly. "I'd be very surprised if I were wrong about the precautions taken by the Duke. Alternating watches, two men in the castle, two in the barbican, two in the watchtower and Antonio makes a round to check on them. Forget about the watchtower, the barbican and the castle will give me four guards to take care of. Even without the collaboration Escarpaz guarantees me, I'd be sure to succeed. With his collaboration all the better!"

It would have taken a miracle for the guard in the barbican to be suspicious of the man with a lantern whom he saw from on high and whom he heard climbing the stairs. This man could be none other than the chief Antonio. When the man showed up on the roof, his lantern left behind in the doorway, the sentinel rattled off:

"Nothing new."

But the "new" came out to a hard punch on the watchman's chin. He was immediately dazed and dizzy. He wobbled. An arm caught him and a hand was clasped over his mouth. When he started to regain his senses, other hands were blindfolding, gagging and tying up his arms and legs. They lifted him up and carried him downstairs into the guardroom. He could guess easily enough that his partner was probably caught off guard in his sleep and bound and gagged on the cot where they threw him. They stripped off their clothes, caps and shoes, leaving them half-naked, side by side, with another rope tying them to the cot. Two gypsies used the clothes to transform themselves into guards.

In the castle Juan Matello had the same success. The uniforms of the two captured guards were worn by two other Bohemians.

Julien Peul was overjoyed. He almost cheered out loud when Matello addressed him in front of the group of waiting gypsies:

"Juliano, my friend, I'm putting you in charge of this. When I come back with the horses, the gate should be open, the portcullis raised and the drawbridge down. Find the right keys if you can (he tossed him the ring) or else pick the locks, break them if you need to. I'll judge you by your work. If it's your fault we have to go back to the slaughterhouse and get back on those cork rafts, you'll be worthless in my eyes. Quick! Choose a man who'll be your assistant."

Peul pointed to a short but stout gypsy with an intelligent face and darting eyes.

Escarpaz approved, "Good choice, señor. Mesterbeï, be worhty of the honor."

"*Vamos!*" Matello ordered. "Don't waste time. Let's go finish this!"

And the whole troupe, except for Peul and the gypsy Mesterbeï, left, went back to the barbican, whose two big doors (built to let pass the horses, carriages and cars) were now open, and then without stopping they returned to the main courtyard.

It was a woman who first saw the glow of the fire. In truth, this woman was expecting the glow. She had known for hours that a fire would break out in San Lorenzo. She knew it because in the morning a young gypsy, her lover, had told her.

This woman was Manetta. She was one of the battalion of chambermaids that obeyed the smiling but strict authority of Blanca. At the behest of Padre Felipe, a fanatic of certain mushrooms, Blanca had allowed Manetta to go out into the forest and pick some of the mushrooms that she was the only who could recognize.

Now, for the past two months Manetta had been the lover and fiancée of Mesterbeï, the handsomest of the young Bohemians who had come six weeks ago to camp for a long rest outside the town of Salas. See, this Manetta had distant relatives who were gypsies, the blood of Egypt was in her veins.

Via the lover, the suitor, the soon-to-be husband Escarpaz had made Manetta his accomplice. This complicity had started only that morning. Manetta had spent a good half hour longer than she was supposed to picking mushrooms. Using a skillful blend of flattery and firmness, of promises and threats, and of course dealing with a woman passionately in love who by blood as well as love was fully committed to him, the young gypsy, trained by Escarpaz, told Manetta enough and gave her specific instructions for what to do during the night to help the intruders.

But would Manetta, seized by guilt, reveal everything to Blanca who would in turn inform the Duke? Bah! Escarpaz was not worried. Manetta had the blood of Egypt in her—to betray her race, the bosom that fate was pushing her to return to, would be like losing her life and with it the happiness of loving and being loved.

Therefore, in San Lorenzo Manetta was the first to see the glow of the fire. Although, while waiting for the event in which she was to play a role that might have been crucially important, she had to get undressed, go to bed and pretend to sleep. Her room had six other small beds in it, so Manetta had five other servants like her in the room every night. This night, once the others were asleep, Manetta opened her eyes and did not close them again.

The room was relatively big, taking up part of the top floor of the Lord's wing. There were two mullioned windows that opened onto a small service yard separated from the main courtyard by a ten-foot wall with a narrow door. It was through these windows, not equipped with shutters, that Manetta saw glow of the fire.

She propped herself up on an elbow and waited to be sure. When there was no doubt about it, she leaped up, screamed and went whirling around the dimly lit room while her fellow maids were startled awake and started panicking without knowing why. But when Manetta started yelping, "Fire! Fire! The castle's on fire!", they jumped out of bed, screamed like panicking lunatics and ran out of the room in their nightgowns, following Manetta.

But the terror of the gypsies' accomplice was completely fake. The girl had a three-fold mission: to sow panic among the servants of San Lorenzo, to pretend to be terrified and spread chaos, and finally to open and close certain doors to lock the servants in their quarters and create an easy access in certain parts of the castle for the Bohemian arsonists and invaders. Manetta behaved in such a way as to earn the esteem of the tribe of Zapatan and the love of her fiancé.

Soon after the first cry of alarm, all the girls and Blanca herself were running hither and thither around the servant quarters spreading panic, terror and chaos all at the same time while the male servants found themselves unwittingly blocked by closed doors without keys to unlock them. On the other hand, there were other doors, closed just a minute earlier, that were open, particularly the one between the main courtyard and the small yard outside the kitchens and other rooms where daily duties were performed. There was a short hallway between these rooms and the dining rooms (one big and one small) that led to the salons, the main vestibule and the grand staircase. Lastly, from the office there was another stairway that led up upstairs.

Eventually, Manetta—still pretending to run wild—scrambled up the main staircase all the way to Sylvie's rooms, leading five men dressed as game wardens. These five men were Juan Matello and the four gypsies who had put on the watchmen's clothes.

Now, without their knowing, the little gypsy girl Huronilla was following the fake guards even though she was supposed to have stayed with Escarpaz.

The Bohemians had set fire to the hayloft next to the stables. Within minutes the flames were shooting out of the roof and licking the castle walls.

Then the wind blew them against the front of the Lord's wing. The stables were thrown open and the horses and mules bolted into the grounds. Not all! Two horses, chosen from the best by an expert eye, were tied up by Escarpaz in a corner of the main courtyard next to the path coming out of the barbican and the castle.

With this done, Escarpaz and the two men with him went back to the butcher-house and threw the cork rafts into the water, tying them together with a single rope. Then they waited for either the arrival of Matello, in case he had not got into the castle, or a signal meaning the job was done and they could beat a retreat. The fire was started, the stables emptied and two horses were ready to go—the role of Escarpaz inside the castle was finished.

When the fire was raging and when howling Manetta started her abominable scheme, the Duke Pedro d'Arandar was sinking into that early sleep that is so calm and so deep for men still physically active in their 50s. He was only woken up by the noise of Padre Felipe and the head servants banging on a locked door in the hallway outside his rooms. At first he thought it was a nightmare that he was only slowly waking up from. But in one of the three windows, which was left open during the night, he saw the flickering flames of the fire and he snapped awake immediately.

"Fire! There's a fire!"

Out of bed in a flash, he was dressed at once, clumsily but enough to go out. He would see, command and act.

"First Sylvie and Pierre!" he told himself.

But outside his rooms he bumped into Padre Felipe in the hallway arguing with several men. Two more, down the hall, were kicking a door and smacking it with their swords. Three men were holding candelabra with two, five and seven lit candles.

"Hola, everyone! Be quiet and stop what you're doing!" the Duke shouted.

At the voice of the master all the fury subsided. When asked, the chaplain could only say that everyone was anxious and worried about the doors being inexplicably locked from the outside.

"We'll find explanations later if we can," the Duke cut him off calmly. "We have to get to the fire. It looks like it's centered in the service buildings. Mariano, you're in charge of doing on the left what I'll be doing on the right."

In the hallway were two heavy chests mounted on sculpted feet that in the 16th century were called "cabinets". They were empty, placed there as precious museum pieces. The Duke grabbed one, lifted it up and dashed off to ram it into the door separating the hallway from the landing of the grand staircase, past which was the hallway that led to Sylvie's rooms. The door boomed and cracked. A loud bang followed, then another crack. The butler Mariano, being as strong as his master, had just rammed the second chest into the door leading to the service stairs. Three times more for each of them, the Duke and the butler throwing all their weight behind the oak "cabinets" against the thick, carved doors. They finally gave way almost at the same time. Behind Mariano all the servants ran down to the courtyard, passing by the office and the kitchen.

They went carrying the flickering candelabra. The Duke and Padre Felipe were surrounded by darkness.

However, a faint light was moving on the grand staircase. The Duke ran and leaned over the forged-iron railing. He saw at the bottom of the stairs a few of his guards in uniform, one of whom had a big silver stripe on his sleeve, glimmering in the candlelight held up high in his left hand. In the middle of these guards the Duke spotted a woman with blonde hair cascading over the dark fabric of a coat and a second woman in a white shirt carrying a white bundle with a child's head sticking out of it. The group was rushing across the vestibule on the ground floor.

"Good!" the Duke thought. "My brave Antonio was thinking first of Sylvie. That's good!"

Believing he was speaking to his game warden, whom he recognized by the silver stripe, he cried out:

"Antonio! Antonio!"

The man with the silver stripe stopped, turned around and looked up. But at the same time he lowered the candle so that his face was lost in the shadows. The Duke, therefore, could have no inkling of his gross error. He kept shouting:

"To the chapel! Take la señorita to the chapel! If it's cold, light a fire in the chimney of the sacristy."

"I'll meet them there," Padre Felipe told the Duke.

"That's right, dear friend. Go now. Comfort the lady. Even if the fire is big, only the common buildings are in danger. The castle itself has nothing to fear. Plus, the chapel is set apart from all the other buildings. Go, Padre. Me, I'm going to the fire as quickly as I can."

Returning to the hallway the Duke ran to the service stairs, bounded down the fifty steps two at a time, darted through the office and the kitchen and the small yard and came out into the courtyard right in front of the fire. Mariano and the valets had only just arrived. They had still done nothing. Women in nightshirts or half-dressed, men wearing only pants, huddled in a corner, stunned or milling around haphazardly, grooms, man-servants, gardeners, mule drivers, kitchen girls, all the servants were there. The barns and two stables were ablaze with towering flames.

The Duke spotted a servant girl he knew. "Manetta, where's Blanca?"

"Lord, I don't know," the trembling girl mumbled.

"Go search for her. In the castle you'll be safe. Find her! Got it? Run, you ninny! Tell her to go to the chapel and you go with her. Got it? Run!"

Not worried about Sylvie, Pierre and the nanny, not at all anxious for Blanca, the Duke considered, commanded and did what was necessary to get the servants to locate and fight the fire, whose cause he would deal with after it was put out.

For a full hour the Duke was busy at work. The service buildings set aflame ended on one side on the path following the ramparts and on the other end at the wall that separated the courtyard from the small yard. The backs of the buildings were bordered by another yard, longer than it was wide, where they kept the pigsty, the chicken coops, the rabbit hutches and the sheep pen. Swept up by the wind, the flames were growing taller and reaching out to lick the front of the castle. But it was built of granite and the fire had nothing to feed on. A few windows shattered and some shutters burned, but it was damage that would not spread and was really not very serious.

Two years ago the Duke had installed a modern fire hose, which was connected to a very simple piping system through a water intake fed by the river. The Duke had quickly calmed and organized the servants to fight the fire while saving the pigs, sheep and other animals that a strong gust of wind could put in jeopardy.

When the flames were nearly extinguished and the fire was confined, under control, the Duke was surprised not to see Antonio and realized that there were some guards missing among the rescue workers.

He pulled aside Mariano the butler, gave him some orders, then marched across the courtyard, down the path and was soon in the darkness of the main courtyard. It was, in fact, almost pitch black.

He wondered, "Where are they? Did they stay in the chapel with Sylvie and Padre Felipe? What for?"

The fire was almost out and the stars were too dim to shed any light. Besides, the Duke's vision was still blurred by the flames he had fought for the last hour. Still, he knew the place and kept walking fast in a straight line to the chapel. Again he was surprised that the windows of the chapel showed no signs of an inside light. Obviously, it was unlikely that Sylvie Saint-Clair, her son and the nanny, joined first by Padre Felipe and then by Blanca, were sitting in the sacristy without any kind of light.

"And Antonio? And the guards?" the Duke said aloud. "What's the meaning of all this?"

Thus a concern was sparked in him, which quickly grew into agonizing bewilderment. And the bewilderment was suddenly turned into horrified terror when he almost stumbled over a body on the ground. He leaned over and recognized Padre Felipe, bound, gagged and blindfolded.

"Oh no!" he said.

Automatically he looked around. In the dim light of the stars that his eyes were now accustomed to he saw Blanca sitting against the chapel wall, also tied up, gagged and blindfolded.

"No Antonio, no guards," the Duke thought to himself.

But he immediately went stiff.

"And Sylvie? And little Pierre?"

Then his intuition kicked in, not about the factual details but of the general meaning behind it all. It flashed through his mind: "The fire was started on purpose to cause chaos so they could kidnap Sylvie and Pierre."

Right away he thought of the exit. So unbelievable, so enigmatic were these events that the only reasonable conclusion could be the gatehouse, the only place where, the Duke believed, anybody could leave the castle.

Why did he not think of the butcher-house and the low door? The hypothesis of intruders swimming across the river with a woman and child in tow was too far-fetched to even come to mind. Besides, at this point the Duke's mind was full of conflicting and chaotic ideas and completely befuddled. He could concentrate on only one thing at a time and this one thing was very simple: the gatehouse.

He freed Padre Felipe and Blanca as fast as he could. They could tell him nothing more than that they had been grabbed, tied up, gagged and blindfolded by unknown assailants, as he could see for himself. So, he ran.

Finding the big gate wide open he did not bother to check the guardroom in the barbican. He went straight to the entrance where he found the portcullis raised and the drawbridge lowered.

He slapped his head and groaned, "It's done! They took them... Sylvie and Pierre... But who did this? And how?"

The door of the guardroom was half open. He pushed it with his foot. The four-sided oil lamp cast its gloomy light. On the cot were two men, half-dressed, tied up and gagged.

At these various sights, which focused his scattered thoughts, the Duke regained his composure. From now on he did nothing unnecessary and said nothing in vain.

The two men were set free. They did not have much to say. They went with the Duke to raise the drawbridge, lower the portcullis and close the gate. They also accompanied him to the barbican and freed the other two guards who were tied up in that guardroom. Another interrogation was as uninstructive as the first.

The fate of Antonio remained a mystery. But now the Duke knew that the five men in uniforms he had seen in the vestibule at the bottom of the stairs with Sylvie, Pierre and Adele were kidnappers and the one with the silver stripe could not have been Antonio.

After dealing with the two sentinels in the barbican the Duke went to talk to Padre Felipe and Blanca who told him in detail about their arrival at the darkened chapel, at separate times, but neither had seen the attackers. Manetta, who had found and talked to Blanca, was no longer around.

"But Antonio? Where's is he?" the Duke asked.

He let the butler and his assistants worry about the fire, which was almost completely extinguished. The barns and stables were left in smoking ruins where a few cinders still glowed.

The Duke went to the top of the watchtower and found the two sentinels. During the fire they had stayed at their post to signal in case the flames spread to other parts of the castle grounds. The Duke commended them and asked about Antonio. He found out that the game warden had made his usual rounds between ten and eleven, shortly before the fire broke out.

"Well then," he ordered, "let's look for him everywhere."

They looked. And, eventually, they went into the laundry where they saw the opening made in the grill of the air vent.

"That's big enough for a child to get through," the Duke observed.

They saw nothing else suspicious so they went into the butcher-house. The low door was open. And at last they discovered poor Antonio in the pig scalder.

Ungagged, unbound and free of the blindfold, first he exploded in a storm of furious curses. After a short while, a little calmer under the commanding gaze of his master, he told what he knew. Not much since he had only heard and they had said so little and in whispers!

But still, adding everything together the Duke got a picture of what obviously happened: except for the betrayal of Manetta whose disappearance was inexplicable, and putting aside the fact that they had no idea who the kidnappers were, having left no clues behind but the anonymous clothes thrown on Antonio—all in all the Duke's picture was pretty close to the truth.

Moving on from the theory of what happened to what they should do next, the Duke d'Arandar gave orders.

"Antonio, you and all the guards get on the horses! Take torches and weapons and ride out! The bandits have only one hour headstart. The whole pack, too, Antonio. The dogs will easily get on their track if they follow the horses since we'll know which horses they took."

It was simple: the animals had fled out of the stables during the fire and run all over the grounds. The stable boys and mule drivers had brought them all back. They were counted. The Duke checked them all. He found that two were missing, two of the best hunting horses.

Now, the dogs were used to following the horses. Antonio just had to get the pack to sniff the right stalls for the clever bloodhounds to understand what they had to do.

Fifteen minutes later a troop of fifteen men, eight of whom carried torches, rode through the portcullis of San Lorenzo and unleashed a dozen bloodhounds. As a pack, after sniffing the ground and the air, the dogs found the scent of the two horses and they bounded off down the trail.

CHAPTER XI
The mother and child

Sylvie's room was too far from the servants' sleeping quarters for the cries of Manetta and the others to wake up the mother, child and nanny.

A few loud knocks at the door of the antechamber pulled Sylvie out of her quiet slumber. One of the windows of her room was cracked open. Right away she saw the flickering, flashing glow that looked exactly like a fire.

In her pajamas, throwing a coat over her shoulders, trying not to tangle her beautiful long hair that was untied and flowing over the coat, she went to open the door.

Some men were there who looked like game wardens, but poorly lit by a single candle in the hand of one of them. She saw the silver stripe on the sleeve.

Someone said, "Come quickly, madame, come quickly with the child, there's a fire in the castle."

She did not even have time to look at their faces.

Besides, she did not know the game wardens well enough to identify them. She had only seen their chief, Antonio, two or three times and his face were not exactly engraved in her memory, so in the present situation, an emergency in the dark, she could not realize that the face of this man wearing the silver stripe was completely unknown to her.

Moreover, the threat of danger to her son, herself and the nanny made her turn around as soon as she heard those ominous words. She ran to the connecting door to the room where little Pierre was sleeping. Adele heard the knocks. Confused and anxious, she was sitting on the bed, dimly lit by the thin flame of the oil lamp.

"Quickly!" Sylvie said, "Get Pierre dressed!"

When the baby, whining and crying after being so rudely shaken out of his sleep, was dressed and wrapped in his hooded cape fringed with lace, Sylvie put on her shoes, tied a scarf around her neck and fastened the coat that was still on her shoulders.

In the meantime and with enough self-composure, Adele also dressed quickly before picking up little Pierre.

"Let's go!" Sylvie said.

In no time, the two women were surrounded by the guards. The fake Antonio was careful to stay behind the group, holding the candle over their heads.

They started walking fast down the hallway leading to the grand staircase. They scrambled down it to the sound of pounding doors, apparently from people trying to open them. But Sylvie did not speculate on the reason behind the uproar. She was preoccupied with leaving the Lord's wing to find refuge in a part of the castle that was safe from the fire.

But she did not ask where exactly they were going.

At the bottom of the stairs she heard very clearly the Duke's voice shouting to Antonio to go to the chapel. It was exactly what she wanted and needed to hear. So, she hurried her step, keeping a close eye on Pierre, who was quiet now and smiling wide-eyed at his mother. In the arms of Adele, pressed against her chest, he was warm and safe. The incident, which meant nothing to his infant brain, was clearly amusing him like any change amuses a four-month old baby for a few minutes.

Therefore, without any misgivings, without any suspicions that she and her son were in danger, Sylvie Saint-Clair, surrounded by "game wardens" and followed by "Antonio", left the castle, crossed the main courtyard and headed for the chapel.

The glow of the fire lit the courtyard enough to make it easy to walk without stumbling. But when they got near the chapel, a few feet away from two saddled horses being held by a man whose hands and arms were the only thing visible since his face and body remained hidden in shadow, Sylvie suddenly had the premonition, the intuition that it was a trap, a snare, a peril.

She turned around to talk to Antonio. And since all her senses were suddenly sharpened at this point, she realized that the man with the silver stripe was not the game warden. Her eyes widened, her arms rose up and she opened her mouth to cry out... But the fake Antonio, who had got rid of the candle, muffled her scream with a quick and firm hand.

At the same time he shouted orders in a language that Sylvie did not understand.

Immediately sunk in the depths of horror, her whole being went numb. After the hypersensitivity she had just experienced, her body reacted by collapsing. But her mind held on and stayed aware of everything happening around her. Grabbed, gagged and tied up in a matter of seconds, she was lifted off the ground in the powerful arms of one of the fake guards who was already seated on a horse.

"My son! My son!" she wanted to scream.

She did, in fact, scream but the gag muffled her desperate voice. Anyway, she heard the rider who was holding her captive declare, "Don't worry, madam, your son's not in danger and won't be taken away from you. Adele is on the other horse holding him in her arms. Don't do anything foolish, your lives are at stake."

The young lady straightened up and stopped struggling to break free of his iron grip. But she looked around as much as could and managed to see that Adele was indeed straddling a horse and being held in the arms of a man sitting behind her, his hands holding the reins in front of her.

The two animals were already out of the main courtyard and on the path that led to the gatehouse. This realization, forcing itself on Sylvie's mind, brought back all her self-composure, all her strength of character. First of all, she cursed herself for becoming flustered in the courtyard when she might have managed, with a clear head, to resist, struggle, maybe stop the kidnapping.

It was the first time in her life she had been overwhelmed like this by emotions that took away all her self-control. But was it not also the first time that as a wife and mother she had to confront a reality that was shattering all her happiness? No matter! She would not forgive herself. But her thinking raced on, she did not waste time scolding herself.

Right away she thought of the consequences of what had happened: she thought of the future.

"What are they going to do with us? Did Leo also fall into a trap? Are they going to torture him using me, torture me using him and torture both of us using Pierre?"

The sinister villa of *The Sycamores* suddenly popped into her head, the memory of that pile of ashes, then the story of Leo's meeting with the mysterious, fearsome Korridès. She imagined the emotional and physical suffering they would inflict on Leo, on herself, and, horror of horrors, maybe on little Pierre! But why? Why worry about the future? She was starting to panic again, like back in the courtyard.

Deep down inside, she convinced herself to stay calm, to get hold of herself, to see things clearly, to reflect and calculate. She was back in control of her mind. And for the first time she tried to see the face of her kidnapper.

But she could see only a shadow, a dark blotch under the lowered visor of the cap.

They were riding at a fast trot on the forest path, wide but winding, down the rolling hills that led from San Lorenzo into the heart of the forest. At certain spots, the unclouded stars in the southeast allowed her to see the path cutting through the tall trees. But the light from the stars was so dim that the man's face was nothing but grayness. She wanted to talk to him but the gag prevented her.

Then, once again, she thought only of Pierre. He was crying now. And the mother was stricken to hear him almost wailing. She managed, however, to suppress her pain, telling herself that the child was not suffering too much since he was being held tenderly by his nanny. At a certain point Sylvie could see Adele very clearly. She felt like the nanny was fully aware of her duty, which was to give all her attention to the baby, to think of nothing else, not even of herself. It was this firm and sincere conviction that gave Sylvie back the natural strength of her character and the conscious exercise of her will.

She told herself, "I can do nothing right now but stay calm and strong, see and hear everything, evaluate everything so that I can take advantage of the slightest mishap to turn things around in our favor. It's all a mystery. The fire, the kidnappers, where we're going, what they'll do with us... And Leo?"

The situation for a wife and mother could not have been more tragic. And yet, it became infinitely more tragic in the next few minutes...

While she was completely absorbed by the tumult of her thoughts and feelings, a tumult that she tried and finally succeeded to make some sense of, Sylvie had lost track of time and place. But when the horses suddenly stopped, she did have the impression that they were far from the castle? They were in a clearing at the top of one of the many bluffs that form the foothills of Mount San Lorenzo for several miles around the castle. As the clouds cleared off the starry sky cast light on this June night that was finally bright enough for Sylvie to see the face of her abductor. She saw a dignified, energetic face with assertive eyes. She did not have time to linger over this face because at that very moment the guy jumped out of the saddle without letting go of his captive.

He put her on the ground and said, "Be patient for a few minutes, madam. I'm sitting you so that you can see your son in the arms of his nanny. See how he's sleeping right now so you have nothing to worry about. The guard I'll put on you for a few minutes is well bred. Don't be afraid of being hurt, not you, your son or even your nurse. You are very valuable hostages!

"And to prove to you that you're not dealing with common thieves and also that I know my power, I'll introduce myself and my companion: I am Juan Matello from Burgos and this is Julien Peul, my secretary.

"At daybreak, I hope, we will arrive at a place where you'll find a haven, I dare say, much better than San Lorenzo despite the noble courtesy and devoted affection shown to you by the Duke d'Arandar. Then, you're going to write not only to Leo Saint-Clair, your husband, but also to a Dr. Korridès in Versailles from whose claws I have just freed you by making you my captive... Think about what I've just said and see you soon."

The man had spoken in French with an accent that Sylvie believed was tinged by Portuguese. His voice was dignified, his gestures restrained to fit the words. His extraordinary and very unexpected speech reassured Sylvie, even more so as she saw her dear little Pierre sleeping in the arms of Adele. The nanny was still on the horse but the rider had dismounted and was holding the reins. This man looked very young to Sylvie. Like the man who had just spoken to her this one did not appear threatening.

The young lady told herself, "They want to put pressure on Leo to ensure his neutrality in this strange and tragic affair that we go mixed up in by entering the Sycamores that night of May 21. If I'm right, Leo will agree, of course. Clearing up the biggest mysteries in the world would horrify him if he could do so only through the suffering, however minimal, of his wife and son! Let's hope it works out!"

Meanwhile, Juan Matello dashed across the glade and onto a path that led to another, smaller clearing. There he saw a white-bearded man standing in the middle: Escarpaz.

The Portuguese and the Bohemian approached each other, hands held out and smiles on their faces.

"So, it's over?" Escarpaz said. "You did it? The guy I had holding your horses came to tell us in the butcher-house. We jumped on the rafts right away and made a clean getaway. But tell me, have you seen Huronilla? She's missing. Except for her we're all here with all our things. We left nothing behind that could put the Duke on the trail of Zapatan's tribe. And we can be sure that no one saw us. So, all's well, señor... except Huronilla. So, once again, have you seen her?"

"No," Matello shrugged his shoulders. He did not care a wit for the gypsy girl. He added, "Our business is finished, patriarch. As for the money, I have enough on me to pay you right now and I'll take back that paper you had me write and sign."

Escarpaz narrowed his eyes and sneered, "Oh, you have a promissory note on you that's worth 100,000 pesetas at the Bank of Spain? So, I'll have to go to Madrid."

"Oh no, no need to go so far," the Portuguese sneered back.

Their hands were still clasped, their eyes staring hard at each other. Escarpaz had not bothered to wonder where Matello's left hand was.

Then the left hand shot up into the air, came swinging down in a well-calculated arch and buried the long blade of a Catalan knife into the Bohemian's neck. A quick flick of the blade turned it in the wound and sliced deeper. The carotid artery was severed clean and his throat slashed. Blood gushed out but Matello was already jumping to the side and pulling back his hand armed with the blood-stained blade.

Escarpaz did not even gurgle. His knees bent, he slumped and fell on his side, his neck split open like an overripe pomegranate. There were two or three convulsions before he went limp and his body lay lifeless.

Very calmly, Matello wiped the blade clean on his victim's clothes and threw the knife a few feet away next to the path that led to a shortcut into Salas where the gypsy tribe was camped.

Then, being careful not get a drop of blood on himself, Matello slipped his hand into the Bohemian's coat pocket and pulled out a dirty pocketbook, opened it to verify that his signed IOU was there and stuck in his own pocket.

But at that moment, one, two shrieks rang out. They were awful shrieks of pain followed immediately by groans and cries for help.

"What's going on?" the Portuguese wondered.

He balked. But only for a few seconds. Then he ran. There was no doubt about it: some tragedy was playing out in the clearing where he had left Sylvie, Pierre and Adele guarded by Julien Peul.

When Matello got to the clearing he saw Sylvie rolling on the ground, making furious efforts to free herself; he saw Julien Peul and Adele running all over the place like lunatics, like the damned, swearing, moaning, shrieking and sobbing, their hands covering their eyes. The frightened horses were snorting and neighing. The sight of Matello leaping at Peul must have put the fear of God in them—they tried to break free.

But Matello was ready for this. He grabbed their reins, tied them to a tree, then turned and grabbed Peul by the shoulders.

"Oh, good God, what's happened? Look at me! Talk! What happened?"

Peul groaned, pushing away his hands. "Pepper! Pepper in my eyes! Oh, it hurts! Water! Please, get some water!"

Seeing the pain-stricken face where huge tears glistened in the dim light of the stars, Matello lost his composure for an instant. A new voice calling out a trembling appeal for help snapped him out of his daze.

The voice was shouting, "Untie me! Come on! Come here and untie me!"

It was Sylvie. In her violent struggle she had loosened the gag.

"Come here, untie me!"

Matello left Peul and knelt next to Sylvie. "No, I won't untie you. Talk. What happened? Your son?"

"A girl jumped out of the bushes. I recognized her. It was the gypsy who told me '*Aplasta la vibora*.' She threw something in the eyes of that man and Adele. Adele fell off the horse with Pierre! But the girl caught Pierre... and ... she ran off. Now untie me! I have to catch her!"

Matello was as confused as he was furious. He could not believe what Sylvie was telling him: that Huronilla had stolen the child. It could only be, he believed, on behalf of Escarpaz. But Escarpaz was dead. Obviously the gypsy girl would hide first, with her prize, in some secret spot in the mountains that she would only leave much later to join up with the tribe as they fled to some other region. Follow her now? No use. He said so.

"Madame, it's a setup against me, not you. Following the gypsy girl will be useless. I know Huronilla. It's night and she knows where she's going. We don't even know what direction to take."

"Untie me!" she screamed.

"No! We'll get your son back. But if I untie you, I risk losing everything. Anyway, it's likely that the basic facts will soon be discovered in San Lorenzo. They'll be searching for you. I figure I'll stay free as long as I've got you. Oh, please, stop torturing yourself. I'm going to put the gag back. If you fight me, I'll have to do a little jujitsu move and knock you out. I'm sure your friend Gnô Mitang has told you about those."

But the poor mother was driven half-mad by her son's abduction, by the idea that she would not be with him, by the ghastly fear that he could suffer and die, that he was already lost forever!

"Untie me! You're a liar! It's you who did all this. It's a heinous put-on. You want to get rid of my son for... for... Don't you see, they'll kill him! Untie me! No? Ha, you crook, you evil villain! Help! Help me!"

He grabbed her by the neck and she understood. Her desperate cry died in a wheeze. And she went limp, passed out.

121

Very calmly, he put the gag back on her and went to help Peul.

Thanks to the tears forced out by the pain, the young man had finally washed away the fine, irritating, stinging, burning powder. His eyes were almost blind, but the pain now was bearable.

"Julien, my friend," Matello said, taking him by the hand, "Be strong! We have to get out of here. Come on, I'll help you get back on the horse. All's not lost. I'll get the kid back. I'll know where he is in a few days. For now, the important thing is not to get caught by the Duke d'Arandar and his men who will be hot on our heels very soon. Now on the horse! Keep the nanny in front of you since we can't leave her here. She's in a daze of despair and sorrow so she won't put up any resistance."

A couple of minutes earlier Adele had just sat on the ground, wiping her eyes mechanically with the corner of a big scarf that she had wrapped around her head at the castle. She moaned, really dazed, so overwhelmed that she was almost senseless. She did nothing when she was picked by Matello and hoisted in the saddle, nor when Peul, still moaning a little himself, hopped on behind her and held her fast in his left arm so that she would not fall.

"Can you see enough to follow me?" Matello asked.

"Yes," Peul said. "I was hit with less pepper than I thought at first. My eyes feel like burning cinders but I can see and I'll tough it out."

"Well, then, let's go! Stay close behind me."

Matello had got in the saddle with Sylvie in his arms and planted her in front of him.

To his suffering companion he said, "We've only got to trot for fifteen minutes, then we'll let the horses go and they'll find their way back to San Lorenzo. Our mules are waiting for us. It'll take three hours to get to the place where I'll know if Fate is working for or against me. The child, I repeat, will be recovered. I'll even bring back Huronilla for you to take whatever revenge you want. The main thing is for Sylvie Saint-Clair not to escape. And you see how I've got her... You've done well, Julien Peul. I've decided you're my chief lieutenant. If I manage to get two leagues from this place in the next three or four hours, I'll have succeeded and your fortune is made."

"May your demon brothers be listening," Peul muttered.

"I like your expression," Matello snickered. "Let's go!"

Twenty minutes later the two riders with their captives were at the edge of the ravine where they had left the cave a few hours before to join Escarpaz and his band of gypsies.

"Dismount!" the Portuguese ordered.

Sylvie was still unconscious and Adele stupefied. When they got off the horses Matello lay the young lady on the ground and with a brusque "Giddyup!" it slapped the haunches of the horses. They bolted down a path, guided by instinct.

"We have to get going," Matello said.

"I think so too," Peul agreed.

A few minutes later, sitting on the mules with their captives in front of them, the two men were off again. From the ravine they entered one of the roughest regions of the mountain. So far they had only traveled over rolling, wooded hills, not so rocky, where the forest paths, as wild as they were, still allowed them to trot or even galop.

But the horses would have broken their legs here where the mules were scrambling. Luckily for the animals and for the humans they were carrying the sky was finally clear and the myriad of stars were shining brightly around the risen moon. They moved fast over the rough, barely traceable path that was often "eaten away" by rocks and bushes, a path that sometimes tumbled down into steep canyons, sometimes climbed up rocky bluffs that looked inaccessible. For three hours and ten minutes exactly they did not stop. Matello was in front and all of a sudden shouted with joy and triumph, which echoed through the pure air of the mountains in the spring dawn.

"Viva! Bravo! Bravissimo!"

With his eyes still aching, though seeing clearly now, Julien Peul gaped at the surprising spectacle—totally unexpected—of a big, white airplane sitting in a huge, empty space that marked the edge of the savage land they had been traveling through. This space was like the high pasture lands of his native Auvergne.

The shouts of joy and the beautiful airplane made him think that the crazy, risky adventure was finally at an end (despite Huronilla's abduction of Pierre) since the Portuguese was where he wanted to be.

Juan Matello would have been less joyous and triumphant, even at this moment when he did not have to fear being hunted by the Duke d'Arandar, if he could have read Huronilla's mind from afar and if he could have seen her, by some miracle of clairvoyance, walking in the mountains.

After invading the castle she was supposed to stay with Escarpaz. She followed him, Matello, instead and kept well hidden. So, she witnessed, without anyone seeing her, the transformation of Matello, Peul and the three gypsies into game wardens. Then she saw the beautiful blonde señorita and the nanny carrying the baby leave the castle, cross the courtyard then get kidnapped.

When the gypsies were leaving the castle and Matello and Peul were taking away their prisoners, Huronilla just jumped on a mule and followed the trail of the horses.

Used to riding all kinds of animals since she was an infant, especially the horses that were almost always stolen by the Bohemians, the little gypsy girl was a veritable Amazon. She had no problem riding and guiding the mule, sometimes slowly, sometimes fast, to pursue the horses without being seen. And so she saw them stop in the clearing. She slipped onto the ground, tied up her mule with the long, wool belt she wore around her waist from back in the butcher-house, and then went to spy on them from the bushes.

Before the kidnapping in the castle had begun, she had already formed her plan. Foreseeing the need for a surprise attack, she brought a little bag of pepper tied tightly inside her shirt.

From her hiding place she watched attentively every move made by Matello and Peul. When she saw the young man left alone to guard the prisoners she figured it was the right time to put her plan into action. She pulled out the little bag, opened it and poured the pepper into her hands. Jumping out of the bushes she blinded Julien Peul first, then the nanny who screamed in pain, falling off the horse and dropping the baby at the same time.

In mid-air, literally, Huronilla caught the baby and immediately ran to where the mule was waiting. She untied it, jumped on, squeezed her knees, grabbed the mane with her right hand and, holding the baby tightly to her chest in her left arm, she set off towards Salas.

Still far from the village, she veered off to the left and took a mountain path that she knew well because she had searched it out two days before. She trusted the mule, used to such rough terrain, and quickly put distance between herself and the region between San Lorenzo and Salas that was most frequented by men. In other words, she headed into the wildest, roughest, most deserted and least known part of all the Sierra de la Demanda.

However, she did no go far. Barely half an hour after stealing little Pierre she stopped the mule and slipped off. She was on a rocky plateau, standing on a kind of overhang that looked out on a deep gorge where a rushing river roared through the bottom.

At the other end of the plateau, the mountain was hollowed out into a spacious cave that was very dry because of its orientation at noon. The solid rock had no leaks. In good weather this cave was surely a safe and sound refuge. But with the southeast winds that raged often in this region, it would have been less welcoming. This first cave, at the opening, continued into the depths of the mountain through a series of natural corridors with countless branches forming a real maze in the darkness.

The day before, when she had found the cave and chosen it for her refuge, Huronilla had prepared, at the back, sheltered behind a rocky that acted as a screen, a thick bed of dry, soft leaves. On this bed she put little Pierre who had fallen asleep to the mule's rocking motion. She held the baby so tenderly that even when she got off the mule she did not wake him up.

Now freed of her breathing burden, Huronilla went back outside, unfastened the Catalan knife from her skirt, opened it and in one swift motion pricked the mule's rump. The animal brayed, reared up and then bolted off in the direction it had come.

Huronilla knew that they could not follow her trail because most of it was over rocks on which the mule left no trace. The path, moreover, was rarely used. In fact, the path was a natural ravine that could sometimes be used by men and animals but was not a usual route for anyone because it led far from hunting grounds or any inhabited regions.

Having got rid of the mule, the gypsy girl returned to the back of the cave, stuck her hand into a hole at the height of a man and pulled out a small pile of matches and a yellow candle, probably stolen from a church. After lighting the candle she put the matches back in the hole and protected the flame with her left hand as she crept into a narrow crack that led to an underground corridor that itself opened onto a small, round space with a kind of alcove to the left. In this alcove was a second bed of leaves and standing nearby was a big goat, muzzled like a dog and tied by rope knotted around a jagged rock sticking out of the wall.

"*Bueno*," she said softly.

In the middle of the round room she put the candle on the ground and secured it with a compacted circle of the fine sand that covered the ground. Then she went back to the first cave, gently picked up the infant and in the candlelight flickering through the corridor she carried Pierre into the round room without bumping into anything. She put him down, still asleep, on the bed in the alcove.

"*Bueno*," she said again.

And her cheerful face looked completely satisfied.

She petted the goat, went back to the cave and made several trips, bringing all the dried leaves of the first bed into the alcove. She did not leave behind a single leaf. With great care she added every last one of them to the bed.

She knew that since the ground was smooth rock her comings and goings left no trace; thanks to the wind the dust was piled up in the corners and at the foot of the walls. The dawn was bright enough now for her to see that she had left no clue to a human presence in the first cave. Once she was sure of this Huronilla went back into the round room with the pile of matches. She picked up the candle and sat right next to the baby. She looked at him and smiled with that doting tenderness that the maternal instinct puts in the heart of most girls.

Then, having made the five signs of the cross (forehead, chest, both shoulders and mouth) she leaned the candle in a corner against the rock, put the matches next to her on the ground and blew out the flame. Happy to have done what she wanted to do, the gypsy girl lay down, closed her eyes and fell asleep in no time.

The sun was already high in the sky and the daylight was spreading dimly through the second cave when Huronilla was woken up by the baby's cries.

In fact, little Pierre had regular feeding times. It was breakfast time for him. He had stopped sleeping and was upset that his mouth could not find its source of food.

The gypsy girl sprang to her feet.

In the alcove, the light was not bright enough for her to see the infant very well. So, she lit the candle, gave Pierre a little smile while tickling his chin, unwrapped him, picked him up and sang to him as she walked over to the goat.

Very often among the Bohemians it happened that a mother lacked milk. Therefore, a goat (the tribe always had some around) replaced the deficient mother. Many a time Huronilla had taken a baby to feed on a goat. Natural instincts kicked in, adaptation was fast and the animal itself was as calm as could be to play the role of wet nurse.

But the feral atavism that that gypsy babies can access did not come to the aide of Sylvie Saint-Clair's son.

He must not have found the goat's teat to be as soft and sweet as he was used to. But the instinct of the little creature, who was still an infant, his hunger, the submissiveness of the goat, the experience and patience of Huronilla, whose right hand was squeezing out milk, all this finally produced the desired result: Pierrot started sucking greedily, which soon satisfied his voracious appetite.

The gypsy girl laughed merrily. When the baby was full, she took him into the big cave, sat in the sun and rocked him on her knees, singing softly a song from Bohemia.

CHAPTER XII
A bullet right between the eyes

Meanwhile in Paris, in the course of taking care of his secret, political business, Gnô Mitang went to the main branch of the New Universal Bank, easily spotted one the employees named Maurice Benoit who endorsed checks and took him aside for a few minutes. He showed him the letter written by the Nyctalope with the signature accompanied by a cabalistic sign.

"Monsieur," replied Benoit, a tall, serious young man with very candid blue eyes and an intelligent face, "I am at your service. I see my address is written at the bottom of the page. So, you know where to find me outside of banking hours. Night or day, monsieur, I repeat, I am at your service. But if I get anything that might be of interest to you, how can I find you in case it's better for me to go to you rather than wait?"

"Right you are," Gnô said, very satisfied with this Benoit, how he looked and talked. "I live at the Central Palace. You just have to call. Here's my card. If I'm out, my secretary will answer. And like you, day or night, I'm at your disposal."

This first contact took place on May 30 in the morning.

Gnô Mitang had arrived rather late the night before at the Bourget airport. The next day, after going to the New Universal Bank a little before noon, at the drop of a hat, he invited Maurice Benoit to lunch. He had the highest opinion of the intellectual and moral qualities of Saint-Clair's private correspondent.

On June 1 they did not see each other but they talked briefly on the phone:

"Hello, what's new?"

"Hello. Nothing, monsieur."

June 2, a short meeting at the bank. No letter, no telegram, no message of any kind had arrived from Saint-Clair.

But on June 3, at 8:30 a.m., Gnô Mitang was informed by one of the switchboard operators at the hotel that a monsieur named Benoit was asking to see to him.

"Send him up right away!"

This morning visit from the bank employee must have meant he had received a message at home from the Nyctalope. Gnô Mitang figured it was bad news when he saw Benoit's face, more serious than usual and very pale, his eyes glassy.

He did not ask questions, just held out his hand, shook the young man's hand and said, "Hello. Give it here."

"Here you go," he replied just as curtly.

He handed over an unmarked, unsealed envelope. Forcing himself to stay calm, Gnô took a piece of paper out of the envelope: it was an official form for all wireless messages. He unfolded it and read:

"Absolute necessity that you come immediately and quickly. Friend."

It was addressed to Maurice Benoit, 14 Rue Desrenaudes, Paris. It had the word "friend". But Gnô had been told by Saint-Clair that "friend" meant the Duke d'Arandar and that "Benoit" was really Saint-Clair.

The Japanese said nothing to the bank employee about the dark and menacing mystery that the Saint-Clair family was involved in. But Benoit was smart enough to understand that such an imperative demand meant trouble, even more so as Gnô Mitang had betrayed his grave concern by many little signs, not to mention his silence, to the observant young man.

After reading the message, Gnô pondered it for a moment. Then he muttered, "Immediately and quickly, yes! But where is Saint-Clair?"

Life has surprises: the Japanese had barely breathed the question when the telephone rang in the room next to the small salon where he had received his visitor. He went to answer it.

Benoit heard him say, "Send him up right away."

Two minutes later, without a word spoken in the salon, the door opened and Leo Saint-Clair the Nyctalope stood in the doorway.

It was a scene that Maurice Benoit would never forget—the slightest details, the colors and light in the room, the faces and reactions of the two men staring at each other in front of him.

At the look on Gnô's face, which he knew so well, Saint-Clair stepped forward and closed the door. He did not beat around the bush.

"What's wrong?"

"This!" the Japanese answered.

He held out the telegram and Saint-Clair read it. His lips shut, his eyes too, and an expression of great sorrow and desolation crossed his face. But briefly. His eyes snapped open, hard and vibrant, and his face suddenly turned to stone.

"Are you coming with me, Gnô?"

"Naturally!"

"Let's go. I saw some cars for hire in front of the hotel. We'll be at Bourget in no time and we can rent a private plane. Do you agree?"

"Absolutely. But, please, give me time to grab a coat, hat, gloves and a few things for the trip, like my checkbook."

"I'll wait for you!"

In the two adjoining rooms Gnô had set up his secretary and butler. He called them. He gave orders to the secretary while the butler got together the necessities for the trip. It took less than five minutes, during which time the Nyctalope talked with Maurice Benoit, thanked him, briefly told him that Sylvie and Pierre were certainly in danger and then gave him instructions for any eventual action.

After shaking the hand of the young man, who followed them to the hotel exit, Saint-Clair and Gnô Mitang climbed into a big, beautiful car for hire. It took them to the Bourget airport where they had to spend ten minutes filling out the forms to rent a fast, long-distance plane, which had been made available to the public on January 1.

The got introduced to the pilot, to whom Saint-Clair made it plain that they needed to go as fast as possible.

"Destination: Burgos. There's no airport or even a landing strip," Saint-Clair said. "But nearby are some fields, big enough and clear enough to land without too much trouble... What's the maximum speed you can reach with this plane?"

"160 mph," the pilot replied, "but I haven't pushed it too hard."

"Well, you can push it to the limit this time. I'll give you a 100-franc bonus for every mph you reach over 160."

"That's fine, monsieur. You'll be more than satisfied," the pilot smiled.

As the crow flies, keeping in mind the unavoidable deviations, the distance from Paris to Burgos is 560 miles. Leaving at 10 a.m. from Le Bourget, Saint-Clair and Gnô were stepping onto an open field half a mile from the cathedral towers of Burgos at 12:30.

To get to San Lorenzo from Burgos they could only use mules. Of course, part of the trip could be done in a car, but wherever the car had to stop they risked not finding any saddled mules to rent or buy. So, the surest, simplest, quickest solution was to buy mules in Burgos and do the whole trip on their backs.

"It'll be hard on the mules," Saint-Clair said, "but we'll make them cover up to thirty miles in four hours, over the plains and valleys and the mountain that separates us from San Lorenzo."

Finding his usual mule driver, Saint-Clair bought the two best animals in his stable.

At 4:57 p.m., according to his watch, Saint-Clair jumped off his mule as it collapsed 300 yards from the drawbridge of San Lorenzo. Gnô's mule held on for another 100 yards.

They ran over the drawbridge and straight into the arms of the Duke d'Arandar, whose red eyes were glistening with tears.

There are scenes one does not describe because words fail to express the intensity. If one tried to describe them, the reader would be disappointed. One has to put oneself in the place of the characters and identify with them. Only in this way could anyone understand what Leo Saint-Clair was feeling in the magnificent smoking room of the castle of San Lorenzo when the Duke, unable to hold back his own emotions, recounted the abominable hours he had lived through since he realized that Sylvie, Pierrot and Adele had been taken.

The Duke was heroic enough to leave out no details. He seemed to want to punish himself for letting the enemy slip through this hands. Still, without losing his natural dignity, he talked like a guilty man, tormented by regret, berating himself and finding no excuse.

He finished up, "My dogs were sent on the trail of the horses stolen by the kidnappers. They led us far into the forest. We followed, winded and worried, trying hard not to lose sight of the dogs. We trotted on, not realizing that the trail led in a big circle. Moreover, night came on, although clear, it changed the places we were used to seeing in the daylight. In the end, we were stunned and dejected to find ourselves back in front of the castle and staring at the two riderless horses walking across the drawbridge.

"The dogs ran after them, jumped and barked with joy at finding their prey. We'd lost the trail but it'd brought us back to the start.

"In the meantime, the kidnappers and their victims had obviously abandoned the horses at some point on the run and escaped into the mountain either on foot or more likely on mules hidden beforehand to be picked up later.

"We took off again, searched for hours again and we ended up on a vast, empty plateau. Here the dogs were at a loss, running around in circles, stopping and barking. The mystery was impenetrable. The bandits and their captives had obviously come to this plateau. But what happened to them? All my experience as a hunter, all the noses of my dogs, all the instincts of my game wardens were utterly useless. Nowhere around the barren terrain could we find the mules' trail because it was certainly on the backs of mules that that the bandits had set off from some hidden hollow.

"Around 11 a.m. I sent one of my best riders to Burgos to get a telegram to you. I myself with Antonio and the other game wardens kept on searching all around the plateau until night fell. Nothing! Nothing! Absolutely nothing! If I weren't conscious of my duty towards God, you and your family, I'd have killed myself on the spot. Saint-Clair, my friend, I am so sorry and deserve to be cursed to hell by you."

Saint-Clair and Gnô had listened to the dramatic and grievous story with the strength and courage to remain impassive. But whereas the impassivity of the Japanese was like a statue of Buddha, that of the Nyctalope was like a sculpture whose face was frozen with all the pain a man could suffer when everything he loved most dearly in life was threatened.

When he had finished, the Duke choked back a sob and doubled over, with his elbow on his knees, his face buried in his clenched hands, and the proud and noble old man cried.

Now, three knocks spaced apart rapped at the door. The Duke shuddered, stood up straight and out of habit called out, "*Entre usted!*"

The heard the faint sound of a door opening. The curtain was parted and Padre Felipe appeared.

"Señor," he said, "a *caballero* is asking to see you immediately. He says his name is Don Joao Matello, a noble Portuguese."

The name was completely unknown to the Duke who, recovering his dignity and a little of his composure, had the presence of mind to say, "This *caballero*, whom I don't know, did he tell you what he wants?"

Solemnly, the chaplain answered, "He has come to talk about Señora Sylvie Saint-Clair."

All at the same time, the Duke, the Nyctalope and Gnô Mitang stiffened up.

"Show him in!" the first shouted.

"Very well, señor," the monk said very calmly and solemnly. "I'll get him and bring him to you." Stepping back, he disappeared behind the curtain.

The few minutes that passed awaiting the man who came unexpectedly to talk about the Señora were laden with both mortal anguish and feverish impatience.

Now the monk was back introducing Don Juan or rather Don Joao Matello, the Portuguese. He strode in with his head held high and his face dignified. He was bare-headed, holding his wide-brimmed black hat in his left hand. He wore a black velvet hunting outfit and laced-up boots. Tall and muscular, he gave off an aura of strength, agility and energy.

He stopped three or four feet from the Duke, the Nyctalope and Gnô who were facing him in a single line. He looked calmly at the three men, one by one, and chose the one in the middle, meaning the Nyctalope, to speak to in French.

"Monsieur, before anything else, I feel compelled to warn you that no matter what you hear you must keep your composure. It's possible, probably even certain that a couple of minutes from now you're going to feel the irresistible urge to kill me. But you're going to resist this urge because if I die you'll never see your wife and child again."

Saint-Clair shuddered. His teeth clenched and his limbs went stiff. The Duke, being more impulsive, less self-controlled, stepped forward and the growl that came out of his mouth along with his two clenched fists rising up were unmistakable by Gnô, the reasonable observer, who jumped in front of him, grabbed his arms, gripped them tightly and looked hard into his eyes. This glare was enough to make the Duke aware of the gross error he had almost made by pouncing on the man who had just spoken such dire words.

It took Saint-Clair a full minute to calm down from the harrowing emotion that was shaking him down to his soul. He calmed himself enough for his mind and will to confront the unbelievable tragedy of the situation. He opened his mouth twice and took deep breaths. Then in a low, rumbling voice, his eyes hard and riveting, he said:

"Monsieur, my two friends and I have, as you hoped, the restraint to hear you out. But say only what is necessary. What you've already said leads me to believe that the fate of my wife and son is in your hands. It would be very dreadful for you if one word too many made me forget, even for a split second, that my family means everything to me... Now, talk!"

Juan Matello bowed in honor before the Nyctalope's character. Then he said, "I alone am the judge of what is necessary to say and you must listen calmly. However, I have to assure you that concerning your wife, she has suffered no abuse, she is well taken care of. For your son, it's not for me to say, but I know with absolute certainty that he's out of danger and in a few hours, one or two days at most, he'll be back with his mother. So, monsieur, your heart can rest at ease. Now, if I may ask the Duke d'Arandar to treat me like the noble visitor I am and offer me a seat because you and I might be having a very long talk."

He gave them a brief smile, both snooty and snide, shrugged his shoulders and added:

"It's not very comfortable to stand here stiff as gamecocks ready to fight. I come as a negotiator to make a proposition. In order for you to judge its true value, I need to tell you how and why I took your wife and son, Monsieur Saint-Clair, even though I hold no grudge against you. But enough said as an introduction, if you please…"

Turning to the Duke he finished with:

"Monsieur Duke d'Arandar, I am honored to meet you."

"Please sit down," the Duke said. "Leo, my friend, and Gnô Mitang, take a seat."

Before his three extraordinary guests sat down, the Duke himself dropped into an armchair. His politeness had no warmth to it:

"Señor Joao Matello, we are listening."

With poise that proved how strong he felt in his position, Matello sat down and put his hat on a stool next to the armchair. He took off his gloves and laid them on top of his hat. Then, crossing his legs, resting his hands on the arms of the chair, he looked and sounded like a diplomat reciting facts, defining a situation and commenting on it in the company of other diplomats representing nations much less powerful than his own but that he still respected, valued and did not want to offend by any thoughtless remarks.

"Messieurs, my name really is Joao Matello. I was born in Lisbon and I own quite a lot of property near Oporto. I was involved in the successful plot to assassinate King Carlos and his son Luis Felipe. I worked for the revolution of October 1910 and the establishment of the republic. I afterwards took part, often as chief, in several conspiracies. Exiled twice, sentenced to death thrice in absentia, I never gave up the ambition I'd had since my youth. But with age, experience, time and finally the change in political ideas around the world, my ambition also changed, in its form but not in its goal. In short, I want to establish a dictatorship in Portugal, similar to the worker and farmer Soviet regime, and become, personally, the dictator.

"Now, messieurs, everything is prepared. Cells, sections, networks, a secret central committee, everything is organized. But to set off the final revolutionary movement and guarantee its success, to buy arms and munitions, supplies and a few morals, to pay for some neutrality here and complicity there, to

132

reward certain actions in advance, I need… 100 million French francs, which makes around 20 billion Portuguese reals."

After pronouncing this enormous sum, Matello stopped. Stiff as statues, not twitching even a finger, Saint-Clair, Gnô and the Duke sat there without saying a word.

So, Matello, as calm and serious as ever, went on:

"To get the money, I figured it best to partner with the sect of Hashshashins, which I heard about, by chance, during my revolutionary activities in Portuguese East Africa. Leo Saint-Clair, if we can be civil together, I'll tell you all about these Hashshashins who took over, with even greater proficiency, where Leonid Zattan left off. For the moment, I'll just say that I was ordered by these Hashshashins to kidnap your wife and son and I did it. But…"

After a moment of silence he continued:

"But I decided that my successful exploit should profit myself alone and not the sect. As a result, on my personal orders and for my own benefit, I'm asking for a ransom for your family and I set this ransom at 100 million francs."

He obviously believed (nothing seemed more logical) that the Nyctalope was about to speak. But Matello had not finished. He raised his hand to be understood and in that phenomenal serenity he carried on:

"Madame Sylvie Saint-Clair is in a safe place. I challenge even the Hashshashins to try to take her from her. Your little Pierre will soon be back with his mother and Adele who hasn't left her side. For the ransom of 100 million, payable in Lisbon in French currency, or Spanish at the current exchange rate of course, the mother, child and nanny will be given back to you in perfect health, I assure you. The exact location and the protocol of the exchange will be determined in a few minutes after you give me your word of honor to…"

The Nyctalope cut off the Portuguese in mid-sentence with an unequivocal gesture. His voice was hoarse, his eyes cold, "Enough, monsieur! Listen to me. I won't bother with any protocol and if you're the revolutionary dictator you say you are, you'll dispense with formalities, too. All right, you've played your game of kidnapping, betrayal and blackmail. And you won. I lost, I'll pay. You will bring back my wife and son and the nanny here in San Lorenzo, right away, without delay. I, Leo Saint-Clair the Nyctalope, give you my word that within a month 100 million francs will be deposited in your bank."

Gnô Mitang raised his right hand. "And I give you my word of honor as the Marquis Gnô Mitang, president of the secret council of His Majesty the Emperor of Japan."

"And mine, too. I, Pedro IV, Duke d'Arandar, give my word of honor," the Duke stood up.

"Nevertheless," Saint-Clair resumed, "you go first, monsieur Matello, because I can see in your eyes that you will do as I want and accept the full value of our words of honor. You're going to talk first, clearly, simply, succinctly and completely. You're going to talk and first tell us everything about the kidnapping and then everything you know about the sect of Hashshashins. In my opinion, you're just a stooge who saw a chance to double cross this sect. It's their business you cheated and it's on you they'll wreak vengeance. For me, once I've paid your ransom and got back my wife and son and nanny, I'll forget about you. But I'll punish the Hashshashins who are really responsible for everything, who I'm starting now to see why they are my enemy. You're going to talk. And we're listening."

Not at all ruffled but quite the opposite, very content, Juan Matello leaned forward a little and with spirited urgency said:

"Gladly, monsieur. I will be as brief and complete as possible. But allow me to start with the Hashshashins. Then I'll tell you about your family. I think it better this way because I'm sure that you'll want to go into action immediately after hearing me. Let's deal first with the Hashshashins then."

"So be it!" Saint-Clair said coldly.

Gnô Mitang had taken pen and paper out of his pocket and was ready to play stenographer for Matello's disclosure. It began:

"I'll be brief, messieurs. Here's everything I know, everything anybody can know I must say... about the sect whose supreme leader is a woman, Titania!"

And Joao Matello gave facts, names, places and numbers. He revealed the secret signs, passwords and other privileged information about the organization. With a document that he took out of his wallet and handed to Saint-Clair, he delivered to them the keys of all the codes used by the different levels of the internationally expanding sect. In short, he thoroughly and profoundly betrayed the dreadful, dangerous secret society of high-ranking officials that he had been a member of for the past several months.

The Nyctalope thought, "This guy must really believe in himself. If he's wrong, he'll be dead within a week. Korridès will find out about his betrayal and have him killed."

But when Matello said, "That's it for the Hashshashins," Saint-Clair simply said, "Now tell us what you've done with my wife and son. Then you can go get them and bring them back to me here."

"Your wife, yes," Matello replied tranquilly. "But your son, since you're going to find out anyway and I accept your word to pay the ransom, for your son, we'll have to find him..."

"Find him?"

Saint-Clair jumped up and grabbed Matello's shoulders in a grip that could be as deadly as an eagle's.

"Find him, you say! What, they took him from you?"

"Calm down, monsieur, calm down," Matello spoke softly without moving a finger to get out of the Nyctalope's grip. In a soothing voice he continued, "I understand your violent reaction, but it's futile. Please listen. The situation, I assure you, presents no danger to your son."

"I hope not!"

Once again controlling his emotion, which was torture, Saint-Clair let go of Matello and sat back down between Gnô and the Duke.

Casually, as if this had nothing to do with a crime, as if he were not the main perpetrator of this deed, the Portuguese told them in detail about what he knew had happened at San Lorenzo the night before last. He held nothing back, not the complicity of Manetta the maid (who had since disappeared from the castle), nor the murder of Escarpaz by "Juan" Matello himself. He told everything, start to finish. He concluded, believing that he knew who was really behind it all:

"It's clear that Huronilla was obeying the orders of Escarpaz. Obviously, he wanted to have a hostage until he got his 100,000 francs promised by me on a signed paper. Escarpaz is dead. He even got buried last night by the gypsies who are still on the move, in case they want to take revenge on me, even though I gave up on the idea of putting the Spanish police on their trail because of this death of Escarpaz, for which I would've had two false witnesses to declare them guilty, but never mind. Escarpaz is dead and buried, that's all there is to say. The important thing is that his tribe of Zapatan is within your reach again. Now, I know the gypsies are still camped near Salas. As for Huronilla, she's hiding with the kid in some mountain hole where the gypsies are obviously giving her food and stuff. One of the young gypsies has certainly also been promoted to nurse-maid for your son, monsieur. I'm sure that with a little cleverness and a lot of money you'll find Huronilla and therefore your son before I even get back with your wife."

What made it worse now for Saint-Clair, Gnô and the Duke was that they could not show their utter repulsion for this murderer-thief Joao Matello. But at least they could finally put an end to a meeting that, despite it being absolutely necessary, was torturing them with humiliation and shame.

Saint-Clair was the first to stand up.

"Monsieur, we have nothing more to say to each other. Bring me my wife. I will deal with finding my son. But be aware that when you get back here we'll be holding you hostage in San Lorenzo until we've got my son back."

Matello was so sure of his hypotheses about Huronilla and little Pierre that he did not bother to acknowledge this last remark.

"Very well, monsieur, but I'm not worried. As fast as I'll be bringing your wife back, I'm sure you'll be able to throw your son into her arms when she gets here."

"I will show you out," the Duke said.

"I'm honored, Duke," Matello bowed.

He had enough good sense not to hod out his hand to Saint-Clair and Gnô. He swiftly bowed his head to each of them, swept up his hat and gloves, turned his back and marched to the door that the Duke was holding open.

Only then did the Japanese close the notebook, put the cap back on the pen and stuff both back in his pocket.

"Leo," he said, "tomorrow I'll send a message to the Japanese embassy in Paris to tell the emperor that I'm taking a leave of absence for an indefinite period. Together, if you want, we can wage war against the Hashshashins."

"If you hadn't offered, Gnô, I would've asked."

In silence, lost in thought, they awaited the return of the Duke. When he was back in the room, they made a mutual agreement, without even discussing it, dictated by willpower: go straight to the gypsy camp outside Salas, surround the tribe and if money and persuasion don't work, then by force they would find out where Huronilla was hiding Pierre.

So as not to talk about a man, whatever his ambitions, who deserved to be hanged or guillotined, they made no mention of Joao Matello.

Saint-Clair and Gnô were shown to their respective rooms where a specially assigned valet brought them leather gaiters, spurs, a rifle, bandolier for cartridges, a Browning with a full clip.

The Duke was firmly resolved to act like they were under martial law with respect to the Bohemians in case they showed the least resistance, even if it meant having to deal with the Spanish authorities later. All the game wardens were recruited with Antonio at the head. All armed with rifles and Brownings, they jumped on their horses at the same moment that Saint-Clair, Gnô and the Duke got in the saddle.

Of course, the Nyctalope, Gnô and the Duke, each on his own, were wondering many things about Matello, where he had taken Sylvie, how he was going to bring her back, but they figured Sylvie would fill them in on all the intriguing details later. Anyway, they did not doubt the sincerity, as self-interested as it was, of the despicable bandit who acted like an ambitious revolutionary.

Their individual thoughts were so obsessive and they were so hesitant to share them that during the entire ride from San Lorenzo to the gypsy camp, no one said a word. Despite the rocky road, they kept their horses at a good, steady pace. The squad of guards followed close behind. The whole troop charged into the steep valley where the tribe of Zapatan had been camping for several days.

In mourning for their patriarch the gypsies were showing their sorrow and regret by being still and silent. Men, women and children had to fast for two days during which time, according to custom, they lit no fire and did nothing. All of them were sitting or lying next to their tents, huts made of branches and their big carts with woven fiber floors and canvas roofs.

Nobody showed the slightest reaction when the armed game wardens spread all around them.

Flanked by Saint-Clair and Gnô, the Duke d'Arandar stood his horse before half a dozen Bohemians who were older than the others and sitting in front of the cold ashes of an extinguished fire.

"Hola, gitanos!" he said loudly. "A child of my race has been stolen by one of your girls, the one called Huronilla. Tell me right now where she's hiding the child and I'll give you 1,000 duros. But in five minutes, if I'm not completely satisfied with your information, you will all be my prisoners, taken to my castle and shot one a day, starting with the youngest until you talk. In the meantime, my friends and I will search the mountain. When I've found the child, I will turn over to the police anyone who's still alive—you will be prosecuted for arson and kidnapping."

To make such utterly illegal threats, but which he was determined to carry out no matter the consequences, the Duke looked and sounded like the feudal Castilians who fought against both the Catholic kings desiring to unite Spain and the enemy Moors of these same kings.

All the gypsies knew about the disappearance of Huronilla. The mystery was as incomprehensible as the death of Escarpaz whose corpse had been found by three of their young men out poaching. But they did not know that Huronilla had stolen this child the Duke talked about, this child that Matello had kidnapped with his mother and nanny. This is what was said with sad dignity by one of the elders who had taken over for Escarpaz as patriarch of the tribe.

He concluded, "Señor, we are in your hands, our sons, daughters and grandchildren. But by the ancient gods of Egypt whose memory our fathers handed down to us, by Martha and Mary, patron saints venerated by the Bohemians, I swear to you that what I say is true! Cursed forever be that bandit who seduced our Escarpaz to drag some of our men into this sordid affair! What's more, we are all ready to search with you for Huronilla. And then we will all atone for the faults of the few by doing whatever work you ask of us."

Then a young woman who had just stood up kissed the hand of the patriarch said, "Not only are we missing Huronilla, but we're also missing a dairy goat, the best one. If she stole a baby she also took the goat to feed it."

At these words, which he understood even though spoken in a kind of mix of Castilian, Majorcan and Catalan, Saint-Clair almost shouted with joy because in this information he saw confirmation of the gist of Matello's guess about little Pierre and the gypsy girl. He believed like the Portuguese that Escarpaz had ordered Huronilla to snatch Pierre as a hostage to guarantee payment by Matello.

Now, in this case, it was clear that the young gypsy could not have gone far up the mountain.

"My friend," he said to the Duke, "this old man and the woman speak the truth. Let's accept their help seeing that the whole tribe was not in league with Matello and Escarpaz. Let's split the mountain into two sectors. Antonio, his guards and half the Bohemians will take one and you, Gnô, the other gypsies and I will search the other sector."

"Yes, yes," the Duke agreed immediately.

He called over Antonio and pointed out specifically what part of the mountain he was to explore. The patriarch and the Duke split up the men and women of the tribe into two groups: one gathered around Antonio and the other stayed with the Duke, Gnô and the Nyctalope.

The Duke shouted instructions.

Antonio was to zigzag to the northeast and cut across diagonally towards the castle until he got to a spot on the mountain that was the top of a steep triangle with Salas and the castle of San Lorenzo forming the base. The others would explore an equal extent of the mountain to the northwest.

Saint-Clair's watch showed 7 pm when the two groups separated to start their search.

But right away both troops were taken by surprise, a very rare if not unheard of and never before seen event in the Sierra de la Demanda: a huge airplane appeared in the west, flew over and disappeared in the east. It was flying very low, barely over 300 feet altitude, through the wide corridor formed by the successive valleys...

They watched it. They whispered about it. But since the sun was setting and would soon disappear, since their minds were occupied by their duty, the plane was only a very brief diversion.

"Let's move!" Saint-Clair ordered.

"Anda!" Antonio shouted.

And they went their separate ways.

They did not think of eating. But they had not brought any provisions anyway.

Everyone was fully, passionately concentrated on the search.

Nevertheless, they applied enough method, care and attention that not a stone was left unturned, not a bush was unexplored, not a single hole in the ground was not plumbed.

Night fell at 9 p.m. after a long twilight because of the clear sky. They came from different sides to the huge, barren area where the Duke and his game wardens the night before, had found the mysterious, incomprehensible end of the trail left by the two kidnappers carrying Sylvie and the nanny.

And all of s sudden, at the edge of this space, coming out of the woods, Antonio showed up, worn out, hatless, with one broken spur and no rifle or bandolier, an Antonio who was panting in front of the trio of Saint-Clair, Gnô and the Duke.

He babbled, "Señores! Señores! A cave down there... The one they call The Wind Cave. Definite signs that it's Huronilla's hiding place. I found a goat tied and muzzled next to a pile of good grass for it. I saw the bed for señorito Pedrito and the gypsy niña. Outside the cave I found this, which was hanging on the thorns of a gorse."

The guard lifted his right hand and started waving a strip of cloth with a lace border.

Dazed, Saint-Clair, Gnô Mitang and the Duke stared at the cloth, which looked even whiter in the brown hand holding it. Saint-Clair and the Duke recognized the lace border of Pierre's blanket.

But Antonio had paused only to catch his breath. He added, "Halfway down, under an overhang that forms a big ledge in front of the cave, we found Huronilla covered in blood. Her shoulder and chest, two bullets fired at point blank range!"

In front of Antonio, all around Anotnio, there was ice-cold numbness. But before anyone could say anything or make the slightest gesture, there came a piercing shriek from the middle of the barren zone, which made everyone turn around and look. And they saw two Bohemians walking fast, carrying the body of a man between them. When they got closer they broke into a run and dropped the man at the feet of Saint-Clair.

Horrified, shuddering in bewilderment and anguish, he and Gnô and the Duke recognized the pale, bloody face of Joao Matello.

In a low voice, as if speaking to himself, one of the Bohemians said, "We examined him. There's no question, this man was shot dead, right between the eyes."

Antonio, who had caught his breath again, grabbed and shook the Duke, ranting, "She was still alive. I touched her. She opened her eyes and made a great effort to say: '*La vibora! La vibora! Aplasta la vibora, matala!*' then her head fell back. I got back on the horse and came straight here... but I could still hear the gypsy gasping, 'The viper! She killed me! The viper! Kill her!'"

CHAPTER XIII
The Viper's map

Leo Saint-Clair proceeded with a thorough investigation after discovering that Huronilla and Matello had been shot dead. The gypsy girl and the Portuguese were brought back to the castle and examined by Padre Felipe who performed duties as a doctor as well.

"The man's dead for sure," he said, "but the girl's still alive."

What a blow! Once the wounds were washed they could see that her injuries were only superficial. One, to the head, had caused her to blackout. But none were life-threatening. Even better, nothing was broken and if her head injury was not serious she would be back on her feet in two days and as good as new since she had not lost much blood.

"Will she wake up soon?" Saint-Clair asked, watching the examination with the Duke.

"Right away," the chaplain replied.

He had a well-stocked and modern pharmacy in the castle of San Lorenzo. He gave Huronilla a shot in her left arm and two minutes later the girl opened her eyes.

She gasped, *"Aye, la vibora!"* And she started to cry. They made her drink a cordial.

The Duke spoke softly to her, "Calm down, niña. You're at the castle. You're out of danger. Tomorrow you'll be able to get up. I'll keep you here with the servants of Doña Blanca if you want… If you'd rather go back to your tribe, I'll give you money enough to take care of you for a while… Hey, don't cry. Everything's all right. Do you feel strong enough to talk? Yes? Well, tell us what you did and what happened over the past few days since the night of the fire… Will you talk? Will you tell the truth? The whole truth? Yes? That's a good girl… Go on, talk, we're listening."

Doña Blanca had put the girl in her own room on a little bed in the second alcove where one of the youngest servants usually slept. She was the only woman in the room. When the Padre gestured to her, she arranged the pillows so that Huronilla could sit up comfortably.

The Duke went to check that nobody was listening at the doors, in the hallway or in the room next door because he was as suspicious now as he was trusting before the calamity. He locked the door and went back to the foot of the bed next to Saint-Clair and Gnô Mitang. Padre Felipe and Doña Blanca were on either side at the head. And very simply, frankly, Huronilla spoke.

She started her story with the river and sneaking into the laundry. Then she told everything that happened until she settled down with little Pierre in the back of the second cave. She paused, sipped the cordial, which Padre Felipe was holding, and continued:

"I wanted to keep the baby to bring him back here to the castle but I had to wait a few days until Escarpaz and the three others left the area and the tribe to go live like rich men in Barcelona, which they planned in secret. You know, the whole tribe wasn't working with Escarpaz. Me and many others obeyed him because he was the patriarch and he scared us…"

"He won't scare you anymore, or anyone else," the Duke said, "because he's dead."

"Escarpaz is dead!" the girl cried out, doubtful.

"Yes, probably killed by Matello, who is also dead, by the way."

"Oh! I'll bet it was *La Vibora* who killed Matello… I understand now what she was trying to say."

The eyes, face and voice of Huronilla showed extreme surprise, joy and excitement at this news.

The Duke shuddered, "*La Vibora?* You say that a lot. We don't understand."

"You will, señores. Listen! I was sitting calmly outside the cave, in the sun, at dawn, rocking the baby in my arms and singing a song to him when I saw a plane in the sky. It was flying very low. It disappeared to my left, over the mountain, then it came back. It made me laugh. It turned around right over my head and then disappeared again, but behind me this time. It was flying so low that it looked like it was trying to land. I know the mountain very well. I said to myself, 'If it wants to stop, it can. Right over the cave there's a barren plateau, long enough and wide enough…' I know a plane needs space to land. Escarpaz, who knows everything, told us a lot about airplanes. But then the baby woke up and started crying. He was hungry. I went back into the cave where the goat was tied and I fed the baby. When he was full, I went back out… And out of nowhere I was face-to-face with *La Vibora*…"

"*La Vibora*… The viper!" the Nyctalope said. "Who is it? Tell me right now!"

Captivated by his tone of voice and by his gaze, both imperative and soothing, Huronilla answered:

"She's a woman, a Russian, very beautiful and very sly. In Barcelona, around two months ago, she talked with Escarpaz for a long time in secret. But I was hiding near them and heard everything. It was about using the tribe, someday in Spain or in France, to kidnap a rich French woman and her son, a baby. And the Russian woman described the French woman so well that I recognized her right away when she passed through Salas the other week with her baby, a señor, a nanny and a mule driver… Well, this Russian, I call her *La Vibora* because I heard Escarpaz tell his nephew, his henchman in the tribe, 'This time *La Vibora* is making a good deal for us'. From other things he said I knew he was talking about the Russian, mean and devious like a viper. But wait… I recognized the French señora again on Sunday when the whole tribe went to the castle. Do you know I tried to warn her tell her to crush the viper, to kill her?"

"Yes," Saint-Clair said, "yes. *Aplasta la vibora, matala!* And now we understand maybe everything. So, go back when you came out of the cave, Huronilla."

"*Bueno.* What was I saying?"

Doña Blanca, panting with curiosity, replied, "You were saying that you suddenly found yourself face-to-face with *La Vibora.*"

"Oh, right. I recognized her right away because I'd seen her in Barcelona. I recognized her even though she was dressed like a man, wearing a weird leather cap. I think she must've come on the plane. She had a gun in her hand. Before I could move or speak she blurted out:

'Huronilla, give me the child. Here's a 100-duro bill for you.'

'No,' I said, 'the child's mine.'

'It's not yours. It belongs to a woman who is living in my house and whom they stole it from before you took it.'

'Well,' I said, 'that's because the mother of this niño is your prisoner. I know it, so go! I'll save the baby! You won't get him!'

"I jumped to the side to slip between her and the rock, to run out of the cave and into the mountain where I knew the woman would never catch me. And I heard her shout, 'You're going to get you both killed just like I killed the other. I'll have that child dead or alive!'

"She fired the gun. I felt like a lashing in the shoulder, then another in my back. I had an idea. I put the baby on the ground and turned around to jump on *La Vibora* and gouge her eyes out with my nails because I thought I was going to die. But she fired again and I felt my head... I don't know anything else. But, señores, tell me, did she get the baby, heaven's little angel?"

Nobody answered. She read it in their eyes, which were teary. She knew the truth.

"*Aye, aye de mi!*" she groaned and then passed out.

"Christ have mercy!" the padre murmured while Blanca broke down sobbing. He turned to Saint-Clair, Gnô and the Duke and said, "Señores, I think you won't get anything more out of this poor girl until tomorrow."

"You're right, father," the Nyctalope said. "Don Pedro, Gnô, let's go." Then, in the hallway, "We have something to do, my friends."

"What?" the Duke asked.

"Something immediate, despite our fatigue and despite the late hour. Run to the gypsy camp, surround it again and make a thorough search. You were right, Gnô, since there's a woman at the center of all this intrigue, in whose web I've been driven more than I've been driving for almost two weeks, it's very possible that this woman is Diana Ivanovna Krosnovief, the Red Princess, the fiancée of Leonid Zattan. In which case, from Korridès to Escarpaz, all the men I've seen mixed up in this affair are cogs in the machine, a well built machine.

142

But such organizations don't often exist without notes in diaries, memos, papers and documents, more or less secret, in some kind of file. We have to search the tribe of Zapatan."

"Right!" Gnô sounded satisfied. "Now for some action. And we'll go full tilt. Let's leave right away."

"Right away!" the Duke agreed enthusiastically.

The game wardens were still eating bread, ham and cheese and drinking a little wine, rifles slung over their shoulders, standing around the servants' dining room. As soon as they were told, they were on horseback again with new torches burning. The Duke and the Nyctalope with the Japanese at the lead of the troop galloped out of San Lorenzo. They had to slow down in the rougher terrain. Night was just surrendering to the dawn when the Bohemians found themselves surrounded once again before anyone could escape the sleeping camp.

On hearing the noise, the new patriarch was the first to come out of his caravan, which was lavish and sparkling clean compared to the other motley, shabby vehicles that formed the tribe's "traveling train". He was called over, rudely, right away, by the Duke d'Arandar.

"Hey, you! I didn't ask your name yesterday. What is it?"

"Candeyro, señor."

"Well, Candeyro, line up everyone on the left, in the open space over there. Everyone, no exceptions, and hurry up!"

"But, señor…"

"No buts! Do it! Or I'll take the whole tribe to Burgos under police guard, which I'll get here in a jiffy, and you can deal with the courts if you don't want to deal with me. We're not going to hurt anyone unless we find something… We're here to make a thorough search to see if we can find any useful papers. Hola! Where's that guy going? Antonio, get him!"

The young gypsy who tried to escape was fast but hesitant. He ran but did not know exactly what direction to take. Antonio had no trouble catching him and bringing him back.

"Who are you?" the Duke asked.

"Elizon," the gypsy answered proudly.

"He's the nephew of Escarpaz," the patriarch added.

"Ah, a good catch," Saint-Clair remarked softly. "We'll start the search with him."

"Absolutely! Antonio, don't let him go."

The Duke waited for all the members of the tribe (except for Elizon), pushed and pulled by one another to obey the shouts of Candeyro, were huddled together in the empty space on the edge of the camp.

"Antonio," Don Pedro said, "you and your guards keep a close eye on everyone. Don't let anyone, not even a child, sneak away. I'll take care of this kid. Go on."

The Duke, Saint-Clair and Gnô Mitang were left alone with Elizon, whose left arm was held in the Duke's tight grasp.

"Candeyro!" the Duke yelled.

Dignified but sad, cursing the deceased Escarpaz who was the cause of all this grief for the tribe, the patriarch stepped forward.

"Brother," the Duke spoke kindly now, "search this kid since I'm sure you know how to do it. Whatever you find, toss it at my feet. I trust in your loyalty, but still, I warn you that the two men and I are watching your every move. Please, search him."

"As you wish, señor."

Elizon straightened up and his face betrayed his worry. Should he run? He couldn't. He lowered his head and spread his arms, resigned, surrendered to the fatalism of his race.

The dutiful and thorough search did not take long. The kid was only wearing pants and a coat, both in fairly good condition. One sigficant detail: the two inside pockets of the coat were reinforced with canvas and fitted with buttons. From these pockets Candeyro pulled out two flat, carefully tied, oilcloth packages. The other pockets and the cloth belt gave up only trivial items, except for the big switchblade knife.

"That's all," the old gypsy said.

"I believe so," the Duke replied.

Saint-Clair bent down and picked up the knife with the two packets. "The kid can take back the rest."

"Sure," the Duke nodded. And to the Bohemian, "Go back to your family, kid." Then to the patriarch, "Your caravan used to belong to Escarpaz?"

"Yes."

"Let's go."

Although the light was already brightening outside, the inside of the caravan was dark. Not for the Nyctalope since his eyes knew no darkness, but for his companions, so Gnô turned on a flashlight. The search was meticulous and complete. They found nothing suspicious, therefore nothing interesting. The caravan of Elizon's mother, a widow, was also searched in vain. They went through others and the tents, searched half a dozen of the tribe who were called out by the Duke as close to Escarpaz. Nothing turned up.

"I'm putting odds on what's in those two packets," the Nyctalope said. "But we should first find out if Elizon or the other friends of Escarpaz can give us any useful information."

"Right away," the Duke said.

He lined up the seven suspects in front of them.

"Listen up! 100 duros to anyone who can tell me something about what Escarpaz was doing, something I don't know, about the kidnapping."

They all talked with apparent sincerity, with the desire, obviously, to earn the 100 duros. They said that what they knew. Elizon himself could only add this:

"Escarpaz made me swear often that if he died without giving his last wishes to the next patriarch, I should take this package from his caravan, which he told about only to me, and burn it in secret without opening it."

No matter how hard he interrogated Elizon, that was all he could say. His six accomplices had nothing to add about the bandit Escarpaz, barely conscious of their complicity.

"Bueno!" the Duke wrapped up. "You've been cooperative and honest. You'll each get 25 duros and you, Elizon, 50 for the last information. Candeyro, your tribe is free. But break camp until I say so. I want one of you to come to the castle every day and stay there for 24 hours. You won't be a hostage because I don't need that to make sure you'll obey. No, you'll be a messenger between me and the tribe. All the men and women here are now working for me until the lady and her son along with the nanny are found. To keep you out of trouble I'll give five duros a day to all the tribe. You can weave baskets and blankets and bring them to the castle where you'll be paid a fair price. I don't want the people of Salas to suffer from you staying longer. I will punish the whole tribe if they're victims of any theft. Is that understood, Candeyro?"

"It is, señor, and thank you for your generosity. I know you could put us in prison for arson, at least some of us, so bless you."

"Bless you!" they all cried out.

"Very well. Keep listening... Two pieces of good news: first, your best dancer, Huronilla, owes her attacks of drowsiness to a drug that Escarpaz was giving her to make her blind and mute at certain times. Therefore, you don't have to worry anymore that she'll die during one of these crises. Second, she's alive and only with minor injuries. In less than a week she'll be fine. I'm taking care of her at the castle."

Thanks were shouted out while the Duke mounted his horse. Saint-Clair and Gnô did the same.

The Duke said to the Nyctalope, "Now the whole tribe is on our side. If need be, it'll be a bigger help to us than it was to Escarpaz."

"Thanks," Saint-Clair responded curtly.

"We should examine that package soon, shouldn't we?"

"Yes."

"Uh, at the castle?"

"That's right."

"Antonio, get on your horse. We're off to San Lorenzo."

Right after they got to the castle and drank a cup of hot coffee that Blanca had prepared for them, the Nyctalope, the Duke and Gnô Mitang shut themselves up in the smoking room.

Saint-Clair and Gnô opened the two packets at the same time. They contained papers, one a bunch of loose pages, the other arranged in numbered envelopes. The three friends made three piles. Page by page they started going through them. They threw in a basket all the papers that seemed to concern only the tribe of Zapatan—there were many: paid bills, expired passports, authorizations to camp or trade. Escarpaz must have kept all this, which was useless, to make forgeries, as could be seen by some of the (often crude) changes to dates and names. As for the documents that were, at first sight, of possible interest, they put them in the middle of the table.

After this first selection, they sorted again.

They put aside the papers whose text or drawing—see, there were drawings—were incomprehensible at first glance. They would study them more carefully later.

In the end, Saint-Clair had before him only four documents.

The first was a photograph of a woman with a stiff paper envelope labeled number 1. On the back of the image, with no photographer's mark, was written in red ink, in big, clumsy letters, very clear and legible: *La Vibora*. The woman was pictured only from above the shoulders, which were bare under a chiffon "drape". Pearl necklace, pendant earrings, pearl headband in the long hair styled like Empress Eugenie, rather anachronistic, probably for some fancy ball because the photograph was relatively recent. The beautiful woman was around thirty, at most, and had "something very modern, very trendy about her" as Gnô Mitang said.

Saint-Clair concluded, "We'll show it to Huronilla. I think she'll recognize the woman from Barcelona and at the cave. Thanks to some of these papers about the tribe we know that the words *La Vibora* were written by Escarpaz. The old coot couldn't have known two vipers. Until proven otherwise I'll figure this 'Second Empire' woman is Diana Ivanovna Krosnovief, the Red Princess."

"I think so too," Gnô said.

The Duke had nothing to say on the subject. He took the photograph and slipped into envelope number 1.

The second document was a list of names and words with a normal envelope marked number 4. The list had a title reminiscent of a distant and terrible past:

Sect of Hashshashins
Sunday (Vibora)
Mittwoch Donners
Diens Freitag
Montag Sams
Fidawi de Hasan ibn Sabbah

It was all typed. Only the parentheses next to Sunday were written in red ink in the recognizable script of Escarpaz.

English and German were not unknown languages to Saint-Clair and Gnô. Moreover, the Duke knew as much as his two friends about the history of "Hasan ibn Sabbah", the "Fidawis" and the "Sect of Hashshashins".

The Nyctalope said, "From Sunday to Sams, the seven words are a mix of English and German. One of them, the last, is shortened. They're the seven days of the week from Sunday to sams, samstag or Saturday… We can assume that they're *noms de guerre*, the secret names of the seven individuals who are the chiefs of the new sect of Hashshashins, otherwise called Assassins. The word *Vibora* written next to Sunday proves that the woman in the photo, probably the woman seen by Huronilla, is called Sunday in the High Command of the sect. The Fidawis mean the servants, the fanatics of Hasan who was the supreme master of the historic sect… So, the new cult followers call themselves this as well.

"Let's be as careful with this document as with the photo. It adds weight to the hypothesis that you, Gnô, expressed in Nopals and it confirms part of what Joao Matello revealed to us."

The Japanese bowed. And the Duke put the list into its envelope.

The Nyctalope picked up the third document. But instead of examining it alone like the first two, he spread it out on the table.

It was heavy paper folded in quarters from the biggest envelope numbered 7. Unfolded it was a foot long on each side and perfectly square. The folds were so heavily creased that they had to pin it down on the four corners to keep it flat.

It looked like a very simple geographical map or the linear outline of a place.

There were only two lines: One, a closed circuit making a very simplified image, a basic drawing of a Vauban-type fort; the other, an irregular line cut off at both ends, forming a half-circle under the fort, with its jaggedness clearly delineated by the shading under it, just like the inside of the fort was cross-hatched.

At the top right of the drawing Escarpaz had written in red "*La Vibora*".

For a few minutes the three men examined the document without saying a word.

Finally, with a sparkle in his eyes and a bitter grin on his face, Gnô asked quietly, "Do you have an idea, Leo?"

"Yes," Saint-Clair answered.

"Do you want to tell us?"

"Gladly. Have you two read the novel of Alexandre Dumas titled *The Viscount of Bragelonne?*"

"Yes," the Japanese and the Spaniard said together.

"You probably remember the episode of Belle-Île-en-Mer, the fortified island that good Porthos was working on for Fouquet or thought he was working on to make it impenetrable?"

"Yes."

"Well, I read it too and in a curiously illustrated edition. I remember a picture that was supposed to represent this fortified Belle-Île with the coastline on the right. Except here the coastline is under the polygonal fort on *La Vibora* map. The map reminds me of the novel: it shows an island fortress with a jagged coast underneath. I guess that by writing *La Vibora* on it Escarpaz wanted to tell some accomplice that this island is the lair of the Viper."

"That's what I think too," Gnô said. "But it was only guess. I didn't remember Belle-Île, which adds some colorful support to the hypothesis. And you, Duke?"

"I have no idea," Pedro d'Arandar said simply. "But I'm with you. It's obvious, really. The shading of the fort and the irregular line under it looks like the map of a coast."

Saint-Clair spoke softly, "There's no doubt about it if we compare the Viper's map to this other document that is here in my pile of papers. You haven't seen it yet but I read through it when I first came across it. Read this!"

The Nyctalope pushed over a paper taken out of envelope number 8. Again in red ink, it was all written by Escarpaz in Spanish. Gnô knew the language well enough. He and the Duke read it at the same time and as he read, he muttered a translation:

"To be seen by the island, get to the Cape of La Vibora. To show you're a friend raise and spread your arms three times like a cross."

Since he had received the Duke's tragic call back in Gnô's room in Paris, Leo Saint-Clair had not smiled. But now he was smiling and the crease on his forehead softened.

He said, "The Cape of La Vibora! Isn't that shown clearly on the map where Escarpaz wrote it in red? No doubt about it! Now, my friends, all we have to do is identify the geographical location of the drawing, a fortified island off a semi-circular coastline..."

Gnô broke in, "If we consider it proven that the island is the secret hideout of the Viper, Diana, the Red Princess, then it's very likely that she's holding Sylvie and Pierre and Adele on it, first in collusion with Matello, then alone when she was sure that he wouldn't betray her. That's how I see things, logically."

"Yes," the Nyctalope and the Duke agree together.

Saint-Clair added, "Matello didn't say anything to us about this island because that's where he had imprisoned my family."

"Exactly," Gnô said. "This secret island can't be too far away. Sure, the Portuguese was in a plane, in the plane that Huronilla saw, the plane that we ourselves saw. *La Vibora* shot him dead. But we know that, if his betrayal succeeded, which we must imagine he wanted, Matello would've brought Sylvie back to us within eighteen hours. And lastly, remember that the kidnappers were fleeing to the west and it was from the west that we saw the plane... Therefore, wherever Sylvie, Pierre and Adele are being held is to the west. And again: an eighteen-hour round-trip with night coming on, a needed pause, with landing, getting off and on... That's not a lot of distance to cover even in a fast plane. Duke, do you have an atlas?"

"Of course!"

Don Pedro jumped up, opened a bookshelf, grabbed a hefty atlas, dropped it on the table and opened it.

"Spain," he said.

"Thanks."

Saint-Clair, accepting Gnô's reasoning, was already leaning over it, continuing the hypothetical but oh so logical theory:

"The Atlantic coast. Spain, north and west. I won't consider the Portuguese coast, it's too busy, with a railroad all along it. By definition a secret island has to be in wild, deserted country, far from any kind of traffic. Now, the Basque, Asturian and Galician coasts are full of uninhabited and unknown nooks and crannies, right Pedro? A lot of them must be pretty inaccessible. That's where we should go looking."

"That's right," the Duke said.

"And without delay," Gnô encouraged.

He stood up, walked around the table and put his hands on Saint-Clair's shoulders.

"Leo," he said affectionately, "you're tired. Only your willpower is keeping you awake, thinking and talking. Your nerves are shot. The same goes for me. And look at the Duke. Let's all get a few hours rest. We've dealt with the main problem. Now we just have to go in action, hard and fast! But we'll be working poorly in the state we're in. Let's get some sleep."

"Let's do that," Saint-Clair stood up.

"You're right," the Duke agreed somberly.

Less than fifteen minutes later, each in his own room, the three men fell last asleep.

The Nyctalope was the first to get up. Broad daylight was pouring in through the open window. He looked at his watch, which he had not even bothered to take off in his almost unconscious condition.

"Three o'clock! I slept for six hours. That's all right. I feel well rested now. I think I saw a tub in the bathroom yesterday. A little cold water will refresh me completely. My mind is clear. We have to be in San Sebastian tomorrow morning at the latest and be on a plane by noon to explore the Spanish coast down to Vigo.

"But I need Vitto and Socca. My two allies will be indispensable. I'm sure they're at Saint-Jean-Pied-de-Port. I'll send them a telegram from Burgos so they'll arrive at the same time as Gnô and I at San Sebastian. On the train, after Burgos, I'll examine the other documents with Gnô. Maybe we'll get some new information.

"I do hope we'll figure this out. I feel we're on the right track. Ah, if this Viper from hell has hurt Sylvie or Pierre in any way, I'll kill her with my bare hands, slowly and painfully. There are cases in which the justice of the Spanish Inquisition is a good thing—justice in the service of hatred and revenge."

"Oh, I hope it doesn't drag on. If all our hypotheses are right, what's this woman's goal? What Korridès told me? To make us, especially me, suffer? Does that mean the woman who was following me on the highway from Orleans was the Viper? Diana the Red Princess? Oh well. Curses on both her and Korridès!"

From then on Saint-Clair was on the go. He saw Huronilla one more time but she had nothing more to say although she did formally identify *La Vibora* as the woman in the photograph. With Gnô Mitang who would, of course, be with him until the end of this harrowing adventure, Saint-Clair bid farewell to the Duke d'Arandar. Don Pedro was staying at San Lorenzo to keep an eye on the Bohemians and hold a few gypsies in reserve in case the Nyctalope needed some strong-arm support.

On the night of June 3 Saint-Clair and Gnô Mitang were in Burgos and the following morning in San Sebastian. The mysterious documents were examined for two full hours during the trip but remained incomprehensible to them.

Gnô said, "We'll have to come back to them with more time."

"Yes. For the time being, let's get some sleep. There's nothing more we can do until the morning."

In San Sebastian they met up with Vitto and Socca who had received the telegram from Burgos and drove the roadster at breakneck speed.

Some time ago a commercial and tourist seaplane station had been built in the bay of San Sebastian. Saint-Clair found a brand new plane, the latest model. Vitto and Socca were first-rate mechanics and the Nyctalope had flown a hundred times as an amateur pilot. Gnô was a captain pilot in the Japanese army reserves.

At 1 p.m. on June 4 the *Goéland III* took off from the bay, circled twice to gain altitude and headed west through a clear, calm sky with perfect visibility.

The plane, perfect for "grand international tourism", was a six-seater in two compartments separating the passengers from the pilot and assistants. When examining the plane he was about to fly off in, Saint-Clair told Gnô:

"You and me up front, Vitto and Socca behind us. The two other seats will be for Sylvie with Pierre and Adele... or else we won't be coming back!"

"I get it," the Japanese said softly.

The big windows gave a good view of the whole coast and the land under plane. They were so well arranged that pilot and passengers only had to turn, lower or raise their head to see everything in the sky and on land.

In front of them Saint-Clair and Gnô had spread out a very good map of the northwest coast of Spain.

When the plane was cruising at 120 mph, Saint-Clair said, "It's not possible that the Viper Island is between Saint Sebastian and Santander or even Gijon or San Esteban. Up to this last little port the coast is riddled with naval and train stations and small towns, skirted by the railroad, and so very busy, very well known. The existence of a secret island around there is just not possible."

"I think so too," Gnô said. "But between San Esteban and Ferrol, between Corogne and Cape Finisterre and south of there..."

"Yes, no trains, no ports, very few villages, wild, uncultivated mountains, all kinds of coves and creeks, long reefs that force ships to give a wide berth... If our speculations are valid, that's the only place on this peninsula that they'll be confirmed."

"I think so too."

"So, let's get to San Esteban fast, then we'll slow down and fly lower from there."

"In case we do find the Viper Island, Leo, do you have a plan of action?"

"Simple," the Nyctalope said. "If the drawing of the coast is accurate, we'll have no problem identifying the island or the fort enclosed in the semi-circular coast. We'll check it out from a distance and a high altitude so as not to make them suspicious. Then it'll depend on the site, the time, the weather, all the circumstances. Do have anything better?"

"No, that seems reasonable."

"So, let's get to it." He turned his head slightly and said, "In any case, Vitto and Socca, do a good job as spotters. You've got a map. If any configuration of the coast looks to you like the drawing with an island nearby, shout it out!"

"Don't worry, monsieur," Vitto said.

From San Sebastian to Gijon, as the crow flies, is a distance of 560 miles. The seaplane took five hours to cover it. No mechanical or atmospheric incidents. No alert from Vitto or Socca.

From the air Gijon is easily recognizable by the maze of train tracks that weave through the valley. Between Oviedo and the sea and on the coast there are many villages. Only twenty miles lie between San Esteban and Gijon to the east. They were covered quickly. After San Esteban there was no railroad.

"Vitto, Socca, be on the lookout!" Saint-Clair said.

Very rugged because of the mountains with numerous valleys that tumbled down, often steeply, toward the sea, the wild, inhospitable, deserted coast was carved into jagged headlands and swampy coves. The seaplane was flying at only 20 mph and barely over 300 feet altitude.

They cruised over the rare towns—just small fishing villages—spaced apart along the arid coast. Luanca, Nuvia, Figueiras, Ribaldeo, with a short railway that ran to the mining and forest village of Villaodrid... and other villages even farther apart, until the coast, after Cape Ortegal, turned to the southwest and hollowed out to form the long, wide and lovely bay where Ferrol and Corogne face each other.

"Stop!" Saint-Clair said. "Night's coming on. Rest until tomorrow. What we know for certain is that the secret island isn't off the Asturian coast. Let's hope it's hiding in Galicia, which is so rugged and jagged around the dangerous waters of Cape Finisterre."

"Let's hope so," Gnô chimed in.

The two men were sad and tired. Tired especially from the disappointment caused by their sadness. Another day gone by! Another night with nothing to do! In the meantime, what was happening to Sylvie, Pierre and Adele in the clutches of the dreadful Viper, of the hypothetical but no less dreadful Diana Ivanovna Krosnovief?

"We'll anchor in Ferrol?" the Japanese asked.

"No. Nor in Corogne," Saint-Clair came back firmly. "If, as I hope, the secret island is around Cape Finisterre, it's probable that *La Vibora* and the Hashshashins have accomplices in these ports, these naval ports, fortified towns, the only real towns in the northwest of Spain. We'll risk being spotted, reported..."

"So, we'll spend the night at sea?"

"Yes. It's calm, the night's clear and there's no wind. They said that the *Goéland III* feels like a big boat on the water. Let's go out there and we'll take turns on watch. Keep the running lights on like on board a military patrol boat so that any ship passing by won't ram us and send us into the deep... Tomorrow we'll cover the westernmost point of the peninsula... God willing, we'll find the cursed island!"

The *Goéland III*, piloted by Gnô for the last two hours, skirted over the sea like the seagull it is named after, and set down on the relatively calm waves two miles west of Corogne.

The sun was just going down on the horizon. It looked like it was diving into the sea, very fast, a big, red, rayless orb. A gossamer mist was rising on the purple screen of the glowing sky. Gradually, this glow faded, the mist vanished and the stars started twinkling. The spring night was promising to be serene. The ocean itself was flat, the waves forming barely perceptible ripples. Not a breath of wind. A sailboat sat motionless, barely visible, far to the north, almost unreal—to the eyes of the four men breathing the fresh air through the big opening of a kind of movable flap that formed part of the "roof" of the seaplane.

For men like Saint-Clair and Gnô Mitang, Vitto and Socca, the riskiest decisions, the most dangerous solutions are simple, natural, ordinary, as long as they follow factual logic. Now, logic deemed that the seaplane not attract any attention from anyone, that it go unnoticed during the night and somewhat during the day. Anchored in sight of Ferrol or Corogne was prudent, therefore, in a certain way, but illogical as far as the goal of the expedition. They figured it was better to face all the perils of one night at sea than to risk alerting any would-be accomplice of the Hashshashins in case they had anything to do with the kidnapping, which was highly likely.

They ate: bread, sardines, canned chicken, pineapples in kirsch, fresh water. A pipe for Saint-Clair, a cigar for Gnô, cigarettes for Vitto and Socca. Coffee kept warm on the electric stove for whoever was on watch…

In their bucket seats, comfortable enough, Saint-Clair, Gnô and Socca settled in, wrapped in blankets. They were asleep in no time.

The first two-hour watch was kept by Vitto. From the darkness of the plane he scanned the less dark night outside. The running lights of the *Goéland III* cast dancing glimmers on the black water where the reflected stars flickered. The plane floated easily, balanced, bobbing softly with little creaking. No anchor was needed or even could be used because of the depth of the ocean. Therefore, it was drifting but not to their detriment, first of all because it was slow and slight, secondly because it was to the open sea and not landward.

The hours rolled by. After Vitto came Socca, then Gnô. The Japanese let the Nyctalope sleep until daybreak. Two steamships passed by, coming from the northeast. The sailboat had disappeared. There was nothing else remarkable. When Saint-Clair finally woke up on his own, after a long, calm, sorely needed rest, he found his companions ready and the coffee warm.

"Hello. Anything new?"

A quick washing up, an even quicker breakfast and they were off!

June 5, under the 11th degree longitude west and 43rd degree latitude north, the sun had risen at 3:45 a.m. The *Goéland III* took off and rose in the air at the same time as the sun peeked over the mountains beyond which was Saint Jean de Compostella.

At 4 a.m., so fifteen minutes of a low, slow flight along the rugged coast that formed the vast headlands of Galicia, Vitta cried out, "Heads up! An island in view… The coast looks like the map drawing."

"Socca, Vitto, get to your stations!" Saint-Clair ordered.

The Nyctalope and Gnô leaned toward the windows full of anticipation and their sharp eyes scrutinized the land, sea and the geometrically shaped island!

The plane flew over…

They only had around one minute for useful observation. It was enough. Neither Gnô nor Saint-Clair had the slightest doubt. The resemblance of the natural layout to the drawing of Escarpaz was clearly identical.

"We've got it, Gnô," Saint-Clair panted.

"Yes we do, Leo. Even the Cape of La Vibora is obvious."

"I saw that."

"What do we do now?"

"You'll see…" He turned to Socca, "Another ten minutes going south at a higher altitude. Come back higher and higher. We'll watch it through binoculars. Then set down coming back north to south… a long, long descent… We'll anchor the plane in some hidden cove. Then we'll try to get as close to the island as we can, we'll watch, consider, discuss and act depending on what we find…

At last! At last! We've got it! As long as Sylvie, Pierre and Adele are there. Lord, Lord..."

Clasping Gnô's hands hard enough to crush them, Saint-Clair the Nyctalope broke out in sinister laughter.

CHAPTER XIV
The mother, the wife, the viper

The westernmost point in Spain is not, as is generally believed, Cape Finis-terre but indeed Cape Torinana, located twenty miles or so farther north. Be-tween these two capes, the coast cuts in sharply for six miles. It forms a wide-open bay furrowed with coves and bristling with promontories.

There is no coast steeper, lonelier or more desolate in southern Europe. The Galician mountains end there in the water, often in vertical cliffs. No towns, not even a fishing village is in the jagged bay. Nobody lives on the mountain overlooking it. No boat, big or small, ever enters it. Cargo ships, battleships, passenger ships, sailboats, they all pass farther out to sea. Even the Spanish and Portuguese coasters avoid this dangerous shore whose two opposite capes, Torinana and Finisterre, extend viciously into the sea with perilous reefs.

For all these reasons, no doubt, the small, rocky island sitting deep inside the bay was called *Isla Perdida* (Lost Island). Looking from the ocean it was indistinguishable from the land because on the west, north and south sides it was separated only by a narrow, winding canal, at most 600 feet wide. From the land nobody ever saw it because the region is uninhabited for many miles around.

What misanthropic fantasy or what pirate savagery had given a noble Gali-cian sailor from Corogne who lived, they said, in the 16th century, whose real name has been deformed by legend, the reckless and stubborn idea to take this deserted Lost Island that belonged to no one and to build a fortified castle on it? And in a very original style! It took a century to understand the design of the il-lustrious military engineer and Maréchal of France Sebastien Le Preste, Lord of Vauban, as a fortified architecture whose main characteristics are the polygonal perimeter and the slight elevation of all the buildings above ground.

In the 18th century Lost Island was acquired by a Portuguese Lord, Domin-gos Matello, a famous explorer but long forgotten, who expanded and made more comfortable the barracks: he transformed them into a small castle whose oddity, like the barracks it replaced, was that it contained only a ground floor with terraced roofs.

Around the polygon the island extended as an irregular polygon itself, less than a quarter mile wide on average and the whole surface a sloping bank made of smooth rock over which, during high tide, the ocean waves crashed and left their foam on the bastion walls as the spray reached all the way to the castle ter-race.

On the west side, facing the farthest cove of the angular bay, was a small harbor accessed by a narrow inlet just wide and deep enough for a mid-sized schooner. But the arm of the sea between the island and the coast was so deep and the inlet designed so that a small ship could go in and out even at low tide.

And this Lost Island was the prison in which Joao Matello had incarcerated Sylvie Saint-Clair with her son Pierre and the nanny Adele on June 2.

Since passing out while Matello and Peul were transporting her on the plane where they had placed her comfortably enough, Sylvie regained consciousness maybe fifteen minutes after takeoff. She was ungagged and unbound. The first thing she saw was Adele next to her, her eyes red and her face puffy, the poor thing completely dazed, from time time shaken by an uncontrollable sob.

On the contrary, when Sylvie woke up she was in full possession of her memory, her courage, her self-control, her mind and emotions.

She understood that it was useless to talk to the nanny. She merely took her hand and held it in her own. Then she sat up a little in her seat, looked at Matello and Peul sitting across from her, side by side, with their backs turned to the front of the plane. A headband was tied around the young man's eyes, surely to soften the corrosive effects of the pepper. He appeared to be sleeping. Matello, on the other hand, was wide awake and looking at Sylvie.

She stared at him coldly for a few seconds. He held the scrutinizing, hostile gaze of the young lady.

Then, in a firm voice, she said, "When are you going to get my son?"

"Tomorrow." And he explained, "We'll get to Lost Island around nine. Getting you set up there, which wasn't planned, and getting me some rest means I can't leave til tomorrow for Salas where I'm sure I'll pick up the trail of Huronilla. So, tomorrow night or the next day at the latest, I'll give you your son back."

"You should take Adele with you. My God, as long as her milk hasn't dried up from all this horrible emotional trauma..."

She looked worriedly at the nanny. For a few minutes it was only Sylvie the mother who was thinking and only this: how are they feeding Pierre during all this time? How am I going to do it if Adele is run dry or if her milk's gone bad?

"Monsieur," she turned back to Matello, "the life of a three-month old child is fragile. I don't know where you're taking me or what you plan to do with me or my son. We'll deal with that when you've given him back to me and we can be sure that he'll be fed properly. But if my son dies, there will be no word to express the loathing and hatred with which my husband and I will hunt you down. You are madly deluded if you think there is anything you can do to render us unable to punish you. Whatever power you have, whatever plan you're working on, keep in mind that its success and your very life depends on the life of my son."

"Madame..."

"Be quiet! Nothing you can say means anything right now. Make sure you get my son and that he doesn't die, that he doesn't get hurt in any way. Nothing else matters. For the moment, let me take care of Adele. Do you have anything here to help her? Some warm water for her eyes? A sedative for her nerves?"

Humbled and also finding Sylvie admirably strong and reasonable in her motherly love, Matello answered respectfully, simply and quickly, "Madame, there's an electric kettle and a complete medical kit."

"Well, what are you waiting for? Heat up some water and bring me the kit."

"I'll be glad to help, madame."

After three hours of flight, the dual-purpose plane (regular plane with its automatic landing gear and seaplane in its hull and floats) first set down on calm water and then cruised up the sloping bank of Lost Island and finally stopped in front of an opening in the wall where the barracks had been ingeniously transformed into a small aircraft hangar.

Adele was already less maudlin and out of her daze, but she still needed care, reassurance, encouragement in order to go back with Matello to become nurse and nanny again, if, that is, her nursing abilities were intact. Sylvie was acting like a sister to her. She did not think of the circumstances. The mother in her was concerned only with the milk to keep her son alive!

On the ground floor they gave her two adjoining rooms, comfortably furnished not in a modern way but in the style of Louis-Philippe, King of France in the 19th century. Sylvie did not even notice the anomaly.

In the evening Adele was back to normal. And thank heavens, Sylvie was sure that the fright of the abominable night before had had no harmful effects on her body. The two women ate and drank. Then they slept. The next day, when Matello came to fetch Adele, they said their goodbyes with hope for the future.

Sylvie Saint-Clair was so preoccupied with this hope, from which she drove away every pessimistic fear, that she did notice the change in Joao Matello... the tremendous change...

The man, usually so calm and self-assured, so clearly confident in himself and his destiny, so proud and haughty, this man was pale, agitated, his darting eyes were full of both worry and anger. His shoulders were hunched and he spoke quietly, saying only what was strictly necessary, unlike earlier when he always seemed to wax eloquent before Sylvie...

What had happened on Lost Island to transform Matello in this way?

Sylvie did not ask because she did not see it.

Still the mother hypnotized by her lost child but who would soon be together again, Sylvie was waiting, just waiting. She was, body and soul, on hold—and nothing else, nothing more. Sitting in front of the window from which she could see the ocean through a slot in the fortress wall—the ocean over which the plane would make a wide turn as it came back and descended—Sylvie did not move. She did not go to eat at noon at the table that a young, smiling, though timid Galician girl had set with a beautiful tablecloth, heavy silver and precious porcelain full of appetizing treats. No, she waited, her eyes, her attention, her soul focused on the sea. This wait did not cause her anxiety. She was sure, convinced, absolutely certain that maybe this afternoon but today surely the plane would be back and she would see in the hangar, clearly visible down below, Adele carrying Pierre back to her.

In fact, such was the case. The plane came back, skated over the water, rolled up the slope and disappeared into the hangar. Moments later Adele came out with Pierre in her arms.

Only then did Sylvie move. She stood up at the window. Happy and not at all surprised, she saw the nanny cross the bare space that separated the main castle from the barracks. When the corner of the building hid her from sight, she turned around, walked to the door and opened it

She called out, "Adele! Adele!"

"Madame, little Pierre is just fine!"

"Oh, thank God!"

The child was handed over by the smiling nanny. With tears of joy, overwhelmed by her emotions, babbling tender nonsense, laughing joyously, Sylvie kissed and coddled little Pierre. Then she held him out and looked at him. He opened wide his sparkling eyes and waved his little pink hands. The mother did not see the dirty, torn jacket, she saw only her living child, healthy and smiling instinctively, out of habit and obviously because he recognized his "mama".

All of a sudden Adele was pushed aside by a hand on her shoulder and Sylvie, who at that moment was starting to cuddle Pierre to feel his warm, breathing body against hers, Sylvie Saint-Clair saw a woman walking towards her. The face and eyes of this woman had such an intense expression of wry and cynical joy, such a cruel, savage, ruthless joy, that Sylvie felt a violent jolt run through her entire body and immediately the loving mother turned into the passionate spouse. By some native intuition, only accessible to people who combine high intelligence with extreme sensitivity, she knew that this woman was the enemy. Her mind was no longer babbling, "Pierrot" but shouting "Leo"! An inner cry for help, a cry of fear and foreboding, but also an incitement to courage, calm and self-control.

Holding her child against her chest like a shield, Sylvie stared stonily at the woman who stared back savagely.

Sylvie was the first to speak. "Who are you?"

The woman laughed insolently, shrugged her shoulders and replied in a melodious voice but guarded, as if veiled, making her words sound like a threat. "Bravo! Just as I imagine Sylvie MacDuhl. I see her in Sylvie Saint-Clair. Both of you deserve an answer, madame. But my name will mean nothing to you. I am Titania."

It was Sylvie's turn to laugh and shrug her shoulders. She added contempt and cockiness to her voice. "Titania? Why, that's a stage name."

"Or a *nom de guerre*," she shot back gruffly. And then more frigidly she said, "In fact, you're right. Titania, a stage name, why not. But for you, Sylvie Saint-Clair, it will be a stage set for tragedy."

Her dark eyes flashed and changing her tone of voice again, she spoke again, more serene and serious, "Please sit down. We have to talk. This woman," she motioned briefly toward Adele, "can listen. She's of no importance. Besides, you'll give her your son if his squirming or crying bothers our conversation. Don't mind if I take this armchair. And now, are your ready to listen?"

"I will, madame," Sylvie said, sitting in a chair near the table and holding Pierre in her arms, rocking him gently, out of habit and maybe unconsciously. "I will but first a question. Who is keeping me prisoner? Is it you or the man calling himself Joao Matello?"

The pretty, purple lips of Titania smiled briefly and the woman answered simply, "Joao Matello is dead. He betrayed me, so I killed him. His accomplice, young Peul, doesn't matter. I'll tell you more about them later. It is I and I alone who are holding you prisoner here, madame."

At this first, unexpected information from Titania, Sylvie did not bat an eyelash. She was expecting all kinds of surprises. She knew more were coming, which would surprise her less. She was aware that a great battle was underway. She thought of Leo. She hoped, believed, was sure that he was free and on the move. She, Sylvie, while waiting for deliverance, had to be ready for anything, to face anything, to retain her strength and morale against all odds.

She said, "Madame, I'm listening. Please speak calmly so as not to wake up my son who is sleeping."

Titania nodded, "You're tough. But look at me and understand that nothing you do or say is going to prevail over me.

"I've already taken a good look at you," Sylvie replied. "You're beautiful, strong, still young... For reasons unknown to me you're playing a game that's completely mysterious to me. Hatred, murder, mystery, criminal deceit and abuse of power—you are all these in my eyes. So, explain yourself, madame, since you've asked me to listen and I've agreed."

"Very well," Titania said. "It's a pleasure to battle with you and it'll be even more pleasurable to make you suffer. I'll explain. I'll tell you a story. A very short story that I'm sure won't bore you."

After a brief silence:

"When the man who is now your husband defeated Leonid Zattan, did you ever hear of Diana Ivanovna Krosnovief?"

Hearing this name Sylive could not help shuddering and for a second her eyes showed surprise. But she answered in a calm, normal voice, "Yes, madame, he called her, I believe, the Red Princess."

"Indeed. Did you know that Diana Ivanovna was deeply, passionately in love with Leonid, Prince of Issyk Kul, and that she loved even more, perhaps, the certainty that once married to Zattan the conqueror she would be a kind of reigning dictator herself, side by side with her husband, over all of Asia and Europe, which would become an Asian colony?"

"I did hear about this one day from a Polish man, Ignace Kiewicz and his wife, the sweet and pretty Nadine."

At Sylvie's response Titania suddenly turned pale and squinted, then guffawed abruptly before resuming her tale.

"So, you can understand what Diana Ivanovna had lost on the day that Leonid Zattan, defeated, despoiled and defenseless, was sent to prison on an island where he died soon thereafter. But what you can't understand, probably because you don't know certain things, is what the Red Princess suffered during the fall of Zattan."

With her face frozen in impassive gentleness as she rocked her sleeping son and her perfectly tranquil blue eyes staring into that pair of dark eyes, both stone-cold and fiercely ablaze, of the strange and beautiful enemy, Sylvie Saint-Clair uttered:

"In fact, I don't know."

"Listen up," the other snapped back. "By a despicable betrayal this Ignace Kiewicz and his wife Nadine captured Diana. They pretended to be friends and allies, devoted to Zattan, but they were lying. They pursued Diana with an invidious, ruthless and patient hatred. When they felt that Zattan was about to be crushed by the Nyctalope they showed their true natures. Diana was their prisoner, then the prisoner of his brother, Stanislas. This Stanislas made his prisoner suffer unspeakable tortures, mental, emotional and physical torments, unimaginable, cruel and sophisticated... But the Red Princess survived with her mind intact. And it was a good thing because after three months of living at the mercy, so to speak, of her executioner, her torturer, Stanislas Kiewicz died. He died in tragic circumstances that allowed Diana to escape. Are you following me, Madame Saint-Clair?"

"I hear every word you say."

"Great. Free now, the Red Princess went to work straightaway on rebuilding new bases for the universal terrorist organization that Leonid Zattan had not put into action in time. She succeeded. By unbreakable bonds she united with a relatively unknown scientist who is, in truth, the greatest, deepest, boldest genius of our time. She set two goals. The first, to take revenge on the men and women who were the direct cause of Zattan's downfall and of her own suffering in the hands of Stanislas Kiewicz. Secondly, to do what Zattan had not done, that is to conquer Europe through Asia and put Asia under the rule of a single authority that she herself, Diana would hold the reins of. I won't lie to you, the second goal is still in the works. But the first, oh, the first is like a flaming bull's eye two hundred feet away. And Diana Ivanovna is starting to shoot! She's already hit it once and she's got in her sights to hit it three more times. More will follow. Ha..."

Another short, vicious laugh broke out before she went on, panting a little.

"The first bull's eye was Ignace Kiewicz. He's dead. Someday you'll see with your own eyes, which will be even more beautiful than they are now, you'll see how he died. The second bull's eye was Nadine his wife. And the third... ha... the third target... and the fifth... Yes, the fifth because I'm still not absolutely sure about the fourth even though the trap is now set for the prey to fall into... So, the third and the fifth targets are..."

She stopped there, leaned forward and changed her tone.

"But me, madame, if Titania is a stage name as you say or a *nom de guerre* as I say, do you know who I am?"

Although she was getting scared more by what she imagined than by what she heard, Sylvie remained the calm, affectionate mother who was listening to an interesting story while rocking her sleeping baby. She had been waiting for this direct question asked by Titania. She did not hesitate to answer.

Serenely she said, "It's not too hard to guess, madame. You are Princess Diana Ivanovna Krosnovief."

Leaning even farther forward toward her victim, "Good. I figured you wouldn't hesitate. But now, guess who are the third, fifth and then the fourth targets for my flaming arrow... Can you guess? No? Yes? Come on, don't turn pale... your eyes are flickering... You don't dare pronounce the names? Well then, I'll tell you."

She raised her hand and pointed her finger.

Her voice had turned hoarse as she growled, "The third target is this Pierre, your Pierre, Pierre Saint-Clair. He will die slowly in front of you and your husband, whom I'll capture soon. And Leo Saint-Clair the Nyctalope will be the fourth. You'll watch him suffer like Nadine watched Ignace. You'll watch him die like she watched her husband die. And then you, Sylvie Mac Duhl, whom Leonid Zattan might have betrayed me for if his victory had been crowned, you, Sylvie, will be the fifth. You will die slowly like Nadine will soon die."

She stood up and walked, pointing with her right index finger because at her first threat Sylvie had jumped up and was starting to back up, trembling, horrified, and her maternal instinct compelled her to hide the face of sleeping Pierre under his jacket. She retreated all the way to the back of the room. Next to the window she ran into the wall. Since the Red Princess had stopped too and was brushing the jacket with her outstretched hand, Sylvie jumped to the side and shouted:

"Don't touch my child, don't touch him, or else..."

"Or else what?" Diana sneered.

"Well..." Sylvie's eyes flashed. Then she put the baby on the bed and ordered, "Adele, take him!"

Suddenly she turned around and pounced.

It was not in vain that Sylvie had kept her body supple and strong. As spouse and soon-to-be mother, she had kept exercising moderately but daily. After the birth of her son, when nature's whim deprived her of milk and thus kept her from feeding her baby, she again worked on giving her classically beautiful body, which maternity had not blemished or impaired, the athletic training she had been so proud of when younger.

And it was indeed an athlete who attacked the Red Princess.

Stunned right off by a well-placed punch, Diana groaned, covered her face, wobbled... A shove sent her to the floor. Sylvie was on her in a flash, her hands wrapped around her throat and squeezing hard. She was not acting out of blind rage. She was clear-headed, cold, determined. She figured his woman was the Enemy who had been secret up until now and out of vanity and foolishness had just revealed herself. Suddenly Huronilla's words, at first mysterious but now very clear, came to mind: "*Aplasta la vibora, matala!* Crush the viper, kill her!"

Sylvie was thinking, "I won't crush her but I'll strangle her to death!"

She had no idea what would happen afterwards. She was thinking of nothing but the deed itself. It was plenty. Kill the viper, destroy the enemy of Leo, herself, Pierre, that was all that was needed... And her two long, beautiful hands transformed into a steel vise. Sylvie was killing the Red Princess!

In vain was Diana energized by the threat of mortal danger. She struggled, twisted and turned, tried to break the lethal grip.

Sylvie was straddling her enemy's chest, her knees planted solidly on the carpet, her arms hard and stiff like iron bars. She was as solid as rock and she was squeezing.

All of a sudden the Red Princess was beaten: her eyes twitched; her arms went limp; her whole body stopped moving...

It was then that two huge black hands seized Sylvie by the shoulders and yanked her back, squeezing her hard enough to break her bones as she was pulled away from her victim. Pulled away, lifted up like a sack of flour by a giant. The two monstrous hands threw her on the bed, rolled her in the blanket and tied it closed.

"Adele! Adele!" Sylvie called out, not losing her head, which was sticking out of the wrapping, "Come and see for yourself! Come, come!"

Though choked by terror Adele obeyed. She emerged from a corner of the room and rushed over with little Pierre in her arms. The child was woken up and starting to cry and shake.

"Adele, get on the bed, climb over me and sit there, yes, next to the wall... And feed Pierre so he'll calm down. He's safe now. The viper is dead! I killed her!"

2 fr.

TITANIA   Jean de LA HIRE

ÉCRASE LA VIPÈRE !...

Collections hebdomadaires du
LIVRE NATIONAL
ÉDITIONS JULES TALLANDIER
75, Rue Dareau, PARIS (XIVᵉ)

PART TWO: CRUSH THE VIPER!

CHAPTER I
The electric speedboat

Alas! No, Sylvie had not killed the Red Princess and Diana Ivanovna was not dead. The giant Nubian who had come to rescue her had saved her life. Just in time! Two seconds later the strangling would have been successful and death would have replaced life. But before the first of these seconds had ticked by, life was still there. It only took a light massage of the throat and chest for this life to reassert itself.

The Nubian had quickly ripped the top of her dress to bare her chest and he worked like a professional in massaging her heart. Less than two minutes... and Diana gasped and opened her eyes.

Awake and immediately aware, in a hoarse voice she said, "Thank you Hamed! You saved my life."

"I came just in time, mistress."

"Where is she?"

"On the bed."

"You didn't kill her, I hope."

"Oh no, didn't even beat her. Rolled up tight in a blanket."

"And the baby?"

"Uh, I don't know."

"Stop, that's enough. I feel fine. Help me up."

He stopped massaging, which the conversation had not interrupted. Standing up, he held out a strong hand to Diana who grabbed it with both of hers and lifted herself up. She was a little wobbly, but the giant's arm supported her. And her eyes met those of Sylvie.

Silence. Staring. Defiance and pride in those blue eyes. Hatred and menace in the dark eyes.

Then, "Sylvie," the Red Princess said, her voice still hoarse and short of breath, "you've lost."

"Not yet, Diana!" the prisoner shot back. "As long as Leo's free..."

"I'll get him."

"I doubt it. And as long as he's alive..."

"I'll kill him."

"Unless he kills you first!"

"Your child, Sylvie…"

"You won't touch him as long as his father's out there because you know that if you even scratch little Pierre, Leo will make you wish you'd never left the Pole's torture room."

"But I told you I'm going to capture your Leo."

"So be it! Until then, you won't lay a finger on my son, nor on me or the Adele because the child needs both of us… I've lost, true, and I do believe that you're going to be on your guard now. And Leo will beat you!"

"Well, I accept your challenge," Diana acknowledged.

Keeping one hand on her throat and using the other to hold her torn dress closed, the Red Princess smiled at the Nubian and said, "Hamed, come with me. Leave her here. She can get the nanny to unwrap her."

Sylvie had no problem getting "the nanny to unwrap her" since the calm and soothing voice of her mistress reassured her. The life of the prisoners was organized on the spot.

Sylvie said, "Adele, stay calm. Think only of taking care of us and Pierre. Either I'm sorely mistaken or they'll give us whatever we need. This evil woman will do nothing against me or my son until she's got hold of my husband. But my husband is stronger and he'll set us free. I'm sure, absolutely certain of it. What just happened will never happen again. We'll be treated well as prisoners so that when she wants to have her way with us, we'll be good martyrs, completely conscious and capable, physically and mentally, of suffering for a long time. But my husband will set us free and he'll kill this woman before she'll dare to even touch us…"

For the moment, at least, Sylvie was right. Her prison was comfortable, the food impeccable. She realized this the next day, June 4. In the big room, heated during the night by an electric radiator, a Galician servant brought a breakfast of excellent chocolate, condensed milk, honey and fresh bread. The prisoners learned that—what had been less and less practiced even in Spain—the bread was handmade in the old way on Lost Island. The honey came from Aragon, stored in plenty in the supplies barracks.

The Galician spoke Castilian, a language very familiar to Sylvie. "Do you need anything, madame? I have orders to relay to the steward your requests. We will do everything we can to satisfy your desires."

Decisive and practical, Sylvie asked that they vary the meals, that the food be simple but carefully prepared, that they bring soft sheets and towels for Pierre, that they set up a crib next to the nanny's bed in the next room, which was safe because it was really just a big alcove with no other door except the one opening onto Sylvie's room.

June 4 was spent asking for, receiving and arranging the things to help Pierre and Adele feel less deprived.

Titania did not show up.

But the next day, Sunday June 5, at 1 p.m. the Red Princess was announced by a servant. Five minutes later she came in. She took only a couple of steps past the doorway. She looked at little Pierre who was naked, laughing and babbling on Sylvie's knees, smiling and fidgeting constantly. She looked at Sylvie herself, than at Adele who was sewing (they had brought her a kit) diapers from pre-cut fabric of fine, soft cotton.

Without a trace of anger or menace in her eyes or voice, she said simply, "Madame, before springing the trap to catch the Nyctalope, I wrote him a letter. I told him you were in my possession with your son and nanny and you were being well cared for. But I warned him that if he or his friends tried to find and come to your prison and if his attempts seemed in any way threatening to my projects, I would take you immediately to another prison, much less comfortable, even more inaccessible, where you three would suffer a great deal. I added that I wouldn't hesitate to take away your son, even if meant his death, if he dared search for and eventually discover this second prison. Do you understand?"

"Yes," Sylvie said as calmly and simply as Titania herself.

"Good. Do you want to write something yourself? You'd authenticate my letter and your husband would get news from you personally. Of course, your note will have to be very short, no details about where you're being held, this place that I know the idiot Joao Matello called Lost Island. Anyway, that explains why I let the Galician servant of yours give you some information about the daily life here on the island. So, do you want to write to your husband?"

"Yes. Adele, take Pierre."

"Here's my pen and some paper." The surprising Red Princess—although she wasn't surprising the Nyctalope's wife—handed over a pen and small notebook.

Standing up, unruffled, with a firm hand Sylvie wrote:

"My Leo, do as the love for your wife and son bids you. They are treating us fine. Despite the ordeals of our kidnapping and the initial imprisonment, our physical and mental states are good because even with the threats they're making against you, maybe because of these threats, we have hope in you! Adele can still nurse. Pierrot is still a cute little glutton. I love you. I'm waiting for you. I have faith. Sylvie."

She gave the pen and notebook back to Titania. "Here's the note you can add to the letter."

The Red Princess smiled. She had read it, upside down, while Sylvie was writing.

She said, "You're strong. Nevertheless, you're mine. And soon I'll have the Nyctalope. Your strengths combined won't be enough to endure what I've got in store for you without you going insane... According to my latest information your former pretend employee, the so-called chauffeur of your husband, that Gnô Mitang is at Nopals in Saint-Jean-Cap-Ferrat. No doubt your husband will join him there. Maybe he already has. That's where I'll send the letter. It'll push the Nyctalope right into the trap I'm setting for him, which will incline his friends like the Duke d'Arandar, who is searching zealously for you right now, to curb their enthusiasm."

But Sylvie did not seem to hear. She had taken the baby back from Adele and was once again sitting in the big armchair, making faces and tickling her Pierrot.

Titania sneered, turned around and left. The outside lock clicked loudly, even more loudly than when the Galician girl had locked the door.

"Watch out!" Gnô said. "It's getting really narrow!"

"It widens out again after this bottleneck," Saint-Clair replied.

"Sure, but will we make it through?"

"Let's hope so."

A minute later Socca said, "We've made it."

It was noon, June 5. For several hours, sliding and bouncing the plane on the waves, the four men were searching for a safe haven for the *Goéland III*, a hiding place like the Nyctalope had envisioned so that they could put into action his plan concerning Viper Island. South of Cape Tarinana, getting closer to the bay of the secret isle, Saint-Clair and his friends were inspecting all the inlets, one by one. The beautiful, calm weather made it easy to navigate over the water.

The searchers were starting to despair of finding a suitable spot on this side of the coast, meaning north of *La Vibora*, and were considering going back to Cape Torinana so that they could get back in the air, make a wide detour and start searching to the south around Cape Finisterre, when they saw an inlet that looked much deeper and meandering than what they had seen so far.

Gnô was piloting. With a wave of his hand Saint-Clair got him to turn the Goéland III into the channel. It twisted between high, steep cliffs dropping into deep water. After two turns the waves were barely felt. After the third it was dead calm. Naturally, the place was totally invisible from the ocean. But the channel became so narrow that the four men thought the plane might not pass through. But it did. Then it was floating on the still water of fairly round bay like a giant well with straight, smooth walls made of the cliffs over 300 feet high. This architectural whim of nature in this dream location made the four men gasp in wonder and contentment.

Rimming the bay, fifteen to twenty feet above water level (and it was high tide at the moment) the circular rock walls were deeply hollowed out, forming a vaulted half-tunnel with a base almost seventy feet wide.

"Look, there!" the Nyctalope shouted. "That's a first class, natural shelter for our plane! Not will the *Goéland III* be safe here from storms but the over-hang will hide from any potential passers-by in the mountains or in the air. What luck!"

"A good omen," Gnô smiled.

"Yes, a good omen," Saint-Clair repeated gravely.

The plane was soon anchored in the deepest recess and moored to rocky outcrops.

"Let's have lunch," Saint-Clair said. "But a quick one. I'm eager to get out there and see the island as close as we can get in the strait separating it from the land."

"I'll go with you," Gnô volunteered.

"Of course. And Socca too. You, Vitto, will stay here."

"Very well, monsieur."

Although hardy, the meal was brief.

"Monsieur," Socca said, "I noticed that just before the narrowest spot in the bottleneck there's a small inlet crossing it with a creek running into it. We can get there with a skiff, which would be easy to hide in the rocks. If we follow the creek up we can get to the top of the mountain."

"Good, let's get the skiff ready."

Vitto and Socca pulled a half-folded bundle out of the upper hatch of the plane. The two men neatly unfolded it and tightened the thumbscrews of the braces and tensioners. Then they had a small boat with two paddles in which four men could easily squeeze in if they did not move around much. But one or two could sail it even in rough waters.

"Gnô and Socca, arm yourselves. We have to prepare for the worst. Brownings and a blade. I'll bring the binoculars as well. Ready?"

"Yes, Leo."

"I am, monsieur."

"Get in! See you later, Vitto."

"Good luck!"

"Thanks."

The Nyctalope slipped softly into the boat. He sat in the middle with Gnô in the back and Socca kneeling up front paddling. Within minutes they had reached the bottleneck, which was almost too narrow for the big plane but plenty wide for the skiff. They entered the cross-channel on the south side. When they got out of the skiff, they laid it upside-down in the jumble of rocks where the creek came pouring into the cove. The ravine was steep and rocky, hard climbing. The three men made the ascent fast and furiously.

"Watch out when we're on top," the Nyctalope said. "Don't stand up right away. We won't know how far away the island is or if we'll be hidden or out in the open with respect to it. We should come out slow and stealthy."

And so they did.

First, lying flat on their bellies, then kneeling at the top of the cliff, the three men saw straightaway that they were overlooking this landscape: a deep ravine plunging down the mountainous terrain into a relatively low headland beyond which was a deep, jagged bay where the secret island lurked like a monstrous beast, like a nightmarish, geometrical crab...

The headland was none other than the Cape of La Vibora of the Escarpaz documents.

The Nyctalope's face had turned pale, fraught with emotions. He thought, "Undoubtedly, that's one of, if not the main, hideout of the Hashshashins, the enemy's stronghold. Is the enemy really Huronilla's *La Vibora*? The Red Princess of Gnô's hypotheses and Matello's confession? Are Sylvie and Pierre really there? Probably. If Matello told us about this island when he was revealing everything about the Hashshashins, it's because he himself had hidden Sylvie and Adele here and then the Viper brought Pierre after taking him from the gypsy girl... Yes, it all makes sense!"

He took out the binoculars. Aiming and focusing them he announced aloud:

"I see what must be the main building of the fort, which I'm surprised wasn't mentioned in Vauban's *Memoirs*. The island is quite extraordinary. What's even more extraordinary is that we knew nothing about its existence. It's unknown to all authorities, at least in Spain. There are customs officers on the coast, like on every coast, even the wildest, most deserted shores of modern nations. How did the customs office, its directors, the Spanish government... how did Elisée Reclus' geography and all the tour guides not mention this architectural island oddity? We'll have to find out, Gnô... when we've got time..."

"Maybe it'd be useful," Gnô said, "to get some information right away from the Spanish officials. If our guesses are correct and Matello didn't lie, this island is the lair of criminals and the home of a well-organized, international conspiracy. It's weird enough that a civilized nation would let it exist in its territorial waters but it would be too weird if it didn't know that it existed."

"Right you are," the Nyctalope said, putting the binoculars back in his pocket. "But in the meantime, let's follow our plan."

"Okay."

"So let's get as close as possible to the bay and island. Cape of La Vibora is too open, no trees or bushes and the rocks are smooth. Forget the cape. But down the ridge of the headland where we are, we'll go around the bay to that spur down there that's covered with pines and oak trees. We can go through the trees to the water's edge exactly where the channel is narrowest between the land and the island. Gnô, any objections?"

"No."

"Let's go! And don't forget to stay hidden behind the rocks and bushes as we go. If the island is what we believe, it'd be unthinkably stupid not to have eyes watching day and night over this crazy fort. Since our enemies are supposed to be intelligent and prudent... Do you hear me, Socca?"

"Yes, monsieur."

"You go first and if you've got any suspicion at all, stop!"

It was a tough, tiring walk that wound around, climbed and dropped over the distance of two and a half miles. It took more than an hour but they finally reached their goal: the farthest point of the wooded spur at the end of the bay, facing what one would call the "back" of the island, which was longer than it was wide, pointed sharply out of the fort on the ocean side but rounded into a half-circle on the shore opposite the coast.

There the strong currents raced through the two hundred yards of the channel. The wooded spur ended in a high cliff from which the men could see the whole island, all its angles and the linear details of its geometric shape.

Between two bushes, in the shade of a maritime pine tree, the three men were lying flat on the bellies next to one another, their eyes glued to the mysterious island.

The relatively short distance allowed them to see perfectly well with the naked eye. The central building, the barracks and bulwarks, the sloping rock and especially the tiny port were clearly visible. In the port there was a speedboat with an engine that was probably electric. It was long, slim, with beautiful lines and could probably navigate the sea in any weather.

At first the three observers saw no movement. Nothing on the terrace of the main building, nothing in the round courtyard, nothing on the walls, nothing in the port or on the slope. However, the windows were uncovered, the glass reflecting the sunlight.

Gnô whispered, "Seeing this island, even from here, you could imagine that from the bridge of a ship out at sea it would blend right in with the rocky coast because they're the same color and the island's really low."

"That's true," Saint-Clair agreed.

And again they fell silent, continuing their surveillance.

But then at the end of the little half-moon bay a small door in a barracks opened and three men stepped out. One was dressed as a yachtsman, the two others as common sailors. They looked like they belonged to one of the private luxury yachts, which are not rare in the tourist season on the coasts of Spain and Portugal. They could have left from San Sebastian or even Nice, Monte Carlo, Marseilles or Barcelona, and sailed around the Iberian Peninsula on a pleasure tour.

"Good," Saint-Clair said, "they're getting in. I'll bet that speedboat is used to bring supplies to the island. In Vigo or La Corogne those three guys can plausibly say that they're coming from a big luxury yacht anchored in a nearby bay. In case the authorities get curious, they just have to pull out some forged papers and be polite. Gnô, if the speedboat takes off with those three men, we should take it. You were asking me about an action plan and I told you I'd be inspired by circumstances. Well, what do you think of my inspiration?"

"Excellent. In any case, they've got to have eyes and ears constantly on alert on the island. Plus, if our hypotheses are correct, keep in mind that the great scientific brain of Korridès ought to have set up an electronic or electromagnetic defense system working automatically. Therefore, if we try to take the island by force, no matter how clever, brave and daring, we'd probably be running into impenetrable barriers and an impregnable surveillance. Conclusion: the idea of capturing the boat seems like a good idea no matter how you look at it."

"After that," Saint-Clair said with a smile, "we can wait for more circumstances to inspire us. So far, they've been pretty good to us."

During this brief conversation the three men down below did indeed get into the speedboat. When it was clear from their actions that they were going to take off, leave the port and head out for an unknown destination, Saint-Clair said:

"Ah, there's no time to lose. Whether they're going north or south, we have time, if we run fast, to get to the plane, pull out of the cove and sweep down on it as soon as it heads for Corogne or else make a wide turn at sea and catch it off guard before it reaches Vigo."

While talking he started crawling away, followed by his two partners. When they got into the woods they stood up and ran as fast as the terrain allowed until they got back to the skiff. It took a lot less time to go back than it had to come because they knew where the tough spots were. Moreover, they knew where to stay hidden from any would-be watchers on the island.

Once in the skiff they paddled hard to get to the plane. In two minutes the skiff was folded and put back, the *Goéland III* unmoored, the anchor pulled up and the plane was skimming fast over the water.

As soon as they got out of the narrow pass Saint-Clair, who was piloting, turned the plane north. In the meantime, his companions keep a close eye on the sea. On leaving the island, as Saint-Clair had said, the speedboat could go either to Corogne or to Vigo. In the first case they would spot it quickly. In the second, they would have to wait five minutes for it to get farther away from the island. Then they would take off, get some altitude and inevitably spot the speedboat, which they only had to sweep down on from the sea.

This waiting time was pushed to seven minutes by Saint-Clair. Then he said, "We can take off now. If the boat was coming this way, meaning towards Corogne, we'd have seen it as soon as we got out of the channel."

"That's right," Gnô said. "It's certainly heading for Vigo."

At that very moment the *Goéland III* took off and soared up diagonally into the calm sky to the north, then veering to the left, to the east, and making a wide curve over the ocean that would take it south of the island between Cape Finisterre and Vigo. The plane was two-thirds through this wide curve when Gnô, the watcher, Saint-Clair still at the wheel, and Socca watching the controls, announced in his tranquil voice:

"Leo, the speedboat is in sight, headed south. It's going fast, leaving behind a long wake."

"Good," Saint-Clair said.

And his eyes sparkled, his lips smiled, two signs of being combat ready, especially when victory was assured.

"Good. We'll capture the boat and the three men. I'm sure that'll come in handy. In any case, at least we'll get some valuable information."

In its course the *Goéland III* had basically made a complete tour of Cape Finisterre and could have dropped onto the speedboat two or three nautical miles from the cape, but Saint-Clair and Gnô had a quick discussion and preferred to attack as far as possible from the island and so closer to Vigo.

Gnô consulted the map and said, "The best place looks like around Cape Corrubedo. It's right in between Vigo and the secret island. If the boat's really going to Vigo or even to Pontecedra, which is a little farther north, it'll skirt by Cape Corrubedo while the bigger ships, there are three of them in sight right now, are far out to sea."

"Yes," Saint-Clair agreed. "Good thinking. The place is perfect so that nobody comes to the rescue. But since the boat is a lot slower than us, we can come in from the south and catch it heading north."

And so they did.

The two clocks on the *Goéland III* showed 4:12 p.m. when the plane descended toward the sea. It landed not far from the speedboat on the starboard side and glided over the waves to it. When the two crafts, at the same speed, were no more than 20 fathoms away from each other, Gnô, Socca and Vitto climbed onto the hull in front of the hatch where there was a movable guardrail to hold onto.

Socca, whose voice could boom very clearly, started shouting, "Ahoy! Ahoy! Speedboat! Stop right now or we'll open fire!"

Kneeling on the flat hull, their bellies against the railing, the three men shouldered their rifles. Maybe the guys in the speedboat were considering putting up a fight because while one of them stayed at the helm, the two others ducked, as if to grab weapons.

Socca's voice turned harder, more menacing, "Stand up! And put your hands up or we'll shoot!"

It had an immediate effect. The sailors stood up. One of them made a show of dropping the rifle he had picked up, then he raised his arms.

"Stop! You, stop the boat!"

Gnô was an excellent shot. He fired and the small English flag that was waving in the front of the boat was struck, its short pole cut clean off by the bullet. The demonstration did the trick. The man at the wheel leaned to the left, pulled two levers and in the back of the boat there was a big eddy. Almost immediately the speedboat was only drifting, then completely stopped by propellers spinning in reverse.

The ocean was calm enough for the boat and the plane to idle together harmlessly.

Saint-Clair's voice was heard by Gnô, Socca and Vitto saying, "Cap Corrubedo has two headlands. I see a little bay between them, should be deep enough and no waves. Tell the speedboat to go in there and I'll follow."

The order was transmitted by Socca. The elegant officer of the speedboat obeyed. Constantly in the sights of the three rifles, he maneuvered the boat into the back of the bay. There, as was expected, the plane could drop anchor and the speedboat remain almost directly under its wing in front of the passenger door on the right.

Saint-Clair and Gnô jumped from the plane to the speedboat while Vitto and Socca, still on the flat part of the hull, kept watch, rifles at the ready. The Nyctalope and the Japanese carried no weapons. They knew now that they had no need.

Standing in the back of the luxurious, powerful speedboat, they had the officer and two sailors before them, also standing and lined up. The two sailors were around forty years old, the officer much younger. He had an expression that was both insolent and forlorn. The sailors looked unhappy and ashamed.

Saint-Clair addressed the young yachtsman, "Monsieur, you and your two men are my prisoners. Whether or not you know about the combat you're mixed up in, I'll warn you that my partners and I are acting under a martial law that's nothing like the laws of civilized nations you might call upon. For you that means we won't hesitate to do what we deem necessary, like shoot you and toss your bodies overboard."

With these menacing words, the three men turned pale but the "officer" still had the presence of mind to say, "But who are you and what do you want? It is indeed against every law for you to attack us like pirates."

That might have sounded like proof of courage but the young man's voice was choked and his eyes so brimming with fear that Saint-Clair and Gnô saw only a kind of nervous bluster, a phony front of bravado meant mostly for the two sailors to respect their boss. It was even more obvious by the terrified expression on the young man's face when he heard this response:

"I am Leo Saint-Clair the Nyctalope and this is what I want from you: You will tell me everything you know about the sect of Hashshashins, which you are working for, and about the secret island you just left."

By pronouncing the name of the sect Saint-Clair was testing the waters, so to speak. The results were significant. The young man did not deny knowledge of the Hashshashin nor did he show any surprise but rather, if possible, more fear and confusion. Thus, Saint-Clair and Gnô knew that their hypotheses were very likely to be corroborated. And now there was no reason to beat around the bush.

Saint-Clair went on, "The three of you, sit down. We're here to talk but it won't take long. So, sit down!"

It was an order that the three men obeyed at once. Behind them was a bench sitting against the wall of the small deckhouse. Gnô and Saint-Clair had a semi-circular bench usually used by the captain and pilot of the boat.

"What's your name, monsieur?" Saint-Clair asked in an authoritative voice while his hard eyes drilled into the officer, banishing any thought of lying.

The young man said, "I'm Julien Peul."

"Oho!" the Nyctalope reacted. "Just before dying, Joao Matello mentioned you. How we treat you will depend on how honestly you answer our questions."

Julien Peul, completely submissive, dropping his hands and staring at his feet, muttered, "Monsieur, you're stronger than me. Ask away, I'll answer."

Saint-Clair wasted no more time, "Are my wife and son on the secret island?"

"Yes… on Lost Island."

"Well treated?"

"Yes."

"Where were you going?"

"Vigo."

"Why?"

"To send some mail and get some supplies."

Seeing a gesture that needed no accompanying question from the Nyctalope, Peul continued:

"Monsieur, in the mail there's a letter for you. It's addressed to you at the Nopals Castle, Saint-Jean-Cap-Ferrat. Since it's yours, you can have it right now."

The tone of his voice was pathetic but also a little snide.

Saint-Clair and Gnô were both thinking, "What a weird kid!"

Julien Peul bent down and opened a small chest screwed onto the inner starboard wall. He pulled out a few envelopes among which he chose one and handed it over. Gnô grabbed it with all the others.

Then one of the two sailors stood up, gave a military salute and in a voice trembling with emotion but also betraying a firm will, he said, "Monsieur Nyctalope, I'd like to say something."

As eager as he was to read the extraordinary message arriving so unexpectedly, Saint-Clair held off satisfying his curiosity. He stared at the sailor, a man with a rough, candid face, thick, black beard and mustache and blue-gray eyes looking directly at him.

"Speak!" the Nyctalope said.

"Well, monsieur, whatever he says to you and whatever he does, Julien Peul is our boss only by special delegation, revocable at any time, so I have to warn you about one thing that I'm sure he'll agree…"

"And what's that?" Saint-Clair was very interested.

"Monsieur, get as much as you can out of the present situation but don't think we're going to say or do a thing that might help you do whatever it is you're planning to do on Lost Island. Might as well shoot all three of us right now. We prefer death to the risk, however slight, of facing Titania after betraying her."

Turning his head and looking down at Julien Peul, he put his heavy hand on his shoulder.

The young man was white as a sheet. But he spoke clearly, "Monsieur Saint-Clair, he's right. I'll say the same thing. I'd rather die right now than risk the wrath and vengeance of the Red Princess."

The first sailor turned to the second, "And you?"

He nodded and muttered, "I'd rather kill myself."

"What's your names?" Saint-Clair asked.

"I'm Loustal," the first sailor said, "and my comrade is Marod."

"Are you French?"

"Yes. Both from the Cévennes, the same town. We used to poach. We got caught by a game warden, really bad luck! When we got out of prison we were hired by a guy from Sète. And now we're on Lost Island. We get good pay, which is piling up, but we're like prisoners… until we get old or die, whichever comes first."

"And if we free you?" Gnô asked. "If we put you out of reach of this scary Titania?"

He said, "You're never out of her reach. And we have good reason to be scared. Anyway, I think that's enough talking, maybe too much. Don't ask anything more, please. Marod and I won't say a word, I swear. As for Peul, I advise him to keep his mouth shut."

Julien Peul was calm now and his mind made up because he probably felt he had less to fear from the Nyctalope by keeping quiet than from the Red Princess by talking. He concluded, "Loustal's right. Do what you want with us and the speedboat because you're stronger, but don't bother asking questions, I won't talk."

Saint-Clair and Gnô looked at each other. The former was still holding the envelopes passed to him by Gnô. The latter smiled and cast a glance at them.

"Yes," Saint-Clair said.

He tore off a corner, split it open and took out a piece of paper that he unfolded. Meanwhile, Gnô kept an eye on the three captives even if they were constantly in the sights of Vitto's and Socca's rifles. The Nyctalope read. He kept a straight face, expressed nothing, but a slight tremble in his hands revealed the emotional impact. When his eyes reached the bottom of the page, they went back to the beginning and read again. Then he pulled out the pin that was holding a much smaller square of paper and held the paper in his hand. With the other hand he gave the bigger piece of paper to Gnô and said:

"Read that. Diana Ivanovna thinks I'm in Nopals with you. She isn't so well informed after all. But read."

As impassive as Saint-Clair but certainly less touched because as much as he cared for Sylvie and Pierre, they were not his wife and son, Gnô read the following:

"To Leo Saint-Clair the Nyctalope, in care of Gnô Mitang, Nopals Castle, Saint-Jean-Cap-Ferrat (Maritime Alps). June 5.

"Monsieur, your wife, your son and the nanny Adele are in my power. Their health is fine. It will remain so until you are my prisoner. So, don't worry about them. As far as in my power, your wife has and will have nothing to grieve except her separation from you and the unknown future, which should scare her.

"It will be good for you to discourage your friends from searching for your family. At the least hint that their search is pointing in the right direction and consequently that my plans are threatened, I'll put your family into a much less comfortable prison—they'll suffer terrible hardships. And I won't hesitate to separate the mother from her son, even if it mean his death, if the search uncovers this first, current prison.

"With the hope that you will soon be reunited with Sylvie Mac Duhl and little Pierre in my hands, I remain, forever and always, your ruthless enemy. Titania."

After reading this Gnô looked at Saint-Clair.

The Nyctalope was keeping calm when he said, "Now read this." And he handed him the smaller piece of paper. Gnô took it, as touched now as his friend was at first.

"My Leo, do as the love for your wife and son bids you. They are treating us fine. Despite the ordeals of our kidnapping and the initial imprisonment, our physical and mental states are good because even with the threats they're making against you, maybe because of these threats, we have hope in you! Adele can still nurse. Pierrot is still a cute little glutton. I love you. I'm waiting for you. I have faith. Sylvie."

With a grim look and a hushed voice Gnô said, "The pin."

"Here it is."

Saint-Clair gave him the pin that was still pinched between his fingers. The Japanese carefully reattached the paper and refolded them before handing them back and saying in the same hushed voice with the same grim look:

"These two letters should be kept together until you force Diana Ivanovna to read them aloud in front of you before I kill her with my bare hands."

"As you wish, Gnô. In the letter she wrote 'Sylvie Mac Duhl'. Mac Duhl… You have first dibs on Diana, Gnô, since you watched over the daughter of Gregor Mac Duhl from her earliest childhood…"

"Thanks, Leo. Now let's get to work."

"Right away."

And the Nyctalope was once again the Nyctalope, meaning he was the man who, even more than his eyes could see clearly in the dark of night, could penetrate with the keen vision of his mind the mysteries of men and matters at hand. From this minute forward the Nyctalope embarked on a series of actions, slow and progressive or lightning fast and simultaneous, sometimes unplanned but always logical, for which he was an unrivaled genius. How would he proceed to crush the Viper and save his wife, son and himself from the cruel and murderous wrath of this Gorgon? He did not yet know, but what he did know was that he would triumph no matter what his enemy did.

"First off," he said, "let's look at the mail."

The pack of letters that Peul had taken out of the chest was on Gnô's knees. One by one they examined the envelopes. Saint-Clair's plan was to open those whose name and address piqued his curiosity. They would look at the others later. Thus, one of the envelopes made him raise an eyebrow.

"See here, another letter for me. Did you know about this Peul?"

The young man sounded sincere when he said, "No, monsieur."

And he reacted naturally by leaning over to read the address.

Immediately he cried out, "But that's my writing! Well, a very good forgery of my writing because I never wrote that!"

Gnô said, "We have to see this one right away."

Saint-Clair opened the envelope, took out a piece of paper, unfolded it and showed it to Peul. "Is that your writing and signature?"

"Yes, but I swear I never wrote it."

Saint-Clair chuckled and said, "Diana Ivanovna must be a professional forger. Let's read it."

Softly he read aloud:

"Monsieur, I'm taking a big risk writing to you but the hatred I feel for this woman who's making me her slave and is your worst enemy compels me to defy torture and death. I want to tell you that Sylvie Saint-Clair and your son and nanny are being held on a farm deep in the mountains around fifteen miles north of Santiago de Compostela. There are only three men and two women to guard them. Whether or not you free the prisoners, don't forget that the one writing you is a friend of Joao Matello whom your enemy killed. Matello probably talked about me. My signature will authenticate this letter. Yours truly, Julien Peul."

"Ah, come on!" the young man was pale. "What does this mean? Why would Titania bother to forge such a letter?"

"My God," Saint-Clair said, "it's not to guess. The farm she talks about must have been set up as an ambush where the Red Princess hopes to catch me. She's right to think that your signature would make me trust it since from what Matello told me Titania, by killing him, frustrated all the great plans you were expecting from his allegiance. This letter is very cleverly devious. Psychologically it's true, isn't it Peul?"

"Yes," the young man lowered his head.

"Well," Saint-Clair went on, handing the letters back to Gnô, "that's enough. We'll look at the others later. For now, we have to get moving. Let's go, Peul, cards on the table, do you really ahte the Red Princess?"

"Oh, yes!"

"If you could take vengeance on her and help to bring her down without any danger to yourself, just follow an order I'll give you, would you do it?"

Peul raised his head and with sudden self-confidence said, "Yes, I'll do it. But you said yourself that it's only on the condition that Titania can't suspect me."

"Right, right. The condition will be respected. You'll see for yourself... And you, Lousal, Marod, you're so scared of Titania but do you want to be freed of your slavery without running any risk?"

"Oh, yes, yes," the two sailors chimed in.

"Well then, it's very simple. You were going to Vigo? And so you will and do whatever you were supposed to do there. Even you, Peul, send the one registered letter in the pack, meaning the one to me, not the forgery from you but the real one from Titania. You just have to buy an envelope and blank piece of paper. Address it to Gnô Mitang at Nopals. You can give the postage receipt to Titania to prove that you sent it. As for the others, since they're not registered mail she won't find out until much later that they were intercepted. By then it'll all be over because I'm asking you for three or four days to put an end to everything.

"After doing what you have to do in Vigo, go back to Lost Island normally. Of course, you'll say nothing about this meeting. If you three stay silent about this, if nobody betrays..."

"Oh, monsieur," Peul said, "our shared hatred and our common interests will guarantee our silence."

"I ask only for silence," Saint-Clair went on. "I'm not asking you to do anything for me. You're not obliged to conspire with me in any way to help me get on the island. No. Simply, from the moment we split up in a few minutes, forget about this meeting, about this conversation. Act as if your trip to Vigo went off without a hitch.

"I'm sure no one saw or will see us. The sea is deserted, the ships that were passing by have gone. These steep cliffs are completely barren. In a pinch, if by some extraordinary set of circumstances Titania finds out that your speedboat veered off course for a few minutes, you can just say that you had to find a peaceful place to repair a minor problem with the engine. Moreover, the plan I'm going to put into action won't compromise you because once we're separated I'll forget all about you. I don't need you. On my word. Does the word of the Nyctalope reassure you three?"

The faces watching him showed relief. Whatever faults these three men had, maybe even whatever their crimes, they caught a glimpse of a rehabilitation or at least a kind of freedom to start over. Obviously, the slavery the Red Princess was imposing and the constant threat against them made the financial benefits of their peculiar situation a rather bitter boon.

Peul saw very clearly that the ambitions nursed in his imagination were unattainable among the Hashshashins now that he had been compromised by Matello's betrayal. As for the two sailors, the vision of a comfortable retirement as old men gave no comfort to the extreme hardship of their present slavery.

They all answered, "Yes, monsieur, we're reassured. We'll do as you say and stay quiet."

"All right then. Now, any more time together would be wasted time. One last piece of advice. If for any reason you feel jeopardized on Lost Island, be brave and jump in the water, swim for the shore. You can easily get to Vigo on land and lose anyone chasing you. Once there, go to the governor and say that I sent you for temporary asylum in the city jail. The cell will be the safest place against any attack by Titania. I'll get you out when she can no longer do any harm to anyone.

"Julien Peul, you're aware that I can have you arrested and sentenced for accessory to arson, kidnapping and even murder because of your complicity in the death of Escarpaz after the crimes committed in San Lorenzo by Matello and the gang you were part of. Well, I'll forget all about this if you don't do anything to make me consider you as an enemy.

"So, are we all in agreement? Silence?"

Loustal stood up and held up his open right hand, "More than an agreement, monsieur, it's a solemn vow."

"Yes, a vow," Marod made the same gesture.

Clearly as sincere and firm as his two companions, Peul stood up and raised his right hand, "I swear, too."

"Very well. That's that. Goodbye or see you later, depending on what happens."

During this conversation Gnô Mitang had nodded silently in agreement every time the Nyctalope glanced over at him.

"Vitto, Socca," Saint-Clair shouted, "let's go!"

But an idea made him turn around and again face the three men he had so easily subdued. His voice this time was shaded with a hint of emotion.

"I just said that I ask nothing of you but silence. However, I would like to appeal to your human hearts and say this: without compromising yourselves, without running any risks, if you could inform my wife that I'm nearby and she can still have hope no matter what happens at first... Well, do it if you can. Don't answer. Don't promise. Feel free to do nothing. But if you can, do it."

With that he turned his back on the three stunned men and got into the plane. Gnô followed him, then Vitto and Socca. The door was closed, the propellers started spinning and a low rumble rose up.

As graceful as a swan, the airplane glided away from the speedboat. Soon it took off, gained altitude, made a wide turn to the southwest and vanished into a fog bank that the setting sun had drawn up from the ocean.

CHAPTER II
Sovereign land

For a few days the royal family of the Spanish court was at San Sebastian where the city, under agreement with the government, was organizing a big festival for an anniversary concerning Navarre and the Basque country.

Don Gabriel d'Ulloa, former minister, close friend of the king and advisor to the crown, though lacking a formal title and without an official post, had come with the court. But he stayed away from the hubbub before the festival and appeared as seldom as possible because he did not like showing himself in public. He lived a very secluded life in his beautiful, private villa on Mount Ulia, tucked away in a magnificent forest of pines and ferns. With a democratic spirit and generous heart, very intelligent and broad-minded, he was the most popular man of the court in Spain, even though he did nothing to stir up or keep up this popularity. The king heeded him well, enjoying his talks, finding them pleasurable and profitable, whether in private or among a group of friends.

El señor Gabriel was a short, pudgy man, quiet and unassuming, gesturing rarely. He had a mustache and an old-styled beard and a slightly lazy left eye compelled him to wear a monocle. He spoke slowly, sometimes with severe eloquence, sometimes with cheerful irony. He knew men and judged them leniently except when it came to people who were intentionally mean. Then he wielded a heavy hand.

On Monday, June 6, at 10 a.m. in his private salon, which had a smoking room, library and gallery of prints (he loved pictures), Don Gabriel d'Ulloa was finishing up his reading of various Spanish and French newspapers when his butler came in to give him "from a monsieur who doesn't want to divulge his name" a small envelope. Don Gabriel opened it, took a small calling card, looked surprised but happy and said, "Show him in right away."

Less than a minute later Leo Saint-Clair the Nyctalope entered the room. But a Saint-Clair so Spanish with his beard and clothes and manners that at first Don Gabriel thought some salesman might be playing a rude trick on him. His doubt lasted only ten seconds. Then Ulloa started laughing and held out both his hands.

"Your eyes, dear Nyctalope, don't lie. That's how I recognized you. But why the disguise? And to what do I owe this long-awaited visit, which is, I don't have to tell you, most welcome?"

"My friend, something or rather somethings of grave importance," Saint-Clair answered. "May I ask for an hour or so of your time?"

"Two, three, four if you want. Are you ready this morning? And you can stay for lunch since I don't have to leave until later in the afternoon."

"No, thanks. After I talk to you I have to leave immediately. And you won't want to keep me, I'm sure."

"Oh, if you put it that way. May I… you've had a hard time and are still going through it, right?"

"Yes and you can help me put an end to it."

"I'm at your service. Do you want to sit down?"

"Do the walls have ears? Nobody can hear this."

"Wait."

Don Gabriel went to the double doors, opened them, locked other doors in the adjoining rooms, then came back and sat down.

"Speak."

"Here it is."

The Nyctalope told him the whole story, short but to the point, of everything that had happened to him since the night of May 21, that is over the past two weeks.

Not once did Gabriel interrupt him. His embedded monocle made his left eye look more lively; his right eye was solemn, attentive; his body sat motionless in the armchair, arms and legs crossed; he listened. His growing concern showed only in a slight clenching of his jaws and puckering of his lips behind his beard.

When Saint-Clair had finished by saying, "That's it. And I came to you," Don Gabriel uncrossed his arms and legs and spoke sternly:

"Okay, what do you need from me?"

"First of all, explanations and information. Then some help, maybe…"

"I'll give you a simple, honest answer: If it's possible, it's done. If it's not possible, it will be done. The explanations first. What do you want to know?"

In a somewhat hard and bitter voice he said, "How is it that an island within Spanish territory, lying so close to the shore that customs officers can see it with the naked eye and observe everything that goes on there, an island so strange in so many ways, how is it that it can be the hiding place for a gang of criminals without the police or government raiding it?"

Don Gabriel answered, "Because the police and government don't know about it anymore than I did fifteen minutes ago before you told me. Since there's been no complaint against the inhabitants of the island, the police have nothing to do with it. And since there's been no smuggling, customs won't concern itself with it, especially if they've seen nothing the least bit suspicious there. And thus the government stays in the dark."

"I guess so," Saint-Clair said. "But now that circumstances have changed, will they stay out of it or can I count on the help of the Spanish authorities?"

Gabriel d'Ulloa answered frankly, "Stay out of it, certainly. Help? That depends…"

"On what? Why?"

"Because the island you call *La Vibora* or the Secret Island and is really called *Isla Perdida*, Lost Island, this fortified island, my friend, is sovereign land."

"Huh?" the Nyctalope was flabbergasted.

"Yes, sovereign land. Undisputed sovereign land, more so than the Principality of Andorra between France and Spain, more so than San Marino in Italy, more so than Monaco... Look, I know about it because when I was briefly Minister of Foreign Affairs in Spain it piqued my curiosity. Are you listening?"

"Passionately."

"Well, Isla Perdida was given away as a royal prerogative with sovereign rights and without the slightest trace of vassalage to the crown except for a traditional levy... get it? Traditional, one pound silver. So, this peculiar gift of the island, documented in letters patent, which have never since been revoked, was made by King Philip V in 1709 to a Portuguese explorer named Domingos Matello, a naturalized Spaniard, if I may say so. Since then, from father to son, the Matello dynasty, sovereign lords of Lost Island, has continued unabated. Don Joao or Juan Matello..."

Don Gabriel broke off and shrugged his shoulders, remained silent a few seconds, lips parted, and then:

"But you've just told me that Joao Matello was killed."

"Yes."

"*Caramba!* He was childless. The letters patent of Philip V specify that without a direct male heir Lost Island will revert back to the Spanish crown."

He stood up, excited.

"My friend, I said 'that depends' just now when you asked about support from the government because the King of Lost Island and his delegated authorities are free to do whatever they want there and if this King asks our government, as stipulated in the letters patent, it has to help him against any attack. But I wasn't thinking of the death of Matello, the King of Lost Island! With him dead the delegated authorities are deprived of all rights and privileges. With him dead Lost Island is Spanish territory. Help, you asked about? As much as you want! I suppose a torpedo boat on the water and a regiment on land would suffice?"

Despite his heavy heart, despite the gravity of the situation and all the present dangers, Saint-Clair could not help smiling.

He shook Gabriel's hands and said, "My good friend, I don't need anybody, not on sea or land. By help I simply meant an order given to the customs officers on the coast to lend a hand, if needed, to anyone sent by me and also special instructions for the governor of Vigo to do certain things in certain circumstances that I will specify."

"That's nothing. The governor of Vigo and the customs office will get whatever orders you want to send."

183

"Thanks, but we have to keep it a secret. The orders have to be confidential and the men concerned have to swear to speak of them to no one, to give absolutely no clue to their existence, even when they are carrying them out."

"That, too, I will promise to be done."

"Very well," the Nyctalope said. "As for the Spanish government and the civil and military authorities at every level, I'll need them to stay neutral. If there's a battle in the air or on the sea around Lost Island, if there's a gunfight, if men are hurt or killed, nobody can interfere."

"Bah!" Don Gabriel replied. "The region's deserted. You were asking about explanations. Here's one: because of the exceptional political situation of Lost Island and its inhabitants for the last 250 years or so, because of the barren land and the fact that the forest are untouched since there are no accessible roads, and finally because of the very wide circumnavigation forced on all ships rounding Cape Finisterre, the customs officers don't even visit the bay of Lost Island. Anyone who happens to witness fighting there will be given the confidential orders you dictate. So, you'll be free to do what you need to.

"But allow me to say one thing. Under these conditions and particularly with the imprisonment of your wife and son and nanny, if Titania catches the slightest whiff of any action by you, it'll put not only their safety but their lives in danger. Titania's letter that you showed me is categorical. I see why you demand the utmost secrecy. But how are you going to carry out your plan, whatever it is, without alerting *La Vibora*?"

"I have an idea. But I don't know if it's practicable. Any plan against her can run into obstacles that no human power can overcome. In that case, I hope that God will inspire me and I'll come up with something. But let me keep my secret, even from you. There are only two of us who know it, my friend Gnô and me, and we'll be the only two to succeed or fail. In the first case, I'll tell you all about it after the victory. In the second case, maybe I'll be able to come back and get some advice from you. For now, I think I have nothing more to say. Here's a note I wrote. It's short. It's the orders for the governor of Vigo and the customs."

"Have you asked me everything you need to know? Is that all I have to do? Have you thought everything through?" Don Gabriel asked as he took the note.

"Yes, my friend, yes. When I came here I had everything worked out in my mind. The fact of the 'sovereign land' was a big help but it doesn't change my plan or the help I need from you because the crucial condition for what I want to do is to keep it absolutely secret and for me to have complete freedom from the Spanish authorities. But let me ask you a question."

"Go ahead."

"The governor of Vigo and the captain of the customs office, can we get the orders to them today?"

"Yes, today. It's been awhile now that the governor corresponds in code by mail, telegram or wireless with the civil and military leaders. The provincial

184

governors and captains are among these leaders. So, today, this afternoon, they'll get the orders and I will personally get proof of their reception written in code."

"Great," the Nyctalope said. "Thank you. That's all I have to ask of you, so I'll bid you farewell. I came by plane. It's waiting for me in the bay pretty close to its hangar where I bought it only the day before yesterday."

Don Gabriel was curious, "Is it in the plane that you disguised yourself as a perfectly typical Spaniard?"

"Yes," Saint-Clair smiled. "From my travel bag, which I take everywhere. I have a small but full kit that the greatest actors and the wiliest policemen would envy. As for the clothes, one of my men who's the same size bought them for me in San Sebastian. It took me forty-five minutes to change into a Spaniard, but it'll take a lot less time to change back into the Nyctalope. This whole time we've been talking, Gnô and my two friends have been working. On board the Goéland III I'll have everything I'll need to execute my plan. So, we'll probably be in the air before noon and tomorrow night we'll go into action."

Since Saint-Clair obviously had nothing more to say, Don Gabriel gave him a hug and said, "God be with you! When you've rescued your family, do me the honor of coming back for a visit. I'll be in San Sebastian until the end of the month. But if you don't manage it straight off, I'll remind you of what you told me: you come back and remember that I have enough influence to get all the money and power you'll need for your just cause."

"Thanks, Don Gabriel."

"See you later, Saint-Clair."

CHAPTER III
The underwater enigma

As is well known, a diving suit was a kind of hermetically sealed outfit in which one could descend into the water up to a certain depth and stay down there while breathing air supplied by a pump outside the water. It was used especially in construction work when laying foundations underwater and also for doing research.

It consised of a helmet with a window, a waterproof suit, various accessories and a pair of specially built boots. The round, copper helmet was flared below to fit onto the shoulders of the diver. It had four small windows with thick glass. The air came in through a tube connected to an exterior pump, which was placed on a boat, raft or on a dock and was operated by someone. The air breathed and the excess air pumped in was expelled through a valve that could be turned on and off inside the helmet with a simple nod of the head. The lower part of the helmet, covering the chest and upper back, was supplied with hooks used before diving to weigh down the suit so that along with the lead-soled boots it could stay on the ocean floor and be easily balanced. The suit itself was one piece, made of canvas lined with rubber. It covered the entire body except for the head and hands, the first being protected by the helmet. The wrists of the suit, in order to prevent leaks, had rubber cuffs for sealing. A leather belt was worn around the waist on which was attached a brass scabbard with a long knife and the end of a rope to communicate with the men on board or on land. It was with this rope, using a kind of very simple, coded alphabet, that the diver could tell the men above what to do.

Such was the ordinary diving suit, differing only in certain details according to the manufacturer. It was used everywhere.

However, some wealthy and scientifically-minded shipping companies had recently commissioned a different kind of diving suit made of a very strong but light metal and looked more like a set of medieval armor. The multiple joints allowed more normal, flexible movement. The sealing of these joints was made with an inner lining of folds and the helmet was almost the same as the traditional one. But this modern diving suit was free in the water. It was not dependent on men sending air through a pump. There were no air tubes or communication ropes. It bore on its back an air generating tank and had a tiny device inside the helmet to absorb carbon. The air tank was good for 24 hours without a refill. Using a simple valve the diver could discharge a certain amount of air to make him heavier or close it to let the air build up, which rendered him lighter than the water. Thanks to this suit a smart and experienced diver could adjust his weight and thus navigate in the water, not just on the ocean floor, rising and dropping like a Cartesian Devil.

The Nyctalope knew that two of these new metal diving suits were being used in San Sebastian by an English-Japanese underwater construction company that had been hired to build a maritime museum with an underwater aquarium in the Bay of Pasajes. Gnô Mitang had gone to ask the chief engineer to use the diving suits for the next 48 hours.

When Saint-Clair came back from his visit to Don Gabriel d'Ulloa and he climbed into the *Goéland III* where his three partners were waiting for him, the first words out of his mouth were:

"Gnô, is it a yes for the diving suits?"

"Naturally. Look back there!"

The back of the plane had been cleared out to make room for the two diving suits that were set up, ready to go, looking very strange, as if awaiting medieval knights but with the helmets making them more scientifically bizarre.

"They brought them in pieces," Gnô said. "Vitto and Socca helped me put them together so we'd have less to do when we want to use them."

"Perfect," Saint-Clair replied. "Thank you. On my side, I got what I wanted. I'll tell you all about it later. Let's leave at once. We'll eat in the air. I'd like to get to that hidden cove early enough to do what we planned before it gets dark."

"As you wish. Everything's ready. We just have to lift anchor and take off."

"Let's do it!" the Nyctalope said as he sat next to Gnô who was in the pilot's seat.

The trip from San Sebastian to Cape Torinana was much quicker than the first time because they did not have to search for the island. They parked the Goéland III in their special inlet and calmly went about preparing for their nocturnal, underwater expedition, which was the main part of Saint-Clair's plan. When they were ready, Saint-Clair and Gnô were sealed into their suits but they kept the helmet window open so they would not yet have to use the air tank.

The sun had set a half hour ago and the twilight was already giving way to night because the sky was gradually being covered with clouds that would soon veil the stars from one horizon to the other.

"It's time," the Nyctalope said.

The plane had not only been anchored but moored as well. Vitto lifted anchor while Socca piloted the aircraft. He glided over the water without any other sound but the low hum of the propellers and the light splashing of the waves against hull. He got through the bottleneck, left the inlet and turned slowly around the headland, staying as close as possible to the shore until he was almost at the end of Cape of La Vibora. Behind the cape was the deep bay where Lost Island lurked.

"Monsieur," Vitto said, "we're here. Should I drop anchor?"

"Yes. If the floor is good. If the anchor doesn't hold, we've got some leeway before we're too close to the reef."

One minute later Vitto announced, "Anchor's holding."

"Good," Gnô said.

And Saint-Clair, in a very calm voice, "Socca, Vitto, remember everything! In 48 hours, if neither of us is back, go to San Sebastian and do what I told you."

"Yes, monsieur," the two men solemnly responded together.

"Let's do it, my fellow soldiers, my trusty watchdogs, my friends," the Nyctalope held his two hands open, "be brave. See you later."

Vitto and Socca shook hands with him and then with Gnô.

Saint-Clair was the first to close the window of his helmet. Gnô followed suit. Together they checked that the long, sharp knife was well attached in its scabbard to the left side of the belt and that on the right the metallic case was also firmly fastened and closed. Vitto and Socca helped Saint-Clair first and then Gnô get out of the plane and onto the platform. Then, holding hands, the two of them squatted and making the same movements they dropped into the water, as stiff as if they were wearing real suits of steel armor.

Thanks to the perfect balance of the diving suits with the lead soles and the weights hanging down over their chest, shoulders and back, the two divers dropped straight down in the water. It did not last long. The water was only forty feet deep before they felt the bottom under their feet.

They were surrounded by pitch black because the dim twilight did not filter down so far. Well, at any rate Gnô was blind because darkness did not exist for the Nyctalope. His eyes had a very rare property for humans, less rare in the animal kingdom, that allowed him to see clearly in the darkest night.

But so that the Japanese not be completely blind in the underwater obscurity, Saint-Clair taken the small, waterproof flashlight from his chest and hooked it to his back. Like that, walking ahead, he could be not only a source of light but also the sense of direction for Gnô. It had been agreed that if there were danger or any problem with the dorsal light, Gnô would use a rope he had wrapped around his waist to stay connected to his partner. This was useful in case the two divers came to a place where they might get separated but wanted to stay together. And of course, Gnô kept the light on his chest turned on.

The two divers, moreover, had a way to communicate verbally. Each had a flexible metal sound tube that he carried in a small holder attached to his belt. The ends of the tubes were fitted with a device that fit into special valves on both sides of the helmet next to their ears. To speak to his companion, a diver just had to grab one end of the tube and connect it to one of the valves and do the same with the other end to the other helmet. His voice would sound normal inside his partner's helmet. On easy terrain the two divers could even walk with their sound tubes attached. But they had to be careful not to stray farther from each other than the length of the tube. Still, it would not be too serious of a problem: the valves could be closed up from the inside with a simple bump of the head.

When Saint-Clair and Gnô had reached the bottom they stood motionless for a few moments. But they knew what they had to do, so they started walking, the Nyctalope in front, Gnô behind him. Their goal, obviously, was Lost Island. But since they had found no map of the seafloor they had to watch out for sudden ground pressure and abrupt drops into a chasm whose depth might be more than 200 feet, thus surpassing the limit of what the diving suits could withstand. The deeper the chasm the more likely the suits would explode and kill the diver on the spot.

But calmly and carefully Gnô and Saint-Clair could avoid this danger by increasing their air intake and floating over the abyss, swimming in the direction they wanted to go. But if the currents around the island were too strong, would the floating divers be swept away?

"No!" Saint-Clair had declared. "If we paddle with our hands and feet wisely we can get ourselves tossed out of the current by its own centrifugal force."

No matter their mental and physical strengths, the two men were obviously going to face all kinds of dangers on their underwater expedition, many of which were unforeseeable.

They started walking. In this perilous part of the fight against *La Vibora*, her enemies' biggest advantage was the Nyctalope's night-vision. In the darkness underwater his eyes saw clearly and farther than the range of the brightest flashlight. His view obliterated, so to speak, the opacity of the darkened water at night so that he could march confidently, worrying only about sudden drops into a precipice.

The resistance of the water was minimal as long as the two divers kept on the axis of Cape of La Vibora. But when they rounded the cape and were in the waters closer to Lost Island, they started to feel the force of the current. The current went all around the island, first from west to east, then south to north, then east to west. Now, since Saint-Clair and Gnô had entered the bay from the northwest the current was pushing them out to sea. If, on the other hand, they had come in from the south, it would have dragged them toward the island.

Saint-Clair stopped and connected his sound tube. "Gnô, what do you think? Do you think we try to fight against the current to reach the end of the bay and explore the island underwater? Or should we head south to get carried over there by the current?"

Gnô answered, "When you stopped I was ready to give you my sound tube to ask the same question. I don't think we should fight the current. Let's cross the mouth of the bay in relatively calm water and go south to catch the current that'll carry us east to the island... If the bottom starts dropping off we can start swimming."

"All right," Saint-Clair said.

He put the tube back in its holder and the two divers, still one behind the other, were off again. They let themselves be pushed out to sea a little as they went, then they were in still water and the seafloor stayed level enough until they reached the south end of the bay, which Siant-Clair realized when he suddenly saw a wall of rocks in front of him. When he looked up, he saw the stars shining above the water. He could even make out two maritime pines with their branches hanging over a promontory.

Whereas the current had hit the men on the left side earlier, pushing them to the right, now it hit them on the right and drove them to the left. Sometimes walking on rock with shifting sand, sometimes floating a few inches off the floor, they let themselves be borne gently by the current, paddling a little to veer left, meaning to the north, also meaning toward the underwater foundations of the island.

All of a sudden Saint-Clair stopped and turned off the light on his back. Feeling around he grabbed Gnô's hand and squeezed it. Then he connected the sound tube and spoke calmly because he was afraid the helmet was not a good sound box and any loud noises might be heard by underwater sentinels or more likely by well-placed sensors.

"God is smiling on us, Gnô, at least at the start of this adventure. We were hoping to find an underwater access pipe to the island or a special entrance for divers or even an intake duct for water into a distillation room, any kind of passageway for us to get into a building on the island. Well, around twenty-five yards in front of us I see a long rectangular grill... no light."

"That's good. We assumed there'd be something like that but on the ocean side. We guessed right. It's a good sign. Let's go."

"Keep the sound tube attached," Saint-Clair said.

The two divers started off again, heading straight for the grill spotted by the Nyctalope. When they stepped onto a very small stone platform that stuck out from a ledge in front of the grill, the Nyctalope said:

"You can turn on your light again, Gnô. It's just a sewage drain. I'm sure nobody's above us in the water or on the slope and certainly not at the end of this drain pipe. With your light on you'll be able to see almost as well as I and we can work together."

The thick globe on Gnô's chest cast a bright ray light before them. The grill revealed itself in sections as he swiveled his chest from left to right and back again. It was partly built into the rock, partly into the masonry. Two huge hinges proved that it could be opened and closed, but only from the inside. A big, thick piece of metal instead of a lock protected the mechanism from the outside.

The grill was made of a dull white, rustproof metal. There were twelve vertical bars crossed by two horizontal ones, each about an inch and a half thick.

"That's our way in," Gnô said.

"Of course," Saint-Clair replied.

They were talking not just about a drain but about a kind of sewer main that carried all the water, waste, all the human garbage from Lost Island into the sea, evidence of which was seen in the kitchen trash and rags stuck to the ends of the vertical bars or hooked onto the rocky walls and not washed away by the flushed water. Even here was felt the ebb and flow that created spots of still water and all sorts of rubbish stagnated in the crevices. But most of the water was as pure and clear as the sea itself because the waste and garbage were either carried away by the current or eaten by the countless fish, crustaceans and mollusks.

"Let's stay connected to the sound tube," Saint-Clair suggested, "and work on the two middle bars. Any sign of danger and you turn off the light."

"Got it."

The two men simultaneously opened a case hanging on their belt and took out a small, thin saw whose handle unfolded. They started filing away at the bars.

Right away they were glad to see that the metal happened to be rather soft, probably also very light, making it easier to build with underwater, which otherwise, if it were ordinary iron, would take several men and special equipment. In two minutes Saint-Clair and Gnô had each sawed through their bar at chest level.

"Let's kneel down and saw through down below now," Saint-Clair said.

And so they did. But since the two bars were still held in place by the horizontal bars, they had to go at those, too. Instead of two minutes it took them three on this section.

Saint-Clair only had to give a light kick for the crossed bars to fall inside and settle on the floor of the wide duct. Around twelve feet wide, in fact, and much less high, proportionally, so that they had to hunch over when they climbed in to avoid hitting their helmets on the top. They had to walk with their knees bent. Soon they were crouching because the ceiling of smooth rock suddenly dropped down to only four feet high. But then four feet farther on they could stand up straight when the ceiling abruptly rose up very high.

When Saint-Clair and Gnô looked up, one with the help of the electric light, the other only with his nyctalope eyes, they were struck by an avalanche that threw them to the ground and dragged them away. Luckily they both thought of the sound tube being snapped off and this thought, along with instinct, made them grab each other's hand at the moment of impact so that they were swept away together.

They felt like they were in a rushing river. But as quickly as this feeling struck them, another, opposite feeling, took its place—they felt themselves suddenly stationary, as if pinned against something blocking their way.

"The grill," Saint-Clair had not panicked even for an instant.

"Yes, the grill," Gnô replied just as calmly.

The electric light had stayed on. Gnô, therefore, could see as well as the Nyctalope that they were, indeed, both pinned to the grill on theirs sides, three feet to the left of the opening they had made. But water was pouring out around them. It was dirty, full of all kinds of shapeless debris.

"Damn," Saint-Clair said, "it's the evening, the end of the day, end of the work, curfew time. The Hashshashins have refitted Lost Island to modern standards. At certain times, especially in the evening, the automatic flushing of air and water turns on to clean out all the ducts and pipes. We've just been caught in one of these purges."

With this in mind, the situation seemed not only funny but trivial, which helped to purge, so to speak, the emotions that had nagged their hearts at the start of the adventure. This was good because some sentimental emotions are not suitable for perilous projects.

Coming here to save his wife and son, Saint-Clair knew well that it was not only his own life on the line but that of his wife and son as well. This naturally reduced some of his inner strength. He was afraid of making a wrong move, a rash decision that might put Sylvie and little Pierre in danger. If he had undertaken this adventure only to fight for a cause, for example, he would have been, like in the other dramatic exploits in his life, in much better control of himself when he and Gnô strapped themselves into the diving suits.

And now this stupid incident, this material and mechanical thing, this completely unmysterious sewage drain, the simple flushing of air and water to clean out the pipes, this pushed Saint-Clair and Gnô back into action, back into the fight that, no matter the goal, had to be executed without floundering in poetic sentiments.

Then, for the first time since they had found Lost Island, the two men were truly calm, their nerves and muscles relaxed, their mind disciplined, and their willpower able to keep in check any emotion that might arise.

"This flushing can't last more than two or three minutes maximum," Saint-Clair said.

"Probably right," Gnô agreed.

They heard each other clearly despite the water rushing around them. But the artificial torrent did not even last two or three minutes, like Saint-Clair had imagined, before it slowed down, cleared up and allowed them to see six feet in front of them again.

"Off we go," the Nyctalope said.

"Let's do it," Gnô said.

Still next to each other they started walking again, bent double, then crouching and finally standing up and once again looking up to see what was above.

Gnô turned off his light right away because in the distance, to the left, there was something casting a pale, greenish light in the water.

"My word," Gnô whispered, "I feel like I'm in the aquarium of a maritime museum."

"That's it," Saint-Clair replied, "but instead of a museum it's a prison." After a brief silence, "Gnô, I think it'd be better to unhook the sound tube. Just follow me. As long as that light is there you can see well enough, but if it goes out, don't turn yours on right away. I'll flash mine briefly and you can grab my belt. Then we'll figure out what to do."

"Right," Gnô said.

Saint-Clair disconnected his tube and rolled it up into the case. Then he started marching toward the green glow.

Even better than Gnô could have done with the help of his chest light, the Nyctalope saw that they were in a kind of vaulted trench where several ducts from various buildings on the island emptied out. He made out a big, perfectly round opening where the piston of the pressure pump was probably chugging away.

The light was coming from the end of the trench. The Nyctalope could soon tell it was a single spotlight whose pale light looked green from a distance because of the thickness of the water.

Saint-Clair wondered, "Why is this trench lit up like this, apparently all the time?"

He would have like to hear Gnô's opinion on the matter.

He thought, "We can at least speak in whispers."

He turned around to face his partner, starting to take the sound tube out of its holder, but his hand froze and he stood still, alarmed and confused. Gnô was gone!

Gnô could not have been more than two or three behind him but he was not there. He was not on the right or left and not farther back either. The Nyctalope's sharp eyes could see all the way down the trench. He could even make out the access at the very end with the hole in the grill. His friend had vanished.

After a moment of worried astonishment Saint-Clair got hold of himself and thought, "He obviously went back but why? And why without telling me?"

The Nyctalope started walking back the way they had come, soon bending down under the low ceiling until he came to the grill. He looked all around but no Gnô!

He went through the grill, searched right and left on the ledge, peered into the depths of the channel between the island and the shore but he did not see any sign of the Japanese.

"But in such a short time he couldn't have gone far. From the moment we unhooked the sound tube until I turned around couldn't have been more than two or three minutes. No, something's wrong. Gnô didn't turn back. He disappeared in the trench. How? Why? I'll find out."

He went back through the grill and to the trench, but he did not enter. At the spot where the duct rose up after the low ceiling he stood up slowly and then stopped, scrutinizing all the details of the trench.

His first observation was this: "Hold on, the spotlight's turned off."

Indeed, there was no light and the area glowing before was now in the dark. At a distance and through the murky water the Nyctalope's eyes could not even see the thick glass of the spotlight. But in a range of several yards around him he saw everything clearly. The walls were natural rock, sealed in places with cement. In short, the industrious hand of man had completed the work of nature to make this underwater hole a waterproof tunnel that leaked no water under the island. He examined the various duct openings that he had noticed earlier. Nothing seemed to explain the mysterious disappearance of his friend.

"And why didn't I hear anything? If someone came out of a hidden door, sneaked up behind him, grabbed him and dragged him away, he would've fought. His suit would've made enough noise to catch my attention. Was I too preoccupied to hear a sound muffled by the water? Weird, very weird. But I've got to find out. If Gnô fell into a trap, I have to watch out not to get trapped myself."

He pulled his long knife out of the sheath and held it tightly in his right hand. Then, slowly, all his senses on alert, he walked forward. With every step he peered ahead, to the sides and even turned around to look behind him, ready to defend himself against any attack. It took ten minutes to cover the distance that had taken only seconds the first time. Nothing suspicious happened. He got to the round opening that he thought housed a pressure pump. He looked up through the top window of his helmet, which remained stationary on his shoulders so that no would-be observer could tell exactly where the diver was looking.

Saint-Clair thought, "If the danger comes from here, they won't know I'm seeing it."

Then the thing that the Nyctalope had predicted happened. It was so fast that he barely had time to jump back and dodge it.

From the round opening a machine had sprung down. It had eight clamps that opened up as it shot down and when it got around three feet off the ground they snapped shut like jaws. Without pausing, the machine sprang back up and disappeared. All without a sound.

Saint-Clair was stunned for a moment. Nevertheless, as always in dangerous scrapes, his mind continued observing, reflecting and analyzing. Thus, from the opening, which his eyes were still glued on, he slowly lowered his gaze to the ground and he saw that the smooth, black rock was bumpy directly beneath it with a few black points sticking up, only visible to someone actually looking for them.

"Okay, okay, the machine with iron tentacles must be automatic and these black points would be triggers... let's see."

Carefully, keeping his body well out of range, Saint-Clair stuck his right foot out and pushed down hard on the closest point. As soon as he felt the point sink into the ground the open tentacles dropped down, snapped shut and shot back up.

"Damn," Saint-Clair shuddered. "Gnô was snatched up by that. What an infernal machine! But whoever's in charge here, *La Vibora*, Korridès or some other Hashshashin, is going to be warned, maybe at this very moment, that the tentacles got a victim. I know Gnô won't talk, but just his being here speaks volumes because in the letter Titania wrote to me at Nopals she said she knew that we were meeting. I have to get out of here right away or else I'll be caught. But taking off, abandoning the project when it's barely begun... But if I get caught, all will be lost..."

He stepped back but his courage was stronger than his caution and held him fast.

He thought, "I could at least hide in the duct. There are small recesses. I'll see."

As he was deliberating internally, he felt compelled to retry the experiment. He stepped forward again and pushed the black point with his right foot. What happened was the most unexpected phenomenon he could imagine. It froze him to the spot as he gasped in his helmet. The claws appeared but they were carrying something that they dropped when they opened and that Saint-Clair recognized as a diving suit just like his.

"Gnô!" he said aloud.

It was indeed Gnô Mitang sent back.

The claws sprang back up and Gnô pulled out his sound tube at once.

"Stunning," he said. "You were aware I'd disappeared?"

"Yes," Saint-Clair answered, "but after the fact."

"So, you didn't know how?"

"Well, yes, I found the machine that snatched you and tripped it myself to figure it out."

"Ah, that's why!" Gnô almost shouted. "Luckily because that saved me."

"Tell me."

"First, how did you find it?"

"By looking down. Turn around and you can see the little black points in the floor. They're triggers."

"Oh, I see," Gnô observed. "So I stepped on it by chance when we were walking to the green light. And it snatched me up like a feather. Up there I was dropped but I fell on my feet. There was a big, electric ceiling light turned on. I was in a room with a weird machine that filled up half of it. It had a series of clamps that I was checking out while moving away when all of a sudden, right in the spot where I was before, a round trapdoor opened and the tentacle dove through and came back immediately. I was half expecting it to have snatched you up like it did me. But I told myself, 'It's automatic. Let's see if I can make it work from here? Maybe I can get it to drop me back off in the duct where you'd certainly be searching for me.' So, I stood on the trapdoor, right under the clamp, which I grabbed above me and hoisted myself up. It wasn't too hard to get it around my waist...

195

"I was barely ready when the thing dropped down and as I'd hoped, as you saw, it delivered me back here. So, it was you who triggered it the second time?"

"Yes," Saint-Clair said. "The machine is automatic when you press one of those points."

"I wonder why I wasn't grabbed by someone up in that room? It's strange that there's no one watching."

Saint-Clair said, "Maybe there is now. Maybe the machine has an alarm and the person or persons take a little time to get there. Or maybe today they were busy doing something else. It doesn't matter. I have an idea, Gnô. Are you still ready to risk it all?"

"Of course!"

"Well, we've got to get ourselves grabbed by the clamp, both of us at the same time. It's big enough. And then up there, we'll see. I'm thinking that maybe there's no alarm after all. There's no evidence that this machine is a trap for enemies. Maybe it's used to leave the island in diving suits. The island must have all kinds of systems built into it underwater, maybe even electronic sensors. Who knows?

"I checked out the trench but I saw nothing that led me to believe there's another access than the one we came in. Let's both go up. At worst we'll have to start fighting. We've come out on top in other battles that looked and were a lot more mysterious and dangerous than this one."

"Leo," the Japanese said, "if you're saying all this to convince me, there's no need. Just say 'let's go' and I'm right behind you."

"Then, let's go."

Gnô disconnected the sound tube and the two men stood back to back under the round opening. The Nyctalope pressed one of the points. Immediately the weird machine dropped down, opened up and the claws, each furnished with a kind of suction cup, gripped the two men around their torsos and shot back up through the ceiling, out of the dark tunnel and into a lit room. The trapdoor under them closed up before the claws dropped them onto the floor.

There was no one in the room. Saint-Clair and Gnô wasted no time. Events dictated exactly what they had to do. First of all, get out of the diving suits to be able to arm themselves and fight when necessary.

"Oh, that's better," the Nyctalope said with relief.

More comfortable in the blue, mechanic's jumpsuits they were wearing inside the diving suits, they went through a quick series of Swedish gymnastics to loosen up. Then they grabbed their Brownings and hung the knife from the thin but strong belt around their jumpsuits. They wore no hats. For shoes they had on felt-soled sandals strapped around their ankles. Like this they felt ready to face any physical challenges.

Gnô said, "I think you guessed correctly when you figured this was not meant to be the first room of a prison for intruders like us but rather a dressing room for divers. See all the suits over there?"

"Yes," Saint-Clair answered. "And this machine is only for making it easier to get in and out of the trench."

The room was almost square, measuring around twenty-five feet per side. Besides the machine in the middle there were other machines, one of which must have been the motor for the tentacle device. Several cabinets were lined up along the walls where there were also complete diving suits hanging, almost identical to Saint-Clair's and Gnô's.

The Nyctalope commented, "The Hashshashins have got the latest equipment here. Look at their helmets, they're better than ours. They don't even need a sound tube. Either I'm completely wrong or this little device on the inside and outside is a microphone. But let's not dawdle here. It's obvious nobody's coming. I don't think they figured anybody from the outside could get in to use their machine."

"The weird thing is that the room's lit up," Gnô remarked.

"Not so weird," Saint-Clair said. "They must have all of Lost Island wired up with electricity so the inside of the fort is probably always lit, except for the private rooms which would have switches. Do you want to bet that when we leave this room we'll find all the corridors, stairways and other rooms lit up just like this one?"

"Let's hope so. Then I won't have to use the flashlight."

Saint-Clair smiled, "That too, I don't agree with. Better to be in the dark where I can see but not be seen. You can stay right behind me or hold onto a cord or something to follow me."

"You're right, but if the light is on everywhere, they must have switches somewhere. Then, just in case, we can turn the lights off."

"We'll see."

Not for an instant did the two men doubt that they had to keep following the path that Providence seemed to be showing them because was it not almost a miracle that they had entered the very heart of the island without their presence being exposed? They barely even had to break in and it was so easy! Their first goal was accomplished. It was an important victory for them. Now they had to take advantage of it.

"Let's go," Saint-Clair said. "You agree with me, right? We don't use our weapons unless absolutely necessary. We both know all the secrets of jujitsu, so let's try to avoid killing. However, if we have to, use the knife rather than the gun. The main thing is to make as little noise as possible."

"I think so too."

"So, what are we waiting for?"

In the diving room there was a big clock divided into 24 hours and its two golden hands pointed to 23:12 when the two men headed for the only visible door, which was in the middle of the wall the one being covered up by machines. The wall and the big double-door were metal and painted white. There was no special lock because Saint-Clair just had to push on the handle and it

197

opened. As he had predicted everything was lit up, at least in this part of Lost Island. The two men walked down a bright corridor and into a rotunda that had two other corridors leading out of it along with three stairways.

The Nyctalope whispered, "It's obvious that we're at the bottom of the island. Those corridors probably lead to outside barracks. The stairs, though, go upstairs. We must be underneath the octagonal building we saw from the mountain. Let's take the middle stairs."

"Right behind you," Gnô said.

It was lit. they counted twenty-six steps until they reached a landing with three doors. The one on the right and on the left were painted black. The one in the middle was white.

Gnô said, "The middle one, the white one. There's something cabbalistic about it. Let's take that one."

"Yes."

Here again a simple push opened the door. Apparently the masters of Lost Island had complete trust in their security. If, as was likely if not certain, there were guards permanently on watch around the island, they must have thought the octagonal building was safe from intruders because so far they had come across no obstacles. They went on.

Through the white door, Saint-Clair and Gnô followed a corridor, which they were surprised to find decorated with wall tapestries and two impressionist paintings depicting small harbors on the sea. At the same time, they felt they were in a place where people lived a comfortable, luxurious, even refined life. It conflicted so much with the diving room and the rotunda that the two of them could not help expressing their astonishment.

The Nyctalope whispered, of course, but not without a hint of emotion, "Gnô, are we going to end up directly in the rooms where *La Vibora* is keeping Sylvie and Pierre? Do smell that perfume?"

"It's not Sylvie's perfume," Gnô whispered back, "unless she changed it since you've been married."

"No she didn't change it. But you smell it... Remember? It was in the room of Leonid Zattan!"

"Yes, yes."

"Not surprising to think that Diana Ivanovna, the Red Princess would, out of love, use the same perfume as Zattan."

"Yes, yes," Gnô repeated.

"So, at the end of this corridor, behind that heavy curtain, is the room belonging to the Red Princess, *La Vibora*, Titania? We're right next to her."

"Could be."

"And do you think that Sylvie and Pierre are being kept close at hand?"

"Probably."

"Well then, let's go."

"Yes, let's go."

This time Gnô went first. He was calmer than the husband and father. He parted the curtain and again the door opened easily.

The two men entered as the curtain fell closed behind them. They were no longer in the bright light that had accompanied them so far. A small electric lamp like a night light inside a green crystal globe diffused a dim light that allowed Gnô to see that it was a kind of vestibule with many doors, all covered with the same kind of curtain, the same fabric and the same layout, meaning that each was doubled and the left one showed signs of a door frame behind it.

Saint-Clair and Gnô stood next to each other, thoroughly examining the entire room. Even stronger than in the corridor they smelled the perfume. Without a doubt Diana Ivanovna had her rooms behind one of these eight doors.

The Nyctalope whispered, "We have to get to Diana. She's got to be *La Vibora* of San Lorenzo and the Titania of the letter given to me by Peul. She is the Enemy. It's her we have to get to."

"Unquestionably," Gnô replied coldly.

He stepped forward, head raised a little, sniffing at the air. A little farther than halfway through the room he paused, but only briefly. He turned to the right and faced the door that had one detail different from the others: both curtains showed evidence of a door frame behind them.

The two men stood side by side in front of this door. Very gently the Japanese felt for the handle. It took thirty seconds for him to fully press down on the golden door handle and then he pushed cautiously. But this time the door did not open. He looked at Saint-Clair who shook his head. Gnô just as slowly let go of the handle, then took three steps back. The Nyctalope remained at his side.

Unlike all the others this door was locked. But it was from this door that the subtle but pungent fragrance came. They stood looking at the door, wondering how they could open it for a good two minutes.

Suddenly Saint-Clair said, "Come on, let's try again."

"Gladly."

The Nyctalope this time touched the handle. When it was fully lowered he froze, Gnô as well, when he heard a muffled alarm go off somewhere behind the door. A simple coincidence? Or did the second attempt set it off? Puzzled but prudent, all their senses on alert, the two men waited. At first nothing happened. Then they heard a creaking sound and faint footsteps running on a carpet.

"They're coming," Gnô whispered.

"Watch out!"

At the same time they stepped to either side of the doors, half hidden behind the curtains. Their eyes were riveted on the fateful handle. They saw it lower as if by itself and heard the quiet click of a lock. The door opened and in the doorway was a woman in pajamas, her hair tucked into a turban…

Ah! They had no need to look at each other, no need to say a word! The same impulse was triggered. They jumped out and pounced on the woman, grabbing her around the shoulders at the same time and both of them putting their hands over her mouth to muffle her cry. Together they pushed her back into the room. Saint-Clair kicked the door shut behind him and they heard the latch click in the lock.

The woman's legs gave way and she fell backwards with the two men on top of her.

Saint-Clair spoke coldly, "Tie her up, Gnô. I've got her and I'll gag her."

"Right."

Gnô stood up. The room was lit by a bright ceiling light. He saw that it was just an antechamber, but in front of him was a double door, one side of which was open, through which he could see another brightly lit room. What he glimpsed told him that this second room was a bedroom. He ran in. He had no trouble finding some scarves in the wardrobe, which he brought back to tie the woman's ankles and legs together and her wrists and elbows behind her back.

Then he spoke softly, "Her bedroom's in there. A big bed and two couches."

"Good," Saint-Clair said. He stood up and lifted the woman who was no longer struggling. He carried her into the bedroom where he laid her on the bed. Meanwhile, Gnô had locked the door to the vestibule and come back to close the bedroom door.

"Now," he said, "I think we'll be safe. That didn't make a lot of noise."

"Watch out," Saint-Clair warned.

And he lunged to hold the woman who had coiled like a snake and thrown herself off the bed next to the nightstand. But something strange happened—she did not fall. She was held back by the headboard that her hands were hanging onto. She was hanging on so firmly that Saint-Clair and Gnô needed all their strength to pry open her fingers, which were clenched around a kind of apple sculpture, and throw her back in the middle of the big bed.

"What's got into you, madame?" Gnô said. "Your violent fits won't do you any good."

At the same time he pulled his long knife out of the scabbard and as the blade glimmered in the light he continued:

"We've seen your picture. You're *La Vibora*, Titania and you must be Diana Ivanovna Krosnovief, the Red Princess, and no doubt also the Sunday of the Hashshashins. A lot of names! But names don't matter when we've got you in the flesh. Madame, I'm going to let my friend talk, Leo Saint-Clair, whom you may have never met. Allow me to introduce you. Myself, I'm Gnô Mitang, ready to stab you in the throat if you scream because I'm going to pull out the gag so you can answer some questions from my friend Saint-Clair, the Nyctalope, here in your own bedroom on Lost Island, which, as you see, was not completely lost to everyone."

Thus said, the Japanese untied the gag and stood back holding the point of his blade inches away from Titania's carotid artery.

What surprised the Nyctalope at this moment was the expression on Titania's face. Under such circumstances, a woman being caught like this should have looked scared, even desperate since she was in the hands of her worst enemies. But quite the contrary, this face showed only defiance, insolence and triumphant irony. Her beautiful, red lips parted, her white teeth sparkled and a loud laugh exploded from her mouth.

Addressing Gnô she said, "Monsieur, since you have taken the trouble to ungag her, untie my arms and legs as well. I assure you that I won't fight you. Me, a weak woman, all alone and unarmed against two strong men holding weapons. If I called out, they wouldn't hear me. But with my hands free I could press a button on the electric bulb hanging from the nightstand and one of my slaves would come, the best and most devoted one, the Nubian you met, Monsieur Nyctalope, when you went to see Dr. Korridès at *The Sycamores*... But what can this Nubian do against you two? With one good shot you'd kill him on the spot. So, I won't call anyone or put up a fight. I'll do whatever you want, except for one thing..."

These last four words were spoken directly Saint-Clair. But he kept calm.

"First of all, madame, please tell us what we should call you. We know a half dozen names. To simply our conversation, which looks like it's going to be very interesting, one single name would be better."

"Very well. Call me Titania. It's the name that fits me best when it comes to you. Perhaps one day I'll explain why. For now, I'll it say again." She paused briefly before continuing. "I'll do what you want except for one thing."

"What's that?" Saint-Clair asked.

Titania laughed again and raised her voice, "Aha! Can't you guess? Why did you two come here, especially you, Leo Saint-Clair? Wasn't it to free a young woman who answers to the name of Sylvie and a charming baby called Pierre along with his nanny, of course, Adele? You two are very strong. Stronger than I thought. When I set a trap for you I was sure you'd be snared, but you managed to penetrate this impenetrable island and get into my room, make me your prisoner... Yes, you're very strong, but still, I've got the upper hand."

Saint-Clair shuddered. He felt that this woman was sincere, that she was not just showing off, that her tone of ironic and arrogant defiance was not a bluff. He could not wait any longer. He grabbed her by the wrist, which Gnô had untied by now, squeezed it more and more tightly, and snarled:

"Tell me! Tell me now! What is it that you won't do?"

Simply and solemnly, staring at the Nyctalope with her magnificent, cruel eyes, she answered, "What I won't do is give you Sylvie and Pierre."

"Oh, if they're here, I'll get them without you."

"No you won't."

"What?"

"I said no. You won't get them. You won't find them. Nobody will find them. At the moment I have very few servants on the island. Except for two sentinels, everyone is sleeping like I was ten minutes ago when I was woken up by the alarm, which is always set off by the second pressure on the door handle.

"You can tie me up again, leave me here and go take over Lost Island, get rid of the Nubian, the young man named Peul, two sailors and finally two other men who are posted on watch. Then you'll be the masters here. But will you use torture to make me talk? Those who do talk don't know and the one who does know, meaning me, won't talk."

Again the woman fell back on her pillow and started laughing.

Saint-Clair looked at Gnô who was grim. Their eyes met and each of them knew that the other believed what Titania was telling the truth. But everything that had happened over the past few days pointed to Sylvie, Pierre and Adele being on Lost Island. Even their conversation in the speedboat with Peul, Loustal and Marod made no sense unless Saint-Clair's family were locked up on the island. And this island was not a vast continent. However complex the architecture might be, it could not take two men like the Nyctalope and Gnô more than a few hours to search the place from top to bottom, from one end to the other. Unless…

Gnô expressed his thought out loud, "Unless this woman got suspicious or got warned and yesterday decided to move them to another one of her lairs. It's possible."

"Yes, that's possible," Saint-Clair gumbled.

He looked at Titania. She was smiling but the Nyctalope looked so menacing that the smile froze on her face.

In a sharp and stern voice, proof that the Nyctalope had willed his emotions into submission, he said, "Titania, in spite of what you said, I'm still going to search for my wife and son here. If I don't find them, you will die."

As hard as her adversary, the terrible woman shot back, "Sylvie and Pierre will die if I do."

"Maybe," the Nyctalope said, "but if I know one thing about you it's that all your actions for more than a month have led to only one thing: to revel in the sight of me and my wife watching our son die and then the suffering of my wife before my own death. To torture and kill little Pierre, to torture and kill me, then maybe to leave Sylvie alive if she doesn't die of grief. That's your goal. Well, I'll tell you right now—you've failed. If I don't find them on Lost Island and if you don't tell me where they are when I get back, I'll kill you. You won't see us suffer, you won't get your revenge, you'll end your life knowing the shame and misery of failure… As for my family, I'll keep searching and the devil take me if I don't find them. Gnô, tie her up."

"We'll just see about that!" the woman said.

She put up no resistance. After gagging her, they tied her legs together her hands over her head and then to the bed itself so that she could not roll off, onto the carpet and drag herself to some secret button. They used some strong, silk cords they found in the bathroom next door. They checked the exterior doors of her quarters, which consisted of the bedroom, bathroom and a kind of sitting room. The doors were all locked from the inside and they left through the one they had entered, which could be locked from the outside. They were careful to make sure the curtains looked undisturbed.

Thus confident that Titania could not free herself or be easily freed—or so they believed—they started a methodical exploration of the building. Brownings in hand, they went from room to room.

In one of the rooms off the main vestibule they found the Nubian asleep, whom the Nyctalope recognized from *The Sycamores* in Versailles. The man was startled awake by a sharp pain in his belly. He opened his eyes but immediately fell into a coma because Gnô and Saint-Clair both gave him a hard jujitsu chop. The effect was so quick and the coma so deep that a weaker body might never come out of it. Since the Nubian was a giant, they were sure it would not last too long. But, as a precaution, they tied him up with the belt, ties and rolled up towels they found in the room.

Then, stealthy and silent, both careful and daring, they worked fast. First Julien Peul, then the two sailors were found, woken up, given a jujitsu chop and rendered immobile. In a kind of dormitory next to the kitchen and in an office they found a man in his fifties, an old woman and a boy. All three were tied up. In the rest of the octagonal building Saint-Clair and Gnô found no one else.

When the course of their search led them back to the main vestibule, Saint-Clair looked at his watch. "An hour and a half. We've got control of Lost Island. That was fast. Now we just have to deal with the two guards. Let's hope it's just as easy so we don't have to use our weapons. Where do you think they are?"

"Oh," Gnô replied, "I think it'll be easy to find them. There's got to be a guardroom lit up somewhere, probably in one of the barracks on the periphery. Let's go out into the courtyard and start looking."

During their search they had seen a second vestibule that ended in eight steps leading down to a door set back in a Romanesque archway. They had figured it was the main exit of the octagonal building. Now they went back to it. It had a system of locks controlled by a lever, which took a good fifteen minutes for them to find. It was hidden in the vestibule very ingeniously as two sculpted, wooden apples looking like ornaments of a medieval bishop's chair in a niche carved out of the stone. In their meticulous search they happened to touch these apples and one of them sank into the post it was attached to. And thus the huge door at the bottom of the stairs was opened.

"Very good," Saint-Clair said.

"Perfect," Gnô added.

Still holding their guns, they went outside.

The night of June 7 was serenely charming. The calm ocean waves were whispering melodiously over the sloping bank and the rocks on the shore. A light breeze lilted through the pine trees. A myriad of stars were sparkling, diffusing a dreamy light through the air.

Stepping out of the hot, heady atmosphere of the octagonal building, the two men felt a great relief to breath the fresh air of the night, the sea and the mountain. But they were too tense to enjoy the delightful sensation. They were eager to destroy or at least remove any obstacle to their final search.

Of course, during their initial investigations, every time they encountered a new door, they were hoping that, despite Titania's threats and promises, they would find the room where Sylvie, little Pierre and Adele were being held prisoner. But no! They had not found even the slightest hint. In fact, they felt like they had entered every room, seen every nook and cranny of the octagonal building and the truth was dawning that they were not there.

Responding to his own thought and, he was sure, to Gnô's as well, the Nyctalope said, "When we've taken care of the sentinels, we'll search all the barracks and buildings outside. It's possible that a prison was built underneath the island, which the Red Princess might think is untraceable."

"Yes."

That was all they said. Walking slowly, they only had to go around a quarter of the building before they saw a small portion of the courtyard lit up. The light came from a transom window above the door of a barracks.

"That's where they are," Gnô said. "I think the guardhouse just stretches out behind the door and so looks directly onto the slope and the mouth of the bay. That's the only side the island is easily accessible. On the side facing the land, the steep, barren cliffs drop into a strong current, making it almost impossible to get a dinghy in the water and too dangerous to try swimming. From the ocean you can get here on all kinds of boats."

"You're right," Saint-Clair agreed. "I think that to surprise these guys the simplest way is the best. Go through the door if it's open and show them our guns. If the door's closed, we'll just knock and do the same thing when they open it."

"Okay," Gnô said.

And they walked straight to the door. They saw that it had an old-style iron lock. Gnô grabbed the handle, put his thumb on the latch and pushed. The horizontal bar of the latch clicked and he just had to pull the door open.

In the room arranged as a crude guardroom, two men were sitting under an electric light on either side of a table, playing cards, which proved that Titania's feeling of security was shared by these two men who were the very ones responsible for said security.

"*Hola!*" Saint-Clair greeted. "*Alto las manos!*"

The two sentinels were so utterly astonished that they could not even think of obeying. Gnô had to repeat the order while raising his own left hand. Both he and the Nyctalope kept their guns held in their right hands.

The rest was quick and easy. On Gnô's orders the two card players went to lie on the bunks where they were bound and gagged.

"There we go," Saint-Clair said. "I believe we're the absolute masters of Lost Island now. We can interrogate these two guys. If it's not enough, we'll go straight to Julien Peul. I'd be surprised if he or the two sailors don't know where my wife and son are being held on the island."

"Don't get your hopes up," Gnô warned. "Remember on board the speedboat when we told them that we'd be grateful if they'd let your wife know you were here, they didn't say anything. They would've had time. Their silence came out of surprise, emotion, or, as I fear, ignorance. After all, Titania is fully capable of arranging things so that she alone knows where the prison is. She could even be bringing the food and water. And Adele would be taking care of everything else inside their cell…

"Strictly speaking, there's no reason to think that Julien Peul or the two sailors or the kitchen servants or the Nubian or especially these two buffoons know where the hiding place is! So, don't count on getting anything out of interrogating the people on the island. By the way, if there's one thing that surprises me it's that there are so few people on the island, which I imagine could comfortably accommodate hundreds."

"Yes," Saint-Clair said. "You're right, Gnô. And I was thinking of something else, too. Do you believe that Joao Matello, the king of Lost Island, didn't have his own servants here, his own guards? After killing Matello, did Titania make all those people disappear? It's a mystery.

"But let's forget about these two guards. They're really just lackeys. If anyone knows something it's the Nubian. He must be her chief servant since she brought him with her from Versailles. Peul's just a sidekick, the sailors are basically employees and the kitchen help are menial servants to her. Let's go straight to the Nubian. Do you think he's awake by now?"

"I'll wake him up if not. Unless he's dead, which I doubt."

Three minutes later they were back in the Nubian's room. He was not moving, really looked dead. Gnô leaned over, opened his shirt and listened to his heart and lungs.

"The big guy's alive," he said. "Don't try to stop what I'm about to do. It may look cruel but it's necessary to yank him out of this catalepsy, which could last for days and end in death. The blows we gave him are usually fatal, you know that. You also know there's only one way to bring him back to life."

"Do it," Saint-Clair showed no emotion.

"I need a match."

"I've got a lighter."

"Better still. Light it up."

The Japanese had pulled out his long knife. He leaned over the legs of the Nubian and on the bulging calf of his right leg he felt for a particular muscle. When he found it he pinched it between the index finger and thumb of his left hand, then with the sharp blade of his knife he cut the muscle. Blood flowed. Without trying to stop the bleeding Gnô took the Nyctalope's lighter and positioned the flame between the lips of the small wound. It lasted thirty seconds. The giant black body convulsed a few times, then shook violently. With his teeth chattering, the man opened his eyes.

"There we go," Gnô said quietly.

He gave the lighter back to Saint-Clair and slipped his long knife back into the scabbard.

Saint-Clair remembered that the Nubian had spoken French at *The Sycamores* in Versailles. It was, therefore, in French that he asked directly:

"What's your name?"

Dazed, understanding nothing, wondering why he was tied up, why his right calf felt like it was burning up, and how these two men (he thought he recognized the taller one) had got into his room, the giant just rolled his eyes and said nothing.

Calmly, the Nyctalope spoke again, "You know me. I'm Leo Saint-Clair the Nyctalope. On May 22 you met me at the villa of Dr. Korridès in Versailles. Remember?"

"Oh yes, yes," the Nubian furrowed his brow, his eyes turned hard, mean, even hateful.

On seeing this Gnô pulled out his long knife again and waved the blade in front of the man's face. "Don't get any ideas, big guy. Your mistress is in our power. Everyone else here is tied up like you. We've taken control of Lost Island. So, behave yourself and do as you're told if you want to live. Leo Saint-Clair asked you your name. Answer."

"Hamed."

"Very well," the Nyctalope said. "Hamed, we're going to untie your legs. The cut we made in your calf to wake you up won't keep you from walking. It'll hurt a little and you'll limp but it'll remind you that any wrong move will get you stabbed or shot. Gnô, please untie his legs."

With a swipe of the blade the Japanese severed the straps around Hamed's ankles.

Saint-Clair went on, "Now stand up. Walk straight ahead and take us directly to where my wife and son and nanny are being held prisoner."

Hamed did not put up a fight. The knife and the gun pointed at him, his desire to live, the probable certainty of the Nyctalope's victory over Titania, and finally the sapping of his mental and physical strength due to this unexpected dilemma, all this made him a virtual slave to the will of the stronger. So, he stood up and started walking. He was so naturally tough that he did not even feel the injury to his calf. Moreover, Gnô had finally bandaged it to stop the bleeding. Therefore, Hamed walked.

Out of the room, which led into the main vestibule, he was about to pass by Titania's room without stopping when the Nyctalope decided it would be better to show the Nubian what condition his mistress was in.

"Hamed, come here."

He led the Nubian, followed by Gnô, into the room to see Titania bound and gagged.

"You see? Now let's go."

The woman had opened her eyes and her defiant glare drilled into the Nyctalope. It lasted a split second. Gnô and Hamed were already in the vestibule. The Nubian went down a corridor that Saint-Clair and Gnô had already explored. They had entered all the rooms and found only workshops, laboratories, a utility room, just things to keep the island running.

Well, this corridor ended in a room that was much longer than it was wide and its white walls were bare. But from the ceiling hung gymnastic apparatus. On the thick, shag carpet was scattered various weight-lifting equipment.

Hamed had barely entered the room when he stopped abruptly, looked around, then down. Saint-Clair and Gnô had stepped forward and were watching him. He looked stupefied. He only had to take a few steps forward to stand facing the wall opposite the door. He looked around again and then started feeling along the wall. He stepped back, shook his head and muttered:

"I don't get it."

"What? What don't you get?" Saint-Clair asked.

"What I see here," the Nubian answered. "What I'm seeing... Yes, it's the exercise room, but... Listen, monsieur, I only went into the room with the prisoners once, I swear, one time only. And I swear I went through the exercise room. Then there was a very short corridor to the room. But see, there's no door here except the one we came through. No other door! Maybe I'm wrong? Maybe I was going somewhere else when I came through here..."

While he was talking, slowly, shakily, unsure and uneasy, Saint-Clair and Gnô were observing him closely. There was no doubt—the Nubian was being honest. He was not pretending.

After silence settled over the room Gnô said, "Maybe there are two exercise rooms and you're confusing this with another?"

"I don't think so. But it's true I've only been on the island for four or five days. Yes, today is the fifth day since my mistress and I got here. Maybe I don't know the whole island. I haven't been everywhere. I really don't know... If you kill me, it'll be unfair... I'm telling the truth."

Saint-Clair put his left hand on the man's shoulder, "Calm down, Hamed, calm down. We're here to get explanations, to find out everything. We'll do it without having to kill you, I hope. Listen and think hard before answering. Who was in charge of taking care of the prisoners? Not you since you only saw them once. Hold on, why did you go to see them. Tell me now."

The man raised his hand and opened his mouth to speak but hesitated.

"Wait, wait! What's the name of your mistress?"

"In Versailles her name was Jane Korridès?"

"Right. And here?"

"Here, when we talk about her we call her Titania."

"And do you know her by any other names?"

The Nubian shook his head.

"Fine. Now talk"

"Well, monsieur, my mistress told me to follow her, to stay behind the door, to listen and only come in if she called me. I just followed her. I thought we came through this exercise room. We went through a door that I can't really remember where it was. She made me stay in the corridor. She went into the room and closed the door. I heard some shouting and maybe a struggle. I just stood there. But then a scream made me jump and barged in just in time to save my mistress from the hands of the lady who had knocked her down and was strangling her…"

"Bravo!" Gnô cheered.

"That's Sylvie all right," Saint-Clair said. "Go on."

"I left with my mistress and that's all. Did we go back through the exercise room? I don't remember. I was holding my stumbling mistress. She was leading the way. I was just looking at her. And I never went back to that room."

"When did this happen?" Saint-Clair asked.

"Well, is it past midnight?"

"Yes."

"So, today's June 7?"

"Exactly."

"Well then, yesterday, June 6, the day before, June 5, no, it was the night before, so June 4."

"Okay. And since then, you're sure you've never been back to the room?"

"Absolutely sure."

"And have you seen the lady, the child or his nanny?"

"No."

"So, I'm back to my first question. Who was in charge of taking care of the prisoners? Was it just the nanny?"

"No. The relay between my mistress and the lady, between the kitchen and the prison-room was carried out by a Spanish servant I heard called Carmetta."

"And where is she? We've seen every room but no sign of her though we found all the other servants."

"I don't know, but I think she used to sleep on a bunk in the corridor outside the room. In the little corridor I told you about off the exercise room."

"Oh, come on," Gnô exclaimed. "There's got to be another exercise room! It's not impossible. We could've missed a small side corridor and it could be the one leading to another exercise room."

"Yes, that's possible," Saint-Clair pondered. "So, from what we've just heard, Hamed only recently came to Lost Island with Titania, but Loustal and Marod were here already with Joao Matello. We can suppose they were part of his staff. Let's go ask them."

"Let's go," Gnô agreed. And then to the Nubian, "Hamed, start walking. We tied them up with Peul. We'll forget about Peul who only got here a few hours before you did, but we're going to interrogate the sailors. You know where they are, right?"

"Yes."

"Good. You go first, that way we won't get lost."

A few minutes later Saint-Clair and Gnô, right behind Hamed, were back in the sailors' room. It was to the right of the big vestibule that led to the main door. It was a rather big room, very comfortable, with two beds, two wardrobes and adjoining a modern bathroom. Obviously, Loustal and Marod, although just underlings, were respected by Matello and no less by Titania since she had left them this room that they had been living in, apparently, for a long time. In fact, the walls were decorated tastefully but very personally. Everything about the room was personalized.

For the moment Loustal and Marod were lying half-dressed on their beds, tightly bound and gagged. Perhaps such strict measures were not necessary with them and Peul? But Saint-Clair and Gnô had thought that, in case their luck changed, it would be better not to let anyone suspect these men of betrayal.

Now, therefore, they continued to act as if they had never met the two sailors. They asked them their names and spoke to them hard and rudely because of Hamed's presence. But from their clearly honest answers it was obvious that the two sailors did not know where the prisoners were being held.

"And yet," Saint-Clair said, "you're sure they're here on the island?"

"We didn't see them in person," Loustal replied. "We talked about them with Carmetta, the Galician girl who was in charge of them."

"And this girl, where is she? Where's her room?" Gnô asked.

"A little room next to the cook's room."

"That room was empty," Gnô said. "We saw it. And this Carmetta can't be found anywhere."

"That's all we know," Loustal muttered.

Leaving them there, Saint-Clair and Gnô took Hamed to see Julien Peul. They got a second edition of the tale told on the speedboat. But this edition was new, revised, corrected, edited and complete.

While pretending not to know Saint-Clair and Gnô, but convinced that they would, in the end, vanquish Titania and the Hashshashins, Peul held nothing back. A few obscure points were clarified in his account.

"Alerted the night of May 22 by an order sent over the wireless as a musical phrase," he told them, "I went to watch the border of Cerbère and Portbou. On May 28 I recognized you, Saint-Clair the Nyctalope, on the sidewalk outside the train station in Portbou. You were tailing some guy. I saw you knock him down. I kept out of sight. And then I lost you because you got in a boat so I stuck to the guy you handed over to the Spanish police. I talked to him in the train in code so the guards didn't understand a word. And that's how I took his place with Joao Matello, the main agent of the Hashshashins in the Burgos region.

"This Matello saw some things in me that he liked, which got him to divulge certain secrets to me and me to entrust myself to him. His goal was to betray the Hashshashin, to keep for himself all the credit and profit for kidnapping Sylvie Saint-Clair and her son and to make you pay a heavy ransom with which he could support a revolutionary movement in Portugal where he was planning to become dictator.

"On June 2 we brought Madame Saint-Clair and the nurse here by plane. The child had been stolen from us by a gypsy girl who'd blinded us with pepper while Matello was off killing Escarpaz, the patriarch of the Zapatan gypsies.

"But a few minutes after the two women were locked up here and while Matello and I were getting ready to take the plane back to search for the son, Titania, the queen of the Hashshashins, arrived on Lost Island also by plane. She'd caught us off guard. She interrogated the men who'd seen the prisoners arrive and guessed that Matello was going to betray her. She took me aside and threatened with death I told her the truth.

"Matello's personnel had been cut back to the minimum, down to four: the Galician servant girl, the couple in the kitchen and their son. All the others, guards, officers, soldiers—it'd been like a military garrison here under Matello—had already gone back to Portugal to work as revolutionary agents.

"Titania pretended not to know anything about Matello's traitorous projects. But she said she wanted to go with him to recover the baby from the gypsy girl. I knew that before they even found the child Titania had shot Matello to death. I'd stayed on the island. Titania had showed me mercy but as a result I hated her and swore to betray her the first chance I got."

Peul broke out in cackling laughter, which did not lack remorse, and spouted, "My life is really weird. I started off with dreams of conquest, honor and glory but I've just gone from one betrayal to another. You know everything now. What do you want from me?"

Saint-Clair and Gnô were not expecting such a disgraceful and pitiable confession from the wayward young man. They were starting to think that too much time had already passed between their arrival on the island and the eventual rescue of the prisoners. This rescue had to happen without further delay. They had not interrupted Peul during his speech but as soon as he had finished Saint-Clair ordered:

"Get up and take me to the room where my wife and son are being held prisoner."

"But I don't where it is!" Peul insisted. "When Matello brought me here he left me in the guardhouse while he locked up your wife. When Titania came back with the baby I was still staying there and I never found out where they were locked up."

"But," Gnô said, "you're sure that they were locked up here on Lost Island."

"Oh yes, I'm sure of that."

"And no one took them away?"

"No," Peul answered confidently. "Besides, you can only get off the island with the speedboat or by plane. The speedboat only went out one since I got here and that was for Loustal and Marod to get supplies in Vigo. As for airplanes, the one belonging to Matello and the one Titania with her Nubian Hamed came in are both in the big barracks transformed into hangars. Have you seen the hangars?"

"Yes," Saint-Clair said, "and we saw the two planes."

"So it's there's no question that the prisoners haven't left Lost Island."

"Right," Gnô said.

At that moment, the Nyctalope's patience was wearing thin. Grief and anger were battling in his soul, stirring him up and pulling him down at the same time. But still his voice was calm when he said:

"That's enough. Now, Gnô, we've got to make sure that no one on the island is in any position to bother us. So, Peul, we're going to tie you up again. You, too, Hamed. You're not going to be eating for a few hours, so if you get hungry or thirsty, be patient. I don't mean you any harm. When this is all over I'll probably just let you go, but behave yourselves and don't try to get free because Gnô and I will be coming back to check on you from time to time. Any sign of revolt will earn you a bullet in the head. Do you understand me?"

Peul, without saying a word, plopped down on the cot and crossed his legs to be tied up, which they were. Hamed was taken back to his room where he was also tied up. Then Saint-Clair and Gnô went to see the two sailors, the watchmen and the kitchen help. All were immobilized.

"Now," Saint-Clair said, "we're going to go through everything again, room by room, but first let's plan it out. We'll do it this time to be sure that there are no hidden rooms. What do you think?"

"Yes, yes, that's the only thing we can do."

"Very well. But first I've got something to say to Titania."

The two men went back to *La Vibora*'s room. Diana Ivanovna appeared to be sleeping. Her beautiful face was calm, her breath steady.

"Oh, oh," Saint-Clair groaned while raising a fist over her, "this is the first time in my life that I'd feel pleasure in killing..."

The woman opened her eyes. Saint-Clair saw that she wanted to talk. Without trying to be gentle, he tore the gag from her.

"Speak!" he ordered. "What do you have to say?"

"Well," her voice imitated sweetness, "kill me. Kill me if you dare because I'll never talk."

"Don't tempt me! I might just do it anyway. Listen up."

He leaned over her, his right hand gripped her shoulder and he growled:

"Twenty-four hours. I'm giving you twenty-four hours during which time my friend and I will search Lost Island inch by inch. If I haven't found my wife and son in twenty-four hours, I'll come back to see you. If you don't tell me where they are, I swear on everything I hold sacred in this world that I will kill you!"

He straightened up and stomped out of the room. Gnô did not follow him right away. He stayed with the Red Princess, checked the bindings, tightened the knots and said:

"I won't bother with the gag. You can scream. Nobody is coming to save you and you'll never break free. One more thing, madame, in case my friend Leo doesn't have the nerve to kill you, I'll do it myself. I'm Oriental. I'm not as sensitive as Europeans. I'll shoot you in the head or stab you in the heart. But I'll make you suffer first and I'll be damned if I don't wring the information out of you."

While speaking the Japanese must have really glowed with cruelty in his eyes because Titania, who had held the Nyctalope's stare, closed her eyes faced with Gnô's.

Outside the room he found his friend.

Saint-Clair said, "We could trust the two sailors, convince them to talk."

"Good idea," Gnô approved.

When they were back with the two sailors Saint-Clair said, "Loustal, Marod, we're in control of Lost Island. Titania and Hamed are out of action. Do you want to side with us? Do we have to show you Titania tied up on her bed to help you to decide?"

The Japanese had taken out their gags.

Loustal answered, "Neither my partner not I doubt you, monsieur. But it would be nice to see Titania like that."

"Well, follow us."

Unbound, the two sailors followed Saint-Clair and Gnô to *La Vibora*'s room. When they saw that Titania was really the Nyctalope's prisoner, they did not hesitate. Before her glaring eyes Loustal told Saint-Clair:

"Monsieur, we're with you. We've been servants of Matello and this woman for too long. We ask you, however, not to use us against her personally. Then we'll work with you in good faith and do whatever you say."

"Very well," the Nyctalope agreed.

They all left the room. Saint-Clair gave instructions to the sailors to take the speedboat and bring a note he wrote to Vitto and Socca in the cove. It was an order for them to come to Lost Island on the plane.

The two hangars were already occupied by Matello's and Titania's planes so the *Goéland III* would roll up the slope and be anchored as firmly as possible. At least it was the season in this latitude that windstorms and squalls were rare. Plus, the bay was well sheltered by the cliffs around it. Thus the plane could stay outside without being damaged.

Of course, on this night of June 7, Saint-Clair and Gnô needed rest, but they did not think about it. Their taut nerves kept them going and they were eager to discover the secret of Lost Island and finally free Sylvie, Pierrot and Adele. Two men like them were not being presumptuous in hoping, even knowing they would succeed withing twenty-four hours. There was good reason that strong minds spent their youths cultivating the science of observation, deduction and logic. Since the prisoners had, by all accounts, been brought to Lost Island on June 2 or 3 and not left, they had to be there.

As well designed as the octagonal building, barracks and basements were, even if they were partly built like mazes, what the builders had cooked up other men could also imagine.

"Let's not wait for Vitto and Socca," Saint-Clair said. "We should get to work right away."

The first thing they did was to go to the electrical control room. After studying the various switchboards they turned on every single light on island. Then they went into Titania's study/work room and started looking for a document that they were almost sure was there: a map of Lost Island. But after an hour of careful searching they were forced to admit that there was no map.

"Okay," Saint-Clair said, "we'll just have to make a map as we go along. We'll measure every inch of the island and I hope I won't have to keep my word and stab Diana Ivanovna in the heart."

CHAPTER IV
The grand alarm

In the villa of *The Sycamores* in Versailles, in the strange, secret, underground room where they had held on May 29 the council of the Hashshashins, presided over by Sunday, a very similar council was held again on the night of June 6.

Over the course of the last week, one of the sect members, the one answering to the name of Freitag and called number 6, had died suddenly of an embolism. Now, the law of the Hashshashins required that when one of the seven was taken away by death, he had to be replaced by a new member within eight days so that the Council of the Seven was always complete. On this night, therefore, the solemn choice of the new member had taken place. He had been chosen from among the European Fidawis by a vote of those present, of course only after making the list that never included more than three or four names and was drawn up by Sunday alone, dictatorially. Thus, the nomination of a new Hashshashin was always prepared in advance by Titania in case of her absence, as was the case here to replace number 6. The name and the social status of the new Freitag was unimportant.

Introduced by Rosario first into the villa, then into the secret underground room, the Convoked was recognized by three Hashshashins, including Number 2, Montag, a.k.a. Dr. Korridès. To the two others he was completely unknown. He was a man of medium height, looked in good health, well built and energetic, his clean-shaven face revealed a quick and cold intelligence. No rite had been performed. Summoned by a special wireless, he came from Brussels because he was Belgium. He was welcomed with smiles and outstretched hands. Montag introduced him to the two members who did not know him and then he had to undergo the three prescribed ordeals.

These ordeals were designed to test in the Convoked his physical endurance of pain, his emotional resistance to unexpected fear and his natural power facing sudden and horrendous dangers.

For the physical ordeal they submitted the Convoked to torture by fire. This ordeal was performed with a branding iron in such a way that the candidate was burned very painfully in several parts of his body but without hindering his ability to move. When it was over, they bandaged the wounds, which eased the pain a great deal and avoided future complications.

The emotional ordeal was done with a kind of lie. Most of the judges, meaning at least four of the six (but this time it was four out of five with Sunday absent), pretended that the ordeal by fire was not honorably endured and that the Convoked was therefore rejected. Since this rejection meant immediate death to preserve their secrets, Montag announced to the candidate that he had the right to express his last wishes before he was killed. Then three Hashshashins were given Brownings that they aimed at the condemned man. How the man reacted to this unexpected death sentence was a demonstration of his emotional strength.

If this ordeal was suitably endured, they went on to the third. If not, meaning if he showed any weakness, the sentence was really carried out and they shot him dead. But if he survived the second ordeal, he passed onto the third, which was to judge his strength of character. This third ordeal seemed milder but was, in truth, the most formidable. More than one candidate had failed. It seemed mild in the sense that it only consisted of a short speech by Montag. But in this speech Dr. Korridès gazed steadily and ominously at the candidate as he enumerated the various dangers that the members of the Grand Council faced: dangers inherent in their various missions, the danger of falling into the hands of the law in different countries or falling prey to semi-savage fanatics, the danger of not satisfying the Grand Mistress of the Hashshashins, whom they called Sunday in the council but had the common name of Titania. In this last case they could expect the most excruciating tortures before dying and more often than not this torture and death was carried out in front of the eyes of the victim's loved ones.

This speech usually lasted around twenty minutes. It sounded even more dreadful because the others kept absolutely silent and stone-faced the entire time. Moreover, the mystery surrounding the meeting, the strangeness of the place, everything the candidate knew or suspected about the Hashshashins, of whom he had been one of the main Fidawi for a long time, and finally the dark gaze, somber voice and haunting face of Korridès all made the speech into highly charged evocation of the many dangers faced when given the honor of being one of the seven council members.

Of course, if in the expressions on his face, in the twitching of his eyes, any sign of weakness or a clumsy, careless or sullen comment, the Convoked One did not satisfy the third ordeal, he was killed mercilessly. For, the law of the Hashshashins demanded that every Convoked One be put to death if he was not elected unanimously. Only one voice against and the Convoked One was condemned without appeal. All these precautions were necessary for the seven council members to be absolutely certain that they formed a union of physical and intellectual power without the slightest flaw.

The Belgian passed all three ordeals with flying colors. He was elected unanimously by the five present members. Montag told him that he would henceforth be known as Freitag, number 6. Then the council proper was held as usual, examining the news from around the world during the previous week.

Montag, Diens, Mittwoch, Donners, Freitag and Sams were busy working when a shrill alarm suddenly went off. The deafening noise echoed through the entire basement. Some of them just froze, but others cried out, "The alarm! The grand alarm!"

Montag stood up and raised his right hand, "Silence! Let's wait. It might just be a warning."

After their initial reactions of surprise, Diens, Mittwoch, Donners and Sams sat down and looked at Dr. Korridès who was still standing. Freitag had also stood up but he did not understand what was happening because he did not know what the shrill ringing meant or why they called it "the grand alarm". It must have been very serious judging by the unrestrained emotion on the faces of the others. Anxious and curious, Freitag waited. Not for long. It lasted thirty seconds of anguished silence and then the six men (including Freitag) shuddered when the dire alarm rang out again.

It sounded like it came from everywhere, out of the walls, the ceiling, the floor. It was brief. Afterward the silence felt like death. Pale, his hands trembling a little, Montag would have failed the second ordeal at this moment. Still, he pronounced in a steady voice:

"My friends, our dear Sunday is threatened with death and our work is in danger."

Freitag, feeling the emotion in the air, did not try to control himself, "Look, I'm new here. I don't understand. Please, explain it to me."

Everyone looked at him.

In the same quiet voice, but panting a little, Korridès said, "That's true, you don't know. Well, listen, I'll be brief because there's no time to lose. We have a one-of-a-kind secret lair. It's the headquarters of the Hashshashins. It's sovereign land, meaning we make our laws there without any nation on earth interfering in our actions. In this place is our treasure. In this place is a special prison we made where we can hold high-valued hostages or captives whose confinement or death is of the utmost importance to us. In this place, finally, is my latest invention, the most beautiful, most useful, the one I'm most proud of. So, to signal to us that the treasure, hostages or my invention is at risk of being stolen, we built a mechanical and wireless system to warn us of the threat. And so we've been.

"Right now, then, Titania is in the secret place that is called Lost Island. And it's from this island that the grand alarm is coming. I know Titania, we all know her, for her to set off the alarm she must be in danger of death.

"This island, Freitag, is around Cape Finisterre at the northwest end of Spain. All six of us are going there. No more talking. Are you ready to obey?"

Having spoken (during which Dr. Korridès had recovered, at least in appearance, all his composure and self-control) he walked off to the left end of the room, opened a cabinet, then a wall panel and thus revealed a telephone. He pressed a button and spoke into it immediately:

"Hello? Hello? Do you hear me?"

"…"

"Very good. Is it you, Dermoz?"

"…"

"Good. Congratulations. I'd have been sorry to see you caught off guard. We're leaving in an hour. There will be six of us. Yes. Do you have everything necessary?"

"..."

"So there's nothing you need us to bring you from Paris?"

"..."

"Very well. Get the plane ready so that we can take off at once."

"..."

"Perfect. In an hour, Dermoz."

Korridès put back the panel, closed the cabinet, crossed the room and pulled and pushed some books on the bookshelf, which immediately split into two and separated, revealing a section of the wall. Korridès took one step forward, pressed a previously hidden wooden slat on the parquet floor and a closet door opened. The tall, wide, deep closet was an arsenal.

"Arm yourselves," Korridès ordered.

There were different models of Brownings, clips and packs of bullets. There were also swords and stilettos. Lastly, there were rifles with explosive cartridges.

Freitag was the last one there but like his colleagues he took a Browning, half a dozen clips and two packs of bullets. He put them all in his pockets, although it was a little burdensome.

When they were all armed, Korridès closed the closet, put the bookshelf back in place and said:

"We have nothing more to do here. Your coats are upstairs. Before sunrise we'll be at Le Bourget and five hours later, I hope, we'll be landing near Lost Island. From this moment on don't forget that we're soldiers and I'm your chief. Above all, don't forget that, like me, you have sworn your life to the sacred cause of the Hashshashins. Whatever dangers we're going to face, tell yourself that your death will be helping everyone, especially if it helps to save Titania, without whom the Hashshashins and their work would've long ago crumbled to dust."

Mittwoch, number 4, raised his right hand and with exalted gravity said, "May we die so she can live! Long live Titania!"

Diens, Donners,Sams and Freitag lifted their hands in turn and faced Montag, chanting, "Long live Titania!"

Montag was the last to pronounce in the same tone, "May we die so that she can live! Long live Titania!"

And the six men left the underground chamber, went into the courtyard of *The Sycamores*, then into the garage where there were two cars: one a two-seater sports car, the other a sedan that could comfortably seat eight passengers. The Hashshashins all climbed into the latter. Diens took the wheel with Montag next to him. Mittwoch, Donners, Sams and Freitag slid into the backseat and the car started.

Before leaving the villa Dr. Korridès had a case from his workshop. It had the size and appearance of a portable typewriter. He kept the case carefully protected between his feet.

The maid Rosario was left alone to close up *The Sycamores*.

The pilot Dermoz, an Austrian but naturalized French, somewhat known in the aviation world for certain performances, was in reality a Fidawi Hashshashin. He was a front man for the sect as owner of a private hangar and a big, modern, private plane at Le Bourget airport. They believed that Dermoz was rich and he supplemented his income by flying wealthy tourists around the world. That was why no one was ever surprised to see him over the last six months take off at odd times in his eight-seater plane with an electric motor, always bound for distant locations.

It was no different this morning. Besides, no one was there to witness the departure of the *Vulture*.

When the Hashshashin council traveled all together, one of the six served as the mechanic because all the members were both scientists and technicians, either in mechanics, chemistry, physics or even balistics. All of them could fly a plane, especially Titania when she was part of the expedition. Thus Dermoz could not only be assisted but replaced if need be. When the *Vulture* was in the air heading south at 140 mph, the Hashshashins started talking. The plane, fitted with two state-of-the-art electric engines, flew almost soundlessly. They could, therefore, hold a conversation in a normal voice inside the cabin.

The members had, for a long time now, regained their self-control. Naturally, they started forming hypotheses about what had caused Titania to set off the grand alarm.

"In my opinion," Sams said, "it's got nothing to do with the Nyctalope. It's true we haven't heard anything specific for a few days and we don't know exactly what the Fidawis in Spain are doing, but it's also true that Titania for some reason decided not to keep us informed of what she was doing on Lost Island. I think Matello must have betrayed her."

Mittwoch asked, "Are you sure he betrayed her?"

"Absolutely," Sams replied. "Don't forget that Titania left for the island because she suspected a betrayal. It'd been 48 hours since she'd heard from Darlecq in Irun, Julien Peul in Portbou, Escarpaz the Bohemian and Matello in Burgos. Well, Matello is the sovereign ruler of Lost Island, remember. We know that before entering our sect he personally financed a project for a Portuguese revolution. If Titania's suspicions were right, she could've found the situation on Lost Island extremely dangerous to our cause and therefore sounded the alarm."

"That's all fine," Diens said, "but what I want to know is where's the Nyctalope. According to the last report he was seen entering the Nopals chateau in Saint-Jean-Cap-Ferrat. Since then, no news."

Montag turned around in his seat and said flatly, "We'll have Saint-Clair working against us directly only if we've got his wife and son in our hands."

"Of course," Donners said, "but what scares me now is that Sunday, your wife, my dear doctor, hasn't given us news for four days since she got to Lost Island."

Montag furrowed his brow, then shrugged and grumbled, "The only flaw in the queen of the Hashshashins is her pride in winning. The harder the game, the more she wants to win it by herself. All of you, except Freitag the newcomer among us, you all know that in the small operations in which she was directly involved she had hourly conferences with the council. On the other hand, every time it was something really important, we only found out the details after it was over. Remember that last Mexican revolution in which we had rightly placed so many hopes that were fully realized. Titania took charge of that all alone and we went two days without any news. When she told us about the victory of our partisans, the whole thing was over, so fast and efficient that the news agencies around the world were learning about it almost at the same time as us."

"That's true," Sams said.

"In the current case," Montag continued, "it's a matter of killing one man who could be a serious impediment to organizing the next international revolution, which is our ultimate goal, really our only goal! Well, as long as Titania doesn't have the Nyctalope in her hands, made a prisoner, sentenced to death and beyond rescue from anyone, then she won't be giving us any news. And if she's set off the grand alarm, it's only because her life's in danger and our projects are seriously compromised."

With intervals of silence, both short and long, the conversation of the Hashshashins carried on this subject, each expressing his idea whenever a new thought sprang to mind. And not just to talk but because these men knew very well that by calmly and coldly expressing their thoughts they would shed as much light as possible on the situation and thus prepare themselves psychologically for whatever was to come.

Dermoz did not seem to be listening. He participated in no conversation. He concentrated on piloting the airplane, which he did with the utmost skill. Sometimes he asked Diens, the mechanic, to look at this or that mechanism. He waited for the report, sometimes made a comment, then fell right back into his silence. Dermoz was not usually very talkative. He worked with a cold, calm but consummate passion and they knew that he had come into the sect for the sake of personal hatred after watching his hopes be crushed by the military authorities of his country. He was, in short, a bitter man, a calculating rebel who was waiting for his affiliation with the Hashshashins to satisfy his individual grudges.

Taken off from Le Bourget, the airplane flew over Mans, Nantes, then soared off over the Atlantic Ocean, around the Bay of Biscay, and veered directly for Cape Finisterre. Like all truly modern planes the *Vulture* was amphibious, meaning it could also land and navigate on water like a boat. Here the *Vulture* had no need to prove its nautical skills. The trip was without incident and the landing, although very difficult, was a perfect success. Of course, Dermoz had practiced on another plane, lighter and easier to handle, to manage this landing.

The place: a plain forming a wide, shallow basin in a narrow crater between two mountain summits. It was a high plain, completely isolated. Roughly rectangular, it measured over half a mile long and half that in width. It was in the middle of the mountain range that looked directly over Cape Finisterre and Cape Toriana and therefore the bay of Lost Island, which was concealed between the two capes. To the west of the landing plain the mountain formed a kind of rocky lookout point and it was among these rocks that they had set up a wireless radio to communicate directly with Lost Island. The station was completely invisible among the rocks, even up close, because it blended in perfectly. This wild terrain was hard to get to except from the plain and was usually only occupied by two men: one to operate the wireless and the other to get supplies. These two men were replaced every month from the troops normally garrisoned on the island. But these troops had been recently sent to Portugal by Joao Matello, a detail not yet known to the Hashshashins.

When the *Vulture* had stopped, the Hashshashins set out. Dermoz remained alone. They would send back the supply man to help him anchor the plane onto the landing strip. Hurriedly, Montag, Diens, Mittwoch, Donners, Freitag and Sams headed to the station. In a small crater the station was built to look like the surrounding rocks. Even the window, as narrow as arrow slots, looked like holes and cracks created by the whim of nature and not by the hand of man. The main building had a tower, which looked in ruins from the outside but was internally solid and comfortably housed the two bedrooms and sophisticated wireless station.

The poles and antennae were hidden very cleverly: invisible everywhere except in the crater itself but enough exposed that they could send and receive messages without interference.

At the doorway to the tower the Hashshashins were met by the two men. The wireless operator was a Frenchman called Lavignon; the other was a Spaniard named Dontes.

They saluted military style when Montag, whom they both knew, made the cabalistic sign of the Hashshashin on his chest and forehead.

"Dontes," he said, "go help the pilot anchor down the plane. You, Lavignon, take us to your office. You have some explanations to give us."

The office, i.e. the room where all the wireless equipment was kept, was on the third floor of the tower, above which was the terrace accessible by a small, spiral staircase. There were two armchairs and several stools in the room. Montag took one of the armchairs and pointed to the other for the wireless operator while the five Hashshashins sat on the stools.

"Lavignon, tell us about the radio messages you've sent and received since June 2."

"Monsieur, on June 2 I received a message in the evening from Lost Island announcing the arrival of Titania. I acknowledged reception as usual. Since then, nothing except, of course, the signal for the grand alarm, which I expect is what brought you here so fast."

"The signal wasn't preceded by any spoken or written message?"

"None," Lavignon replied.

"But surely, after the signal you were watching Lost Island day and night?"

"Of course. Ten days of supplies had been brought here on June 4. Dontes and I, therefore, had all our time to observe the island through the telescope. We saw in the round courtyard two men we didn't recognize going back and forth. It was right after that that we got the signal for the grand alarm. That's all."

"That's not much," Donners said.

"That's nothing," Mittwoch added. "These strangers must've have been people sent by Matello."

"Oh, I've got one thing to say about Matello. Maybe I should tell you everything I noticed about the matter. It's written in the logbook here. Let me read it to you."

Lavignon leaned over, reached out and grabbed a big book from the table. After flipping the pages he read:

"May 31: the pilot Loustal and the mechanic leave the island in a plane.

"June 2: the plane is back. Come out of the hangar, cross the courtyard, enter the residence are Joao Matello, a young man I don't know, two women I've never seen. Almost right away a second plane arrives and I see Titania cross the courtyard with her Nubian.

"June 3: Titania's plane leaves. Crossed the courtyard to get on it: Titania, Matello and one of the unknown women. This evening Titania is back with the woman carrying a baby in her arms. I don't see Matello.

"June 4: nothing to note. I don't see Matello anywhere. Seems he's not on the island.

"June 5: the speedboat takes off for supplies in Vigo. I spot a plane twice out at sea. It disappears to the north as if it dove into a crevice on the shore.

"June 6: nothing.

"June 7: 1:30 a.m., middle of the night, signal of the grand alarm. Early in the morning two men I don't know come and go in the courtyard, in and out of the residence, enter the barracks. A little later the speedboat takes off with Loustal and Marod on board. An hour later they're back, with a plane that looks like the one I saw the other day. The plane is tied down by Loustal and Marod and two other men I've never seen before."

Lavignon closes the logbook and says, "That's it, monsieur."

During his reading, the Hashshashin grew more and more agitated.

Montag spoke up right away, "The two women, the expedition taken by Matello and Titania, they must've gone to get Sylvie Saint-Clair, her son and the nanny!"

During the flight in the *Vulture* the new Hashshashin, number 6, Freitag, had been initiated by his colleagues into the Nyctalope affair. Although he was too modest to take part in the present conversation, he was well informed so that he understood everything they said. That was why the reading of the logbook was as fascinating to him as to the rest.

Mittwoch spoke next, "That's it, for sure. But where's Matello? Why didn't he come back with Titania on June 3? And what's happened since then? And those two strangers?"

"That's right, that's right," Donners and Sams chimed in.

Diens and Freitag were whispering together about the third plane that they went to fetch.

Confusion reigned for a few minutes, but Montag controlled himself, raised his hand and announced with authority:

"Messieurs, silence, please. There's only one thing for us to do. It's to start watching and maybe we'll recognize the four men Lavignon didn't know, if they show themselves, that is. Whatever's happening, since the grand alarm hasn't been clarified, this seems to me the best course of action given the presence of the four strangers, the absence of Matello and the arrival of the third plane. Again, it's reasonable to think this is the work of Matello who might've gone to Portugal and delegated some accomplices against Titania. At any rate, our queen, my wife, is a prisoner of these strangers. Maybe they've killed her... But before being rendered powerless or being killed, she managed to push one of the secret buttons scattered around, which sent the signal for the grand alarm. But enough talking. Let's get up to the terrace and keep an eye on Lost Island."

The station was equipped with a powerful telescope mounted on a tripod and left permanently on the terrace, sheltered in a small booth. There were even some good binoculars in the storeroom.

Along with Lavignon, the Hashshashins climbed up to the terrace. Dr. Korridès went to the telescope and put down a very small, very strange device, a little like a bizarre machine gun mounted on a tripod, which he had taken out of the case he had carried with him from *The Sycamores*. His colleagues lined up on either side. Lavignon jumped over close to him as well. Everyone had binoculars. The seven pairs of eager eyes observed Lost Island.

The lookout point from where the telescope and binoculars trained their lenses stood four hundred yards above the tiny bay in the middle of which the island squatted. Without thinking for a second about the magnificent panorama of the exceptional view of the picturesque coast, the seven men concentrated all their attention on the few square yards of Lost Island.

It was 9:42 a.m. on June 7.

CHAPTER V
Another little pile of ashes

When Vitto and Socca, assisted by Loustal and Marod, had carefully anchored the *Goéland III* on the sloping bank of Lost Island, they were taken by the two sailors into Titania's sitting room/library.

After meticulously examining the barracks and convinced that there was no secret room where Sylvie, Pierrot and Adele could be hidden, Saint-Clair and Gnô could now concentrate all their efforts on the octagonal building and the basements, which were still quite mysterious. They decided, therefore, to hold a kind of council to clarify the situation, give opinions and try to remember anything that might be useful. At this council, besides Saint-Clair and Gnô, were Julien Peul and the two sailors, along with Vitto and Socca of course.

Saint-Clair and Gnô had overcome their anger, grief and anxieties once and for all. It was a matter of not letting their emotions disturb their logical thinking in any way. They had to proceed with the search not as father, husband or friend but with the same cold equanimity, the same keen observation and reflection as a chemist with a strange and curious compound trying to extract an ingredient whose existence is logically necessary.

Julien Peul was freed by Loustal and brought to the room.

"Peul," the Nyctalope addressed him, "we're holding a council and you can participate. I invite you to give your honest opinion. You can fool me, betray me, there's no threat against you. I'll just remind you that we are in control of Lost Island now. We are in control of Titania. I know almost nothing about the Hashshashins. In a few hours, I think, the French government will be informed so that they'll get their hands on all the leaders of the sect. So, it's in your interest to cooperate. What you say and do will determine how I treat you. For the moment, I'm forgetting all about your past, even the role you played in what might be the most horrible calamity of my life. Now, take a seat and take part in this council, right next to Loustal and Marod. Everyone, please sit down."

The seven men sat down, forming two groups slightly separated. On one side, Saint-Clair and Gnô, flanked by Vitto and Socca. Across from them, Julien Peul between Loustal and Marod. The room was now lit with sunlight coming through the open French door on the balcony. This French door faced the ocean and was high enough that one could see the *Goéland III* beyond the courtyard and barracks and beyond that the vast blue sea under the still rosy morning sky.

On the table Saint-Clair had put a big white piece of paper on which Gnô had drawn a rough map of Lost Island. The central building was only sketched in with an octagonal figure.

"Messieurs," Saint-Clair began, "here's where we are as far as our main concern. Our investigations into the room where not only my wife, son and Adele are imprisoned but also where the servant named Carmetta is hiding, have had positive results in the sense that we now know that further search must be limited to the octagonal building and the basements. The barracks are architecturally too simple to be hiding any false doors, so to speak. But it's not the same with this octagonal building and the basements. The architecture of the various rooms that look adjoined is very complicated. It's possible, in fact probable, certainly logical, yes, that the prison room we're looking for is a secret room hidden like a secret drawer that we don't know where exactly it is and won't find it except by demolishing the piece of furniture itself."

"Exactly," Gnô said.

"Well," Saint-Clair went on, "I won't hesitate, if need be, to demolish every building on this island, brick by brick, as they say. But I think we don't have to resort to such desperate measures, a long, hard task anyway, if we can apply intelligent observation, methodical investigation and logical thinking.

"Of course, we're taking as a given that the prisoners are still on the island. We've got witnesses who say they saw them come here but never leave. So, they're still here. We have to find them.

"Peul, Loustal, Marod, think hard, try to remember anything that might have something to do with my wife, son, with Adele or even with Carmetta having to take care of them."

He looked at Gnô, Socca and Vitto and added:

"Let's take five minutes to consider this."

Peul leaned back in his armchair, looked up and started thinking with his eyes closed. Loustal had both elbows on the table, his face in his hands, showing only the short-cropped hair on the top of his head. Marod crossed his arms, sat stiffly, furrowed his brow and stared ahead, seeing nothing.

They heard the ticktock of the modern clock built into a kind of 16th century, forged iron coat of arms that made an odd ornament between the two bookshelves. The metallic clicking, steady and monotonous, was accompanied by the muted rumble of the ocean waves breaking against the shores. The weather was nice. Scents from both the sea and forests mingled with the cheery sunlight in the luxurious room. All this was a stark contrast to the tragedy that the men gathered there were suffering through.

Saint-Clair and Gnô perhaps felt this contrast and were savoring it like the artists they were. But they showed no sign. Calm, impassive, hands on the table, they looked at the others and waited.

One, two minutes passed and the third was about to tick off when Loustal suddenly looked up.

"Monsieur," he looked at Saint-Clair, "can I say something?"

"Certainly."

"Several times, just out of curiosity, I did go looking for the window of the room where your family must've been locked up. I know every single one of the windows and French doors of the octagonal building. Walking around the outside I can tell you which room each of them belongs to. And I never did find a window to a room or rooms that could be the prison. But I saw them all…"

He stopped talking. Saint-Clair and Gnô had listened to him attentively.

Gnô asked, "What's your conclusion?"

"I conclude that the prison doesn't have a window facing outside."

"Very good," the Nyctalope said, "thank you."

Loustal blushed, put his elbows back on the table and buried his face again.

Then Peul straightened up and looked at Saint-Clair, "Loustal's right. I did it too. And it's weird, I completely forgot. Loustal just reminded me. So, I can confirm what he said and I'll add that yesterday morning when I ran into Carmetta, I was joking around and said:

"You must miss elevators on Lost Island.

"Why?" she sounded surprised.

"Well, because going up and down twenty times a day to serve the prisoners…

"Oh, I won't have to go up and down much anymore because the prison isn't one where you stay for long.

"That's good for you," I said.

"At the moment I didn't think much of the short conversation, which started because I thought the prison was in the basements, which I knew little about… From Carmetta's response it's easy to see that the prison really is underground but it's only a temporary one."

"Very good!" Saint-Clair said. "Thank you."

"One more thing," Peul went on, proudly satisfied that his information seemed more important than Loustal's. "Yesterday morning also, a little before noon, I was in this room where Titania had summoned me to give me some orders for the next supply run to Vigo. While she was giving me these orders, which had nothing to do with all this, Carmetta came in and asked if she could give Madame Sylvie… she did say Madame Sylvie, a second pair of scissors. Titania shrugged her shoulders, smiled briefly, grabbed a pair that was lying on the table and told her, 'Sure, give her these.' Then Carmetta left.

"It wasn't more than a couple of minutes, of course, from the moment Carmetta left with the scissors and when I left with the orders. And I saw her in the vestibule dashing through the door leading to the office. She didn't have the scissors in her hand. Therefore, she had given them to your wife. Going to give them and coming back in two minutes, I think that proves that the prison isn't far from this room.

"The octagonal building is huge with a jumbled maze of hallways, vestibules and all kinds of rooms. If we look at the position of this room, which I believe is at the far west side of the building, I figure the prison is somewhere in the middle. I also figure that it's partly underground and partly on the ground floor or at least easily accessible from the ground floor."

And he stopped talking.

"Very good!" the Nyctalope said again. "Thank you."

He turned to Gnô and they smiled at each other. With just these two accounts of Loustal and Peul they had grounds to believe that the search for the mysterious prison was narrowing significantly.

The five minutes were up, but since Marod was still stiff and staring at nothing, still lost in arduous thought, Saint-Clair kept waiting. It did not last much longer than the first time. Exactly six minutes passed in total silence when Marod suddenly uncrossed his arms, slammed his two fists on the table, leaned forward and drawled:

"Me, the day before yesterday I heard Titania tell the Nubian, 'Yes, she saw me through the window, crossing the courtyard when I arrived with the nanny and the kid. It doesn't matter. But being able to see outside might end up being a problem. I'll get rid of the periscope.' That's all."

"Ah!" Saint-Clair exclaimed, "How did you hear this?"

"I was bringing around the tail of Titania's plane and the door of the hangar was wide open. She and Hamed were walking along the bulwark. I heard them when they were right over me. Of course, I didn't understand a word and thought nothing of it. But now I think it might be helpful to you."

"It certainly is," Saint-Clair said. "Thank you."

He looked at Gnô whose eyes were sparkling. He put his left hand on the right hand of his friend on the edge of the table and whispered to him:

"This third piece of information corroborates the other two. From now on we can accept the fact that the prison is in this building, probably in the middle, and it's only connection to the outside is through a periscope. But the periscope is set up in such a way that the prisoners believe they've got one or more windows looking outside. That's what we've learned from these guys' memories."

"Hey!" Peul cried out, "That periscope, I saw the outside of it!" And he jumped up.

Saint-Clair and Gnô stood up along with the others. They were all trying to hide the emotion that was flooding the room.

Gnô demanded, "You saw the outside of the periscope?"

"Yes, yes, I'm sure of it," Peul affirmed. "I was wondering what that pipe with several branches was because the tips were glinting strangely. Damnation, it was the periscope! Come on!"

In the grip of an understandable fever, Peul ran out. Loustal and Marod, being more disciplined, stood their ground. Vitto and Socca were waiting for orders from their boss. Saint-Clair and Gnô only had to glance at each other.

"Let's go," the Nyctalope said.

It was obvious that Peul was heading to the round courtyard in order to point out the strange tube sticking out of a terrace or one of the eight walls.

Therefore, the six other men went after him through the vestibule. They all stood still just outside the main door, which Peul had left open, and watched the young man march straight to the barracks.

The were thinking, "When he reaches them, he'll turn around to look at the terrace and the three or four walls in his line of vision. Then he'll see the periscope, point at it..."

Indeed, he almost ran into the barracks facing the octagonal building when he stopped, turned around, took a few steps to the left, then the same number of steps to the right, walked into the middle of the courtyard and...

And Saint-Clair, Gnô, Vitto, Socca, Loustal and Marod saw the most unexpected, incomprehensible and quite frankly frightening thing they had ever seen.

Suddenly, Peul froze, went stiff and in a split second turned black, like an ebony statue. Immediately afterward, dark fumes wafted off his body at the same time as a long, tall flame spurted up. Then the flame went out. The fumes dissipated. Julien Peul was not there. His body was not there. There was only some obscure, bewildering thing—all that remained was a small pile of ashes in the shape of a cone. A small pile of ashes on the ground...

CHAPTER VI
Anger… and confusion

While watching from the lookout point of the wireless station, the Hashshashins were talking at the same time. They were reopening, but this time confidently backed up by certainty, the subject of Matello's betrayal, a betrayal that had dragged down the Spanish and Franco-Spanish Fidawis. Names were cursed: Julien Peul, Paul Darlecq, Escarpaz and others.

"If only one of them didn't betray us," Mittwoch said, "we'd have been warned somehow in Versailles."

"And our Titania wouldn't have been caught off guard when she came to Lost Island," Sams said. "She fell into a trap here. First, Matello gained her trust, probably even got her to give him some mission seeing that he didn't come back with her on June 3. But she came back full of confidence, feeling victorious, with Saint-Clair's son, but fell victim to a trap that Matello must've set a long time ago."

This speculation was logical since the information they had to go on was all explained by Matello's treason.

None of this information led the Hashshashins to imagine that Saint-Clair the Nyctalope and Gnô Mitang had gotten onto Lost Island. Hashing over their suppositions and deductions, the six Hashshashins, the wireless operator Lavignon, the pilot Dermoz (who had joined them), and even Dontes the supply man got more and more worked up into anger, a spiteful anger, greedy for punishment and revenge against Joao Maello, who was unfortunately not on the island, and his accomplices, whom they hoped to bring to their knees in a few hours.

Now, in the mind of Dr. Korridès, who shared his thoughts with his colleagues, a plan was forming, a plan that had the two-fold goal of pulling Titania out of danger and of punishing all of Matello's accomplices. Then they would figure out how to get hold of Matello himself and make him suffer the harsh law of the Hashshashins who punished all proven betrayals with death but only after atrocious torture.

In the opinion of his wife, his friends and himself, Dr. Korridès, otherwise called Montag in the council, had only one fault: the sudden and violent bursts of murderous rage that, in some situations, pushed this man, usually in control of himself, to act with impulsive madness. The phenomenon lasted a few seconds. All of sudden, from being calm and cold Korridès was all aquiver, almost out of his mind, with uncontrollable anger and his body, obeying the impulses of his fury-possessed mind, did something that calmed him down just as suddenly. Afterward he regretted whatever he did because it was almost always a blunder.

When he had Titania at his side he felt watched by a higher nature than his and was voluptuously delighted to be dominated by her. A kind of love languor soothed him, making these pernicious fits of anger impossible and that was why Diana Ivanovna, who knew her extraordinary husband perfectly well, never failed to be at his side when a situation might get him too worked up.

But on June 7, on this tragic morning, Diana Ivanovna was bound and gagged in her bedroom on Lost Island when Dr. Korridès, five hundred yards away on the mountain, was observing through the telescope a sight that at any moment could have spurred his anger. In fact, this anger was latent in him and in all his companions. They manifested the phenomenon of collective suggestion, collective passion. And it was a grave danger because Korridès' anger was growing, aggravated by all the angers prowling around him. Little by little, the speculations and conclusions were infused with this latent anger. Voices became rough, hard, full of hatred and menace.

By one of those unconscious gestures that, when we realize it, gives the impression that Fate or Providence has guided our hand, the doctor had put his right hand on one of the levers of the device that he had set up on the terrace next to the telescope and aimed in the same direction. With perfectly natural synchronization his right hand was moving the lever in the same direction as he moved the telescope so that the small diaphragm opening pointed at the same spot on the island.

In the group of men discussing or arguing about the facts of the same hypothesis, there were occasional silences during which their minds came up with new ideas to put forth. One of these silences had fallen upon the Hashshashins. And that was when the emptiness ceased to exist... In the round courtyard on Lost Island the emptiness ceased to exist. In the empty space between the barracks and the octagonal building the Hashshashins had seen nothing and no one so far. All of a sudden the space look filled up. But it was only one person entering the emptiness, meaning a man had come out of the building and was walking toward the barracks.

"Hey, hey," Diens said.

"Who is that?" Sams wondered aloud. "I don't recognize him. And yet I saw everyone on the island when I paid a visit to Matello about a month ago for four days..."

"Be quiet!" Korridès ordered.

Their observation from behind the telescope and binoculars sharpened. But they could only see the back of the man in the courtyard.

They were thinking, "He's going to enter that barracks. When he comes out we'll see his face."

Sams muttered, "Maybe I'll recognize him..."

But the walker did not enter the barracks. When he was almost touching the wall he swung around, stood still for a moment, then stepped to the left, to the right, and started walking back to the middle of the courtyard.

And from the mouth of Korridès issued a kind of roar. His whole body quivered. His left hand clenched the tube of the telescope. His right index finger moved a couple of inches onto a black button on the back of the device, below and to the right of the lever.

There was no flaming jet, no explosion, no flash. There was just a faint, dull click. And down below, on Lost Island, in the round courtyard, the person whom the Hashshashins were watching turned as black as an ebony statue, exhaled dark fumes, shot out a flame... and the fumes dissipated, the flame went out. There was nothing left but the bare and empty ground. But the discerning eyes of the Hashshashin spied on the ground, where the man had been standing a few seconds ago, a small pile that they all knew were ashes.

For a full minute there was silence, surprise and nervousness.

Finally, Sams muttered, "Oh, doctor, why? Don't you realize that that's going to give away our presence?"

Korridès' face was as pale as a corpse. Tears of rage and humiliation poured out of his eyes. And the Hashshashins heard him mumble:

"Yes, that's going to give away our presence. My anger compelled me once again to commit one of those blunders that will destroy in a few seconds what it took me weeks to accomplish."

"But why this time? Why here?" Sams did not hide his irritation.

Korridès mumbled again, "Because I recognized the man. He was one of my favorites, the Fidawi of Cerbère and Portbou..."

All the Hashshashins, except Freitag, gasped, "Peul!"

And they understood, they forgave, they even approved, in hindsight, of Montag's anger. Indeed, they knew that Julien Peul was the youngest of the sect, the pet of Korridès who used to protect him, unbeknownst to Titania, and was counting on him becoming one of the Seven.

In the present circumstances, however, after the speculations and deductions they had made, the presence of Peul on Lost Island, when he was supposed to be trailing Saint-Clair, this meant betrayal.

Peul, a traitor! Oh, the mad and murderous rage of Dr. Korridès seemed natural to the other Hashshashins.

Sams consoled, "Doctor, I understand, we all understand. Too bad! If your impulsive action was really a blunder as you say, we'll do our best to fix it."

"Thank you," Korridès said. "I will try, too, like you, along with you, to fix it."

But Freitag, the newcomer, who was immensely interested in all the scenes he had witnessed since his initiation in the cellar of *The Sycamores*, spoke up for the first time. Speaking to himself more than to his colleagues, he said, "What's going to happen now down there?"

Down there, meaning on Lost Island, nothing happened at first. The courtyard to the west of the building, between it and the barracks facing the sea, remained empty with its pile of ashes...

Under the porch, halfway down the stairs that led outside from the grand vestibule, Saint-Clair, Gnô and the others were both stunned and scared. Only the Nyctalope and the Japanese understood what the sudden transformation of Peul into ashes meant. Vitto and Socca took a few minutes to remember Saint-Clair's meeting with Dr. Korridès at *The Sycamores* in Versailles. But they did remember, especially the pronouncement by Korridès about the death of the man transformed into ashes in that salon. And they understood what Gnô and Saint-Clair had realized immediately: Dr. Korridès and his macabre machine were nearby.

As for Loustal and Marod, who knew nothing, who barely knew the name and importance of Dr. Korridès, they just stood there in a kind of daze that their terrified minds could not snap out of.

Ten minutes passed like this. Vitto and Socca waited for Saint-Clair to make a decision. He and Gnô were thinking, not about Julien Peul's obliteration but about the meaning of the deed.

The Nyctalope finally put his hand on his friend's shoulder and said, "Gnô, I don't get why Korridès, who must be sitting up in those mountains behind us, used his machine against the kid. Even if the doctor knows exactly what's going on here, which I doubt, there's no reason for him to kill anyone because by killing he's warned us of the enemy presence, which we were previously unaware of. I'm surprised that he didn't think of this."

"Everything's a mystery in this adventure," Gnô said simply. "Don't try to understand. Explanations will come when they will. What are we going to do? Don't you think it'll be too risky for anyone to go into the courtyard now?"

"Obviously. But since they can see us if we go out there, we should try to see them without leaving. Now we can assume that Korridès, probably with a few men, is up on a mountain to the east of Lost Island. There's a rocky ridge over 1,000 feet up that looks a little like a fort in ruins that could easily hide a building of some kind. I wouldn't be surprised if there's a wireless station up there in constant communication with Lost Island. Maybe just opening some door down here, particularly in Titania's rooms, set off a distress signal that went from this station to Paris. That would explain Korridès being on the mountain within hours of us entering Titania's rooms for the first time. Conclusion— let's try to see them."

"Yes," Gnô agreed. "For that we'll have to go to the other side of the octagonal building."

"Let's do it." And turning to Loustal and Marod, "Hey, you two, a little more self-control. Pull yourselves together! You're going to see more of this! Vitto and Socca will explain to you what happened later. Do you hear me? Do you understand? Can you answer me?"

These questions were justified. The two sailors looked like complete idiots. But with Saint-Clair's vibrant, commanding voice, they flinched, seemed to wake up, and their faces twitched into their normal, alert, intelligent expressions.

A few seconds later Loustal answered emphatically, but in a voice still hoarse from the shock, "Yes, yes, monsieur! We hear and we understand. Isn't that right, Marod?"

"Yes, sure," the other said.

So, Saint-Clair said, "On the side of this building facing the mountain, is there a window or something from which we can see the coast without being out in the open?"

Loustal replied, "Yes. There's the docking bunker. You can get there through the basements. There are two windows and door. One of the windows has an unobstructed view of the mountain."

"Great. Go find us some binoculars or a telescope. And you, Marod, take us to this bunker."

"Yes, monsieur," the two men answered together.

Loustal added, "In the docking bunker are all kinds of navigation equipment, binoculars and such."

"Good! Let's go. And close the door here behind us."

Vitto and Socca took care of that. Since the door was opened electronically, it locked automatically. They only had to make sure the double doors were both completely shut for the bolts to slide into place, making it nearly impossible to break down without demolishing it.

The six men rushed from one end of the building to the other, went down a small staircase to the basements and then the hallway leading to the docking bunker.

Of course, none of them had forgotten about the periscope. Saint-Clair and Gnô were thinking that it was urgent to clarify it because it might prove to be enough to find where the prison was. But with this deadly, pressing threat against the island and everyone on it, they were forced to delay the search for the periscope in order to solve, if possible, the problem of Korridès' presence.

By the time they were in the bunker, the two sailors had completely recovered their self-control. Marod, who never spoke without being asked, made an exception to his usual reticence to tell Saint-Clair:

"Monsieur, I can tell you that on the mountain, up in that kind of tower you can see, which looks natural but is really the work of man, there's a wireless station in direct contact with Lost Island. There's a telephone, too, that's connected to the station."

"Why didn't you say something before when I was conjecturing about the existence of a station?"

"Uh, monsieur," Loustal butted in, "we didn't hear you."

One of the windows was open. They opened the other. With Saint-Clair and Gnô at the first, Socca and Vitto at the second, they focused their binoculars, but none of them saw anything but the rocky spur of a tower that did indeed look like a whim of nature. Nevertheless, it was highly likely that Korridès, with some companions no doubt, was there with his mysterious, lethal machine that was able to reduce a living being to ashes without a flash or explosion.

After sharing their observations and thoughts, the four men kept watching the suspicious tower while pondering the matter. It did not last long because Saint-Clair soon spoke up.

"All right, my mind's made up. Gnô, my friend, you stay here with Socca and Marod to defend the island in case of attack and especially to guard Titania and Hamed. Don't forget to check once in a while that they're still tied up good and tight. And maybe you can do a little more investigating, some more measuring. And try to find the periscope. The Nubian might have destroyed it, in which case you can try to get him to tell you where it was. It'd be a real stroke of bad luck if in so short a time the tube can't lead us to the prison."

"Very well. And you?"

"Me, I'm leaving Lost Island with Vitto and Loustal. We're taking diving suits. We'll come to land behind the Cape of La Vibora, get rid of our suits and sneak up the mountain until we uncover Korridès' hiding place. Once there, I'll figure out what to do. Loustal, are you ready to work as loyally and bravely as Vitto?"

Loustal did not hesitate. He looked him straight in the eye and confirmed, "Since I'm sure now, at least I'm hoping, that I won't be falling into the hands of Titania, I'm thrilled to be free of my slavery. And since I owe this freedom to you, I swear I will be loyal to you. Marod, do you feel the same?"

"Yes," the other said. "I feel the same way. I, too, will be loyal to you."

"Good," Saint-Clair said. "I believe you both. See you later, Gnô. I don't know how long it'll take us or what will happen, but I hope we'll be back soon to resume the search for the prison, if you haven't already found it. My wife and son are on Lost Island. By trusting the isalnd to you, I'm putting their lives in your hands."

"Don't worry, Leo. I'm your twin here. And good luck up there."

Fifteen minutes later the Nyctalope, Vitto and Loustal in diving suits left the island through the underwater cave and the grill that Saint-Clair had opened before. They let themselves be carried by the current around the island, first from south to north, then from east to west, and put their feet on the ground in the submerged part of Cape of La Vibora. They came out of the water after walking behind the cape. Then they got out of their diving suits, checked the knives and loaded Brownings in their belts and started off on dry land.

Luckily, Loustal had been to the station twice as a supply man. He acted as guide and provided details that inspired great hope in the mind of the Nyctalope. But it still took them an hour and a half of hiking to reach the summit, to the east of the plain, which they had to skirt around to get behind the station.

Saint-Clair was the first to peek over a jagged line of rocks to get a good look at the high plain that Loustal had told him about and he had to force himself not to shout for joy. Yes, joy, because at the very moment his mind devised a bold and brilliant action plan. Two heads popped up on either side of his—Vitto and Loustal.

"My friends," he said, "here's what we're going to do. First of all, go close to the station and climb up on the rocky ridge that Loustal said is only a few yards above the terrace. We'll see what's there and then I'll tell you what to do. If things are as I suspect, we'll head to the airplane we saw on the plain, cut it free and fly away. Like that we'll be taking away from Korridès and whoever he's with, however many there are, their main advantage because without the plane they'll be stuck here. As for the mysterious machine, Korridès won't aim it at the buildings on Lost Island since he knows that Titania is there. He certainly won't risk killing this woman for whom, as far as I can tell, he's got a deep and passionate love. By holding Titania and getting hold of the plane, we'll render Korridès powerless, at least to a certain extent. Do you both get it?"

"Yes indeed," they both replied.

"Well then, let's go!"

Loustal took over as guide again. It was not a hike this time but real mountain climbing and very hard and dangerous to reach the ridge. They had to stumble over fallen rocks or through mazes of monoliths. It did not matter! All the hurdles were overcome. After a final climb that required all their strength and agility not to break a bone, the three men were comfortably enough installed on the top of a rocky crag, thirty yards or so to the southeast of the tower and buildings of the wireless station. They saw the whole surface of the terrace used as a lookout point and could count the men standing, kneeling or sitting together on the terrace.

When one of these men turned his head to speak to his neighbor, the Nyctalope recognized Dr. Korridès and could see that to his right was a kind of camera mounted on a tripod. There was no doubt that the device was the mysterious machine that shot an invisible electric or solar ray, from near or far, capable of annihilating any object. Then he counted the men. There were nine of them, including Korridès.

Loustal murmured, "There's the supply man and the wireless operator. The other aren't from here."

"They came on the plane," Saint-Clair explained.

Vitto spoke calmly, "Monsieur, they've got their backs turned to us. You've never missed a shot with your Browning at this distance. Me neither. If Loustal shoots half as well as us, we just have to chose a man, aim carefully and fire at the same time. We'll kill or seriously injure them all in less than a minute."

The proposal was very tempting to a husband, father, citizen, a man who, like Saint-Clair the Nyctalope, had to save his family, the peace of his country and probably all humanity since his wife, son, France and the whole world could fall victim to Korridès and his sect.

But as turbulent and dramatic as his life was, the Nyctalope had never side-stepped danger or nullified a threat by doing something that he considered un-just. Now, he thought that firing on men without warning, in the back, was un-just.

He answered Vitto, "No, my boy, no. I've never killed except in cases of indisputable self-defense. We could very well take careful aim and fire calmly and put all nine men out of the game without much risk to ourselves. Maybe you'll think my conscience is too touchy, but it won't be the first time, right? Well, no, for the rest of my life I'd regret killing enemies in this way. Let them live. Anyway, we're going to steal their best asset."

And a weird smile crossed the Nyctalope's face while his eyes sparkled with grim mischief.

"Listen to me carefully," he said. "You're both going to leave and run di-rectly to the plane. Cut it free and get it started, then wait for me."

Vitto was used to obeying without hesitation or explanations. Loustal saw that this kind of obedience was the only reasonable reaction when the Nyctalope gave orders.

The two men, therefore, both said, "Yes, monsieur."

And they started down the hill. Keeping on eye on their descent, Saint-Clair kept the other eye on the famous terrace where the Hashshashins (he be-lieved they were all Hashshashins) were lying in ambush, in a way, binoculars and telescope in hand, along with Korridès' machine of death and destruction. He saw Vitto and Loustal cross the high plain, get to the airplane, cut it free and start turning it around. Like this it was facing the long part of the plain so that it would be ready to take off. Then he saw them disappear inside the cabin.

"Very good," he said to himself. "Now I can do something."

He took out his Browning, checked that it was undamaged, then took out the bullet in the chamber and replaced it with another, making sure that there were still seven bullets. He braced his elbow on the edge of the rock and took aim. He took his time, then looked away, breathed deeply, aimed again and fired one after another without his wrist moving a fraction of an inch. He pulled the trigger six times. It took only four seconds, but it was more than enough.

Down below, on the terrace, the weird-looking camera on the tripod, the mysterious, murderous machine, the death device was hit, shattered and smashed to the ground.

Satisfied, the Nyctalope did not stay one second longer in his sniper spot. He slid down to the bottom of the crag, leapt like a mountain goat across the jumble of rocks, stepped onto the plain and started running, still holding his gun.

From the high gap between the plain and the small forecourt of the station, several shots fired out but Saint-Clair was already out of range, at least for shooters like that, nervous and rushing, far from being a serious threat. He reached the plane safe and sound. The cabin door was wide open. He hoisted himself up and closed the door.

"Let's go!" he shouted.

Vitto in the pilot's seat, Loustal next to him, watching the dials, the plane shook as the propellers sped up, rolled, took off, slowly spiraling higher and higher, then veered away until it came back down a few minutes later to glide gently over the calm water of the bay to the west of Lost Island. It drifted a bit, then its landing gear touched the sloping bank, rolled up and Korridès' plane stopped right next to the *Goéland III*.

Words could not describe the anger, surprise, stupefaction, rage, humiliation and furious hatred of Korridès and the Hashshashins.

Pondering once again the impulsive reaction of Korridès in striking down Julien Peul, the six Hashshashin, the pilot, the wireless operator and the supply man were silent and confused, not moving. Through their binoculars or with the naked eye they were staring at the glinting whiteness of Lost Island in the sun.

Here in the springtime morning serenity, in the silence and solitude of the sea and mountains where the faint rumbling of the ocean broke against the rocks and the pine trees murmured in the breeze, all this natural harmony was lost on those human senses... All of a sudden six shots erupted and destroyed the mysterious machine that made Korridès the most lethal killer in the world.

With his whole body vibrating, he turned around. On both sides of him the others turned around, too. They saw nobody else on the terrace. Naturally, their eyes scanned the rocks. But they saw nobody there either, in the crevices, on the ledges, on the big pile of rocks that hid them from the plain, they saw nobody, nowhere.

But up above, on top of the rocky crag that overlooked the terrace, there were tiny, faint, wisps of smoke, barely visible, rising in the air and almost immediately dissipating.

Korridès groaned. Furious curses spat out of the twitching mouths around him. One of the Hashshashins howled like a lunatic. All of a sudden everyone grabbed their guns and jumped to the stairway where they knocked each other over, scrambled down to the bottom and started running. But their stupor on the terrace, their chaos on the stairs and their nervous, stumbling steps was enough for the unknown enemy to get a big headstart.

When they got to the end of what could be called the forecourt of the station, they saw the vast plain before them and in the distance a man running toward the airplane. Their reflex was to raise their guns and start firing, almost without aiming, almost at random. The man kept running until he disappeared behind one of the wings.

"Let's go! Come on!" Korridès yelled.

But the plane was already picking up speed, then it took off before the Hashshashin could do any damage with their wild shooting.

It was the moment for each of the Hashshashins to show how they reacted in face of real calamity. Sams and Freitag were aghast; Donners was crying;

Mittwoch was cursing in German; Diens was cursing in English. As for Montag, he just stood there, arms crossed, looking sullen, staring ahead but seeing nothing. He was, in short, the calmest of all. Even if a storm was raging inside him, he did not let anything show. And then there were Dermoz, Lavignon and Dontes: a little distant from the Hashshashins they were dazed. They stood there on the plain glancing at each other or at the sky or the ground or at nothing at all.

Finally, Dr. Korridès uncrossed his arms and said, "Let's go back in. We'll talk it over. But we can't deny anymore that we're dealing with the Nyctalope. The man who broke my radioactive machine gun, the guy who just jumped on our plane, is none other than Leo Saint-Clair the Nyctalope. If we don't do something today to defeat him for good, we're done for. Let's go."

Turning his back on the plain, Korridès marched quickly back to the wireless station but stopped at the door of the tower. He ordered, "Dermoz, Lavignon and Dontes, get the rifles with explosive cartridges and keep watch at the entrance to the gorge. Like that you'll have a good view of the surrounding area. Any human being who shows up, fire on sight."

He said nothing more. He turned around again, entered the tower and went up to the terrace. The other Hashshashins followed him. Up there, under the clear, sunny sky, in the beautiful light of the day, they huddled together. Questioned by Korridès, the five others, one by one, excused themselves, confessed that they had no idea what to do.

Only Diens added, "We can't say that the Nyctalope has freed his wife and son. When the grand alarm was set off automatically, the prison and the treasure cellar on Lost Island were cut off. And your greatest invention, doctor, is ready to use. We all know it. We know that it's the supreme secret, the ultimate resource for the Hashshashin. Titania is certainly in the hands of the Nyctalope but it's just as certain that she won't talk. So, we still have something to negotiate with, if not for a victory at least for an honorable retreat that will not only give us back Titania but also keep the Hashshashins intact.

"Montag, you'll build another radioactive machine gun and all of us, after holing up for three months, six months, maybe a year, to plan and work, after Lost Island is ours again, we'll restart the global action, this time even more secret, more vigilant, more daring and also stronger than ever."

And Diens ended it there.

"Very well," Montag said. "What I was thinking, dear Diens, you just said out loud. Our goal should be to negotiate, not to fight. See our plane down there? See it next to the one that probably brought the Nyctalope here? How hard will it be for them to take off, fly over here and drop on us the 24 bombs that are on board the *Vulture*? We're in a deserted region. The few customs officers who sometimes come around have surely been kept away by some agreement between the Nyctalope and the Spanish government. If we were attacked, not only would no one come to help us, but one of us might happen to escape but he couldn't resort to any authority. Outlaws we are, outlaws we'll remain. So, under the present circumstances, we're at the mercy of the Nyctalope's offensive. In the cold light of day, that's how things stand. We can't demand anything by force. It's our wits we'll have to rely on."

After a brief pause:

"My friends, is anyone against me raising the white flag? If the same flag is raised on Lost Island, I'll go down there to negotiate. One of you will be chosen at random to come with me."

Glum and enraged at the same time, they all bowed their heads and agreed.

"Fine," Montag said.

He went downstairs and opened a cabinet where they kept fifty or so different signal flags rolled up and labeled. There was a white flag there, longer and wider than the others. That was the one he took. In a corner of the room several metal flagpoles stood bundled together. He grabbed one and went back up to the terrace. Right in the middle of the space was a hole lined with brass and springs. After attaching the white flag to the pole Montag stuck it in the hole. The soft but steady breeze unfurled the immaculate cloth. It started fluttering and flapping in the bright sunlight so that everyone on Lost Island could see it.

CHAPTER VIII
95 + 95 = 200?

Back on Lost Island, Saint-Clair, Vitto and Loustal hurried to tie down the *Vulture*, which they had captured so brilliantly. Convinced that they were no longer at risk of being struck down, burned up and evaporated, they walked normally back to the octagonal building. They stopped in the round courtyard in front of the pile of ashes that used to be Julien Peul. They stared at it for a minute. Then Saint-Clair leaned over and with three fingers of his left hand he picked up some ashes, which he put in his right hand. He contemplated them for a bit, then blew them into the air.

He said, "Just like the ashes I found in *The Sycamores*."

Then he stepped around the pile and entered the building, followed by Vitto and Loustal. He went straight to the salon where he found Gnô alone.

"Well?" the Japanese asked.

"Well," Saint-Clair responded, "we did a bang-up job." He gave a quick summary of destroying the death device and stealing the plane. "And you?"

"Me, my friend, during the short time it took you to do what you did, I didn't do much. I made sure Titania and Hamed were tied up tight, but I let the kitchen help go free. They're just poor folk, completely terrorized, who were working for Matello and are really shaken up that they have to serve Titania. I told them she killed Matello. The cook cried. It turns out she was Matello's nanny. Amidst her sobs she spat out a lot of curses on Titania. I used the opportunity to give them a little speech. Result: they're fixing us lunch. I can't tell you how badly I need one. I guess you must be pretty hungry too. And Vitto, Socca, Loustal and Marod... Now that we're in control of the situation, we need to get our strength back. We won't get any rest until we've found Sylvie and Pierrot."

"You're right," Saint-Clair nodded somberly. "I could eat. Afterward, as you say, I can concentrate all my strength, physical and mental, on solving this mystery of Lost Island since the solution will bring back my wife and son."

He was quiet for a moment in order to keep his emotions in check.

Then he asked, "And the periscope?"

Gnô shrugged, "The Nubian wouldn't talk. He's back to his old self. He's sorry for obeying us earlier when he was out of sorts. He told me I could kill him if I wanted because he wouldn't say or do anything to betray his mistress since he vowed his life to her. Well, there are things said in a certain tone of voice, with a certain look in the eye, that you and I both know what they mean. It was obvious: the Nubian won't talk. Guys like him are immune to physical torture and have nerves of steel. Making a guy like that suffer would be utterly useless because it would mean nothing to him and he won't talk. So, I just left him on his bed.

"It was after that that I saw the cook. Then I called back Socca and Marod, who were still in the docking bunker, and we went to search the terraces for some sign of the periscope, but then I saw you crossing the courtyard and came down here, figuring you'd come here too."

At that moment, Socca appeared in the doorway. "Monsieur, up on the mountain, there's a white flag."

"Let's go see," the Nyctalope said.

They did not go into the courtyard but up to the roof. The roof consisted of several terraces, concentric and superimposed, meaning the lowest was at the level of the gutters and the highest right in the middle of the octagon. Four steps led from one to another on the various sides of the octagon. Only the lowest and highest terrace had railings that looked like natural, jagged rock. The whole, like all the buildings on the island, was made of gray rock veined with red and black, exactly the same as the cliffs. This explained how Lost Island was invisible to ships passing by out at sea because lying low in the water at the back of the bay it blended in with the surrounding coast.

Long before reaching the top terrace the five men saw the white flag fluttering on top of the highest peak of the nearest mountains that overlooked the bay to the east.

"They're surrendering," Gnô said. "That might just mean they want to talk first."

Saint-Clair spoke coldly, "Dr. Korridès knows all the mysteries of the island. He must be thinking that even though we've got Titania in our power, he's got it in his power to give us back Sylvie and Pierre. So I agree with you, Gnô, the flag means they want to negotiate. I think I saw in the docking bunker a cupboard with signal flags. But wouldn't it be easier to communicate by radio? Surely there's something hidden in the salon that can get in touch with the station up there."

"Surely," Gnô said. "But let's raise the white flag anyway."

"Socca and Vitto, get on it!"

"Monsieur," Loustal said, "there's a white flag in that cupboard. I'll go get it. We'll have to hold it up by hand because there's no flagpole here."

"Very well," Saint-Clair nodded.

While going back down to the salon, Saint-Clair told Gnô, "It's not really necessary to waste time looking for the radio device. It'll probably take us a while to find it. Better to tell Titania what's happening and ask her how to communicate with her husband."

Gnô smiled, "But let's admit, Leo, considering how bad things look for her, it'll be a little pleasure to tell Diana Ivanovna about recent events."

Gnô was not wrong and the pleasure the two of them felt was greater than he had imagined because this time the Red Princess was hit hard. Admittedly, it was a hard hit that the Nyctalope gave her when he sneered:

"Madame, I'm pleased to announce to you that your husband and the Hashshasins, undoubtedly warned by an alarm you set off when we captured you, arrived this morning at the wireless station on the mountain. Your husband was reckless enough to kill Julien Peul with that machine that reduces a man to a small pile of ashes. But it was easy for Gnô and me to figure out where the lethal ray came from. So, with two of my men I went up on the mountain and shot to pieces that machine. Then I stole your husband's plane, the *Vulture*, which has been sitting on Lost Island for the last fifteen minutes. Your husband raised the white flag from the station and we'll answer in kind on the rooftop terrace here. This means that I'm willing to negotiate with the Hashshashins, or at least make a stab at it."

He stopped talking. Meanwhile, Titania, lying motionless on her back in her fetters, had open her eyes wide. In her eyes, in the shape of her parted lips, in every feature of her face, she expressed shock, anger, fear and finally a kind of superstitious awe. Of course, this woman knew all about the Nyctalope's reputation. She knew how remarkably and yet simply he had defeated Leonid Zattan. But the estimate she had of her own worth and her diabolical pride had always made her think that a woman like herself would be stronger against the Nyctalope than a man like Zattan. And here now, for the first time, she felt doubtful, fearful, uncertain, one after the other in less than a minute, and suspected that Saint-Clair the Nyctalope might just be more powerful than her.

But Titania was strong. She rose to the occasion. Saint-Clair had barely finished when the woman fought back the sudden panic arising within her from this revelation of such an unexpected downfall. Her jaws clenched, her teeth gnashed, her face turned hard first, then relaxed and serene. When she looked up, her gorgeous eyes shot the Nyctalope a look of almost joyful irony.

In a lyrical voice she simply said, "Monsieur, I congratulate you. In this momentous game we're playing, you keep scoring points. But don't forget that my husband and I are holding the trump card. Anyway, you need to go and talk with Dr. Korridès, the number two of the Hashshashins, of whom I am the number one, the queen."

She smiled, looked at Gnô and in the same tone continued:

"Monsieur Mitang, see that Louis XV clock on the wall to your left about chest high? Push the knot of the ribbon under the face, the one tied around Cupid's quiver. The face will open, along with all the works inside and you'll see a space inside that's a hidden wireless radio. You just have to talk. You'll be heard up there on the mountain by my husband. His answer will come right through the clock."

And so he did. As Saint-Clair looked on attentively Gnô did what Diana Ivanovna had instructed and after a "Hello? Hello? Dr. Korridès?", a metallic voice chimed out of the back of the clock, "Hello? I'm here. Who's speaking?"

Gnô moved aside and bowed an invitation to his friend. Saint-Clair stepped over to the clock and answered quickly:

"Saint-Clair the Nyctalope here. I've just raised the white flag on Lost Island in answer to yours. What do you want?"

The thin voice came back, "I want to negotiate. With one of my companions I'd like to come over to Lost Island. Can you send the speedboat to the point at the northwest end of the bay?"

"Well, yes, the Cape of La Vibora as Escarpaz called it. Consider it done. And done right now. I have no time to waste."

"Right now, yes," the voice said.

"Very well. This conversation is over."

"Over and out, monsieur."

Saint-Clair put everything in the clock back where it was before and turned to Titania.

"Madame, I will be kind enough to meet your husband here in your bedroom. Like that you will hear everything we say and you can even take part in the conversation. See you soon."

Saint-Clair and Gnô left the room. They went up on the terrace. Loustal was holding up the white flag high in the air.

"Vitto, Socca," the Nyctalope ordered, "go down to the docking bunker and get the speedboat. Tell Marod to help you. But don't take him with you when you leave. You're going to the cape to wait for two men. One you know, Dr. Korridès. Be careful. Tell them to keep their hands in the air. When they're in the speedboat search them and, of course, take away any weapons. Then bring them back here to me."

"Got it," the Corsicans affirmed.

"Loustal, roll up the flag and put it back. We don't need it anymore."

Saint-Clair and Gnô were left alone.

Gnô said, "The periscope opening isn't on any of the terraces. After the useless interrogation of Hamed I came here and inspected everything meticulously. It must be hidden in some architectural detail on the facades. Shall we check?"

Saint-Clair replied immediately, "No need. As impatient as I am to open the mysterious prison for Sylvie, Pierre, Adele and the servant, I think we should wait to talk to Korridès. Either the conversation will reveal everything to us or we'll have to fall back on our own resources again. If the first happens, we don't need to search. If the second, we won't have lost too much time. Better to stay here and keep watch. We don't know if Korridès and the Hashshashins haven't got a gang of mercenaries somewhere on the coast. Let's imagine so and make sure no one's trying to sneak in here in diving suits. We did it, so can others. So, I propose we figure out a way to put that tentacled grappling machine out of order. At least no one will get in the same way we did."

"Good idea!" Gnô said. "You really are back to your old Nyctalope self, my friend. Nothing gets past you."

Down in the diving room the two men worked fast, not to block the machine but to dismantle part of it. It only took a few minutes with the help of a monkey wrench and screwdriver they found in a well-stocked tool cabinet.

Satisfied with this, they went back up to the terraces in order to keep watch over Lost Island while Vitto and Socca were picking up the Hashshashin representatives. The wait, however, became for them a new and special search, from a bird's eye view so to speak, of the whole island. Following through on an idea that had been brewing in his mind for hours, the Nyctalope brought up a range-finder (a telemetric device used to measure distances) that he had found in the physics lab. He made a few calculations, wrote them down in a notebook and finally responded to Gnô's questioning looks.

"Remember, my friend. The island is two hundred yards long. Forget about the width for now. Anyway, it's roughly the same. Later on, if our conversation with Korridès is futile and doesn't shed any light on the mystery of Lost Island, we'll go and measure the inside of this building, room by room, lengthwise, meaning from east to west. We'll make a map, mark out certain some reference points like foundation walls or rooms extending out farther than others and things like that. We can get a theoretical straight line of the whole interior length. If the prison is somewhere on this theoretical interior line, since we haven't found it, we'll find that the interior length is shorter than the exterior length, meaning from the inside we're missing something. By process of elimination we'll have to run up against a wall behind which is the prison. What do you think?"

"I think," Gnô said, "that you're absolutely right. The architecture of the other buildings is very simple. We've already been through them twice and know that the prison isn't out there. Moreover, we explored the underground part of Lost Island well enough that the rough map we made didn't show any enigmatic anomalies. After seeing all the rooms, hallways and stairs, we can be sure that the prison isn't there either. It's not underwater because we know that the only thing built there is the passage used to evacuate waste and for divers to get out.

"Therefore, the prison is in the octagonal building, probably on the ground floor. We've both seen that it's impossible to make a detailed map of the ground floor. We tried and came up with different layouts. It's because all the rooms and vestibules, the hallways and alcoves, they're like a maze. Remember when the Nubian couldn't tell us exactly if he went through the exercise when he came out of the prison. None of the others could tell us exactly where the servant Carmetta went on her duties to the prison. So, it's a maze. Where in this maze is the prison? Your method should lead us to some wall hiding it."

While Saint-Clair and Gnô discussed their options, their fortitude, especially the Nyctalope's, kept the analysis calm, clearheaded, precise and perceptive, as if it concerned a theoretical problem and not the very lives of Sylvie, Pierre and Adele and probably Carmetta.

Soon the speedboat came around the cape and entered the bay. Saint-Clair and Gnô could see four men on board: Vitto and Socca, of course, along with two men in suits and fedoras.

"Gnô," Saint-Clair remarked, "look at the smallest guy. That's Korridès."

"Horrid little man!" the Japanese was looking through the binoculars that he had kept with him the whole time. "Yes, horrid. Look at those eyes. And his forehead... a first-rate villain!"

"You can just call him a monster," Saint-Clair snarled. "But by destroying his killing machine I trimmed his claws, filed down his fangs. I'd be interested to talk to him about more than just our present dilemma."

"He's going to try to bargain. And from the looks of him I don't think it'll fair."

"We'll see. Let's wait for the boat to dock, then we'll go down to the salon."

"Okay."

They waited. Meanwhile, they watched the Hashshashin representative, Saint-Clair with the naked eye, Gnô with the binoculars. As much as Korridès was puny with a disproportionately big head, so his companion was tall and well-built, with wide shoulders, gray-blue eyes and a red beard and mustache.

Gnô commented, "The other guy's a German."

"He looks like it, at least. The sect is international, don't forget. The so-called Seven, including our Red Princess, must come from the seven points of the wind rose, being the winds of storms, hurricanes and destruction. Oh, the maniacs! The maniacs! When life is good, in union, in fraternity, in peace, there will always be the Lucifers, the Zattans, the Titanias, the Korridèses along with the monsters who will follow their leaders!

"Look, I don't know if hell exists physically or if it's peopled with demons, but what I'm sure of is that the demoniacal mind is a reality and we see it here on earth, among men, to wreak havoc and sow hatred and woe."

He went silent. Gnô said nothing but nodded his head with a severe expression on his face. The two friends contemplated quietly. Then, as the speedboat was veering into the dock, Gnô lowered his binoculars and said:

"They're here. Let's go down."

"Okay," Saint-Clair replied.

In the salon they waited for less than a minute for the others to enter. Introductions were made first. Korridès started off, with a kind of peevish arrogance, yet fumbling to take off his hat.

"Monsieur Leo Saint-Clair, you know me. I am Dr. Korridès. My companion is Monsieur Mittwoch."

"All right," Saint-Clair said coldly. "My companion is Gnô Mitang. But let's not talk here. I'd like our conversation to be heard by your wife, Monsieur Korridès, the woman called Sunday in your council, the woman once called Di-

244

ana Ivanovna Krosnovief whom some gypsies called *La Vibora* and who is also known as Titania, but whom we, meaning Gnô and I, know as the Red Princess.

"Monsieur Mittwoch here is number 4 in the Hashshashin council, isn't he? No need to answer. I'm just telling you this so you know I'm well informed. Now, please turn around and go into the bedroom of the Red Princess. Vitto, Socca, you go first. We'll be right behind you."

In *La Vibora*'s room Korridès and Mittwoch showed no reaction at the sight of Titania. They obeyed Saint-Clair when he ordered:

"Take these two chairs at the table, messieurs, facing the bed. Vitto and Socca, leave us. While Loustal and Marod are patrolling the walls, you go up to the terrace. If anything happens, one of you come down to alert me. If it's strangers coming, wave them a warning to stay away. If they don't obey, shoot. Got it?"

"Got it," the two said together.

Vitto and Socca left. The heavy curtain settled over the closed door. Saint-Clair glanced at Diana Ivanovna, noticed her dark eyes twitching a little and her face turned horribly pale. Then he looked at Korridès and Mittwoch and nodded to Gnô who was holding his gun, standing next to Korridès and on the lookout for any suspicious movements.

The Nyctalope said, "Dr. Korridès, I'm listening."

He answered in a hoarse voice, vibrating with suppressed anger, "I'll be brief. You're going to free my wife, get off Lost Island and forget all about me and the Hashshashins, at least for the moment because later, if you want, we can restart the war. In exchange for Titania, Lost Island and my airplane, I almost forgot that, I'll surrender your wife and son and nanny. That's it."

"Not enough and too much," Saint-Clair's calm was more daunting than anger. "It's not enough what you're offering to surrender, as you say. You'll also have to give up your weapons, abandon your projects and submit to my justice. And it's too much to demand Titania, Lost Island, the *Vulture* and your freedom. Is that your final offer? Is it an ultimatum or a proposition?"

"It's an ultimatum."

"And if I refuse?"

"Well," Korridès replied with less calm, "I and my colleague will leave here, as is our right as negotiators, and the war will continue."

"Okay," Saint-Clair was as serene and unemotional as ever, "the war between us will continue. I'll keep Titania, Lost Island and the *Vulture*. As soon as you two are back on the cape, where the speedboat will drop you, I will declare the war on again. Don't forget that I've got four airplanes at my disposal and one of them, yours, is loaded with bombs, if I'm not mistaken. You and your colleague won't get far on land. And the others up in the station won't live long. Twenty bombs, I believe. I'll only need five or six to wipe you all out."

"So be it!" Korridès shot up like an angry asp. "But Sylvie Saint-Clair and your son will die of hunger and thirst in their prison!"

"No… or rather…" the Nyctalope stood up and walked over to the bed. He put his right hand on Titania's forehead and went on, "if my wife and son must die, it's truly the will of God. But by my will, you and your Hashshashins will all be killed and your wife will be stabbed in the heart."

Silence. Huffing and puffing filled the room. With his right hand still on Titania, the Nyctalope stared at Korridès. The monstrous doctor was livid. A shiver running through his body made his teeth chatter. He turned his head and looked at Mittwoch.

The big man uttered, "*Mein Gott!*" He suddenly shrugged his shoulders and spoke to Saint-Clair in a nervous voice, "Monsieur, the law of the Hashshashins, Article 9, says: If the number 1, Sunday, dies suddenly or is taken prisoner by enemies without the possibility of immediate release, the six can delegate one of them to act as supreme authority in place of Sunday. If the delegate is not unanimously accepted, the council will make decisions on majority vote. If it's three against three, the oldest Hashshashin's vote will decide the issue.

"Monsieur, the six haven't delegated anyone to take over for Sunday, who is a prisoner without the possibility of immediate release. And the council has not voted on this ultimatum that Montag just declared. Therefore, this ultimatum is only provisional. You shouldn't consider it definite until the council adopts it, at least by majority or by the oldest Hashshashin if equal. Now, monsieur, the oldest Hashshashin is me, Mittwoch. Our Sunday, Diana Ivanovna Krosnovief, married Dr. Korridès and brought him into the sect a few days after she and I founded it. Conclusion: Montag is just a spokesman in the same way, dare I say in a much less significant way, as I am. There you go."

The doctor was not expecting this blow. He was almost always communicating to the council the direct will of Titania when she could not do so herself and he was used to being obeyed without question. He did not think of Article 9. Being reminded like this was so disorienting for him that he automatically looked at his wife, whom he called Jane. He pronounced this name like a call for help.

"Jane! Jane!"

All eyes, even Gnô's turned towards the Red Princess. But her eyes were closed. And a rare occurrence, no doubt, her face was all tensed up as if she were in serious pain and her mouth twisted into unspeakable bitterness.

Coldly, the Nyctalope said, "Korridès, look, your wife isn't answering. Look at her face—defeated."

They waited in silence. On the bed Diana Ivanovna lay perfectly still even though her restraints left her enough room to turn on her side if she wanted or move her head. No, the shapely body remained immobile, sagging, without any reaction at all. But tears started slowly rolling down her pale, painful face. Louder than any words could express, the Red Princess was admitting defeat.

After choking back a sob, with his head bowed Dr. Korridès muttered, "Monsieur Saint-Clair, you haven't said what you want in answer to my ultimatum. What are your conditions?"

The Nyctalope answered simply, "You're going to tell me right away how I can free my wife and son. All the Hashshashins will be brought to justice. The fate of Diana Ivanovna, her husband and their five accomplices will be decided by the French courts. Lost Island isn't at issue since it's owner and sovereign lord, Joao Matello, is dead."

"Matello's dead?!" the two Hashshashins exclaimed.

"Yes, dead and by the hand of your wife, Korridès. So, the fact that he's dead means that Lost Island will revert to the crown of Spain. It'll become one of the private properties of King Alfonso XIII. You see, all of us here will evacuate the island and I'll give it to the proper authorities, as it should be. The *Vulture* and the plane Diana came on will be given to the French government along with everything the Hashshashins possess. These, monsieur, are my conditions. Are you ready to comply?"

Korridès hesitated to answer. Mittwoch was also perplexed. They could not accept total surrender in the name of the Hashshashins. But there was someone who did not think twice—the Red Princess. Had the Nyctalope's demands made her realize, materially so to speak, all the consequences of her defeat? It was too much for her pride. She rose up in revolt. The agony of defeat, which had overwhelmed her for a moment, was weaker than her pride. She opened her eyes and screamed. She writhed on the bed, managed to sit up, then fell back, stiff as a board. She turned her head to see everyone present and in a bitter, harsh, spirited voice she pronounced one word:

"No!"

After a momentary pause she went on:

"Better to die, all of us, and right now than to go to prison or the scaffold after a torture of humiliation, shame and sordid suffering. Maur, you won't talk. You and I are the only Hashshashins who know the secret workings of the prison hiding the treasures of Lost Island. The secret will die with us. And don't forget, Maur, that after five times twenty-four hours the automatic mechanism runs down and everything will blow up. Ha ha! Lost Island, Sylvie Saint-Clair and cute little Pierre will be burned alive and ripped to shreds and their blood and guts will rain down upon the sea with all the wreckage of the Hashshashins' treasure. Leo Saint-Clair, kill us, but kill us now! You will know nothing. Maur Korridès, my husband, won't talk. I won't talk. The others know nothing important... So, damn you!"

She had a kind of wheezy gasp and her whole body shook for a while until she fell motionless again, utterly limp, as if dead.

A little pale, clenching his jaws, Saint-Clair had crossed his arms. His gaze moved away from the unconscious woman and was riveted on Korridès, then Mittwoch. The former hunched there like a little runt, the latter standing tall like a proud Pomeranian lord, they were both shaken up. Their faces, especially their eyes, showed their turmoil.

Gnô Mitang, in his always steady voice, said, "Leo, my friend, allow me to give some advice. Send these two men back to the station. Let them talk with their partners. Since Dr. Korridès knows the secret of Lost Island, the Hashshashins just have to decide that he give it up. He should obey their law, It doesn't matter if Diana Ivanovna doesn't talk. We just need Dr. Korridès to talk."

"You're right," Saint-Clair said. "I'll follow your advice, Gnô. Messieurs, you can leave. The speedboat will drop you off where it picked you up. At 4:35 p.m. if you haven't told me over the radio about the secret of Lost Island, the airplane, which will take off and drop enough bombs on you to bring the whole mountain tumbling down on you. Don't try to escape and run away through the mountains. The Spanish police have already been alerted. Any person trying to leave a defined zone around the coast will be arrested and thrown in prison. They'll be subject to my decision—thus the French courts and the guillotine after long suffering as the lady said. Now go. Gnô, please show them out."

Montag and Mittwoch said nothing. They were the epitome of dejection, confusion and anguish. Their trembling hands put their hats back on and with their heads bowed they walked slowly out after Gnô Mitang.

As for Saint-Clair, after checking that Diana was still tightly bound, while she looked passed out, he went into the salon next door. On the table he spread out the different maps that he and Gnô had made of the various parts and the whole of Lost Island. On a big piece of white paper he started putting them all together with the exact proportions of the total exterior length of two hundred yards. On his map it scaled to fifteen inches.

When Gnô came back and announced, "It's done!", the Nyctalope froze his pencil and said:

"I've been busy. We're going to do what we talked about earlier. But first, I'm hungry and want to eat."

"Me too, I'm hungry. Everything should be ready in the kitchen. I'll go see. The dining room is next to it. I'll get it served. We can also send some food to Loustal and Marod on their watch. Vitto and Socca can eat when they get back."

"Good. When it's ready, call me. In the meantime, I'll keep working."

At 2 p.m., after eating lunch when they got back from their expedition, Vitto and Socca took off in the *Vulture* and started flying in circles, spirals and figure eights over the wireless station where the Hashshashins were, in a way, held prisoners.

At 4 p.m. Saint-Clair and Gnô, Loustal and Marod were back in the salon, sitting around the table on which was spread the map that Saint-Clair had finished with Gnô's help, inch by inch. Without saying a word each of them were making calculations on the corners of the map.

Gnô was the first to speak out, "From north to south, 182, interior as well as exterior."

"Me too," Saint-Clair said, "182 south to north."

"Good," the Japanese nodded.

After a brief silence, "East to west, 200 on the exterior."

"And me," the Nyctalope said, "from west to east, 95 + 95 on the interior."

Gnô said, "Well there we go, unless we admit that 95 + 95 = 200."

"Which is unacceptable."

"Or else," Gnô went on, "there is somewhere in this octagonal building on the ground floor a space measuring ten square yards separating the two 95 yards we calculated."

"Exactly," Saint-Clair said. "But since the 182 yards north to south were measured in a straight line, we have to assume that the missing ten yards are on the right or left of this line we used."

"Precisely," Gnô agreed.

"Now," Saint-Clair continued, "it can't be to the left, meaning to the east of the line because I went over that twice, back and forth, and I didn't have to turn once. From the bedroom into the hallway, the workshop, the laboratory, it's a straight line. But here on the map, to the right of the line, so to the west, when I walked east to west I had to turn several times, which kept me going west and I couldn't head north again except after the center of the building and having to skirting around a space of approximately ten yards. Therefore, the small part of the building that we couldn't walk in, the part I had to skirt around is just west of the center."

"Why that's..." Gnô burst out in an almost triumphant laugh, "there, that's the exercise room! So Hamed wasn't wrong after all when his instinct and memory led him straight to that room. So, there must be some mechanical means of closing off part of the building there to make the prison. We can't argue that 182 + 182, so 95 + 95 has to equal 200. The ten we're missing are there!"

Gnô stuck his finger on the map next to the Nyctalope's.

"Let's go right now," Saint-Clair said.

They left the map and the pencils and were in the exercise room in less than a minute. They stood in front of the same wall that had baffled the Nubian when he was here. Saint-Clair picked up a twenty-pound weight and hit the wall hard three times. It made a dull bang. Some flakes of paint and plaster fell off.

"It's a wall," Loustal said.

But Saint-Clair, "It might be supported on a metal frame. Let's see."

He went to one end of the room and walked straight to the other end, swinging the weight against the wall at every step. At the seventh step he stopped. The weight had hit metal.

Gnô smiled, "That's it. You made your point. Hold on, we're going to get immediate confirmation."

He kneeled down and tried to lift up the carpet that was flush against the wall. The nails were small and easy to pry out. But no matter how closely he looked, he could find no groove between the cement floor and the painted wall.

"This proves nothing," he sounded disappointed, "because a perfect mechanism should perfectly fulfill its purpose." He stood up. "Right, Leo? We both think this wall in front of us is movable. It didn't come down from the terraces, which are above us because there would usually be something sticking out or bulging up there, which Loustal and Marod would've noticed and told us about. If, as I believe, the mechanism was operated by Titania by pressing a button somewhere during those few seconds before we tied her down on the bed…"

"Ha, Gnô!" Saint-Clair shouted, slapping himself on the forehead. "I've got it! From what you just said. My God!"

Overexcited, laughing and whooping, no longer the calm, cold man he had forced himself to be for so many hours, Saint-Clair the Nyctalope ran out of the exercise room. Gnô bounded after him and caught up to him in the big vestibule, grabbed his shoulders and turned him around.

In a firm but tender voice he said, "What are you going to do, Leo? What are you thinking? Calm down."

The Nyctalope straightened up. His convulsive laughter dried up and sweat beaded on his forehead. Pale but calm again, looking more docile now, he said softly, "Gnô, remember the sculpted wooden apple on the medieval bishop's chair in the vestibule that opened the door at the bottom of the stairs? Remember?"

"Yes."

"Didn't you see on the headboard Diana Ivanovna's bed, didn't you see that two posts were topped by sculpted wooden apples? And remember that before being tied down on the bed, as you just said, she was thrashing about, twisting and turning and hanging on for dear life to the top of one of the bedposts? For a few seconds like that… she pressed down the apple. It's the switch for the prison."

"Aha!" Gnô blurted out.

And he let go. The two men rushed into Titania's bedroom. The two windows were closed but the shutters were open and the curtains parted, letting in the sunlight on this bright day of June 7 at 4:30 in the afternoon.

The bed was austere, like the rest of the furniture in the room, but big and low, made of sculpted oak. Spiraled columns formed the four posts and each was ornamented with a sculpted apple on top, an apple sitting on an octagon of delicately chiseled leaves. The posts at the head of the bed were twice as tall as those at the foot.

On the bed, among the jumble of sheets and blankets, Diana Ivanovna was in her pajamas with her hands and feet tied to the four posts. Her eyes were open, staring at the two men. She was pale and started to make a kind of grunting sound while her teeth chattered. On seeing what the two men were looking at, pointing at, whispering about, Titania seemed to understand.

On either side of the bed, Saint-Clair and Gnô walked up to the headboard.

"Me first," Saint-Clair growled.

"Okay," Gnô nodded.

Saint-Clair raised his right hand, wrapped it around the sculpted apple, gripped it tightly and pushed down.

Then they heard an excited voice. It was Loustal standing in the doorway. "Monsieur, I'll dash over to the exercise room. If the wall's moved I'll come back and tell you. Marod will stay in case…"

He did not finish his thought but turned around and disappeared.

With his hand firmly holding the apple down as far as it could go Saint-Clair waited, staring hard into the eyes of the Red Princess. Five, ten, twenty seconds passed. Loustal did not come back. Saint-Clair lost patience. Moreover, his mind started reasoning more clearly.

"Gnô, is this the apple that she was hanging onto in her spasms?"

"Yes."

"So, logically, I'm pressing the button that closed it. Don't wait for Loustal, go ahead and press yours."

The Japanese did the same as Saint-Clair had done. His apple sank into the post.

Titania cried out. A cry of despair and fury no doubt. Her whole body trembled, writhed and jerked wildly.

A noise could be heard coming from the exercise room. At first far-off, faint, then it got louder. Before Saint-Clair and Gnô reached the door Loustal showed up, flushed, wild-eyed, waving his arms in the air and yelling:

"The wall's coming down! It's coming down!"

The excess of joy, delight, triumph and emotion brought the Nyctalope back to his usual self-control. He could not hold back, of course, he did not even try to hold back two tears that ran down his cheeks.

Gnô directed his dry eyes at the Louis XV clock. He remembered Korridès, the Hashshashins, the wireless station, the bombing that was supposed to take place at 4:35 if the doctor had not called to reveal the secret of Lost Island.

"Gnô," Saint-Clair spoke calmly while smiling, "call Korridès and tell him we know the secret and that he and the others are now our prisoners. And you, Marod, get up on the terrace and wave the tricolor flag. That's the signal that Vitto and Socca are waiting for if we pulled it off."

Marod saluted and disappeared. Gnô went over to the clock, opened it and spoke clearly, triumphantly:

"Hello! Hello, Dr. Korridès!"

A few seconds later a metallic voice came back, "Korridès here. Who is this?"

"Me, Gnô Mitang, on behalf of the Nyctalope. Are you listening?"

"Yes, yes."

"It's 4:34 p.m. In one minute you were supposed to reveal the secret of Lost Island or be bombed to smithereens. Well, I have the pleasure to inform you that the Nyctalope has discovered it. We've just opened the wall of the prison. And we've signaled the *Vulture* to leave the bombs alone. You and your partners are now our prisoners. Don't try to escape from the station, you'll get fried. Wait up there until we come and get you. Understood?"

Silence. Then the metallic voice, this time trembling, answered, "Yes, understood."

And Gnô closed the clock.

CHAPTER IX
The final enigma

Right away, without thinking of Titania any more than he was thinking of Saint-Clair, Gnô Mitang ran to the exercise room. The Nyctalope was there along with Loustal. They were looking at the bare wall, the wall that the Nyctalope had earlier hit with the weight and that Gnô had declared was movable.

It was indeed movable seeing that it was moving.

"The wall's coming down!" Loustal had shouted. And it was really, truly, unquestionably going down.

All in one piece it was going down in the opposite direction of a curtain rising before the stage in a theater. The gap between it and the ceiling grew larger.

Saint-Clair, Gnô and Loustal instinctively stepped back to get a better view, standing on their tiptoes to see as soon as possible. The three of them were quivering with impatience.

The Nyctalope could not stand it. His voice was cracked with joy and nervousness when he called out, "Sylvie! Sylvie! Are you there?"

Unconsciously perhaps, Gnô also shouted out, "Sylvie, are you there?"

And the three men's hearts skipped a beat. No answer came to these calls.

Without a sound, without the slightest creak or squeak, the wall kept descending, abominably slowly—and the wall was alive with a kind of blind, cold, relentless machine life that, once started, would not stop until it had finished what it was designed for.

The wall came down.

Saint-Clair and Gnô did not repeat their calls. Now they were scared. Loustal was also afraid. Silence, silence and the slow, mute movement of the wall… What were they going to see?

The moment came when the top of the wall was low enough for them to see beyond it. And they saw another wall, a fixed wall that was around thirty feet from the movable wall and seemed to be made of the same material; it was the same color. As the seconds ticked by more of the second wall could be seen, from top to bottom, as the first wall went down.

"Oooh," Saint-Clair puffed. And he jumped over the top of the movable and disappeared.

"Yes!" Gnô and Loustal said together. And together they jumped.

But on the other side of the movable wall they were alarmed to see Saint-Clair frozen stiff.

On both sides were the same gray walls as the first, which continued its sluggish descent. The four identical walls formed a room of around ten square yards. It was lit brightly by the electric ceiling light in the exercise room. In this square room, within the bare walls, there was nothing…

Nothing!

Absolutely nothing!

Like the four walls, the floor was bare cement.

Bare! Totally empty!

Leo Saint-Clair was choked by his emotions but let out a groan of stupefied sorrow. Gnô clenched his teeth. Loustal swore under his breath. The three men stood there without moving, unable to move… and it lasted how long? Seconds? Minutes? They never knew or tried to know—the dizzying and disparate events had dragged them so far and so quickly!

Still, after a few seconds or minutes of this rueful, rigid, stupor, they got what felt like an electric shock. It came from a noise, loud and sharp, instantly identified in their minds, of a metal door slamming shut. And the noise echoed over their heads.

All three of them looked up at the ceiling.

All three of them mumbled something meaningless as their eyes narrowed.

A part of the ceiling was moving. Yes, moving upward!

It made a hole in the ceiling, a geometric hole in the shape of a hexagon.

As the seconds passed the hole became deeper, meaning more and more hollow, higher, meaning the hexagonal part was slowly but steadily ascending… But it was not silent like the descending wall. This time there was a hum, at first low but climbing quickly up the scale to settle on a high note, muted, like the buzzing of a distant swarm of bees… And all of sudden the rising hexagon vanished.

It vanished abruptly and the buzzing stopped too.

The three men were staring into a kind of chimney, a wide, hexagonal opening reaching up into the blue sky of afternoon where thin clouds floated by.

And lastly in this phantasmagorical or nightmarish room the balsamic mountain air, the salty sea air, the pure air, the open air wafted in.

The physical sensation of fresh air making their bodies shiver a little and their chests swell brought the three men back to their senses. It snapped them out of their daze. They were able to think again, to see clearly, to speak normally.

But Saint-Clair's voice shook a little when he said, "Gnô, my friend, I'm afraid…"

Gnô's voice was flat when he said, "Don't worry, Leo. Don't worry about anything. If we start worrying, it'll slow us down and we'll be lost, Sylvie and Pierre will be lost, the whole civilized world will be lost. Then Titania, Korridès and the Hashshashins will have won."

"Hey, Gnô!" Saint-Clair suddenly shouted, "Titania and Korridès and the Hashshashins, we've got them! We've got them! We've…"

Was he going to pronounce the comforting phrase a third time? Maybe. Maybe not. Maybe he was going to say something else. Either way, something happened that cut him off. Something that he and Loustal saw in the hexagonal chimney against the blue sky—a dark shape.

A human shape. The shape of a man kneeling at the lip of the opening, leaning over, arms behind him as if he were holding onto something to keep from falling in.

The dark shape, the man suddenly cried out, "Ahoy! Ahoy down there!"

"It's Marod," Loustal gasped.

"Aah," Saint-Clair grunted. Then, stamping his foot and punching his fists together he swore, "Damn it! Get a grip! All of us, that's enough! I don't understand, but I will, I have to. We all have to. And do something! Hey, you two…"

"I'm here," Gnô responded in his normal, calm voice.

"At your orders!" Loustal barked.

"Finally!" Turning around, Saint-Clair dashed off. The movable wall was gone. The room with the hole in the ceiling and the exercise room were one. The three men ran as fast as they could, up the stairs, down the hallways, until they were on the highest terrace of the building where they found Marod.

Kneeling at the edge of the hexagonal hole in the very center of the terrace, Marod had straightened up and turned his head at the sound of pounding feet. When he saw Saint-Clair, Gnô and Loustal he stood up. He was pale and shaking. He could not respond to their questioning eyes because his teeth started chattering.

Saint-Clair grabbed his hands, squeezed them and stared hard into his eyes. Marod immediately calmed down and got straight to the point

"I came up here to plant the tricolor flag that you see over there in the corner… and I saw the plane with Vitto and Socca who reacted with two loops… when I heard a creaking behind me. I turned around and saw the terrace opening… Yeah, it was opening up. The hole you see here was made quick. The floor slid open on all sides like a camera's diaphragm. I was standing on one of the sides and almost fell in, but I jumped away in time. When it was finished, I was about to take a look when I heard something like a siren, a whining screech getting louder and louder… I finally came back but a whirlwind was coming out of the hole, like from spinning propellers, then a gray-blue thing rose up and shot off to the south. Before I realized what it was it'd disappeared into those clouds you see over there…"

Panting, Marod pointed to the southwest where a big white cloud was hanging in the sky, midway between the zenith and the horizon.

He went on, "Well, my curiosity got the better of me and I looked in the hole. I was still holding the rope I used to tie the flap to the railing over there… You can see it's longer than I needed for the job… Anyway, since it was tied to the railing I held on with both hands behind my back, knelt down and leaned over. I saw some men down there like at the bottom of well lit up as bright as day. That's when I yelled 'Ahoy!'."

He was out of breath from talking so fast and so excitedly.

Saint-Clair let go of his hands and said, "We were the men down there. We also heard the buzzing. And we saw the thing rising up and disappear." He turned to Gnô, "What do you think? A helicopter?"

"That's what I was going to say. Korridès could easily build one like that."

"Right. We'll find out soon enough. Titania's ours. Korridès and the Hash-sashins are prisoners. We'll find out. Come on."

For a few seconds he watched the plane flying majestically over the island, the bay and the wireless station. Looking very calm but certainly very determined, clearly ready for the most horrendous actions, he went down the stairs followed by Gnô, Loustal and Marod.

In the octagonal building he went straight to the room where *La Vibora* was a tied up captive. Gnô opened the doors, which he had locked from the outside by a special mechanism when he chased Saint-Clair after calling Korridès. He was the first to enter the room in front of the others.

"Oh... but..." he was startled.

"Hey, where is she?" Saint-Clair choked out.

The two of them, with Loustal and Marod at their sides, stared at the big bed and could not believe their eyes. Even after everything they had seen, this was so unexpected and catastrophic!

On the messy bed there were only fragments of rope still tied to the bed-posts. A few minutes earlier these were the ropes keeping the Red Princess a defeated prisoner. Now the satanic woman was gone.

Executioners and torturers, with all the pleasure they take or seem to take in the art of making a human body suffer for as long and as painfully as possible, know very well that physical pain can reach a point where the person is anesthetized, in a way, by the excess of this very pain and will no longer suffer. The same goes for the moral fiber. An excess of emotions can suppress all emotions.

Most people would have passed out at a certain point. The Nyctalope did not pass out but he knew that for the first time in his life his calm mind and nerves was due to physical insensitivity. And he kept seeing, watching, hearing, understanding and thinking. His attitude was so utterly superhuman that Loustal and Marod and even Gnô felt like humble disciples in the presence of a great master.

"All right!" the Nyctalope said. "Gnô, come here. Let's look at these ropes. First, Diana chewed this one off. Then she cut the others with a pocketknife she must have hidden in one of her pajama pockets. Remember, we didn't search her. Or else she could've reached the drawer in the nightstand and found it there. Do you agree?"

"Yes, yes."

"Good. After getting free she left the room. Left? Are we sure? Loustal and Marod, start searching."

The sailors got to it right away. In less than a minute they had examined every corner of the three adjoining rooms: bedroom, salon and bathroom. Of course, Titania was nowhere to be found. Gnô checked that all the doors to the vestibule were locked on the inside.

"Okay," the Nyctalope resumed. "She's not in the rooms, so she left. But not by the doors. And as you see, the windows are shut, the shutters closed and there's an iron grill outside of that... So, how did she leave? Obviously there's a secret door. I'm going to look for it."

After a brief silence he looked at Gnô.

"My friend, leave me alone. Take Loustal and Marod and do whatever it takes to bring Korridès and the Hashshashins to the island and stop Vitto and Socca from flying around. When you're done, come back here. In case I haven't found anything, we'll interrogate the Hashshashins. And if they don't want to talk..."

Gnô just said, "I'll take care of it."

"See you later."

"See you later."

The Japanese left with the two sailors and the Nyctalope was alone.

He went and stood at the far end of the bedroom so that he could see it all by just turning his head a little. Arms crossed, with no expression on his face, his eyes sharp, Saint-Clair was turning his head very slowly from left to right, then right to left, again and again... The seconds ticked by, then his head stopped moving, his eyes stared ahead...

He was talking to himself:

"Diana left this room without moving any furniture, apparently, without disturbing anything that's easily movable. Therefore, the secret passage or hiding place has direct and easy access. Behind the heavy credenza there? Behind the heavier bookshelf on the right? There must be some mechanism to open it and a button or switch somewhere. But where? That's the question. It's the same as the prison... I'm looking at four walls, a bare ceiling, a carpet nailed down on the floor... Furniture... Where is it? Let's see, first of all the furniture is either free standing or bolted to the wall or to the floor. I've moved heavier things... Let's go."

Five minutes later the Nyctalope had pushed the credenza and bookshelf away from the wall. No mechanism of any kind was attached to them.

"There's just the bed left. If I can't find anything I'll try the bathroom and the salon."

The big bed was in a deep alcove whose walls were covered in embossed leather. Nightstands on either side. It was mounted on small but strong rubber wheels. The Nyctalope had no trouble pulling it out of the alcove into the middle of the room. And he saw a very ingenious arrangement of electrical wires, different sizes and different colors, twisted into long coil springs that stretched or contracted by moving the bed.

"Here's the secret. Simple and easy, barely hidden, which means it's only temporary, like the prison behind the movable wall. They're not meant to be used long-term but only for a short time. So, it didn't matter to Titania that, after using them, they'd be discovered by her enemies…"

While thinking things out Saint-Clair was working too. He traced the wires connected to the sculpted apples on the headboard and the mechanism of the prison wall. Then he followed another wire, the third and last and he saw that it ended in two lateral iron rails covered in laminated wood. The tips looked like gold-headed rivets but were in fact little knobs that could be easily reached on either side of the bed by someone lying on it.

So, he lay down and turned the knobs slowly. When they were fully rotated, nothing happened. He felt around carefully and realized that they could be pressed in like a piston.

"Got it!"

He pressed the two knobs at the same time. There was a metallic click followed by a soft, sliding sound.

He sat up and looked at the back of the alcove. A rectangular door had opened around three feet high from floor. When closed it was well hidden by the embossed leather and the thick carpet. As for the door itself, it was short and thick (at least fifteen inches), made of steel covered with wood and leather on the bedroom side with its well-oiled hinges on the inside. Thus it opened inward into the cubbyhole.

"Very nice. From inside you can pull the bed back in place. No doubt you can close the door and probably open it from the inside. Be careful…"

Bent double the Nyctalope went in. No light except from the bedroom. But no amount of darkness (as we know) ever bothered the Nyctalope. He examined the space. It was perfectly square, ten feet per side. The walls, floor and ceiling were of cement, completely bare. The wall across from the door had an archway, three feet wide and six feet high, dark as night beyond.

"A corridor. Where to? To wherever Titania ran off."

He examined the door and its steel frame and found the button to open it from the inside.

"Good. Now I have a way back out."

He let the door swing silently closed. Fearing no ambush since it was pitch black and he could see clearly, the Nyctalope walked through the archway. First a steep slope, then there were stairs with narrow steps. After 37 of these steps there was an easier slope that he could hurry down.

All of a sudden, after a sharp turn, he ran into a grill!

It was half open. Beyond it was daylight. And beyond it was a hole, going up and going down. Saint-Clair grabbed one of the hinges and leaned over, looking up and down.

"The pipe, the hexagonal shaft."

He noticed on the walls of the shaft, opposite one another, four steel rails with deep, glistening grooves. He noted the pairs of small cushions sticking out of the walls on each segment of the hexagon right above the opening he was standing in.

He saw, finally, the whole picture.

He summed it up to himself as follows:

"The hexagonal shaft is the home of some flying machine that must be a kind of helicopter. Sylvie, Pierre and Adele were brought here from the exercise room and put on board. A folding ladder? Doesn't matter. They were held prisoner while Titania was in our hands. She got free, came here like me, opened the grill and probably just stepped into the machine, which was held here on the rails, safe against the cushions... and it flew up and away, carrying everyone with it. My God! Sylvie and Pierre! My God!"

When it was necessary to observe, examine, analyze, decide and act, the Nyctalope was unrivaled. But now that the truth, as mysterious as the details still were, proved to be so terrible for the moment and so ominous for the future, Leo Saint-Clair became the husband who lost his beloved wife and the father missing his only son. He became a man wounded in body and soul—he suffered, atrociously.

Backed against the grill at the edge of the shaft, tears welled up in his eyes. He did not even try to wipe them away. Not a sound escape him. He sorrowed in silence and alone.

It lasted many long minutes. Slowly, the grief drew back into the depths of his soul whence it had come and the eyes of the Nyctalope were clear again.

"Come on, Saint-Clair, nothing's lost as long as you're alive. If this woman, spit out by hell, committed the abomination of making Sylvie and Pierrot suffer... or killing them... O cruel God! I will avenge them before I myself die to join them in the other world where loved ones are reunited forever... Because if it's not like that, what's the point of happiness on earth, which is so easily destroyed by the powers of evil! Go, Saint-Clair, go!"

He turned his back to the hexagonal shaft and went back. He opened the hidden door, pushed the bed and stood in the bedroom.

First thing he saw was Gnô Mitang.

The anxious Japanese asked, "Sylvie and Pierre?"

"Apparently carried off by Titania," Saint- Clair sounded terribly calm. "Carried off in a machine that you were probably right to call a helicopter. And did you do what you had to do? Where are the Hashshashins so we can interrogate them?"

Visibly irritated, which was shocking since he never, under any circumstances, displayed any kind of irritation, Gnô answered, "The Hashshashins? I found them up there looking dead."

"Huh?"

259

"Catatonic, I'm sure. An induced catalepsy, voluntarily induced, yes... but deep, total... everyone up there... and for how long? Eight hours or eight days? The bodies are lying side by side on the floor of the station. Looking dead, like I said. But they're alive because their hearts reacted when I gave them a certain jab I know from secret jujitsu. Plus, their mouths are exhaling an odor I recognize."

"An odor?"

"Yes, of Mexican Datura. A certain dose makes you raving mad, but another dose can make you catatonic. Too much can kill you, but then the heart wouldn't react to a secret jujitsu jab."

"So," Saint-Clair said, "we'll just have to wait for them wake up."

"Yes!" Gnô shouted. "Right, but what will happen to Sylvie and Pierre in the hands of Ttitania? How are we going to get them back?"

Still calm, still terribly calm, the Nyctalpe said, "Gnô, my friend, that's the problem. How to get them back? It's the final enigma. First, we were wondering in whose hands they were. We solved that one. But now the great mystery is how to get them away from Titania. Well, Gnô, we're going to get to work on solving this final enigma. We shall succeed or we shall die."

The two men grabbed each other's hands. That was the first time Saint-Clair had seen tears in the eyes of Gnô Mitang.

CHAPTER X
Sylvie and the helicopter

After a short silence Diana Ivanovna wrapped up, "My incisors are strong and sharp. I chewed through the rope with them. It scratched my gums enough to make them bleed, but it doesn't matter. When one rope was cut I could reach the penknife that was in the nightstand with a few other little things. I cut myself completely free. Then I rushed down the secret passage to come meet you in the helicopter's garage shaft. Your husband probably found the passage. That, too, doesn't matter. I'm willingly sacrificing Lost Island and all of its wonderful scientific inventions. I've got you and your son. That's what's important. My helicopter has nothing to fear from any airplane. It's taking us away. Do you want to know where? I'll tell you because at this point I have nothing to hide from you. It's taking us, at 250 miles an hour, to Abyssinia.[4]"

Titania broke out laughing.

With her blood-stained lips and chin from her gums bleeding during those two or three minutes of gnawing at the rope with her tiger's teeth, with her hair still disheveled from all the furious activity, with her body barely covered by the torn, silk pajamas, the Red Princess sat facing Sylvie. The two women were alone in a strange "room".

Think of a wireless operator's cabin set up with air navigation equipment, dials and control levers, a periscope, and many other instruments and devices that were totally unknown to Sylvie Saint-Clair who was pretty knowledgeable about science and technology.

The hexagonal cabin was lit by the fading light of dusk through the six windows. For actual furniture there was only a tall cabinet standing between two windows, a round table and four stools around it. All were dull gray metal and bolted to the floor, which also seemed to be metal just like the walls and ceiling. There was also, in the corner, a trunk.

When Titania had finished laughing, there was no other noise but a humming that was both high-pitched and muffled, accompanied by a kind of resonating vibration. It was all very steady, permanent, monotone and was clearly coming from the outside. Sylvie had got used to this constant drone so quickly that she no longer heard it, even though the helicopter (as Diana called it) had been in the air for only a few minutes.

The two women sat across from each other, elbows on the table. Sylvie was resting her head in her cupped hands, staring icily at the Enemy.

---

[4] Ethiopia.

The Enemy, Titania, had her hands folded on the table and she was leaning forward, unconsciously revealing her magnificent bust, falling out of the torn top of her pajamas like a modern Amazon after a violent battle.

After laughing ecstatically, she talked again, shooting daggers out of her dark eyes at the half-closed, blue eyes of Sylvie, who remained calm and cold.

"Abyssinia! It's a country where neither the old Christianity or modern civilization have managed to destroy the ethnic savagery. It's a country that's been in the throes of a revolution for eight days. An anarchist revolution, fomented, fed and directed by me from afar along with two colleagues from the council of Fidawis on site. But I am the leader, the president, the queen, the absolute dictator. Are you listening?"

"Yes," Sylvie muttered.

"It's just that with your stone face and your bitter-blue eyes, your rigid body and frozen hands, you look like a statue. You're strong Sylvie... but even in this state of excitement, I'm stronger than you in your poised composure. Have patience! I will break you down, and how!"

La Vibora started laughing again.

Then, feverishly, she went on, "In Abyssinia there's a big lake that's called Lake Tana. It sits in the mountains of Amhara where some peaks are over 13,000 feet high. Almost in the middle of this lake is an island we call the 'Black Star', you'll see why... I love islands! Anyway, the island, the lake, the mountains, the whole region is occupied by revolutionaries protected by Korridès' inventions and from there they spread out all over the country. The ancient city of Gondar is ours now. According to the last message I got from Versailles, our strike force is threatening Addis Ababa, the current capital.

"Sylvie Saint-Clair, I'm taking you and the son of the Nyctalope to Abyssinia and I'll lock you up in one of the arms of the Black Star. Adele can feed Pierre. Carmetta will take care of your needs. And you will wait there, far from your friends, until I bring you your husband, bound and gagged."

She rose up gracefully and casually put her hands in the pockets of her tattered pajamas.

She said, "You can imagine how badly I need to freshen up. I'm a fright and really not very decent, don't you think? But you don't mind, do you, for the moment? The moment will last only a few more minutes, if you want me to show to you and briefly explain the helicopter. No? Yes? Yes, of course you do. At least to prove to you first that I'm not scared of revealing certain secrets to you since I know you can do nothing against me and you'll never escape. Secondly, that my Dr. Korridès, the designer and builder of the helicopter, not to mention so many other wonderful machines, deserves such great and profound admiration from me that it borders on love...

"Oh, you think I'm babbling. You're right. But just think how happy I am! Today I defeated the Nyctalope even though I was his prisoner! There's no way I won't conquer him for good tomorrow when...

"All right, I'll shut up. I was about to say too much. I don't want to be too cruel. I want to leave you a glimmer of hope. So, no more talk about the Nyctalope. Do you want to see the helicopter?"

Sylvie stood up and simply said, "Gladly."

"Ha, I knew it!"

What a scene! And oh, how Diana Ivanovna Krosnovief, the dilettante of hatred and cruelty, the dilettante also of physical endurance and mental strength, how she savored the bitter delight!

With Sylvie Saint-Clair next to her or in front of her, she was taking a tour of the flying prison. While showing this most extraordinary of all the inventions of Dr. Korridès, she gave a running commentary. And despite the wretched circumstances Sylvie looked and listened with rapt interest, so rapt that she did not even try to hide it.

"The whole helicopter," Titania introduced, "is made of two hexagonal boxes or cells, one inside the other. The inner one is twenty inches smaller all round than the outer one. The outer one is the actual hull. It's like armor and at the same time, thanks to the special metal, it captures and processes and stores the radioactivity energy from the sunlight, which is transformed into a manageable fluid that the pilot can turn into light or power or both at the same time. And that's the incredible invention—it continually takes the light of the sun and uses it for light, heat and power."

"Oh, but it really is incredible," Sylvie could not help blurting out. "So, the engine of this kind of machine, this…"

"Helicopter, madame, or gyroplane, if you like," Titania cut in. "But we prefer helicopter."

"Fine. The engine of this helicopter is therefore…"

"A solar energy engine. A helioradiant engine. Specifically, it's the sun that powers it, like steam or fuel or electricity powers most engines today. That means we don't carry any fuel. Just a little oil is enough to fly around the world. And we can stay in the air all night long because the solar energy stored during the day is three times more than is needed to fly during those long nights; Understand?"

"Of course."

"I'll finish up about the outer shell and we'll see the inside. So, to the hull are attached the movable side flaps as well as the vertical rudder, called the 'lower', and the horizontal rudder, called the 'rear', whose combined use allows it to move fast and smoothly in any direction. The hull extends in front into a triangular nose where the propeller shaft is installed, directly opposite the rear rudder. Like that the helicopter has a prow or a front and a stern or a back. Its upper part is like a cone where you can find the vertical propeller shaft. Finally, the bottom has six short, thick feet with powerful shock absorbers that it sits on when its parked. Landing is always soft as silk thanks to the vertical propellers that lets the pilot control the descent with absolute precision. No need to talk about the two doors and dozen windows that are perfectly lined up on the inside."

"A dozen windows? I see only six here and I saw three inside on the lower level. And I saw only one door."

"Yes, but there's another lower level. A ground floor, so to speak. It has three windows and a door. Didn't you figure out that's where I took you in an out of the helicopter? Well, come on."

With a wicked grin but always in a sweet and charming voice, she almost whispered:

"You'll see your son on the way."

In short, the inner cell of the helicopter was divided into three parts, one on top of the other, so into the levels.

On the lower level, the "ground floor", were the compartments for supplies, ammunition, all kinds of tools and various objects needed for the helicopter itself and its passengers. They called it the "storage". There was a space with a toilet and sink. Three windows lit the storage and it had a door to the outside.

The middle level, called the "cabin", had a higher ceiling than the storage and was used for living quarters of the people on board. Four sides of the hexagon were equipped with a bunk and a cabinet above. A fifth side was very cleverly arranged into a bathroom with an automatic screen. The sixth side had a cook stove powered by the solar energy and fitted with a kind of exhaust fan. The cooking utensils were kept in a cabinet above the stove along with the cutlery. In the middle of the cabin was a table with five stools.

Finally, the upper level, called the "machinery", contained the power unit and its apparatus, all the navigation equipment, a special wireless radio and a system designed for the unique scientific aspects of the helicopter, an original aircraft that could fly from three feet a minute up to three hundred miles an hour using solar radiation transformed into usable power.

The machinery also had a bookcase-chest and a cabinet-bed with three drawers full of sheets and clothes. Five people, therefore, if they planned well, could live comfortably enough in Korridès' helicopter.

The three levels—storage, cabin and machinery—were connected by a spiral staircase and two hatches with sliding lids.

Like the storage, the machinery had a door to the outside. This level was the only one with six windows, the others having only three. Lastly, to get out of the helicopter from the cabin, the person would have to go either up or down a level because it alone had no door.

It was in the machinery that Titania had told Sylvie how she had escaped. And it was in the cabin that Sylvie saw Pierrot sleeping the arms of Adele who was sitting on a bunk. Carmetta was preparing something on the stove.

"What do you think?" Titania cried out. "Isn't it marvelous? At 6,500 feet altitude, flying at 250 miles an hour, right now over Sierra de Guadarrama in the middle of Spain... a nanny has just fed a three-month old baby and a girl is quietly preparing a meal for four. Notice that the helicopter is flying all by itself, the engine at 82 percent power, the rudders locked. The pilot/mechanic/captain is only one person... and that person is me, the Red Princess! And I've done you, Sylvie Saint-Clair, the honor of inviting you aboard this helicopter. Did you get a good look at your son? You didn't kiss him for fear of waking him up. You were right... So, should we continue the tour? Yes? Let's go down into the storage." She showed Sylvie the way and went down after her, laughing all the way.

When Sylvie climbed back into the cabin she was left alone with Pierre and Adele. Titania kept going up the stairs into the machinery where Carmetta was ordered to follow her.

The baby was sleeping in the arms of the nanny.

"Madame," Adele whispered, "did the wretched woman talk to you about Monsieur?"

Frankly and gravely Sylvie answered, "Yes. He and Gnô Mitang are in control of Lost Island. They were keeping her captive. She managed to escape and get to us being held inside this flying machine... We were wondering what it was when we were locked up in here. Well, it's an aircraft taking us away to Abyssinia..."

"Abyssinia? Where's that?"

"In Africa. Very far."

"Will Monsieur be able to find us?"

"I hope so."

"How will he know where we are?"

"He found out about Lost Island. Why not about Abyssinia? How? I have no idea. But I'm sure he will. Oh, as long as he's careful. As long as he doesn't fall into the trap she's setting for him. As long as he can spot the bait she's laying out..."

"Monsieur is very smart and stronger than this woman, Madame."

"I know, Adele. But she's so wicked, so evil, so diabolically corrupted. She can come up with ideas that would never occur to the mind of a good man. Still, I have faith. I have faith in my husband!"

"Me too. And now that you've told me he knows who he's dealing with, I'm less afraid. Monsieur will free us and he'll kill this woman."

"May God be listening," Sylvie murmured as she put her hands together.

The hatch door slid open in the ceiling at the top of the stairs that spiraled up between the toilet and the kitchen. A pair of espadrilles and black cotton stockings announced Carmetta. She went straight to the stove and said in Castilian:

"Our mistress will eat alone upstairs. Please sit at the table. It will be ready in five minutes."

"Gladly," Sylvie replied softly. "But Adele is eating with me so set two places."

"Yes, madame."

Little Pierre was put on one of the bunks. Sylvie and Adele sat at the table on two stools facing the baby. The meal was simple but plenty and very tasty. The two prisoners ate, perhaps not with pleasure but with that hearty appetite that people often have when they are engaged in a war whose battles magnify instead of diminish their fortitude.

The solar lamps were turned on when the interior shades closed automatically over the windows. Titania had obviously pressed a button up in the machinery.

Carmetta went back upstairs carrying a bowl with Titania's meal. She came right back and said, "Our mistress says good night and wants to give you this."

She handed Sylvie a piece of paper torn out of a notebook. These lines were written on it in pencil:

We're about to cross the Mediterranean from northwest to southeast. We're approximately 3,000 miles, as the crow flies, from Lake Tana in Abyssinia. So, another 12 hours. You have plenty of time to rest. —D.

"That's fine," Sylvie handed back the paper. "Adele and I will take care of Pierre. The same bunks as last night. Where does your mistress sleep?"

"Upstairs."

"And you?"

"Here, madame, in the fourth bunk."

"Fine."

What a night! Sylvie could not sleep. On four sides of the cabin the bunks were set parallel to the walls so that Sylvie had a good view of her son. A night-light was also turned on. Feeling very calmed by the calm sleep of little Pierre, she pondered...

First, she relived all the tragic hours of the past seven days. Wednesday, June 1, the fire at San Lorenzo, the kidnapping, the separation from Pierre; Thursday, June 2, imprisoned on Lost Island; Friday the 3rd, the return of Pierre and Adele, first meeting with Titania; Saturday the 4th, the nerve-racking wait; Sunday the 5th, second talk with Titania and the letter from Leo; Monday the 6th, changing cells, stuck in the mysterious, hexagonal cabin; and finally, Tuesday the 7th, after a day that seemed like it would never end, Titania burst in, her hair a mess, her lips bleeding, her pajamas in rags... and off they went, bound for Abyssinia.

For Abyssinia! This extraordinary helicopter machine of Dr. Korridès was gliding through air, held up and pushed forward by its propellers at 250 miles per hour, in the night, over Africa...

The wild ride made no other sound but the high-pitched but muted buzzing accompanied by the steady, resonating vibration. Her brain had gotten so used to it so quickly that she really had to think about it to be conscious of it.

And not the slightest jolt or lurch. Sometimes, briefly, a sensation of dropping, like in a fast elevator, but it was so brief and so rare that it could have been just an illusion.

The Korridès helicopter...

Lake Tana in Abyssinia...

Lost Island, Leo and Gnô...

Little Pierre sleeping... Adele...

Titania, Diana Ivanovna, the Red Princess...

These were the cardinal points around which Sylvie's thoughts wandered to and fro haphazardly.

After two, three, four hours, her meditation focused on one point: the helicopter.

She suddenly propped herself up on her right elbow. The helicopter?

She thought, "Titania's alone. I'm sure the lid of the hatch to the machinery can't be opened. That's so obvious I don't even have to check. So, for the the moment, there's nothing I can do against her. So be it!

"But we won't be arriving in Abyssinia until 9 am, I'm sure, at least I hope... in any case it's likely that Titania will come down here or send me up there. She'll be itching, once again, to enjoy the cruel and contemptuous pleasure of seeing me powerless and defeated. Then...

"Yes, then, why not pounce on her like I did on Lost Island? Or better still, why not hit her on the head as hard as I can with some heavy object? For example, the carafe is heavy crystal. Full of water, held tightly, with a good, strong swing it'd make a fine club. I'll pretend to get the hiccups, ask for water, get Carmetta to bring it with a glass...

"Titania's so pleased and proud to have escape Leo and have the three of us back in her power, yes, so pleased and proud that she'd never believe I'd try to fight back physically. While she was showing me around the helicopter she took no precautions except to make sure I was never directly behind her. She kept me in sight, but I was free to move around.

"She thinks she's stronger, smarter and faster than me. She probably blames my attacking her on Lost Island on the element of surprise, even though I would've beat her if the Nubian hadn't jumped in... And she thinks that as long as she can see me, see the expression on my face, it won't happen again or she'll see it coming and eliminate the element or surprise...

"Yes, that's right. Titania thinks like this, with reason... But if I put on a show? If I look resigned, defeated, stubborn and cold? Pretending to have the hiccups is easy and I'll look embarrassed to be so ridiculous and childish... Will she guess? No!

"Of course, Carmetta might only bring me a glass of water without the carafe. Possibly. But since the tray is always set up with both, she'll probably just take the whole thing, bring it to us, pour the water from the carafe... And that's when I'll have a brief moment, a split second to grab it and smash Titania's head."

At this point in her strange and stirring meditation, the young lady sat up straight, crossed her hands on her knees and gazed at her beloved son, little Pierre, who was sleeping with that innocent serenity of healthy babies.

She murmured, "My little darling."

She thought of Leo. "He's looking for me on Lost Island. He'll certainly find clues that prove that Titania escaped and we disappeared again. He'll find the trail... Yes, yes, for sure! But still, I have to do something here. I can't just wait around passively..."

And all her attention was focused again on the immediate future.

"Whether I hit her with the carafe or strangle her with my bare hands or stab her with whatever sharp object is in arm's reach, I have to incapacitate Titania if we're in the same room before landing the helicopter. And then the helicopter! I'll have to fly it to a friendly country where I can use a wireless to warn Don Pedro in San Lorenzo, Sou in Nopals, Briard in Versailles, the Marquis d'Ullea in Madrid... What might be best would be to return directly to Lost Island. Why not? As soon as I can control the helicopter. And I will! It should be easy. Even if none of the controls are marked, I know how to fly and can try them one by one to see what they do. There seemed to be plenty of instruments displaying speed, direction, altitude... Most of them I'll know and can quickly figure out the others. Yes, it should be easy.

"What'll be hard or rather depend on a chance that may not come, will be to knock out, strangle or stab Titania. In any case, no matter the circumstances, even if chances look great, to succeed I'll have to stay calm, cool and collected, in absolute control of my nerves, my muscles, my whole body... Now I should get some sleep, yes... Can I really? With this constant flood of thoughts?"

Sylvie stretched out on the bunk. The temperature of the cabin was pleasantly warm. Her bare arms were on top of the sheets. She glanced over at Pierre and Adele, then at Carmetta, and she closed her eyes.

Even though Sylvie tried to surrender, sleep did not sweep away her thoughts, which were as active and alert as ever. But it did relax her body, calm her nerves, soothe her muscles. It was a much-needed physical repose.

When the clock on the wall showed six o'clock and the Carmetta, obviously out of long-standing habit, opened her eyes, yawned, stretched and got up, Sylvie felt in total control of herself, emotionally and physically. Once and for all she decided to risk everything to crush Titania and take over the helicopter;

CHAPTER XI
The struggle, the anguish, the frigid horror

Quietly greeted by Carmetta, who saw that she was awake, Sylvie Saint-Clair washed up, got dressed and played with Pierre who was also awake. But when the hatch door suddenly slid open, she gave him back to the nanny, who put him on her breast. Sylvie watched Titania coming down the stairs.

The Red Princess was wearing a blue "mechanics" jumpsuit, flat-soled leather sandals and a kind of bathing cap made of rubber. She was fresh, alert and full of smiles.

"Good morning," she said in French in her melodious voice. "Did you sleep well? Yes? Wonderful. And the baby? Oh ho, he's having his breakfast. That's splendid." Then to Carmetta in Castilian, "Will our hot chocolate be ready soon?"

"*Si, señora.*"

"*Bueno.*"

Standing in front of her bunk, Sylvie was impassive, a little pale, her blue eyes looked dull and docile. She was thinking, "In Spain, it's the custom, after the hot chocolate, to drink a glass of flavored, sweetened water. I'll ask for one if Carmetta doesn't offer it."

The chocolate was simmering on the solar-powered stove. Diana Ivanovna had a hearty and refined appetite. She made sure the chocolate was thick and creamy, checked that the cookies in the metal can were dry and the concentrated milk was still good and ready to be poured—all this while Carmetta was setting the table.

"Carmetta," Sylvie perfectly imitated a humbly gentle attitude, "you'll be serving Adele, too, won't you? She doesn't have to sit at the table."

"Very well, madame," the Galician replied.

Titania nodded her head. With no immediate worries, she sat down at the table and motioned to Sylvie to do the same. Sylvie sat across from the Enemy. She had to muster all her strength and use all her acting skills to hide her joy, her ecstatic joy because Carmetta was filling the crystal carafe with filtered water from the tap and was soon putting it on the table. Then she placed glasses and cups with saucers. Right after that she served the hot chocolate. The two women were then free to pour in as much concentrated milk as they pleased.

Drinking normally required all of Sylvie's willpower and self-control, like a soldier accomplishing an act whose probable outcome would be his death.

"The chocolate is very good, isn't it?" the Red Princess asked. "Carmetta almost always does a good job. Have some more… Yes, like me… See…"

Titania poured herself a second cup. At that moment Pierre had finished nursing and was lying quietly at the foot of the bed where Adele had put him and Carmetta was serving Adele who was sitting back against two pillows.

Titania was serving herself...

With her right hand she was pouring the creamy, savory chocolate slowly into her cup. In her left hand was a small, wooden spoon used to stir while pouring. Both hands were full as she kept her eye on the liquid, paying no attention to Sylvie...

This was the time to act, to strike, with unknown but grave consequences.

Sylvie reached out with her right hand, grabbed the neck of the carafe, swung it hard and hit...

Crystal shattered noisily into pieces. Porcelain and metal crashed to the floor. Piercing shrieks rang out.

Sylvie heard nothing. Her entire soul was in her eyes that were staring at Titania... who was wobbling, then falling backwards, her mouth gaping open, her eyes rolled upwards, her forehead getting covered in blood.

That was when Sylvie truly learned how dreadfully strong her enemy was! Sylvie thought she was dead. She sat frozen in that trance that murder sometimes causes in the murderer, even when it was a legitimate act of self-defense. But the thought of victory was already rising in her mind and starting to pull her out of this trance...

But then Titania stopped falling backwards, leaned to the right, braced her right hand on the stool, straightened up... and turned her head, closed her eyes, then immediately opened them, alert, ablaze, brimming with infernal hatred...

And while Sylvie sat entranced, while Carmetta and Adele were stupefied, Titania jumped up, ran to the stairs and started scrambling up them.

She was already halfway through the hatch when Sylvie finally shook herself out of her daze. She ran after the Enemy and managed to reach her as she was lunging into the machinery, both arms stretched out and grabbing a lever...

"Aaargh!" she groaned.

She fell to the floor, her hands wrapped around the lever and as she fell, so, too, did the lever drop down as far as it could go.

There was a loud, sharp, metallic click, like a spring snapping. Sylvie heard it. A cold shiver ran down her spine. She was scared to guess, to know. She leaned over Titania who was lying on her side with her arms over her head, her hands still gripping the lever, and automatically asked:

"What did you do, you cursed creature?"

The Red Princess, eyes wide open, one filled with blood that was pouring down from her cap, the other eye glaring, indescribably, inexpressibly, into the very soul of Sylvie, spurted out, "Now... the helicopter can't... will just crash... the end of its course... it's over... it'll crash... it's crashing... 20,000 feet and smack... Sylvie, you killed me but another one, two, a few minutes and you will follow me into death... death... death, yes..."

The eye closed and then the other. Through parted lips she kept muttering. Sylvie could only barely make out a few words:

"We were getting there... victory... I was getting it all back... and now death! My whole life... all of it... was open before me... and now death!"

A gasp.

And there was nothing left alive of Diana Ivanovna Krosnovief. Nothing?

Calm now, determined to keep fighting, even against all odds, Sylvie Saint-Clair wanted first to make sure that the Enemy was really dead. She ripped open the blue jumpsuit, bared that beautiful chest, and leaned over to listen for a heartbeat.

A few seconds passed and Sylvie thought, "She's still alive. Her heart's beating. Faintly but it's beating. Is it just a coma before death?"

Suddenly she straightened up and spoke aloud, "Am I crazy? What does it matter if she's dead or alive? It's me who's going to die! Me and Pierre and Adele if I don't stop this crash."

She looked around. She had only been in the machinery once, yesterday, for fifteen minutes, but she had got a good look and remembered.

A quick glance at the altimeter showed that, indeed, the helicopter was descending steadily but along a curved trajectory.

The trajectory! The helicopter had changed into a dead missile. A missile still in the air but with no power because of the deliberate sabotage by the Red Princess. The helicopter was ending its flight path. It was falling. And the trajectory was curving, second after second, more and more towards the vertical.

But in no time, with that presence of mind, clear vision and levelheadedness that people with strong characters and nerves of steel recover instantly when mortal danger threatens, Sylvie realized that the helicopter was falling but remaining stable, so to speak, meaning upright. It was not tipping over, not spinning around. It was keeping itself vertical.

"Oh, what does it matter? Crashing into the rocks or into a crater it'll make in the ground... My God, what a way to die! Leo! Little Pierre!"

She leaped over Titania's body and was about to run to the hatch and down the stairs to pick up Pierre, kiss him, repeat the name of his father, her husband... But he stopped completely.

Sylvie was staring at an array of various instruments and, especially, the reflector frame of the periscope, the one that could see the land from inside the machinery. Her eyes and mind noticed three things at the same time: one, the voltmeter of the vertical propellers showed that they were spinning not from the engine, which had been disengaged, but merely from the air as the helicopter dove downward; two, the altimeter showed that it was not a free-fall subject to the laws of gravity but slow and impeded—impeded by what if not the movement of the propellers; three, under the helicopter was not land but a large body of water.

These three observations, made in a few seconds, drove Sylvie to the following conclusions:

"If the helicopter falls relatively slowly into deep water, it'll sink, it won't crash, it'll sink! The water must be Lake Tana. A big mountain lake is usually pretty deep. If the helicopter doesn't hit rocks underwater, we'll be saved because it'll resurface and float on the water. My God!"

And some frightful objections also sprang to mind:

"But the separate cells of the helicopter, the doors, the windows, are they waterproof? Will the weather-stripping leak water into the propeller shafts and then into the space between the cells? In short, is the helicopter hermetically sealed? Furthermore, is the specific weight of the machine going to allow it resurface after diving into the water?"

Even though all these observations, conclusions, deductions and objections flashed quickly through Sylvie's mind, time was still running out since Titania had cut the engine minutes ago. The mother thought something different now: if she was going to die in a helicopter crash she was going to do it with her son in her arms, next to her heart... She jumped over to the stairs, ran down them without looking at Adele and Carmetta sitting side by side, petrified, and picked up Pierre who was babbling and waving his arms and legs.

She hugged and kissed him, muttering, "Pierre, my darling... Leo, my love... My joys, my happiness, my life..."

It was then that the hexagonal bottom of the helicopter hit the water. A thunderous boom, the crash of waves caused by the plunging missile, the black depths of the lake... And in the badly shaken helicopter, objects went tumbling, glass broke, two women screamed frantically...

With a clear mind, a skipping heart and held breath, Sylvie waited.

It only took a few seconds for the wait to seem endless. Her mind was thinking and her body went into action.

"Find out for sure if the helicopter is resurfacing. The manometer, the pressure gauge. I have to go upstairs. The switch for the lights, I remember it's here on the right..."

She reached out and pressed a button. The ceiling glowed with an artificial light powered by the day's solar energy. Carrying Pierre, who was quiet now, Sylvie went back up to the machinery. She pressed another button and the ceiling light turned on there as well.

"No sound of gurgling water. Everything sealed. If there are any leaks they're slow and minimal. So, that won't keep it from resurfacing... We're still going down. Oh, so slowly..."

The manometer showed the pressure rising but more and more slowly. The needle of the altimeter was stuck at zero. Sylvie waited for the moment when the pressure also leveled off. After that, if the helicopter was rising up, the needle would indicate a decrease in pressure from the thinning layer of water bearing down on the hull.

The first moment arrived. It was brief, as a moment should be by definition. And right after, the needle started moving again.

"Aha!" Syvlie cried out, "We're going back up!"

She showered Pierre with kisses as he started crying again. But she calmed him with a smile and rocked him with her eyes keeping watch on the rapidly moving needle of the pressure gauge. But it did not last. The movement changed so quickly that the only word that came to Sylvie's mind was "slow". The needle was slowing down.

She muttered to herself, "So, the helicopter is rising more slowly. With respect to the water, it's less and less light. So, will the weight of the machine and the weight of the volume of water around balance out before we reach the surface? If so, the helicopter will stop and just float in the water like an immersed submarine."

The more she thought, the louder her voice became. The last sentence she almost screamed. And she fell back, startled, aghast because a voice answered!

"But of course, my dear enemy, the helicopter will float in the middle of the water. A floating coffin, a moving coffin, a laguna coffin... Oh, I'm so thirsty... Sylvie, give me something to drink, would you?"

Only then did Sylvie grasp the reality: the voice saying these things belonged to Titania. The Red Princess was not dead! The Viper was not crushed! She was alive and talking.

Yes, because after a kind of grisly sob, she was almost begging, "Drink, Sylvie, drink!"

"Okay."

The young lady went down into the cabin. She shook the nanny and the servant who were still sitting together and now holding hands and crying.

"Come on, Adele, we're not finished yet. Have courage! We'll survive, we'll save ourselves. Do you hear me? Do you understand?"

"Yes, yes, madame," the nanny uttered.

Her teary eyes were, in fact, brighter. The voice of her mistress, the mother of Pierre was energizing her.

"Here, take Pierre. I need my hands free. Good, take care of him, play with him. I also don't need him crying." She turned to Carmetta, "Get up! Yes, right now. Titania isn't dead. She wants something to drink. Get her a glass of water."

Sylvie's strong, willful voice was like a slap in the face. The girl jumped up and found an unbroken glass, which she put under the faucet and starting filling with water.

"That's enough!" Sylvie ordered. "Now straighten up this room." She took the glass and went back up into the machinery.

Titania had managed to sit up, her back against the trunk. She was strong enough to take the glass of water and guzzle it down.

In a quiet, halting voice, she said, "There's a faucet up here too. On the left. Some more? Then you can wash my face. The dried blood is blinding me... I stopped bleeding..."

Sylvie gave her more water. She drank half of it more slowly.

"My face now, wash it... Towels in the drawer behind me."

After Sylvie washed her face and picked out the clot of blood in her left eye, Titania spoke again in the same weak, panting voice but now tinged with the accent of the diabolical fighter.

"You know what they say... If a blow to the head doesn't kill you on the spot, it's not serious. So, I probably won't die from the wound you gave me, Sylvie... I'm glad. Like this we can die together... We'll die the same death, you, me and Pierre, and of course Adele and Carmetta... the same death, suffocation... It'll be long, slow and merciless... I guess we'll pass out and therefore suffer less. Too bad. Even if I had to share it, I'd like your suffering to be atrocious..."

"Oh, shut up!" Sylvie was fed up. "If you keep talking, my anger and disgust will get the better of my compassion and I'll kill you like the monster you are."

"We'll see about that," Titania's eyes were closed and her lips froze in a cruel and bitter smile.

Now, Sylvie noticed that the pressure gauge needle had stopped moving. She was knowledgeable enough in science to make a quick calculation of the pressure. The helicopter was dead in the water, 75 feet below the surface.

Whatever the danger, it was not immediate. Sylvie kept control of her emotions, reactions and fears so she could make clear decisions about the situation. She sat on a stool facing all the instruments and controls and told herself:

"When he designed, built, tested and put the finishing touches on his helicopter, Korridès must've imagined all the accidents a flying machine like this could encounter. Well, on earth, water and land are not equally distributed. The surface of the planet is roughly 315 million square miles and the land covers barely a quarter of this, water takes up the rest, approximately 235 million square miles.

"When he built the helicopter he planned to fly over all the waters of the earth. How could he not have foreseen dropping, diving or crashing into the water and all the consequences?

"Yes, I understand that if the propellers were working they'd raise the machine in the water just like in the air. Korridès must've planned for a disconnection, accidental or voluntary. It's not just likely but certain because an inventor like Korridès would want his machine to be perfect. So, there's a way to make the helicopter lighter so it can rise up in the water even if all its functions are broken, making it dead weight. But how?"

At this point Sylvie looked at Titania. The wretched woman was pale, not moving, her eyes and lips closed. She looked dead. But she was alive—her chest rose and fell slowly with her breathing. But slumped on the floor she looked utterly drained of all her former power.

An idea popped into Sylvie's mind. She acted on it immediately.

Softly but firmly she whispered, "Diana Ivanovna!"

The Red Princess shuddered, raised her head, opened her eyes and calmly, coldly looked at Sylvie.

Sylvie repeated, "Diana Ivanovna. It's the hour of death, don't you think it'd be better to live and make amends for a life that, if you really are a monster, ought to horrify you?"

Diana did not answer right away. Her eyes remained calm and cold, her face emotionless. Then, without changing at all, she raised her voice and spoke quickly and clearly, "Say everything you think but do me the favor and don't talk about ethics that mean nothing to me."

Sylvie nodded and explained her ideas about the helicopter. She concluded, "I'm sure my husband will accept if I promise life, liberty and mercy to you, your husband and your friends since it's against them that the Nyctalope is fighting. I'll promise you all this. In exchange, you tell me right now what I have to do to get the propellers working again. It's not logical that the lever being yanked down doesn't have some counter-action built in... So, I ask again, what do I have to do fix the problem?"

Still calm and cold and impassive, Titania answered in the same voice as before, "Well thought. Yes, it can be reversed. It's very simple. But I won't tell you."

"Why?" Sylvie shivered.

"Because I'd rather die."

But these dreadful words were heard by Sylvie as an annoying but deadly serious puzzle that she had to solve if she did not want to die.

She sounded more emphatic, "Why would you rather die?"

Titania had the strength to shrug her shoulders. She pouted wearily, but she said, "When I tell you why, you'll understand that it's futile to press me. And you'll be killing me if you don't let me watch you and your son in your death throes..."

After this horrifying statement she took a few deep breaths before continuing.

"Listen up and try to understand because after this I won't say another word. If I fix the helicopter there'll be a choice: either we go to Tana Island or we return to Lost Island. Landing on Tana Island could be what I demand for what you want. Will you accept?"

"Of course," Sylvie agreed sincerely.

"Good. Well then, here's what'll happen. We'll be welcomed by the revolutionaries. They respect and admire the living, powerful Titania. But in secret they want, like every rebel, to be the leader. That's why rebels and revolutionaries will never form a long-term government, because they'll end up fighting and killing each other before cooperating. When the Abyssinian revolutionaries see what I've become, they'll take the helicopter, they'll take you and the strongest among them...

"Sure, I know who. The grandnephew of Menelik, deceased. He'll take away any chance I might have to recover and live... Then he'll bargain with the Nyctalope, with the Abyssinian government, with his own accomplices. You'll be given back to your husband but I'll be dead and all my projects along with me!

"You understand now why I'd rather die here where at least I'll be comforted by thought that you and your son are dying too... and that Leo Saint-Clair, that man I hate, will never have enough tears to mourn you!

"That's the first alternative. As for the second..."

She breathed deeply again and keeping her voice clear and firm by force of will, she went on:

"As for the second, returning to Lost Island, well, the Nyctalope is victor there. I can tell you that my husband and his partners are his prisoners. The Nyctalope is victor over the Hashshashins and Leo Saint-Clair will be happy to see his wife and son come back safe and sound... Will I get better? Will I live? Yes. And will my husband be set free? Yes again. Will our fortune be left intact? Another yes. Oh but what do I care about a life without revenge? What do I care about a husband who was just a tool of mine? I'd rather die here, Sylvie, knowing that you are dying too... in despair."

She sputtered a laugh that ended in a rattling wheeze. Then she waited, looking forward to the angry and afflicted answer, the curse and condemnation that Sylive was going to spit out. But her wicked hope was crushed.

Very calmly Sylvie simply said, "That's fine. You won't tell me how to save us. I'll just have to figure it out myself."

"You'll never be able to," *La Vibora* huffed.

"Yes I will."

"Go ahead then!"

"I am."

Sylvie stood up. For the past hour or so, her behavior had been sublime.

First, Sylvie went down to the cabin. She was glad to see little Pierre playing with Adele. Out of habit the nanny could not resist the baby's instinctive pestering and had started amusing him. As death was playing out its hand, life went on.

Not understanding what was happening and a natural fatalist, Carmetta was mechanically doing her chores, cleaning up the cabin. Matello and Titania had instilled in her a very strict discipline. The habitual, daily submission to this discipline was doing its job.

"Adele," Sylvie said, "let's have faith. Everything will work out." She turned to Carmetta and spoke in Castilian, "I'm counting on your obedience. From this point forward I am the mistress. Do you understand?"

"Si, señora."

"Bueno."

Maternal love kept her there for a few moments to make Pierre smile before she headed back up to the machinery.

Titania had not budged. Clearly she was extremely weak. Maybe she was not in danger of dying like she thought or pretended, but the shock to her nerves had made any physical reaction impossible for her. The only part of her body that still seemed alive was her eyes. And what life! Full of passionate hatred, infernal joy and cruelty! Huge black diamonds with some deep, inner light! They stared at Sylvie and never looked away.

Sylvie started examining all the controls, one by one, methodically, patiently. When she had studied them all by sight, reflection and sometimes with careful contact, she mentally split into two those that obviously served no purpose for her and those that might have an effect on the current position of the helicopter.

She went through the latter one more time.

A pedal, a wheel, buttons to push, dials to turn, levers moving up and down or right to left, switches and screws... Sylvie tried them all.

All kinds of consequences resulted: inner and outer blinds opened and closed over the windows, spotlights lit up the water and Sylvie saw hundreds of fish attracted to the light and then scared away in front of the windows, needles on the dials showed the rise and fall of solar energy in the batteries—of no use since the engine was out of commission. Nothing, however, changed the position of the helicopter.

"That's that," Sylvie said aloud. "But maybe there's some dead weight or unnecessary engine pieces that could be detached and lighten it so it can rise?"

She swung around to face *La Vibora*. If what she had said was any reflection of reality, maybe it would show in the hateful woman's eyes.

But Titania's wide open, observant eyes kept the same diabolical expression of hatred and cruelty.

"I'm going downstairs," Sylvie said, "into the storage because if there's anything to throw out it'll be down there. But since I don't trust you, even though you look physically incapacitated, I'm going to tie you up."

Four lockers were cleverly disguised at the bottom of the walls on four sides of the hexagon. They looked like normal baseboards. Sylvie had found and examined them. They were full of tools and various objects like wires, insulation, sandpaper, etc.

With some strong but flexible wire Sylvie bound the wrists and ankles of her prisoner, who did not make the slightest move to resist, did not say a word, did not twitch a muscle on her stone-cold face, did not change the expression in her terrible eyes...

And Sylvie went downstairs. When she passed through the cabin, she was glad to see Pierrot clutching onto his nanny and the Galician servant sitting on a stool watching them tenderly. In the storage Sylvie searched rigorously and meticulously, trying to find anything that was expendable. She opened all the cabinets, all the compartments, looked in all the nooks and crannies. She found nothing that could serve her purpose. Unless there was some inscrutable secret, the storage held no heavy mechanisms or machine parts that could be disposed of.

Far from being discouraged, Sylvie was motivated to search harder. This motivation inspired one of those very simple ideas that made her wonder why she had not thought of it before. The heroic young lady formulated it like this:

"Look, if the space between the two cells contains the gears, batteries, propeller shafts, rudder controls and such, then that's where I have to start looking. Why didn't I think of this first?"

Yes, she was right? But how to get into that space?

"Well, in the machinery or in the storage there's a door!" she stated not with hope but with certainty.

The arched line of a doorway was etched into one of the walls. It looked sealed shut with no way to open it. Where was the secret device to open it? Normally, it should be in the storage but she had thoroughly examined everything. No matter! She decided to explore a second time, even more carefully than the first.

"But no!" she said aloud. "Any work between the two cells is impossible because it's only ten inches wide."

That was when the real torment began, in the depths of which all hope was lost and she entered the frigid horror of conscious agony, the slow agony leading to inevitable death.

Despite the justified idea that being able to move and work "between the two cells is impossible because it's only ten inches wide", she still looked for a way to open the hidden door. In vain.

"Let's go look to the machinery where there's also a door I saw."

Going through the cabin again, she once again felt a little light in her soul on seeing Pierrot sleeping soundly in Adele's arms and Carmetta softly singing a Galician lament.

In the machinery, eyes open and still alert, *La Vibora* welcomed Sylvie, who barely acknowledged her and had no plans to untie her. She looked again for anything that might open a door. A disappointing search. Here, too, the door remained closed. Obviously, the diabolical, inventive and cautious genius of Korridès, no matter the possible risks, had set everything up for this very situation to occur where unless someone knew the secret, the helicopter would change into dead weight, impossible to repair.

Now, Titania was the only one here who knew the secret. She wanted and caused the standstill. She did not want the helicopter to move.

More than an hour had passed since she had thought and said, "Whatever it takes to save us, I'll find it." But she had found nothing and there was nothing else to do but wait for death to come, the death of her son, Adele, Carmetta, Titania and finally herself who was stronger and more worked up so that she would last the longest before dying of suffocation.

Wrapped up, entangled and pervaded by these desperate thoughts, with no hope to cling to, Sylvie admitted defeat. Her body shook with sobs. She barely saw *La Vibora* who was laughing soundlessly. She went down to the cabin, took her sleeping child in her arms, sat on a bunk and like a sleepwalker said, "Adele, do you believe in God? Pray, pray now with all your soul, because we're going to die."

Without hearing or seeing Adele, who let out a cry of despair, jumped up and went to hug Carmetta, now frightened and bewildered, Sylvie kissed little Pierre's forehead with the strange thought that it would warm him up even though the cold horror she felt was, she knew, purely emotional. Even with the solar radiators heating up the cabin, Sylvie was shivering.

Time passed.

Terrified and stupefied, Adele and Carmetta hugged each other on the same stool, crying silently. The excess of fear had rendered them almost unconscious.

More time passed.

All of a sudden Sylvie heard a quiet, soft scratching sound overhead. She listened...

Then a voice called out, quiet, panting, "Sylvie... Sylvie Saint-Clair!"

She looked up, stunned.

The trapdoor framed the face, neck and shoulders of Diana Ivanovna. The unstoppable woman had dragged herself, still tied up, to the door left open by Sylvie. Now she was staring down at the scene of the mother and son condemned to a slow death... A look of implacable hatred, savage cruelty and jubilant triumph. And the voice, the quiet, panting voice, spoke again.

"Sylvie, the agony of you and your son is going to last for hours and hours. I'll survive in order to see it to the end... because I'll stay right here and dare you to try to move me... but listen, listen...

"The house of *The Sycamores* in Versailles, remember? The night of May 21... The call for help, the groans, the sobs, the cries of pain... Did I tell you? It was pretty, kind Nadine, the wife of Ignace Kiewicz, the Polish man you knew... Well, she watched her husband die when Korridès reduced him to a pile of ashes... Oh, that was what I was hoping for your husband, Leo Saint-Clair burned alive in front of you... But when we can't get what we want, we have to take what we can get... Oh, Sylvie, I'll settle for this. After all, it's a beautiful sight... while I'm dying... to watch you and your son dying ever so slowly..."

She could say no more. Her voice had become weak and wheezy. But she stayed there, eyes alive in a face lit by the cabin's ceiling light—the pale, sinister face of a corpse.

Sylvie looked down at her son and murmured, "Little Pierre. Leo..." And then, without a sound, she started crying.

CHAPTER XII
Saint-Clair the Nyctalope

Meanwhile on Lost Island Leo Saint-Clair and Gnô Mitang had passed a sleepless night. After the exhausting and emotional events they had lived through without almost any rest for so long, they really did not need to think or talk or move anymore—they needed to sleep. Guarding Lost Island was in the care of Vitto and Socca who, along with Loustal and Marod, were taking turns on watch.

In the morning of June 8, the Nyctalope and the Japanese were physically rested, mentally alert and as determined as ever to succeed in the task that lay ahead: to find out where Titania had taken Sylvie and Pierre in the flying machine, which they had every right to call a helicopter even though these inventions, in the real world, were purely theoretical; and then to defeat Titania and free the prisoners.

In short, since the tragic night in San Lorenzo the problem had not changed. And despite the successive victories of Saint-Clair and Gnô, the problem was worse because it was harder to solve now.

But of course Saint-Clair and Gnô were not discouraged by this new difficulty. Right after breakfast they started working since they did not have to worry about the daily life of Lost Island, which was taken care of by the cooks and their son who had served Matello and only knew Titania as a kind of invisible goddess to whom they had no personal attachment. Influenced by Loustal and Marod, commanded once and for all by Gnô, they knew what they had to do. The provisions could last for days before being restocked. They had flour for bread, fresh fish in a small pool connected to the sea, meat, vegetables and canned fruit as well as chickens and rabbits living in one of the barracks.

The meals were served at the prescribed times so that everyone on the island was fed. The prisoners also got fed. Prisoners meaning Hamed the Nubian and the two captured guards who were Russian, undeniably communists, and seemed suspicious to Vitto and Socca who had interrogated them and advised Gnô to keep them locked up.

Once everything had been set up, Saint-Clair and Gnô, eventually joined by Vitto, Socca, Loustal and Marod, were free to work without distractions.

First of all, the Nyctalope and Gnô made another search for any document relating to the so-called helicopter and the place where Titania might have taken it. The search lasted until midnight. It was fruitless. The prisoners, though they seemed willing to help, swore they knew nothing about it.

Saint-Clair and Gnô walked around in circles between the guards' barracks and the front door of the octagonal building. Loustal and Marod were sitting on the front steps. Marod was reading a newspaper he had bought in San Sebastian on Monday, June 6, during the meeting of Saint-Clair and the Marquis d'Ulloa. Since then he had not had time to look at it.. Now, during the fifteen of twenty minutes that Saint-Clair and Gnô dedicated to walking meditation, he could give in to his long-standing passion: reading the newspaper every day. The newspaper for him was like the pipe for Loustal. So, he unfolded the paper with great pleasure because he was finally going to be able to get a little relaxation. See, these two men, even if they did not show it, were truly suffering to the depths of their souls because of the pain and sorrow inflicted on the Saint-Clair family. And so, Loustal was smoking his pipe and Marod reading his newspaper.

These two new "guard dogs" of the Nyctalope had known nothing at all about the great adventure. During their morning investigation Saint-Clair and Gnô had filled them in on what they had learned from what was done or said by others or seen by themselves on the island. Therefore, they now knew as much as anyone about Titania, Korridès and the Hashshashins, why they did what they did and what they wanted to achieve.

So, Marod had been calmly reading for maybe ten minutes when all of a sudden he bellowed incoherently. His hands clenched the paper as he brought it close to his face to read better.

Loustal looked over, "Hey, what's got into you?"

Marod did not answer but after a few seconds he jumped up, ran to Saint-Clair and Gnô, stopped right in front of them and started shaking the newspaper. His voice shook along with his hands, "Monsieur, read this! Read it!"

The two men leaned closer and together read:

"Revolution in Abyssinia: A captured rebel makes strange revelations.

"Addis Ababa. June 4. Among the men captured recently in a frontier skirmish between a government battalion and a band of rebels, was an ex-sergeant of the imperial guard named Mikael Tabor. Interrogated by the Court Martial Commissioner, who had the right to postpone his death penalty, the man made important revelations among which was one very strange one: the Abyssinian agitators leading the revolution were not part of the Third International but were members of an anarchist cult whose executive council called themselves the Hashshashin, thus associated in some way or another with the fanatical Muslim sect founded in Persia around 1080 by Hasan al-Sabbah, known as the Old Man of the Mountain. As we know, it is from Hashshashins that we get the word 'assassin'.

"Sergeant Tabor revealed that Tana Island, in the middle of the lake of the same name in the most mountainous region of Abyssinia, is not only the headquarters of the rebels but is also the holy city, the temple, the Mecca of the modern Hashshashins."

On reading this article, Marod's mind, as tired as it was, still made the connection. Imagine, then, how quickly and clearly the active minds of Saint-Clair and Gnô saw the same thing. All of them were thinking: "The helicopter went to Tana".

Saint-Clair voiced it aloud.

Gnô chimed in, "They're in Ethiopia!"

"Right," the Nyctalope went on, "but let's not get ahead of ourselves. It's only a theory. It's the most plausible of everything we've come up with so far because it's information that forms a good basis for further analysis. All of Escarpaz's documents and everything we've found on Lost Island have confirmed the existence of something like auxiliary hideouts for the Hashshashins. For example in Versailles or here on Lost Island. And we feel, we've discussed the need for a secret headquarters, a center of operations and a final refuge. Even if none of the documents mentioned it, even if Loustal and Marod and our prisoners knew nothing about it, it's because the Hashshashin council, at least in Europe, kept it totally secret because it's so important.

"Therefore, it's not possible for us to doubt that the headquarters, the refuge, the nerve center of the Hashshashins is indeed Tana Island, a fact revealed by an independent source, a man who lived there on the island."

"Exactly so," Gnô said. "Besides, if we're wrong, it's a round trip of less than 7,000 miles. With the electric plane of Korridès, again only if we're wrong, it'll be a total of 37 hours."

"Right," the Nyctalope agreed. He was feeling as impatient as he was emotional.

Gnô understood. "So, let's stop talking about it and let's get going. And I think it'll be better to bring along Vitto and Socca. We might need backup."

"Right," the Nyctalope agreed again.

And the Japanese, "We'll trust Lost Island and the prisoners to Loustal and Marod."

Fifteen minutes later the electric plane, the *Vulture*, was soaring off from Lost Island. Fast but attentively, Saint-Clair and Gnô had made sure that there were enough provisions, weapons and ammunition for whatever might occur. The electricity needed for normal operation was stored, pressurized you could say, thanks to a procedure invented by Korridès, in the batteries that took up less space than the battery of an 18 hp automobile. A special system had been set up on Lost Island to charge the batteries. Loustal and Marod had often been tasked with this job. They were tasked again but this time against the Hashshashin. The stored electricity was enough to keep the *Vulture* in the air at an average speed of 200 mph for 120 hours.

Impatient to reach Tana Island, Saint-Clair and Gnô were often tempted to push the plane to its maximum speed, but they resisted because they were afraid a long period at top speed could cause some kind of damage. As slight as the damage might be, it would force them to stop and delay their arrival for who knew how long. It was better to take the normal time to cover the 3,500 miles without problems, without stopping.

During the non-stop flight that lasted nineteen hours, Saint-Clair, Gnô, Vitto and Socca took turns at the controls and resting. They ate and drank at regular intervals because they wanted to be in top shape, ready for any eventuality. Even though they had examined the situation from every angle, even the most fanciful, they did not form an action plan. The saying of the Nyctalope, "Be ready for anything but do what circumstances demand", was more than ever called for because it was a logically reasoned but still uncertain fact that they were going to search for Sylvie and Pierre on Tana Island.

The airplane performed marvelously in every way. It flew as smoothly at the end of 19 hours as at the start. They were in the 34th minute of the final hour of the flight, meaning at 9:34 a.m. on June 9, turning in a circle at 8,200 feet altitude, when they had below them, in the middle of the circle they were maneuvering, the island named by Sergeant Tabor as the headquarters and most secret lair of the Hashshashins.

Among the many tools and accessories in the *Vulture* there were some high-powered binoculars. Moreover, the hull had a window built in to see underneath the plane directly or at a 45-degree angle. While Vitto was at the controls and Socca was keeping an eye on the instrument panel, Saint-Clair and Gnô sat in special folding seats on either side of this window and observed Tana Island through binoculars. The island itself was nothing special. The buildings in the center could have been a small town or a big village. There were no signs of fortifications or anything else out of the ordinary. As for the lake, it was deserted except for one thing.

Gnô said, "Before this tragic adventure I'd read, probably you too, some news about developments in Abyssinia. And I imagine that you, too, never paid too much attention to it."

"Not the slightest," Saint-Clair replied. "Revolutionary troubles since 1919 are a dime a dozen in nations getting back on their feet."

"Well," Gnô went on, "looking at the headquarters of this revolution, you'd think it was pretty calm and not very active. Except for that one thing that looks like a torpedo boat, there aren't even boats or ships on the lake. There doesn't seem to be any traffic between the island and the mainland."

"Exactly. But that little torpedo boat, as you call it, notice how it's acting. I've been watching it closely for a minute. Doesn't it seem kind of weird to you?"

"Wait." The Japanese focused his binoculars on the torpedo boat.

To the west of the island, midway between its shore and the opposite coast, the boat was going around in circles.

They watched it for half an hour without saying a word. During this time the torpedo boat stopped four times, each lasting two or three minutes. Then it started making circles again, sometimes concentric, sometimes eccentric, meaning in inward or outward spirals. The fifth stop was longer, already five minutes, and it seemed to have dropped anchor and was preparing to drop divers into the water.

"Weird," Saint-Clair said.

"Very weird," Gnô agreed.

The Nyctalope went on, "We're too high. Let's go closer. There's no danger. The *Vulture* is surely known to some extent by the Abyssinian revolutionaries. We know there's a K and an H painted under the wings and the meaning's obvious: Korridès and Hashshashin. We still have no proof that Titania came here or whoever's on the boat knows that Lost Island and the *Vulture* are ours now. Most likely they'll think some head honcho is on board, maybe even Korridès himself or Titania."

"I think you're right."

"Vitto," Saint-Clair shouted, "descend in a slow, tight spiral as safely as you can."

"Okay, monsieur."

And the *Vulture* slowly descended toward the lake. One, two, three minutes went by.

"Ho, ho!" the Nyctalope suddenly burst out excitedly.

Gnô felt the need to say, "Stay calm, Leo, please."

"But do you see that?"

"Yes, I see."

"That's got to be the helicopter! What else could it be? Coincidence, really?"

"Stay calm," the Japanese repeated.

So, what were they seeing?

Everyone knows that visibility through water is better the higher up the observer is. Pilots flying 3,000 feet over an ocean or lake, if the surface is calm, see much better than someone on the deck of a ship, for example. That's why during the Great War, especially at the end after much experience fighting on water and in the air, the submarines were no more dangerous than seaplanes.

Now, on this morning of June 9, Lake Tana was as calm as a pond in the park. Not the slightest breeze and not a cloud in the sky. The kind of enchanting serenity that not only people but also animals enjoy, as zoologists have often remarked.

Therefore, Saint-Clair and Gnô could see deep into the lake. And in the water there was an object that must have been floating at 80, 90, maybe 100 feet below the surface, an object seen at a 23 to 25-degree angle depending on the spiral of the plane. The object looked cylindrical, like a long tube, but the gripping detail was that it its top and on one side were what looked like propellers.

The silent observation of Saint-Clair and Gnô lasted another three minutes. Vitto and Socca, who were flying the plane, paid close attention to any words that might escape them, even an audible gasp or sigh.

But it was not a gasp or a sigh that came out of Saint-Clair's mouth. He suddenly jumped up, put his binoculars on a shelf and with an expression on his face that could not be interpreted as anything else but "ecstatic will and energy", in his usual sharp, clear voice, both vibrant and commanding, he said:

"Gnô, Vitto, Socca, either what we call human intelligence is only an illusion of our pride or else down there in the water are my wife, son and Titania, with Adele, of course, and the servant girl. We've got to get down there. We've got to take the place of the guys on the boat who are apparently getting ready to dive down to that flying machine.

"My friends, my plan has been laid out. We've already talked about it so we don't need to go over the details to avoid blunders. Gnô, we're representatives of Korridès. We know Titania is in the helicopter, since it really is a helicopter, right?"

"Yes, of course," Gnô was beaming. "It really is a helicopter."

"We'll say that Titania is in there and we came to get her. That's it… You get it… Let's go! Vitto and Socca, you have to put down as close to the ship as you can."

It was done quickly. In the cabin, in a kind of safe, cleverly installed in a corner, Gnô had found a bunch of silk flags. There were all the "colors" of all the nations of the world plus three red ones with a black Saint Andrew's cross, big X, and two letters: K and H. Obviously, this was the Hashshashin flag.

When the *Vulture* was on the water, Gnô opened the door. In a short tube (obviously meant for this) he stuck the pole that he had found in a cabinet and to which he had attached the flag.

The results were instantaneous. On the torpedo boat, since it was actually a small torpedo boat like the coastal defense ships still in service in most the world's navies, all activity was halted. Officers gathered at the railing facing the plane and stood at attention, feet together, right hand open on one side of the white cap with a long bill. Close by, to their left, two men already in diving suits froze, just like the sailors around them who were holding the helmets.

Saint-Clair whispered to Gnô, "This time, my friend, either I'm completely deluded or we're going to win the last round." But his face tensed up and he added, "We have to stay strong. I'll confess that I'm worried. Is Sylvie still alive? And my son?"

"Let's hope so, Leo. Keep the faith."

"Yes, yes, you're right," Saint-Clair affirmed. He straightened up with his usual expression of energetic and authoritative calm.

Before this final conversation, the two men had made a quick calculation. Supposing that the helicopter could fly at 225 to 250 mph, given that it had left Lost Island around 7 p.m. on June 7, it must have arrived at Lake Tana late the next morning. Now it was June 9. So, it had been submerged for at least 24 hours. Logically, it was accidental and something very serious must have happened for Titania (unquestionably she was inside the helicopter) not to bring it to the surface. The torpedo boat was clearly on a rescue mission. So, there was damage, an accident, a wreck. What kind exactly? How bad was it? And what were the consequences on the passengers?

It was after this mental calculation that the husband and father could not help saying to his friend, "I'm worried."

But his worry had to stay hidden. Any fear had to be completely wiped out. Action was needed, action of the kind that not a single mistake could be made, not a second of hesitation could delay it. The Nyctalope had never taken such pains to remain in control of himself.

From the information furnished by the documents of Escarpaz, and from Julien Peul, Loustal and Marod, Saint-Clair knew that French was the official language of the Hashshashins and that all the chiefs could speak and understand it. The Abyssinian rebel fleet could not have been very big. Probably it was no bigger than this one small torpedo boat. So, the commanding officer, and even the two second mates on either side of him, must have been high enough up in the hierarchy to know French. Saint-Clair did not hesitate. The plane was close enough to the boat to speak at normal volume.

"Captain," Saint-Clair said, "to avoid accidents the *Vulture* is going to move a little farther away. But I and my colleague and one of my engineers have to come on board, so send us a dinghy."

One of the two dinghies on the torpedo boat was already in the water with two sailors. The captain shouted orders not in French but in a language that neither Saint-Clair nor Gnô understood, which was probably Ethiopian—brief orders barked loudly. Immediately the two sailors grabbed the oars and maneuvered their dinghy carefully so that Saint-Clair, Gnô and Socca could get in.

During the short wait, Saint-Clair had given precise instructions to Vitto about the plane.

It was on the starboard gunwale that Saint-Clair and the captain made their formal introductions.

"Monsieur," Saint-Clair said, "I am Diens, number 3, and this (he nodded toward Gnô) is Mittwoch, number 4, from the central committee. We're delegates of K. We've come to meet up with Sunday, number 1, who came to Tana in the helicopter with very important prisoners. We saw it while flying over your boat, which naturally drew our attention. Now introduce yourself and tell me what happened."

The Abyssinian officers of the Hashshashins had probably never left Ethiopia. What little they knew of the sect would provoke no suspicions in their minds. Besides, the brief introduction of this so-called Diens corresponded with the present situation.

The captain saluted again and in a bizarrely accented French said, "I'm captain Theodore Zeila, captain of the fleet of independent Abyssinia and in particular of this torpedo boat. This is my second mate Lieutenant Nagast and the Major Ankoler, our doctor."

The two officers saluted and the captain continued.

"We left port early this morning to go pick up a convoy of wounded but on passing by this spot the officer on duty, Lieutenant Nagast, was surprised to see on the clear, clean water a little pool of oil. He informed me. I stopped the boat and the first thing I did was to get a sample of this unimaginable oil and get it examined by Major Ankoler, who is also an expert chemist.

"Turned out it was lubricating oil for a car or plane. How did it end up here? The question had to be answered on the spot.

"We did some probing because from the surface visibility is poor after 30 feet or so. We found that at around 80 feet there was something pretty big sitting in the water. So, we dropped in an underwater camera we've got on board—the scientific equipment on this boat is first class. The photographs revealed the presence of an aircraft, unless it was a strange submarine, but it looked a lot like what I've read about helicopters."

While talking the captain had waved to a man behind him and been handed a few prints that were still wet from the fixing bath. They did indeed show a machine that looked like what was seen in the airplane.

The captain went on, "As you see, I'm sending divers down there."

"Very good," Saint-Clair's voice was deadpan despite his racing heartbeat. "Did you probe the lake here?"

"Yes, monsieur."

"What's the depth?"

"460, 475, 500 feet at three points of a triangle 165 feet per side. The helicopter's in the middle of the triangle with its higher propeller at exactly 82 feet."

"Fine. These diving suits can go down to 120 feet maximum, right?"

"Yes, monsieur."

"Perfect." On the spot Saint-Clair decided, "My colleague Mittwoch and I will dive together shortly. Prepare the spotlights for underwater lighting. Also prepare the chains with clamps so we can hook them onto the helicopter. For the moment I'm going down alone."

"At your command."

No words, no description could give a precise idea of the emotions shared in the look between Saint-Clair and Gnô right before they screwed on the copper helmet to the collar of the diving suit containing the so-called Diens. They stuck the air tank on his back, which would give him three solid hours underwater. His belt was supplied with three rings to which were clipped the suspension cords. These cords were bunched together three feet above the helmet and run through a pulley on a hoist. And the substitute diver jumped in the water... Socca was discreetly but meticulously checking everything.

"It's okay," he said to himself. He was not surprised.

This episode in the tragic adventure was not only unforeseen but unforeseeable fifteen minutes before it happened. Saint-Clair and Gnô Mitang suddenly transformed into Hashshashin chiefs giving orders to the Abyssinian henchmen of Titania and Korridès and getting obeyed without question, which was only logical—it was all so astonishing. But being in the company of the Nyctalope for so long, Socca found the most complicated and astonishing deeds quite simple and normal, and as any brave and intelligent man he adapted quickly. And what else did Saint-Clair and Gnô do but adapt to situations using their bravery and intelligence?

The diver, therefore, was in the water and slowly descending towards the helicopter. For him the fifteen minutes seemed endless. When he was "face to face" with the machine he yanked the signal cord on the left side of his belt three times. It meant "Halt!"

Up on the torpedo boat Socca hollered, "Stop!", since he was the one watching the lever connected to the signal cord.

The men stopped giving slack to the suspension cords.

At that moment, inside the metal and rubber shell, the Nyctalope was hearing his heart beat loudly. He heard it not like it was in his chest but as if it was in his head and every limb. He felt a cold sweat on his forehead and a shiver ran through his body... But a moment later he heard and felt nothing because all his energy was concentrated in his eyes, on his sight.

Grabbing onto one of the propellers with one hand, the other clamped onto the ridge that separated each side of the hexagon, he looked inside a window...

It was dark in the water and dark inside the helicopter, but darkness did not exist for the Nyctalope. In these few minutes that were like no other in the life of Leo Saint-Clair, his nyctalopian power was doubly acute.

And he saw first that there were two windows of thick crystal lined up one inside the other.

"The helicopter's got two hulls," he muttered, unaware that he was speaking out loud.

He looked through the second window.

And he saw Diana Ivanovna. He saw her half lying on her left side on a table. Her bound wrists were held over her head gripping the wheel of some mechanism. Her face and chest were facing the window. Neither was moving. Her eyes and mouth were closed in her pale, gaunt face.

"Dead," Saint-Clair grunted. "And Sylvie? Pierrot? There are other windows."

His left hand pulled him along to the next window. Here he saw only three quarters of the Titania's "corpse", as he thought of it.

"I've got to keep going."

At the third window again he saw only Titania.

"One window for two sides of the hexagon. Therefore, there are only three windows. This compartment has no one else, at least as far as I can see. But there must be other compartments underneath."

He gave two short tugs to the cord, which meant "Give me more slack."

On the boat, at Socca's orders, the sailors obeyed. Slowly, the diver descended. And right away he was at the second level with more windows than the upper one. He tugged the cord to stop. And he froze.

Once again he mustered all his vital forces into his power of sight and he looked. Directly in front of him he saw a full bunk and on either side half of other bunks. On full bunk there was a woman lying on her back, presenting a perfect profile, her eyes and mouth closed. Saint-Clair did not know this woman. Was she sleeping? Dead?

On the half-bunk to the right he saw a skirt, legs, shoes... The shoes allowed him to identify with absolute certainty the woman he saw only half of.

"Adele," he murmured.

On the bunk on the left or rather on the half of it he could see, there were only unidentifiable feet and legs—anonymous because they were under a blanket. Trembling a little despite his total self-control, slid over to the right.

He figured, "To see the whole bunk on the left, I have to go the window on my right, which will be right across from it."

Thinking and acting at the same time took only seconds. Saint-Clair groaned as his hands squeezed the sharp ridges of the hexagon. He was looking at his wife and son. Half-covered by a blanket, Sylvie was lying on her right side, her face half buried in the pillow, revealing only her left cheek, one eye, the bridge of her nose and a corner of her mouth. Her face was deathly pale but her lips had a little color... and her eye was open.

"Dead? Alive?" Saint-Clair felt an anguish that shook his body.

He could not tell if the eye was living or dead because it was staring at the face of the baby and this face could not be seen because Pierre, in the arms of his mother, had his back turned to the window where the husband and father was stiff as a board inside his flexible shell.

How long did the Nyctalope stay there, immobile, panting, staring through the window? One minute? Fifteen? He was unaware and never tried to figure it out.

At some point, his mind started working again and he heard himself saying, "If I get in front of the next window to my right I'll see more of her face and even little Pierre's."

No sooner said than done. But no matter how hard he tried to analyze what he saw, he could not tell if any life was still coursing through her body or glimmering in her open eyes. He suddenly had the passionate, overpowering, brutal need to know, to know right away.

This compulsion came out in a hoarse voice, "Stop looking! Stop wondering! Do something! And fast!"

He yanked the signal cord once: "Bring me up!"

A minute later he was climbing onto the deck of the torpedo boat. His clear and precise gestures left no room for doubt. He did not want them to remove his helmet. No need... No time to lose! Quickly, Gnô in the suit. The spotlights and chains. Get ready!

The crew on the deck of the small torpedo boat, with Socca giving orders and the officers assisting, steered the suspension cords, the chains and clamps and spotlights into place. Quickly, quickly, above all else, quickly!

Working feverishly, although motivated by completely different reasons, the three officers of the Hashshashin navy obeyed no less zealously than Gnô and Socca. In the shortest period possible, everything was ready to go. Saint-Clair and Gnô jumped into the water at the same time as the chains and electric cables.

Saint-Clair knew that it was impossible to talk with Gnô but through their helmet windows they could see each other. They could also use hand signals. Anyway, were not their will and spirit and wisdom focused on the same goal? If only telepathically, they were sure to think and act in unison.

But as strong as the two men were, each feared that the overwhelming emotions of the other might weaken them. They were both thinking, "I can't let myself be affected by what happens, no matter how hideous or happy it might be."

Gnô Mitang, with no clue as to what the Nyctalope had seen, felt that it must be as mysterious as it was terrible. He was tingling with impatience to see and to know. And he could see and know as much as the Nyctalope because the spotlights were shining on three of the sides of the helicopter. The inside was so brightly lit, despite the water, the layers of crystal glass and the heavy air, that as Gnô passed by the windows he could see Titania, Sylvie, Pierre, Adele and the unknown woman whom he figured must be Carmetta.

None of these discoveries slowed him down. Along with Saint-Clair, synchronized with him, Gnô went to work; simple work that turned out to be very easy. The helicopter was not equipped with rings or rods for clamps, but the exterior shaft of the propeller and the bottom of the rudder were perfect for hooking the clamps.

"Pull the chains!" Gnô Mitang ordered.

During the first dive of the fake Diens, they had equipped the helmet of the fake Mittwoch with a telephonic device wired to the torpedo boat. Up above, everyone heard him because the receiver had a microphone and horn from which his voice boomed out as clearly as a phonograph. At the same time, Saint-Clair yanked his signal cord. Raising the divers and the helicopter took place simultaneously. Saint-Clair and Gnô were side by side with their helmets fused, so to speak, to the window through which they could see Sylvie and Pierre directly.

So, they were about halfway up when the thing occurred.

Did Saint-Clair and Gnô cry out? Maybe? They each thought they clearly heard the other cry out. Maybe it was just an auditory illusion. The cry they heard or thought they heard was immediately answered by both of them, but this time unheard, with the exact same words:

"She moved!"

But as soon as they had said this, they both felt it was a horribly cruel illusion. If Sylvie had moved, it was short and barely perceptible since her head and body and arms were in exactly the same position. And it there were movement, it was not repeated. Was it an illusion produced by the rippling water reflecting off the window?

"My God," Saint-Clair muttered, "so, she is dead."

But right after this he yelled, really yelled, just like Gnô next to him.

"She's looking at us! She's looking right at us! She sees us!"

Because this time it was not her body that moved but her eye, opened wide now and slowly drifting away from the baby to stare straight at the window.

At that moment the helicopter broke the surface of the water along with the two divers. Saint-Clair unscrewed the helmet himself before he even set foot on the deck. He pushed off the helmet and was about to scream out, even if it were an incomprehensible howl, he was going to let loose his inexpressible emotion but his eyes met those of Gnô who had also removed his helmet. And the eyes of the Japanese were so obviously, so firmly saying "Watch out! Be careful!" that Saint-Clair's excitement immediately faded. He remembered that he was Diens, number 3, on board a torpedo boat with a crew of revolutionaries loyal to Titania.

With superhuman effort, swallowing all his emotions, he did what the real Diens would have done. Calmly but quickly, assisted by Socca and Gnô, he got out of the diving suit.

Captain Zeila and Lieutenant Nagats were directing the handling of the helicopter, which was far taller than the boat. The two hoists on the back of the boat that had hauled it up and were now holding it steady were not big enough to lift it completely out of the water. One third of the helicopter was still in the lake even though the chains were pulled as far as they could go.

Luckily, Lake Tana was absolutely calm. No waves rippled the water, no breeze troubled the air. Therefore, the helicopter could be docked to the back of the boat and remain firmly attached. While the work was accomplished without any difficulties, Saint-Clair, Gnô and Socca, along with Major Ankober and a guy named Dazot, discussed the easiest way to open the upper door, meaning the door of the compartment right under the conic roof where the vertical propeller shaft jutted out. The other door, which they could see in the clear water, remained submerged. The accessible door above was located so that from the rear port side of the boat they were in front of it. They just had to rig up a gangway suspended by chains and ropes tied to the hoist.

Ankober said, "There's got to be a way to open it from the outside."

"Certainly," the so-called Diens agreed. "But it's probably locked from the inside. It's very unlikely that the passengers inside the helicopter can't stop it from being opened on the outside."

His conjecture was validated because they did indeed find a kind of switch on the right of the door, which should have opened it but did not work. Gnô rechecked that the windows were too small for a man, no matter how thin, to slip through—they were.

"Okay," Saint-Clair said, "but what the helicopter's lacking right now is breathable air."

While saying this he took an iron winch handle that a sailor had brought him. Without hesitating he smashed one of the windows, first up above, then in the cabin below, which he reached on a rope ladder hooked to the boat's railing.

He looked inside eagerly. He forced himself not to cry for joy when the sound of broken glass and especially the rush of fresh air stirred Sylvie out of her torpor. She turned her head a little and immediately recognized her husband. Leo had no doubt about that!

In the meantime, the head mechanic and two sailors had brought over a powerful blowtorch that was set up on the gangway. The flaming jet started attacking the frame of the upper door.

Saint-Clair had called Gnô over. Together they gazed into the cabin and watched Sylvie. They mustered all their strength to suppress the desire to talk to her—they would have been heard. And what could they say to her? All they could do was to try to express in their eyes the joy and affection they felt in their hearts. And to put a finger to their lips to tell Sylvie, who was starting to cry, that absolute silence was absolutely necessary.

They had another jolt of delight when Sylvie, even though she was obviously very weak, held up Pierrot to show that he was alive. This moving scene, so extraordinary in its apparent simplicity, lasted exactly seven minutes because that was how long it took Dazot and Socca to melt the bolts locking the upper door.

When it was done, Socca shouted to his boss, "Hey chief, it's open!"

Saint-Clair and Gnô stopped their silent conversation with Sylvie and climbed back up to the deck. They ran down the gangway with Zeila and Nagast right behind them.

"Messieurs," Saint-Clair said, "these tragic events have been anticipated. I know my duty. I take all responsibility. I have to get Titania and the woman and child down below into the airplane. My colleague Mittwoch is a doctor. He'll revive them if there's still time."

The decision of the fake Diens was surprising because it seemed more logical to care for the asphyxiated patients in the special room used as an infirmary on the boat. But Zeila, Nagats and Ankober were used to obeying orders, no matter how illogical they seemed, so they did not object or hesitate. The transfer was made quickly and orderly.

Titania looked dead but was still alive, which Gnô affirmed; Sylvie was conscious but very weak; the baby was also very weak but breathing normally; Adele, aroused by the fresh air, had opened her eyes but was utterly dazed; Carmetta was breathing but still passed out. The four victims of the drowned helicopter were put in a dinghy along with Saint-Clair, Gnô, Socca and the head mechanic Dazot.

Before the mooring rope was released, the so-called Diens barked at Zeila, "Captain, order your base to put get this helicopter into a safe place where nobody from the outside will see it until we get orders from Titania."

Five minutes later the four women and the baby were lying comfortably inside the *Vulture* and Dazot was heading back to the torpedo boat.

"Let's get out of here, Socca!" Saint-Clair shouted, no longer able to restrain himself.

Vitto and Socca sat at the controls. The *Vulture* took off at the very moment that Saint-Clair and Sylvie embraced. But the hug was brief because her maternal instinct kicked in.

"Little Pierre, oh sweetie, Pierre," Sylvie mumbled, exhausted.

Some strong smelling salts were in the first aid kit that Korridès, ready for everything, kept in the *Vulture*. They revived Adele. Sylvie and Leo, by the strength of their will, were able to bring her back her senses.

"Adele," Sylvie asked, "do you have milk?"

The nanny excitedly bared her left breast. It was swollen. She squeezed and a drop of milk beaded. Smiling, she took Pierre, whose instinct for self-preservation was still strong, and started feeding him. Only then did Sylvie's tears stop flowing.

She smiled blissfully at Leo and Gnô, who were leaning over her, and said, "My God, we're saved..."

Gnô's cures worked for Titania and Carmetta as well. The servant had suffered only mild asphyxiation. Titania had to by taken care of by Sylvie. Her head wound was only a superficial fracture with some exterior bleeding. The concussion had been severe enough to weaken her nerves to the point that she believed she was on death's door. But after being bandaged and drinking a mixture of sedative and stimulant that Gnô cooked up, she fell into a quiet sleep. For a few minutes her eyes had opened and she had seen, heard and understood. She had not said a word.

Eighteen hours later, when the *Vulture* splashed down near Lost Island, Sylvie had told Saint-Clair and Gnô (Socca and Vitto were also listening to every word) all that had happened. Titania had slept, eaten, drunk and taken another strong dose of Gnô's potion, which consisted solely of wisely chosen ingredients from Korridès medicine kit. And she had listened to (again without saying a word) Saint-Clair telling her what they were going to do with her.

Whereas her husband and the other Hashshashins were to be handed over to the Spanish authorities, she, Titania, would be taken to the San Lorenzo castle where they would wait for her to fully recover from her wounds and shock. After that she would be interrogated and then face a secret court martial, consisting of the Nyctalope, the Japanese and Lord of the castle, to decide her fate according to their own conscience and their duty to humanity. If the verdict was a death sentence, Titania would be summarily executed unless she preferred to kill herself, in which case she could drink a very strong poison.

Saint-Clair and Gnô were absolutely convinced of the vital necessity of these perhaps draconian measures as they saw Sylvie and Pierrot regaining their health and good cheer and they knew what real happiness was.

Vitto and Socca steered the *Vulture* up the slope where Loustal and Marod hauled it into the hangar.

Saint-Clair asked right away, "What are Korridès and the others doing?"

Loustal answered, "They're awake, still in irons, not talking. But of course me and Marod weren't authorized to question them."

Lost Island was visited again by Diana Ivanovna on the one hand and by little Pierre and Sylvie on the other. The latter, however, this time, came back not as captives condemned to death and despair but free, victorious and happy. The former returned defeated, as a prisoner, after believing that she had escaped and would defeat them all.

Gnô went alone to see Korridès and the Hashshashins. He brought them up to date and told them what they were going to face. Then orders were given and arrangements made to get off the island as soon as possible.

EPILOGUE

The wireless messages sent from the station overlooking the bay of Lost Island reached the Marquis d'Ulloa in Saint-Sebastian and the Duke d'Arandar in San Lorenzo through Burgos before ending up with the Prime Minister of France. They dealt with certain things to be done in Spain and France, especially in Versailles, in *The Sycamores* villa, in the house on Rue des Bourdonnais, the home of Dr. and Madame Korridès.

Vanquished, subdued and submissive, Korridès and the five Hashshashins, along with the wireless operator Lavignon, the pilot Dermoz and the supply man Dontes, not to mention the Nubian Hamed and the two Russian guards, were handed over to the military governor of Vigo, who put them under strict surveillance in his most impregnable prison. They were judged after a painstaking investigation by both the French and Spanish governments who had made a secret deal concerning them.

The cook, his wife and their son stayed on Lost Island, which became the property of the King of Spain. A dozen or so customs officers took it over until the royal family decided what to do with it.

On board the *Goéland III*, the *Vulture* and *La Vibora*'s personal plane, Titania, Saint-Clair, Sylvie, Pierre, Adele, Carmetta, Gnô Mitang, Socca and Vitto, and finally Loustal and Marod left Lost Island and headed for La Sierra de la Demanda.

Before descending onto the plain that served as an airstrip a couple of miles away, Saint-Clair wanted, rightfully so, to inform the Duke d'Arandar of his arrival. Therefore, he flew over the medieval castle very low. First he circled around it, then went from south to north and dropped a scarf that the Duke could recognize as Sylvie's from when she had wrapped it around little Pierre that fateful night of the fire. A piece of paper was pinned to the scarf on which Sylvie had written:

"Hello, Don Pedro! We're going to land on the plain where the plane once took me away and where Matello was found dead."

The first moment the plane was spotted the Duke, Padre Felipe and "Señora Blanca" were informed. All the personnel of the castle were alerted along with them. The scarf fell on the roof of the chapel. Antonio's young son climbed up to get it and bring it back to the Lord.

After reading the short message Don Pedro shouted, "Antonio, get the horses! And straight to the plain of Aulaguas! Bring the white mares!"

The Spanish word *"Aulaga"* means a gorse bush. The Gorse Plain was named from its vast extent on which grew nothing but this thorny bush, the gorse.

As the Duke left the castle at the head of a half-dozen guards he turned around on his horse when he heard a woman's cry. It came from the young gypsy girl Huronilla who had just jumped onto the back of Blanca's mule.

The Duke laughed, shrugged his shoulders and grumbled, "For once, let the girls be free!"

Moreover, for once, the Duke forgot all about the ceremonies of Castilian courtesy when he got to the big, open plain. He was too happy. When he saw the plane sitting on the bare ground, he spurred his horse into a gallop. Ten feet from the group formed of Sylvie, Pierrot, Saint-Clair and Gnô Mitang, he pulled up, jumped out of the saddle and ran. He hugged Sylvie, hugged Saint-Clair and kissed little Pierre who was crying. And right away, at once, he wanted to know what had become of *La Vibora*.

"I got the message three hours ago," he said. "A special courier brought it here from Burgos. I read 'Victory on all fronts. Everyone safe and sound!' Tears of joy ran down my cheeks. But *La Vibora*, that woman from hell, the cursed, heinous woman, did you kill her? Good and gone at last?"

"No," Saint-Clair replied. "She's here." He half turned and raised his hand.

A beautiful woman, standing proudly, was leaning one hand on the shoulder of the Galician servant girl. Her forehead was bandaged. She was very pale, a little thin, which made her even more beautiful with her slightly red lips and dark, dazzling eyes. Those eyes were staring at the Lord of San Lorenzo, but Don Pedro was worthy of his ancestors who had resisted the dreadful and bewitching Moorish women. He did not blink. It was the woman who had to turn away, which she did with a look of haughty indifference.

Gnô, eternally impassive, spoke formally, "Monsieur Duke, allow me to introduce Madame Jane Korridès, the widow Krosnovief, née Diana Ivanovna Kaline, once called the Red Princess, lately called Sunday, number 1, and Titania and nicknamed *La Vibora*, The Viper. Madame, meet Duke Pedro d'Arandar."

Titania just shrugged her shoulders slightly.

The Duke tipped his hat and in a cold, menacing voice said, "That's a lot of names for a woman. I'll stick to only one, the last one—*La Vibora*".

Then a young, vibrant voice shouted out, "*Aplasta la vibora... Matala!*"

With eyes glaring and fist shaking Huronilla exuded so much hatred that Titania, who had defied the Nyctalope and sneered at the menacing Duke, started trembling, wobbling a little as she squinted at the gypsy girl...

But Don Pedro was already getting introduced by the Nyctalope to Vitto, Socca and Loustal who got to work right away, with the help of Antonio, on anchoring the three airplanes onto the hard ground. Blanca and Huronilla rushed over to Sylvie, the baby and Adele.

The Duke said to Saint-Clair, "Leo, my dear friend, should we get back to the castle? Yes? Good. Do you want to take the lead?"

"It's all yours, Don Pedro."

"Well then, the two white mares, one for Sylvie and Pierrot, the other for… *La Vibora* to whom I will do the honor of serving as squire and guard. Blanca, please take Adele on the mule. You, Huronilla, take one of the game warden's horses and I'll trust you with this young lady…"

"Carmetta, señor," the Galician said boldly and respectfully.

But the Duke did not hear. "Monsieur Mitang, here's the horse of my head game warden. It's one the best of the stable, as good as my own, maybe better because it's more spirited… it's more than worthy of you."

"Thank you, Duke," the Japanese responded and he jumped in the saddle.

"Leo, please, take my horse."

Saint-Clair started to refuse but the Duke insisted.

"Please, Leo. I'll be leading the horse of *La Vibora* with my gun in hand. Look, I've never in my life sworn on the name of God but today I'm looking up at the heavens and saying, 'May God strike me dead if I don't shoot *La Vibora* in the heart and stamp on her face if she tries to get away!' I'm convinced, Leo, that such a woman as this is the incarnation of hell's power on earth and she's capable of anything, of everything until we kill her three times, burn her to ashes and see those ashes blown away by the wind."

The Duke was so serious, so impassioned, so intimidating that no one even smiled at this melodramatic speech tinged with superstitious fear. Besides, the proud and defiant bearing of Titania seemed to warrant it despite her obvious physical weakness.

Before nightfall they were back in the castle. Antonio had left a unit of four guards with the planes to drive off any local peasant or wandering gypsy who happened to pass by. Two horses were left to them so one or two of them could ride back to the castle if need be.

In the castle Titania was locked up in a dungeon room with a high ceiling and bars on the window. Her needs were seen to not by Carmetta, who now had the privilege of denying her, but by Blanca herself.

It was a long night at San Lorenzo because at the behest of Don Pedro, Padre Felipe, Blanca, Huronilla and Antonio all stayed with the group and listened late into the night to the adventures of Sylvie, then of Saint-Clair and his partners. It ended with this decision: a court martial, consisting of the interrogation and sentencing of Titania, would start in two days when Titania would be physically and mentally recovered enough to endure the process. For the first time in what seemed like countless days, the inhabitants of San Lorenzo went to bed happy.

Saint-Clair, Gnô and the Duke were not destined to court martial the Red Princess, to interrogate and judge her. They would never know why Diana Ivanovna, when she founded the sect of the Hashshashins, had taken the name Titania, why her pride desired to make her the modern daughter of ancient Titanus.

At 8 a.m. Saint-Clair and Sylvie had been awake for a short while when they heard a knock at the door of their bedroom. In pajamas Saint-Clair went to open it. Standing in front of him was the Duke d'Arandar, pale and glum.

He said, "Monsieur, *La Vibora* is dead."

Gnô Mitang was informed immediately and the three men rushed into Titania's room where Blanca was waiting. She retold the story with no less emotion than when she had told the Duke.

"I got up as usual even though I went to bed very late, and I came here. Following your instructions (she bowed to the Duke) I came with an armed guard. Another girl was bringing the breakfast I got prepared for the prisoner. Well, the door was open and the woman was on the bed like you see, her face all white and her hands clutching her left breast where the knife was stuck. I didn't touch anything. I went right away to tell Your Lord."

Saint-Clair and Gnô verified that the Red Princess was dead. The knife in her chest was a *navaja*, a traditional Spanish folding knife, with a horn handle and a long, sharp, slightly curved blade.

The Duke knew. "This knife is Huronilla's."

"Hey," Saint-Clair said, "look at this!" He was pointing to a piece of paper on the nightstand.

The three men leaned over and saw crude but confident writing: "*Aplasta la vibora! Matala!*" And under it, bravely, "Huronilla".

The Duke crossed himself and like a judge passing sentence said, "God's will."

As a formality they started a search for the gypsy girl. She was nowhere in the castle. They figured she had slipped into Blanca's room while she was asleep and taken the key to the prison, which she had brought back after killing the Viper. They also figured that Huronilla had left the castle early in the morning, hid at the drawbridge and escaped when a caravan of mules brought charcoal into the castle.

Antonio and some guards were sent to Salas where the tribe of Zapatans had camped the day before. He was informed that the gypsies had packed up and left an hour ago.

"I think we could catch up to them pretty easily," he told the men, "but I don't have orders to do so. Let's go back to the castle."

The Duke did not chase down the gypsies who had certainly taken Huronilla away. The whole affair, the emanation of God's will, was so righteous to him that he felt it would be sacrilegious for him to interfere in any way with the outcome.

Titania was dead. So many things were simplified now but others would remain forever in the dark, obscure, inexplicable.

A few hours later in San Lorenzo they were informed by a personal letter from the Marquis d'Ulloa that Korridès had killed himself in prison using a strange Hindu method that consisted of plugging his nostrils and folding his tongue back in his mouth to choke on it. As a "safety measure" he had gagged himself first.

Whereas Korridès was buried in the common grave of the Vigo cemetery, Titania was buried half a mile from the castle in an extremely wild spot where nobody ever went. It was truly the end of an astounding adventure.

Sentenced behind closed doors in the Vigo prison, the Hashsashins and the prisoners from Lost Island were given a death sentence to be carried out with that rapidity and secrecy the Spanish courts are used to. Only the governments involved were informed at the same time as the Lord and his guests in San Lorenzo. They also learned that Nadine Kiewicz was found in the house in Versailles, locked up in the basement and completely crazy. They had to put her in an asylum.

Thanks to a joint action of the British, French and Italian governments with the support of the Abyssinian government, the Ethiopian revolution was quelled. They found only ruins and ashes on Tana Island; the last rebels had blown it up after destroying all the scientific equipment and their one and only torpedo boat. The helicopter disappeared in this deliberate destruction—they did not even find the wreckage.

Across the whole world, the Hashshashins were stamped out because with all the documents of Escarpaz and others found in *The Sycamores* and the house on Rue des Bourdonnais, they were able to arrest and imprison all the Fidawis.

Gnô Mitang was the first to leave San Lorenzo to go back to Japan via Paris.

Carmetta stayed on at the castle where she joined Blanca's legion of servants.

Saint-Clair, Sylvie, little Pierre and Adele left a few days later for Versailles on the *Vulture*, which the Nyctalope received as a gift from the French government after he had offered it to them. Vitto and Socca were on board as pilot and mechanic.

The two other planes became the property of the Spanish government. As for the *Goéland III*, it had been brought back to San Sebastian by Loustal and Marod who returned with a small fortune to their native Cévennes.

At Versailles, in their family home of Bligny, Saint-Clair and Sylvie lived a life devoted to love and to their son Pierre.

Was it the end of their turbulent, adventurous and dangerous period of life? Was happiness going to be enough for them?

Yes, to some people, more optimistic than observant, who believed that happiness could be a constant and unconditional reality instead of being, as other people believed, being more observant than optimistic, a transitory and relative reality whose value and vitality lay in its variety. In other words, people could be happy only if they experienced woe and their happiness would be real only in contrast to the looming possibility of a new woe.

Montaigne once wrote, *"What do I know?"*

And Ronsard sang, *"Gather today the roses of life."*

Saint-Clair and Sylvie probably knew no more than we do. But the fact is that after the Titania adventure they were wise enough to follow the poet's advice and, being united in love, being attentive to the budding force of their son, they no longer thought about anything else but gathering in the present time all the roses that life offered them.

www.ingramcontent.com/pod-product-compliance
Lightning Source LLC
Chambersburg PA
CBHW060430030726
47495CB00003B/816